ALSO BY THOMAS BONTLY

The Competitor
The Adventures of a Young Outlaw
Celestial Chess

THE
GIANT'S
SHADOW

THE GIANT'S SHADOW

THOMAS BONTLY

RANDOM HOUSE
NEW YORK

Library of Congress Cataloging-in-Publication Data

Bontly, Thomas, 1939-
The giant's shadow.

I. Title.
PS3552.0643G54   1988   813'.54   87-43233
ISBN 0-394-56540-1

Manufactured in the United States of America
24689753
First Edition

FOR MY SON,
THOMAS DAVID BONTLY

Hast du einen Freund hienieden,
Trau ihm nicht zu dieser Stunde,
Freundlich wohl mit Aug und Munde,
Sinnt er Krieg im tückschen Frieden.

[If you have a friend here on earth,
Trust him not at this hour.
Though his eye and tongue are friendly,
He plans strife in deceitful peace.]

—JOSEF VON EICHENDORFF

ACKNOWLEDGMENTS

The author wishes to thank the Council for the International Exchange of Scholars, the German Fulbright Commission, and the Institute for English and American Studies at Justus Liebig Universität Giessen for the opportunity to live and work in the German Federal Republic.

Thanks also to the University of Wisconsin–Milwaukee Graduate School for a summer of support during a crucial phase in the writing of this novel, and a special thanks to Gisela Kuist for her assistance with the German language.

E A S T

Berlin

G E R M A N Y

W E S T

Breiburg ●

Bad Nauheim ●

Fulda ●

Schloss
Riesenschatten

Klarbach ●

Frankfurt ●

● Schweinfurt

● Würzburg

WEST   EAST

Charlottenburg ●

● Treptow

Dahlem ●

Berlin

G E R M A N Y

Munich ●

Berchtesgaden ●

Eric Elias

A CONSPIRACY OF ELVES

PART ONE

1

ights were the worst. After a month in Breiburg, Sam Abbot still walked the streets and sat in bars, came back to his room at the university guesthouse only when his legs gave out. Most evenings he drank alone, but occasionally he found himself in the company of carousing GIs from the base across town. The young soldiers narrated their sexual adventures and spoke enthusiastically of Bahnhofstrasse whores: chubby Mimi, wicked Natasha, good-natured Collette. Abbot thought sadly of the boys' parents, yet couldn't help envying the brash buoyancy of youth. Clearly, this was no country for old men.

Convinced that he could stand only so many such evenings, Abbot took his Friday luncheon at the university *Mensa,* where it was usually possible to scrounge an invitation or two. When it appeared that his colleagues all had other plans for the weekend—Abbot understood that they lived lives of their own—he told himself he could certainly survive until Monday without social distractions. He had letters to write and books to read, groceries to buy and a week's laundry to take care of . . . plenty to keep him busy, including that paper he was revising for the Berlin conference: "The Ideological Crisis in Recent American Literature." Several passages still needed fixing, and Abbot worked in the American Studies Institute's small English library until it closed at four. From the institute he walked to the local *Wertkauf,* where he purchased cheese, apples, a selection of cold cuts, and two bottles of a good but inexpensive Rheinhessen Spätlese. From the market it was a short though chilly walk to the guesthouse, a sleekly modern building of four stories, hiding a row of garages to the left of its landscaped drive. Professor Mikos Pajorfsky, looking quite spiffy in his red cycling suit, was just rolling his yellow racing bicycle from the last garage. He smiled at Abbot and tipped his cap.

"*Guten Tag, Herr Abbot.*"

"*Guten Tag, Herr Pajorsky. Ist es nicht zu kalt für*"—Abbot recalled the German word for bicycle—"*für das Fahrrad?*"

Pajorfsky's grin indicated that he found this effort to communicate in basic German an amusing little game. "*Nein, es ist nicht zu kalt. Es ist ganz warm!*"

Having exhausted his capacity for a discussion of the weather *auf Deutsch,* Abbot nonetheless lingered a moment beside Pajorfsky's bicycle. He knew the little Pole spoke fluent English. In fact they had chatted quite amiably in the TV lounge one evening last week over the dubbed and incongruous German of a John Wayne western. Pajorfsky, whose field was European prehistory, had asked Abbot about several American novelists whose work was now available in Poland. Abbot in turn questioned Pajorfsky concerning certain Celtic burial mounds in the hills surrounding Breiburg. They had scrupulously avoided political topics, though Abbot would have found Pajorfsky's views on such matters interesting.

The archaeologist stood with one foot on the pedal of his bike and squinted up at Abbot. "We are having today no rain, is that right?"

"Rain?" Abbot glanced up at the pale April sky. "No, it doesn't look like it."

"I mean, you are perhaps not having business elsewhere this evening? This is an American expression, yes? When it does not rain you are given a ticket to play baseball?"

"Oh, you mean a rain check!" After their first conversation, Pajorfsky had invited him to his room for a game of chess; it just happened to be an evening on which Abbot had a dinner invitation, so he told Pajorfsky he would take a rain check, then wondered if he should have explained the reference.

"Yes, that's right, a rain check," Pajorfsky said, immensely pleased to have gotten it right. "You are free then to play chess this evening?"

Abbot wasn't sure he wanted to spend his Friday night hunched over a chessboard; besides, the little guy might be much too good for him. "I'm not really a very experienced player," he warned Pajorfsky. "Strictly an amateur."

Pajorfsky gave one of his exaggerated Slavic shrugs, as if to suggest that the world was full of amateurs and some might be more challenging than others. "For me, it is mostly a social occasion, yes? We sip a little vodka, perhaps, and talk about our work, or life in our two countries—" His mild gray eyes had turned anxious and evasive. "You would find this agreeable?"

Abbot sensed that the words were carefully weighed and wondered uneasily what motive Pajorfsky might have in pursuing this friendship. Yet wasn't he being foolish? No doubt the little Pole carried a burden of loneliness as heavy as Abbot's own.

"Okay, sure, let's give it a try. If you beat me too badly, I'll just have to challenge you to a game of gin rummy."

Pajorfsky grinned broadly. "Very good. You would like to come to my room tonight—shall we say at eight?"

"That'll be fine," Abbot said, thinking that at least he would be spared another solitary ramble across the city. He watched as Pajorfsky swung astride his bicycle and glided down the drive, then leaned into the turn that would take him to the Stadtwald —an extensive tract of forested land that darkened the hills north of Breiburg.

Now that's what I should do, Abbot thought as the red suit flashed between the trees and disappeared. No doubt he would feel better if he got more exercise. During his first weeks at the guesthouse he had run regularly in the Stadtwald, working his way up to six kilometers before a late-season snow had made the paths slippery and given him an excuse to abandon his regimen.

He went up the walk to the front door, pausing to check his mailbox for a letter from home. As usual, there wasn't one. Liz had said she wouldn't write until she had certain matters straight in her own mind, and Abbot knew his wife well enough to know that such mental housecleaning could take a long time. He was determined to be patient, to give her all the time she needed to "reevaluate their relationship," as she put it. Still, she might have acknowledged the several newsy letters he had already written her.

Abbot ran his eyes over the nameplates affixed to the double row of boxes: Professor Gware Motumba, Dr. Yan Sing Ho, Professor Ives Gastanard, Dr. Hashib Harandi . . . the exotic roll call seldom changed, though Abbot checked regularly for new arrivals. It was an academic Babel, a polyethnic Ark, and as the sole representative of an English-speaking nation Abbot sometimes felt as isolated as an astronaut orbiting the earth. Down below he could see all the families of mankind going about their concerns and living their lives, but up in the ionosphere it was very quiet and sometimes quite frightening.

My midlife crisis, Abbot thought with a wince, digging for his key. Perhaps he should think of it as a therapeutic quarantine. No doubt he had been a great pain in the ass this past year. Refusing to grow old gracefully, he had succeeded in alienating his family, his colleagues, his friends. Finally he had begun to bore even himself. Drastic remedies were required, and Abbot was sure everyone had breathed a devout sigh of relief when he finally stepped on board that Lufthansa flight and allowed himself to be catapulted across the Atlantic for a six-month assignment at Breiburg University. The scapegoat, driven out of town with everyone's good wishes heaped on his back. Now only he had to suffer his own wretched company.

He unlocked the glass door and stepped into a gleaming tile-and-terrazzo lobby. From down the hall he could hear the flat pings and hollow pongs of table tennis—another titanic struggle, no doubt, between the fleet Filipino and the quick, catlike African. The door to Frau Graushen's office was open, and she nailed Abbot with another of her ominous smiles as he passed.

"Guten Tag, Herr Professor."

Abbot smiled and waved and scurried past. One always scurried past Frau Graushen, as if to linger in her vicinity might be to tempt one's fate. She was a plump, perky Valkyrie with blond sausage curls and rouged cheeks and a cheerfully menacing manner. Though she spoke only German, the proprietress had no trouble making herself understood. With gestures, facial expressions, and steely-eyed courtesy, she imposed her sense of order on the thirty or so foreigners given into her keeping, instructed them in the proper use of the facilities, and let them know promptly of any inadvertent violation of the rules—for which, Abbot was sure, they were all profoundly grateful.

He started up the spotless marble stairs, the shopping bag hanging heavily from one arm, his briefcase from the other. At the first landing he encountered the spicy aroma of Indian cooking from the apartment of the Harandi family. At the second, he could hear Professor Gastanard sawing away at his violin. As he gained the third, the Mitsutashis' elfin child scampered along the corridor ahead of him, then shyly returned his *guten Tag* before ducking into her family's apartment. Abbot turned the key and entered his bachelor's cell with a sinking heart.

He could tell from the strong odor of cleanser and polish that the tireless *Reinemachefrauen* had been through the place in his absence. They'd even done his dishes again, which embarrassed Abbot because he knew it was against Frau Graushen's rules. Perhaps the heavyset one with the dimpled elbows was sweet on him.

Abbot left his groceries on the counter of the galley kitchen and proceeded to his bed-sitting-room, a rectangle of moderate size, simply and functionally furnished in blond, bland Danish modern. The white walls wore only a calendar, on which Abbot had begun to x out his days. One window with dark-green drapes overlooked a row of tall pines where choirs of blackbirds sang at dusk. If Abbot had been a destructive sort of man, he would have found little in his domicile he could damage; if a thief, little worth stealing. If, on the other hand, he had come to Germany in order to experience the fully orchestrated crescendo of a nervous breakdown, the institutional austerity of his quarters seemed to offer a perfect setting. There was even a mental hospital (*Psychiatrisches Krankenhaus*) conveniently located just across the lane.

Abbot set his briefcase on his desk and stood at the window. From this angle he could look across a bleak, wintery orchard at the bone-white buildings of the university: stacked cubes, the stark modernism of postwar German architecture. One saw a great many such structures in Breiburg, since there hadn't been much left of the city after a certain night in 1943 when the allied bombers passed over with a few bombs to spare. It still struck Abbot as remarkable that they let Americans walk the streets in this town—that they didn't catch one on occasion and string him up by his heels.

What am I doing here? he wondered, gazing out at the barren orchard and chalky buildings. *Why have I subjected myself to these months of exile?*

"Now, Sam," his wife had said that bleached February day as she drove him to the airport, "I know this is hard for you, but remember, we agreed that we need this time apart. Besides, it's a chance to explore Europe on your own, without a wife and kids along to cramp your style. Isn't that what you've always wanted?"

Good old Liz, always looking on the bright side of other people's problems, always using his own ill-considered words to drive a stake through his heart.

He really should go out for that run.

If he got started now, he could log his six kilometers before the temperature went down with the sun. He'd be back in plenty of time for his drink, his bath and his dinner before meeting Pajorfsky at eight.

His drink. God, yes, his drink.

You'll have to earn it, you bastard. Get cracking.

Feeling already the exhilaration of strenuous exercise—*Mens sana in corpore sano*—Abbot got into his running clothes and laced up his sneakers. He bounded down the stairs to the front door, where he found Professor Pajorfsky's young research assistant—a raunchy little blonde in her usual vinyl jacket and thigh-tight blue jeans—just ringing the buzzer above Pajorfsky's mailbox.

"I think he's still out on his bicycle," Abbot said as he stepped out the door. "Would you like to wait for him in the lounge?"

The girl took a step back and looked up at him with sharp eyes. On weekends, this young lady usually carried Pajorfsky off in her dusty, dented sportscar to examine one or another of Hesse's prehistoric sites. At least, that was the explanation Pajorfsky had given Abbot one Saturday morning when he happened to see them setting off together.

"No, thank you, is okay," the girl said in her husky voice and heavy accent. "Do you know perhaps which way he goes?" She looked quickly over her shoulder, and Abbot sensed not only her impatience but something stronger—something quite a bit like fear.

"He went off toward the Stadtwald, maybe twenty minutes

ago," Abbot said. "If I see him, should I tell him you're looking for him?"

"Yes, please. Could give him this number? Ask him call Greta. Is urgent, yes?"

Abbot watched as she wrote the number on a slip of paper she'd taken from her purse. Seen close up (it was the first opportunity he'd had), Greta wasn't quite the beauty he'd thought, nor was she as young as she tried to appear. Her blond hair was nearly black where it left her scalp, and she used a heavy makeup to cover the blemishes of a coarse complexion. Somehow these defects didn't greatly displease Abbot, and he wondered if he could persuade Pajorfsky to invite him along on one of their archeological expeditions; the American Studies Institute had treated Abbot very well, but they hadn't given him a cute little research assistant.

He took the number from the girl and slipped it into the deep side-pocket of his sweat pants. "I'll give him your message this evening if I don't meet up with him in the woods."

"Thank you." Her nervous fingers were fumbling a cigarette from her purse, but Abbot, who had quit smoking years ago and seldom carried matches, could only wait until she came up with a lighter. When she failed on several tries to ignite the plastic cylinder, he took it from her, produced a modest flame and held it cupped beneath her chin. With her first drag, Greta seemed to regain her composure. She brushed the blond strands back from her eyes and smiled at Abbot in a way that suggested she had noticed his appraisal.

He pressed the lighter into her palm and began to ease himself around her suddenly seductive gaze. *Run, Abbot, run.*

On creaky knees and aching ankles, he teetered down the walk and turned onto the footpath that led to the Stadtwald. For several strides he could still feel Greta's dusky eyes pursuing him, and he tried, for her sake, to appear twenty pounds lighter on his feet than he was.

A thin crust of snow still clung to the low shrubbery along the path, and Abbot's breath fled through the brittle air in wispy plumes. He jogged past the mental hospital, its ornamented complex of prewar buildings standing secretively behind a tall chain link fence and wooded grounds. Abbot took it for granted that modern Germany looked after its lunatics and imbeciles in properly enlightened fashion, and yet the *Krankenhaus* never failed to inspire in him a vague uneasiness, an almost metaphysical dread, as if it might once have been the site of fiendish experiments and closet atrocities. For the most part, Abbot liked the Germans and admired their cheerful postwar prosperity; yet there were little things that unsettled his soul, evoking harsh images of the horrifying past. Sometimes Abbot could almost smell the blood in which the land was steeped.

Passing through the dank, echoing tunnel beneath the Autobahn, Abbot picked up the pace, stretched out his strides, then burst into the waning sunshine of the Stadtwald. The well-groomed woodland lay silent, strewn with shadows on either side of the ruler-straight path. Though much used on weekends by hikers and bikers, the forest seemed deserted during the week. Abbot ran uphill for three kilometers, the low sun winking through the pines, the slap of his sneakers and the rush of his breath the only sounds in the vast stillness.

He was nearly to his turnaround point, another narrow lane that cut at right angles across his, when he heard a sharp crackle in the brush and his heart jumped in alarm. Almost at once he spotted the small, reddish deer bounding away through the thicket, yet his pulse was still pounding, his body charged with adrenaline, as he swung into the intersection of the two lanes. Perhaps it was that first fright that saved his life, because the big automobile was almost on top of him, bursting through a screen of pine boughs to his right and pushing back the brush on either side of the lane like a battleship parting the waves. Abbot leapt for the bushes across the lane without breaking stride. His body pulled itself clear, but the front fender glanced off his foot, flipping him over in midair. He recognized a Mercedes hood ornament, caught a glimpse of a white, masklike face behind the wheel, then crashed into the thicket, where he sank down through layers of twigs and thorns.

Buried in bramble, Abbot heard the Mercedes skid to a stop some little way down the lane. Too breathless to shout and afraid to move because of the thorns, he lay still as a car door slammed and footsteps approached the thicket. How did you say "lousy bastard" in German? Abbot was still selecting epithets when, looking up through branches like coils of barbed wire, he saw a face appear against the colorless sky. It was not a face to appeal to for rescue or comfort, nor one he felt brave enough to curse. With its bulging bony brow and sunken, shadowed eyes, its long withered white cheeks and mouthful of large, predatory teeth, it was a face from his nightmares, and it effectively stopped Abbot's tongue. In the next instant, he realized that he was invisible to the man on the path. Moreover, he felt quite sure the driver had not stopped to render aid to his victim. There was no hint of concern or remorse on that ghostly vampire's face—only a glare of grim satisfaction.

Obeying the instinct of the wounded animal, Abbot lay motionless in the thicket until the driver, apparently satisfied that the body was out of reach or not worth retrieving, turned and strode back to his car. The door slammed; the engine growled; tires spit gravel. Abbot let the air come whistling out of his lungs. Then very carefully, hoping not to scratch himself any more than necessary, he began extricating himself from the thicket. It was a torturous process, and by the time Abbot was back on the path, the Mercedes had been gone for some time. He could make out its tire tracks in the soft ground, however, and he thought he heard its engine snarl as it changed gears.

He took a few cautious steps along the path. Apparently the car had struck only the thick rubber sole of his shoe; it didn't feel as though any bones were broken. His face stung from several scratches and there was blood on his hands, but most of the thorns had failed to penetrate his bulky sweat suit. Finding no serious injuries, Abbot began to experience the luxury of anger. What the hell was a big, powerful car like that doing on a forest lane reserved for pedestrians, bikers, and official vehicles? Perhaps the driver was a deranged ghoul—an escapee from the *Krankenhaus*—who enjoyed running down joggers. Abbot knew there had to be other explanations, but at the moment he couldn't think of any.

"Shit," he said out loud. And then, surrendering to the impulse to vent his frustration to the silent forest, he yelled, "Crazy goddamn bastard! Bloody Nazi!"

As if in response, a faint cry came from the woods. Abbot's neck prickled. Was he hallucinating? Perhaps just some bird or animal? But when the sound came a second time he recognized it as a human voice. Had there been another jogger on the path?

He began walking along the lane in the direction from which the Mercedes had come. "Hello, anyone there?" Then he tried German: *"Gibt es einige hier?"*

He was passing through an area where the steepness of the hillside and the absence of tall trees had created an exceptional density of underbrush, and at first Abbot didn't see the yellow racing bike hanging from the bushes twenty feet or so below the path. One of the bike's rear wheels was missing, the other twisted to a sort of pretzel. Abbot plunged into the brush and began searching around the bicycle for its injured owner.

"Hello—are you there? Mikos, Mikos—is that you?"

He was answered by a muffled groan, not far off yet maddeningly hidden by the heavy brush. He worked his way down the slope, calling repeatedly, and at last found the little archaeologist at the bottom of a shallow ravine. Pajorfsky was sprawled across the mossy rocks, amid the muck and litter of the stream bed. His head was bloodied, and Abbot could tell by the glaze in his eyes that he was in a state of shock. A ribbon of blood trickled from the corner of his mouth and a pink bubble formed at his lips when, recognizing Abbot, he tried to speak his name.

"Yes, it's me," Abbot said, kneeling beside him. "Are you in a lot of pain, Mikos?"

"No—no pain, my friend. But we shall need another rain check, I fear. I am badly hurt."

Abbot saw that moving Pajorfsky would not be wise; besides, he didn't think he could carry even such a small man all the way back to the guesthouse by himself. He pulled off his sweat shirt and, rolling it into a sort of pillow, slipped it beneath the archaeologist's head.

"I'll go for help," he said. "You just lie quietly and I'll be back as soon as I can."

"No use," the little man said, one small hand clutching at Abbot's arm. "I am dying, I think. There's something I must give you—very important—"

Abbot saw Pajorfsky's other hand fumbling at the zipper of his red jacket. "Never mind," he said, "it'll keep till I get back. You just lie still—I won't be long."

"No!" The little man's hand clung to Abbot's arm with surprising strength. His other hand drew down the zipper until it snagged. He struggled to work his hand inside the opening. "Inside pocket," he said to Abbot, the bloody bubbles forming at his lips. "Please help—you must see. . ."

"Yes, all right," Abbot said, anxious to do anything he could to ease the little man's distress. He worked the zipper free and opened the jacket. There was an inner pocket and it contained a white envelope. Abbot drew it out.

"This? Is this what you want me to see?"

There was no address on the envelope and its flap was sealed, but Pajorfsky nodded. The fingers of his left hand were alternately stroking and clutching at Abbot's bare arm. "Yes, yes, for you . . . from—from—" He spoke a word of two syllables which Abbot didn't quite catch; perhaps it was two words.

"Who, Mikos? Who is it from?"

"The Stork," Pajorfsky said. "It comes to you from the Stork."

Abbot sat back on his haunches.

"The Stork?"

"Open the envelope," Pajorfsky said. "Open and see . . . I will explain."

Abbot knew he should leave at once for help, yet there was something in the little man's desperate insistence which made him tear open the envelope. There was a photograph inside—a glossy black-and-white snapshot. In the shadows of the ravine Abbot was barely able to make out two people standing before a white building, some sort of shop. There was a sign above the doorway that he couldn't read.

Pajorfsky was clawing frantically at his arm. "You know these men? You understand?"

Abbot looked at the photo again. "No, I can't . . . oh, my God!"

He got to his feet and held the snapshot up to catch a better light. But how could this be? He had the vexing sense that what he was looking at was an utter impossibility. He knew the men in the photograph, all right—one of them was Abbot himself. That picture had been taken with Abbot's own camera, nearly twenty-five years ago.

The other man in the picture was Jeremy Sawyer, who had been living in the Soviet Union for the past eighteen years.

"Mikos, how in the world did you ever—?"

Abbot broke off in horror. The eyes looking up at him were frozen still. The last pink bubble at the bloody mouth burst and was not replaced by another. Abbot grabbed the little man's wrist and felt with numb, fumbling fingers for a pulse. But there was no pulse. He released the hand, which fell away like a block of wood. After a moment, he got to his feet and backed away from the body. The envelope lay on the ground where he had dropped it, and he bent over quickly to pick it up, the photograph securely inside.

Jeremy Sawyer?

The woods seemed to darken around him. He heard a wind moving in the upper reaches of the tall pines, a magpie cry out in passing. The rivulets in the ravine gurgled melodiously over the rocks and around the body of the little archaeologist, whose dead eyes continued to stare up at Abbot with fixed exasperation.

Abbot turned to climb out of the ravine, and in that moment panic came down on him. He slipped in the mud and, sliding backward, felt Pajorfsky's fingers still imprinted on his arm, as if the dead man were pulling him back into the ravine. In a frenzy of fear and loathing he clutched at rock, grabbed handfuls of grass and roots, and pulled himself from the ravine. Panting, he pushed his way through the thicket and burst out onto the path.

Which way to run? He was near the junction of the two lanes. One led downhill to the guesthouse, the other cut across the hillside and intercepted a highway from the city. For several seconds Abbot stood paralyzed, unsure which way to turn.

Jeremy Sawyer? The Stork?

A shadow fell across him. Overhead a large black bird, a rook or raven, settled on a pine branch, folded its wings, gave its raucous call.

Abbot ran for the highway.

2

A pparently the sun had set, because Abbot could see a ruddy stain spreading across the western sky as he waited in the police car. Against that lurid glow the tall pines became brushlike silhouettes, the leafless hardwoods clusters of black capillaries sucking daylight from the sky. The young officer was coming back from the thicket, picking his way to avoid the multitude of thorns and spiky branches. He came up to the car on Abbot's side and Abbot rolled down the window.

"You are sure?" the policeman asked in his precise, careful English. "This is where you found the body?"

"Yes, right in there," Abbot said, "about thirty feet downhill—" Lord, how many *meters* was that? "His bicycle should be hanging from the bushes—can't you find it?"

"Would you come with me, please?" the policeman asked.

Abbot got out of the car, feeling the chill night air on his bare arms and the sweat-damp back of his undershirt. It had taken him longer than he expected to reach the highway and flag down a motorist; then he had trouble explaining the situation to the confused young driver. What was the German word for "accident," for "injury"? He kept saying, *"Polizei, Polizei,"* so finally the young man drove him to the police station near the university. There, after more confusion and more futile attempts to speak German, Abbot was finally given an officer who understood English. Together they set out for the Stadtwald, but Abbot wasn't sure the cop knew what he was supposed to find. So far he hadn't called for an ambulance.

By now an hour or more had passed since Abbot left Pajorfsky in the ravine, and he had lost whatever slim hope he might have cherished of reviving the little archaeologist, of bringing him back from the dead. He kept remembering that look of exasperation in Pajorfsky's eyes, and he wanted nothing more than to see those lids gently lowered, the body rescued from its rocky resting place and given the minimal dignity of a hospital morgue. At the moment, it seemed terribly important to Abbot that they do at least that much for the little man who had almost become his friend.

He led the policeman into the thicket. It was difficult to see objects in the murky half-light, yet something as large and bright as a yellow bicycle should have been easy to find. After several minutes Abbot realized that the bike was *not* where he'd last seen it.

"The ravine," he said to the officer. "Let's check the ravine."

This he found without difficulty, but when he had made his way to the bottom there was no body lying on the rocky streambed.

The policeman cast the light of his flash over the mud and debris. "This is where you saw the body?"

"My God, yes—right here," Abbot moaned. "What could have happened to it?"

Now he felt like a fool. Had he somehow led the cop back to the wrong place? Abbot supposed it was possible he could have become disoriented in the forest, yet this certainly *looked* like the spot. He could picture Pajorfsky in his red cycling suit lying *just there,* where several tiny streams trickled over the rocks.

The policeman knelt down to examine the sides and floor of the gully. He ran his light over rocks, weeds, mud, layers of dead leaves, exposed roots. "I see footprints," he said in his careful English. "I see many marks—but most of these we are making ourselves. I do not know what to think."

"Jesus, neither do I," Abbot said. "He couldn't have gotten up and left by himself, that's for damn sure. Maybe someone else reported the accident? Maybe an ambulance got here before us—?"

But the young cop was shaking his head. "No other reports—I checked before we left. Are you sure the man you saw was dead?"

"He died while I was with him," Abbot said. Could he have been wrong about that? Had poor Mikos come back to consciousness and crawled off into the forest in search of help?

Then he remembered his sweat shirt.

"I left it here as a sort of pillow for his head," he told the cop. "Whoever took the body took my shirt as well. That *proves* he was moved."

But the young policeman was obviously losing his faith in Abbot's reliability as a witness. It was impossible to explain these things—the language barrier was just too formidable. Already the cop had decided Abbot was a crazy, troublesome foreigner; who cared what such people saw or didn't see in the woods?

What I need to do, Abbot thought, is to shut up and let this guy handle things his own way. Don't complicate matters. Don't mention the photograph. There will be someone else I can talk to somewhere along the line—someone who can understand what I have to say.

They spent another ten or fifteen minutes in the thicket, looking for anything which might substantiate Abbot's report. The failing light was against them. Each time a branch stung Abbot's face or poked into his side he wanted to give up the search and return to the comforts, such as they were, of the guesthouse. Finally, as they were working their way back to the car, Abbot found a fragment of red nylon dangling like a small flag from a broken branch.

"Here," he said, showing it to the policeman in triumph, "this is a piece of the cycling suit he was wearing—it was red!"

The cop looked at him as if this attempt to validate his story was in very poor taste, but he took the bit of cloth.

In the police car he gave Abbot a rough blanket to put over his shoulders, then got out his clipboard and a report form with multiple carbons. It was night in the forest now, and despite the blanket Abbot couldn't stop shivering. The young policeman laboriously filled out his form by the light of the overhead dome, asking Abbot his name, his address, his nationality and profession. His passport and residence permit? Abbot explained that they were in his room at the guesthouse. He supplied the names of two professors at the institute who could vouch for him. He explained once again how he had nearly been run over by a large blue or gray Mercedes and how he had subsequently found Mikos dying in the ravine. He did not mention the envelope in Mikos's jacket pocket or the photograph it contained. That was something he meant to ponder in private, over a good stiff drink.

17

The report completed, the officer turned the car around at the junction of the two lanes and drove back to the highway. Abbot was cold, wet, frustrated, and angry. Images of the big car and its skull-faced driver, of Mikos lying dead in the ravine, flashed through his mind like scenes from a surrealist film. German expressionism—good God, could he be cracking up? But no, he *knew* there had been a body, and someone had come back to remove it. Clearly, Mikos's death was no accident.

They drove to the guesthouse and the officer came up to Abbot's room to look at his passport and residence permit. Pajorfsky's apartment stood just down the hall from Abbot's door. The officer knocked and waited expectantly as Abbot went in to get his papers. It would have been embarrassing, to say the least, if the little Pole had answered the policeman's knock, but the cop was still waiting when Abbot returned.

"Of course he's not in there," Abbot said, more irritably than he intended. "He's been murdered."

The officer arched one eyebrow, as if to say that all foreigners were, in his experience, subject to hysteria. He looked gravely at Abbot's passport and residence permit, then explained he would need to take them to the station for a day or two.

"Just so I get them back by Wednesday," Abbot said. "I'm leaving on Thursday for a conference in Berlin."

"We will return them to you quite soon. Someone will come to talk to you tomorrow, I think."

He left and Abbot turned the key in his triple dead-bolt lock. Without his American passport he felt peculiarly homeless, nameless, stranded. He could cross no frontiers; he couldn't even return to the States. For a moment he seemed to join Mikos Pajorfsky in some dim, horrible world of shades.

It *really* was time for that drink.

He started running water for his bath, then built himself a sizable martini, using the last of the gin he'd brought from home. All month he had been hoarding that gin, trying to wean himself from his old dependence on his six o'clock cocktail (it was nearly eight by now—he was two hours overdue); yet even Liz couldn't object to *this* drink, he thought, after what I've been through.

Not that his wife objected to drinking in general; it was only

Abbot's drinking that Liz found objectionable, and then only because she had to live with it.

Down the hatch!

With that first bright, barbed sip, Abbot could feel the world beginning to lose its sharp edges; he could feel his muscles relax, his nerves unwind; the very synapses of his abject brain began to purr as they settled back into the throes of an old contentment.

Abbot knew that for the confirmed drinker there were two distinct worlds: the world without booze, which was cranky and tedious, full of hard tasks and grim necessities; and then the world with booze, in which everything became increasingly warm, soft, colorful, lively, amusing—in which one felt that one could live forever, do anything one wished, and never get hurt . . . right up to that moment when the bottom fell out and you toppled into the abyss.

The trick in being a happy drinker was in knowing when to stop, before you reached the abyss. Somehow, over the past year or two, Abbot had lost that knack. Therefore, the only real alternative to life in the abyss was not to drink at all; yet certainly he wasn't ready for such extreme measures. Sometimes it seemed to him as if the abyss was where he belonged.

He took his drink to his desk and turned on its bright lamp, then reached into his pocket for the envelope Mikos had given him. A small slip of yellow paper came out with it and fluttered to the floor. Abbot picked it up and saw it was the number Pajorfsky's research assistant had given him. He remembered how frightened the girl had seemed. Had she known Pajorfsky's life was in danger?

No doubt he should have given this number to the police. Since he hadn't thought of it at the time, he could either call the police now—a daunting prospect, considering the language difficulties he'd already experienced—or he could dial this number and break the news to the girl himself.

Abbot decided to wait on that one. He went into the bathroom and turned off the water, then returned to his desk and took the photograph from its envelope. In the bright light he could easily distinguish the features of the two young men; their slightly foolish grins greeted him like a mysterious salute from the past. This is what you were like twenty-three years ago. And that man was your friend. Abbot could see that the white building they were standing before was a pub; he could even make out a portion of the sign above the door: KI— AR—, probably "King's Arms." He vaguely recalled the occasion. A warm May afternoon near the end of his year in Cambridge; he and Jeremy had gone out on their bicycles to photograph the countryside and had stopped for lunch at a village pub some miles from town. Sitting on the sunny terrace, drinking their pints of bitter and eating their cheese sandwiches (my God, yes, how even the tastes came back to him now!) they had asked some passerby to snap their picture. "A typical pose, by God," Jeremy had said, lifting his stein of beer; "something for you to remember me by, old bean."

It was, so far as Abbot could recall, the only picture he had from his year in England that showed the two of them together. How had it come into the hands of Mikos Pajorfsky?

Abbot sipped his drink and tried to remember. When had that roll of film been developed? Probably not until he was back in the States. . . . The prints, as he now remembered, were in an old photograph album in his attic in Nakomis, Wisconsin; he hadn't looked at them in years. But of course he had sent a print of this photo to Jeremy. They had carried on a sporadic correspondence, and Jeremy had sent Abbot his first book of poems. . . . Ah, now the pieces were falling into place! When he read those poems, Abbot had been stricken with nostalgia for Cambridge and England. He'd gotten out his photo album and souvenirs and gone through them all with Liz. It was their third or fourth year of marriage; Abbot was still in graduate school; Liz, he seemed to remember, was pregnant with their first child. When he wrote Jeremy a letter of thanks and praise, he had included a print of this particular photo. He recalled having written something on the back.

Abbot turned the snapshot over. Sure enough, it bore the faint impression of penciled lines:

> *Two swans in sunshine,*
> *bestride the tide.*

The words were Jeremy's, taken from a poem Abbot had found particularly moving, but the handwriting was Abbot's own. This had to be the snapshot he had sent to Jeremy in the fall or winter of 1965.

Three years later, Sawyer had renounced his U.S. citizenship and sought political asylum in the Soviet Union.

Abbot looked from the snapshot to the framed photograph that stood on his desk: his three children, Jeffrey, Emily, and Charlotte, now considerably older than when they posed that Christmas morning before the tree with Ruggles, the mongrel terrier long gone to his rest. Jeremy had left a child in England—a wife and child, the bastard. His way and mine, Abbot thought, with some obscure bitterness. Never the twain shall meet. Yet now they were both exiles of a sort, and God only knew which of them had had the better lot, or the more to answer for.

Abbot took his drink and the snapshot into the bathroom. He propped the photo up between the faucet and the tiled wall and set his drink on the edge of the tub. Then he stripped off his clothes and stepped gingerly into the steaming water. Though normally he preferred a shower as both quicker and more hygienic, a hot tub did have its virtues when you were cold and tired and had some hard thinking to do. Abbot sank down into the fiery liquid until he could rest the base of his skull against the rim of the tub and his knees, red as lobsters, broke the surface. Ah, that was better. Healing waters; returned to the womb. He took a sip of his drink, closed his eyes, and set himself the task of remembering everything he could about Jeremy Sawyer.

He was still reminiscing when, nearly an hour later, he stepped into the smoky noise of Zum Eulenspiegel, a student restaurant located just down the street from the guesthouse. He hadn't intended to go out again, but his chronic loneliness, and the fact that he had run out of hard liquor, had driven him to forsake the security of his room for the Eulenspiegel's boisterous atmosphere. Remembering his youth had proved to be a melancholy business—not because the memories themselves weren't generally pleasant, but because it all seemed so impossibly long ago. Remembering those days of innocence and reckless optimism, Abbot felt old, cynical, and defeated.

He found a small table in one of the crowded back rooms and gave his order to the buxom, apple-cheeked waitress with the flaxen hair who had begun of late to favor Abbot with the friendly smile she reserved for regular customers and heavy tippers. Watching her broad hips and well-rounded rump glide between the tables, Abbot felt the weight of a month's celibacy tugging at his thoughts. Of course he hadn't promised Liz he would remain faithful throughout their separation, and somehow he sensed that she didn't really require it of him—that she might even condone an affair, if only it would appease his demons and lead to the recovery of his good humor. But how did you shrug off a twenty-year habit of fidelity, or the diffidence that came with thinning hair and a thickening middle, a quiet manner and an old-fashioned attitude toward women? It was easier by far, Abbot had found, to live with those familiar, harmless fantasies . . . even if he felt on occasion that fantasies were precisely what demons fed upon.

The waitress returned with his glass of beer. Abbot took a foamy sip and hunkered down among his memories. What a flock of them that photograph had raised—as if all his images of the past had been waterfowl nesting peacefully on the marshy backwaters of his mind, suddenly startled into flight, a chaotic blizzard of birds, at the first crack of the hunter's rifle. Even now that the skies had cleared a bit, Abbot retained a sense of squawking and screeching, of wings beating about his ears.

He looked around the room at the healthy, handsome young Germans, the bearded boys and bright-eyed girls, eating and drinking in groups of six or eight, laughing, talking, gesturing energetically, the air hazy with cigarette smoke and great ideas above their tow-haired heads. All over the world, Abbot thought, there were places like this, where students stumbled across the eternal verities and assumed they were the first, the very first, to make such discoveries. If his own youth had seemed somehow, in comparison to the common lot, a more distinguished quest for knowledge and understanding, it was largely due to one man.

Only a year or two Abbot's senior, Jeremy Sawyer had been living in Cambridge for several years when Abbot arrived, in August of 1961, green as the midwestern grass that still stained his sneakers, for a year of graduate study at St. George's College. They met at dinner that memorable first night in Cambridge, and it was Jeremy who struck the first friendly note, who offered his compatriot a short course in the ways of the Cambridge scholar and gentleman. It was Jeremy who sold Abbot his bike and his academic gown (left in Jeremy's keeping by a departed scholar), got him a cheap used typewriter and an electric kettle ("If you want decent coffee over here, old bean, you'll bloody well have to brew your own!"), took him around to the college pubs, and taught him the requisite arts of Cambridge—punting and squash. Within a week they were great chums and Abbot's year abroad was off to a roaring start.

It was the kind of friendship, Abbot reflected, that could only happen when one is young, away from home for the first time, and full of a reckless spirit of adventure. One doesn't choose one's companions at that time of life so much as one hones in on them by some sort of spiritual radar, infallibly the people who, in one way or another, will make one grow. Jeremy was such an individual. Though he aped (with a mischievous twinkle) the speech, dress, and manner of an English gentleman, he was in fact a native of upper New York State, a Yankee to the core, and somewhat starved for American friendships. "Oh, I'm a terrible snob," he told Abbot early in their acquaintance, "but the only class I aspire to isn't one on which the Limeys have a monopoly. Has it ever struck you, old bean, that all the truly great artists of the world have been expatriates? At least in the modern age? Genius, I contend, has no nationality . . . or if it does, it had better get rid of it as quickly as it can."

It was Jeremy who became Abbot's guide to the pleasures and treasures of Europe, his private tutor in art, music, history—who first exposed Abbot to those arcane matters that a young vagabond of the 1960s wanted and needed to know. In the process, Jeremy's ideas, tastes, and opinions—and most of all, Jeremy's extraordinary talent—had a profound influence on Abbot's career.

In his undergraduate days on a sleepy midwestern campus, Abbot had nurtured vague, vain hopes of becoming a writer. Once exposed to Jeremy's genius, however, he realized that his own creative powers were distinctly second-rate. Jeremy was always generous toward Abbot's literary efforts, but Abbot himself could see the difference between his plodding, earthbound constructions and Jeremy's quick, easy, as it were angelic flights. Yet it wasn't until the *Wanderjahr* was over and Abbot was on his way back to America that he made the decision that was to alter the course of his life. Lacking the talent to become a writer of Jeremy's caliber, he would pursue a secondary, though perfectly respectable, role in the world of letters—he would concentrate on criticism, scholarship, teaching . . . and it was not so much with disappointment as with relief that Abbot turned, in the next phase of his education, to his new career.

It proved, on the whole, a wise decision. Abbot's graduate work produced the expected doctorate; his dissertation was accepted by a university press. Before long he was established as a respected scholar and critic of American literature, a tenured faculty member at Nakomis State, editor of the highly regarded journal *Excursions,* as well as several standard texts and anthologies. Before an ill-fated plunge into academic politics and administration, Abbot had had very little cause to regret his choice of career.

As for Jeremy, his career also seemed to prosper at first. He completed his Cambridge doctorate and published his first book of poems in the same year. He married a girl Abbot remembered with fondness (we won't dwell on *that,* Abbot thought, taking another sip of his beer) and accepted a perfectly respectable position at a red-brick university in the English midlands. Yet at some point in those years Jeremy's social conscience and literary convictions led him into politics—and not just politics, Abbot reminded himself, but the angry, irrational, sometimes violent radicalism of the sixties. Jeremy's commitment to the movement escalated with the war in Southeast Asia. He marched with British protest groups, got in trouble with his draft board at home, issued angry statements that were widely reported in the American press. When other young Americans were battling the police in the streets of Chicago, Jeremy suddenly appeared on the cover of *Time,* his long, lean face superimposed on a monochrome montage of warring soldiers and protesting students, with the caption: JEREMY SAWYER—TRAITOR OR MARTYR? His defection was at first a shock to Abbot, then an embarrassment, and finally a mystery in which he was to ponder a double sense of betrayal: Jeremy's betrayal of his own bright future as an American poet and Abbot's betrayal of a friend. For in the controversy that raged over Sawyer's flight to Moscow, Abbot himself had taken no part.

Perhaps it was cowardly, but to have defended Jeremy at the time could have been professional suicide. Abbot was just starting his first full-time teaching job, his wife was pregnant with their second child . . . perhaps he overestimated the repressive forces at work in the academic world, but it was no time to indulge in quixotic gestures. Abbot himself had mixed feelings about the war in Vietnam; he didn't sign petitions or take part in marches. In some respects he sympathized with the government's policy, but he didn't pretend to know all the answers. When people condemned Jeremy Sawyer, or when they praised him, Abbot took refuge in his own ignorance. On such issues he simply had nothing to say.

The waitress brought him his dinner. Abbot cut into his schnitzel and ate without appetite, mostly to put wadding between what he had drunk and what he meant to drink before the night was done. He wondered if all these years he'd harbored a guilty conscience because of his failure to speak up for Jeremy. He knew the man, after all; he understood, or could easily guess, his motives. Jeremy's idealism, his cosmopolitan's view of America's shortcomings, and—most of all—his strong conviction that poets should be men of action, firmly committed to some great cause, not just prophets but builders of that better world they envisioned. Jeremy had expounded on these themes many times during their year at Cambridge; indeed, it seemed to Abbot that he could hear his voice even now, accompanied by the hiss of the gas fire and the sighing of the wind at the old stone casements of their rooms in College, as they talked and argued well into the night. Wonderful times, really, and yet how naïve they were then—how innocent! Why, for Christ's sake, hadn't Jeremy grown up? At the time of his defection he was thirty years old. He had a wife and child; his poetry was widely admired. Hadn't he realized how much he had to lose?

"A poet's loss," Jeremy once told him, "is his only treasure. What you haven't lost can't be recovered in art. Lose the world, Sam—lose damn well all of it! That way, you'll always have it to write about."

Nonsense, Abbot thought. Bloody, foolish, childish nonsense.

And yet, when Jeremy proclaimed a point, whether you believed it or not, or whether even he believed it, it was never forgotten. Jeremy's flight to Moscow had been that sort of proclamation.

For some years after his defection, the Russians treated Sawyer as a prize catch and curiosity, the literary equivalent of the Abominable Snowman of the Himalayas. They paraded him through Eastern Europe and the third-world countries, where he dutifully denounced Western imperialism and assured his audiences that many in America felt as he did—that the second American Revolution was just around the corner. Then, with the end of the Vietnam War and the beginning of détente, Jeremy lapsed into obscurity. By now he was—despite the praise his first book had received and despite even the notoriety of his defection—nearly forgotten in the States. Occasionally some commentator on contemporary poetry might express regret that Sawyer's voice had been silenced by exile, or that his new poetry (assuming there was any) was not available in the West. But that was all. Increasingly, Abbot encountered educated people who had never heard of Jeremy Sawyer. It was to remedy this oversight that he dedicated part of one issue of *Excursions* (the last issue, as it turned out) to Jeremy's work, reprinting several poems and Jeremy's once-famous essay, "The Test of Integrity," along with some biographical and critical notes of Abbot's own. The issue stirred some interest in Sawyer's work, but could hardly be said to have resurrected him, nor did it dispel its editor's bad conscience. It was easy enough to defend Jeremy in the eighties, when nobody cared to attack him. It would have been a good deal more courageous, and meaningful, in 1968.

Abbot pushed away his plate and signaled the waitress for another beer. The odd thing was that none of Jeremy's work had reached the West in well over fifteen years. Was he still writing poetry, or had he set his talents to some more prosaic task? Abbot could scarcely believe that the young man *he* knew could have been persuaded to give up his art for, say, socialist propaganda or technical manuals. Not without a struggle—not without some grand gesture of defiance. Had Jeremy run afoul of the Kremlin's censor, and was that the reason for his long silence?

It would be extremely interesting to see what Jeremy had been writing of late. It would be even more interesting, for Abbot at least, to talk to the man—to learn if he was lonely, homesick, haunted by regrets. Did he still believe those doctrines he had preached in his youth, or had life in Russia taught him the error of his ways? Assuming that Jeremy's ways *were* erroneous, which, for Abbot, was always a difficult question.

The waitress brought his beer. A few more of these and he could quit thinking such disturbing thoughts. It occurred to him, however, that he had one long, unlit block to negotiate—the wooded grounds of the *Krankenhaus* on one side of the street, the university's orchard on the other—in order to reach his room. Someone had killed Mikos Pajorfsky. And Mikos had been carrying a photograph of Abbot and Sawyer. Had Jeremy sent Mikos that photograph via someone named the Stork? What other explanation could there be? The photograph could have been meant as a proof, Abbot thought, that whatever message Pajorfsky bore—the message he didn't live to deliver—came straight from the horse's mouth. But then he had to consider a concomitant possibility: Whoever killed Mikos had done so, in all likelihood, in order to prevent the delivery of that message.

And now the killer had Abbot's gray sweatshirt, with the big red Nakomis State printed across the front, from which he might be able to deduce that at least a part of the message had reached Abbot before Pajorfsky expired.

Did that mean his own life was now in danger? He couldn't know for sure whether Mikos's death was connected to the snapshot, yet surely it would be foolish for him to wait too long or drink too much before heading back to his room. Once he was safely locked in for the night, he could get as drunk as he liked. If, that is, he wanted to get drunk at all. Somehow that nightly retreat into the boozer's foggy euphoria no longer seemed so inviting or inevitable.

You have at this point two options, Abbot thought. You can stick around Breiburg to see what this is all about, or you can say to hell with it and catch the next flight back to the States.

If he chose the first, he might want to think seriously about keeping a clear head. If he chose the second, it didn't much matter whether he drank or not, because his life as a self-respecting adult male would be over and done with. He had betrayed Jeremy

27

Sawyer once; if given the opportunity to make up for it, could he afford to betray him again?

He waved over the waitress and requested *die Rechnung*, added a generous tip, pocketed his change, and made for the door. After the boozy warmth of the restaurant, the night air was agreeably bracing. A pale moon, eyeball white, rode above the rooftops of the mental hospital. A thick hedge stood close along the walk, screening a chain link fence topped with barbed wire. Abbot stretched out his legs, saw his shadow loping ahead of him as he left the light behind.

Up ahead, where the road made a broad turn to the right and the lane to the Stadtwald branched off to the left, there was a single street lamp. Beyond its artificial brilliance, the grounds of the guesthouse lay in heavy blackness. The exterior lights were controlled by a device that turned them off after a lapse of several minutes; the switches were conveniently placed so that a returning resident could brighten his way by stages, the night closing in behind him. German ingenuity. It was only necessary for Abbot to cross a band of heavy shadow between the pool of light at the corner and the lamppost switch at the end of the guesthouse walk. And in that band of shadow, Abbot suddenly realized, a man stood waiting.

He was a tall angular man in a dark overcoat, standing just where the lane narrowed to cross a broad drainage ditch, an iron railing on either side. Abbot was still far enough from the bridge to consider altering his course—yet he would have had to walk several blocks out of his way, or jump across the ditch and blunder through the back gardens, to reach the house without crossing the bridge.

To hell with it, Abbot thought. I'm going across.

He plunged ahead with a brisk purposeful stride, hoping to signal the man on the bridge that he expected no nonsense. He had drawn even with the figure—who stood motionless, hands in his pockets, collar turned up—when the guesthouse grounds were suddenly illuminated. A late visitor on his way out, perhaps, or another resident coming up from the garages on the other side of the building. Abbot never saw the person responsible for this timely gift of light. His eyes were held instead by the face in front of him—an ancient, ravaged, grotesque horror of a face, resembling, with its bony brow, shadowy sockets and array of large teeth, a grinning death's-head from some medieval allegory of sin and retribution. It was the man in the Mercedes, the man who had killed Mikos Pajorfsky.

For several seconds neither man moved, both of them immobilized by the explosion of light, and in that frozen moment Abbot noticed several things: first, that the ghastly whiteness of the man's complexion was the result of a glaze of scar tissue which covered his entire face; second, that the snarl with which he regarded Abbot was in fact a permanent feature, the consequence of a particularly deep scar which angled across his left cheek and, catching a corner of the wide mouth, pinched back the upper lip to expose his long, jagged teeth; and third, that the man did indeed possess a pair of eyes lurking deep within those cavernous sockets—Abbot saw them peering out at him like twin demons of fury and despair. The man, Abbot sensed, had passed through an inferno; he was a creature of the Apocalypse—an authentic angel of death.

Though terrified, Abbot had the presence of mind to conclude that his best defense was a show of indifference: He had to face the horror calmly and, above all, show no sign of recognition. *"Guten Abend,"* he said curtly, as he might have greeted any stranger encountered on an evening's stroll, and resumed his brisk pace.

To his surprise, the creature let him pass. The lights still burned along the walk, and Abbot strode rapidly to the front entrance. The key was in his hand. He didn't glance back to see if the man was behind him, but slipped the key into the lock, gave it a quick half-turn as he put his weight against the glass, removed the key as he slipped through the opening, and eased the door shut behind him. Only when he heard the lock snap into place did he turn to see if he had been pursued. But at that moment the yard lights went out, and all he saw was his pale reflection staring back at him, as if he had succeeded in locking out his own frightened spirit.

He climbed the stairs to his room on trembling legs, let himself in and collapsed against the sturdy wooden door with a sob of relief. My God, what an apparition! His mind rejected the image, as if merely the memory of such a creature might threaten his sanity.

At the same time, it occurred to him that, terrified as he had been, he had handled the situation rather well. That cool, casual *guten Abend* had been an inspiration of the first degree; for all he knew, it had saved his life.

He uncorked a bottle of Spätlese and sat down at his desk, wondering whether to call the police. The difficulties he'd experienced earlier this evening seemed to argue against it. What, after all, could he say the man had done? He hadn't actually witnessed the murder, and he couldn't be sure that the man on the bridge had been waiting for him. He looked at the photograph again, sipped his wine, and considered the possibilities, but there were more than his mind could comprehend. He tossed the snapshot aside, and his gaze fell on the yellow slip of paper which bore Greta's telephone number.

He checked his watch and then, with unusual boldness, dialed the number. He heard several clicks, then buzzing, then a male's deep voice: *"Hallo?"*

"Hello, is Greta there?"

"Greta?" The voice was guarded, but responded in English: "Who is calling, please?"

Abbot hesitated. How much did he have to tell about himself to get information in return? "I'm a friend of Mikos Pajorfsky. Greta gave me a message for him this afternoon."

The voice was silent, and Abbot imagined a hand cupped over the mouthpiece, a hurried conference at the other end. Then: "I am sorry, Greta is not here right now. Can I take a message?"

Abbot abruptly lost his nerve. "Never mind," he said, "just tell her I called," and gently replaced the phone in its cradle.

Getting ready for bed, Abbot listened to the eleven o'clock news on the Armed Forces Network, live by satellite from the United States. It was a comforting custom; he had come to rely on the announcer's nightly assurance that the battered planet was still holding together and could be expected to survive for another eight hours, at least. Tonight, the announcer's familiar voice told of a terrorist bomb scare at the Frankfurt airport, another kidnapping in Rome, more sniper fire in Beirut. The American ambassador to the U.N. had proposed an international conference on terrorism; he called upon the Soviet Union to renounce its support of terrorist groups in Europe, Latin America, and the Middle East.

Lots of luck, Abbot thought. How about getting them to repudiate Marx and Lenin while they're at it? But then, he had never been greatly impressed by the realism of American foreign policy under the current administration.

Before turning out the light he sat for a few moments looking at the framed photograph of his children. Jeffrey was in college now, too busy with his courses (so he said) to write. Charlotte, a high school junior, had other things on her mind, and besides, she had been feuding with her father for years. If Abbot was missed at all, it was only by Emily, the youngest, and then just a little bit, at bedtime, when she remembered him in her prayers. "Dear God, please keep Daddy safe from harm—"

Yes, dear God, Abbot thought, turning out the light and crawling under his comforter, give the old bastard a chance, will you? Maybe, with a little luck, he can do something right for a change.

3

Abbot woke to a chill, dismal morning, clouds rolling westward and raindrops spattering intermittently across the window. He was still in his pajamas and bathrobe, absently watching the coffee drip through its paper filter and into the glass carafe, when the telephone rang.

"Professor Abbot? Is Greta here. I think maybe you called me last night?"

At the sound of her husky voice and thick accent, Abbot felt a mixed rush of emotions—as if something he both dreaded and desired was reaching out to him.

"I have some very bad news. Professor Pajorfsky was killed."

He heard her gasp. "Killed? You are sure of this?"

"A car ran him down in the Stadtwald. I came along just after it happened, and I was there with him when he died. He gave me something—something very peculiar, which I wanted to ask you about. . ."

He waited for her reaction. When she spoke again, her voice had taken on a new decisiveness. "We must not talk about this on the telephone. Can you come to Frankfurt today on the train?"

"Frankfurt? Couldn't we meet here in Breiburg?"

"In Frankfurt is better, I think—is safer, yes? There is a train leaving Breiburg at twelve-oh-five. You can be on it?"

Abbot checked his watch. "I suppose so, but I really have a lot of work to do here this weekend. Couldn't we—?"

"Someone will meet you at the *Hauptbahnhof*. He will make himself known to you—then he will explain how to find me. *Wiedersehen*, Professor."

The line clicked off. Abbot replaced the receiver and stood looking out at the low, dense clouds. Sheets of rain blew across the orchard. Hardly a pleasant day for travel, and his Berlin paper still needed work. The police might be coming back with his passport; surely they would want to talk to him again. On the other hand, Abbot didn't see how he could sit in his room thinking calmly through the ideological ramifications of recent American literature when matters much more immediate might be waiting for him in Frankfurt.

He was ready to leave for the station by eleven. Stepping into the hall, he found one of the cleaning ladies and a very distraught Frau Graushen outside Professor Pajorfsky's room.

"Herr Professor Abbot," the proprietress said, glaring at him as if he were somehow to blame for whatever was upsetting her, *"ein Moment, bitte. Sehen Sie diese Tür? Was denken Sie?"*

Abbot followed the direction of her pointing finger and saw that both the doorknob and lock to Pajorfsky's door were missing. In their place was a charred hole, as if something had burned through the wood around the metal plate. Bereft of its latch, the door hung slightly ajar. Abbot felt slightly giddy, remembering how secure he had believed himself last night behind the triple dead bolt lock.

Frau Graushen was sputtering at him again. He gathered that she had already looked inside and that the interior of the apartment was a mess—*"Schrecklich, ganz schrecklich!"* Though Frau Graushen wasn't exactly accusing Abbot of this outrage, she seemed to know that he and Pajorfsky had been friendly; she expected him to have some answers. *"Wo ist Herr Pajorfsky?"* she asked suspiciously, as if Abbot might be hiding him someplace.

"Ich weiss nicht," Abbot said, which was true enough—he had no idea where the little Pole's body had been taken. He expected, however, that when Frau Graushen reported this vandalism to the police, his accident report of the night before would suddenly gain in credibility. It seemed urgent that he talk to Greta before he saw the police again.

"I'm sorry—I've got a train to catch." He started down the stairs with Frau Graushen's shrill vowels echoing in the well. The diminutive Korean physicist and the serene Indian couple looked out their doors, then quickly withdrew their heads, as if they had no wish to get involved in anyone else's troubles. Good idea, Abbot thought, as he left the guesthouse and raised his umbrella against the rain. Perhaps I should learn a lesson from them.

He was at the Breiburg station by eleven-forty. One of the few buildings in the city to have survived the massive bombings of '43, the *Bahnhof* was a dismal pile of sooty stones. Its ponderous archways and dank, cavernous gloom evoked the grim grandeur of the Third Reich, that already legendary epoch of madness and sorrow which Abbot's perverse imagination was always trying to summon from its grave. In the *Bahnhof* the evil of the past was palpable.

Abbot bought his ticket and wandered into the station's small bookstore, where he knew he could find a few English-language publications. Picking up a day-old *Herald Tribune*, his eye was snagged by the garish covers of several pornographic magazines on the upper rack. The new Germany—free speech and free love. One of those cover girls, with the wild haystack of blond hair and the pointy tits, looked a lot like Pajorfsky's foxy little assistant. So is *that* why you're going down to Frankfurt in the rain, he wondered, when you should be staying home to work on your paper?

But no, he insisted to himself as he paid for the paper and headed for his platform, the dubious charms of Pajorfsky's assistant had nothing to do with this excursion. He had good reason to believe that his old friend Jeremy Sawyer was trying to get in touch with him. His response was habitual and instinctive.

He found the track for the Frankfurt train and stood waiting with a dozen or so others beneath the intricate webbing of wires. Always an anxious traveler, Abbot had learned to double- and triple-check everything in Germany, since its transportation systems—while reliable and eminently logical—allowed little margin for error. Satisfied that he was where he should be, he took note of his fellow travelers: two young GI's, probably off to Frankfurt on a weekend pass; a weary overweight woman with two small children and a babe in arms; a very correct and dignified old gentleman in a gray business suit; a family of Greek or Turkish migrant workers; a rather mysterious fellow in a tan trench coat. . . . Abbot ran his eye back along the platform in search of the tan trench coat, but it had disappeared behind one of the steel pillars that supported the fiberglass canopy.

Hello there, what's this? He considered strolling up the platform for a casual look behind the pillar, but then decided it would be better not to show the man he'd been discovered. *I'm learning how to play this game.* Perhaps recent events had augmented his perceptions, sharpened his eye for detail. He retained the image of a tall, broad-shouldered young man, with curly blond hair and a bland, boyish face, whose clear blue eyes had skipped away from Abbot's glance. *Hell, probably just some student from the institute who doesn't want to be recognized by one of his profs. But in a trench coat?* Perhaps he was beginning to see too much in the perfectly normal behavior of strangers, yet Abbot could have sworn the young man was hiding from him.

A bright point of light well up the track announced the arrival of the train. Abbot checked his pockets one last time—his ticket, his German-English phrasebook, his map of Frankfurt, his traveler's checks, the photo of Jeremy Sawyer in its plain white envelope—and then the great, blunt-nosed engine roared past with a blast of heat and hint of grease. A long line of passenger cars headed for Basel, Geneva, Nice, Milan, slid by as the train slowed. Abbot wedged his newspaper and his collapsible umbrella under one arm and stepped forward. When the train slid smoothly to a halt, he grasped the nearest door handle, yanked the door open, then stood aside for the fat woman and her children. This highly Germanic courtesy gave him a chance to glance over his shoulder. The tall blond man in the tan trench coat had come out from behind his pillar and was edging closer to the train. He wasn't looking at Abbot, however. Something further up the platform seemed to have claimed his attention.

Abbot climbed on board and made his way along the corridor. He heard the conductor's whistle and the slamming of several doors. Bending to the window, he observed the young man making a dash for the already-moving car.

Now that's interesting. A gust of air along the corridor signaled that the fellow's leap for the train had been successful. *I don't want to see him,* Abbot thought and stepped quickly into the nearest compartment. The occupants looked up with the usual *guten Morgen*s of German travelers, then returned to their knitting and crossword puzzles. Abbot took a seat by the window and opened his *Herald Tribune*. As the train gathered momentum, the fellow in the trench coat passed along the corridor, looked in, but did not enter the compartment to claim the last seat. For an instant, their eyes met and Abbot was surprised by the cold, quick appraisal he was given, rather like the glint of some concealed weapon.

Shit, what I am getting myself into?

Too late to worry about that now. The train was speeding through the suburbs and Abbot saw gray stucco flats, tiny garden plots with their improvised huts and ornamentation, a rat's maze of fencing, an abandoned factory with broken windows . . . and then abruptly they were into the forest. Abbot turned from the window and scanned the front page of his newspaper. Nothing held his attention; he was too tense to read. He turned to the Arts page and was halfway through the daily book review before he realized the words weren't registering . . . and then the small headline in the adjacent column jumped at him: EXPATRIATE POET TO ADDRESS CONFERENCE. And there in the outdated, yet as it were ageless, photograph that always seemed to accompany news stories on Jeremy Sawyer, was the poet himself—the very one whose even more youthful image rode in its white envelope inside Abbot's coat pocket.

The story was datelined West Berlin, and at first Abbot thought that the conference in question was the one at which he was scheduled to present his paper. The dates seemed to correspond, but reading further he discovered that this conference was being held in East Berlin, under the auspices of the Soviet cultural mission to East Germany. Apparently the Russians had set up a literary conference in East Berlin to parallel the one in West Berlin—another example of the cultural cold war Abbot had become aware of since his arrival in Europe. *His* conference was supposed to be academic in nature and scrupulously nonpolitical; nevertheless, it was sponsored by the U.S. Information Service and had a certain propaganda value for the West by focusing international attention on that "outpost of freedom," West Berlin. The Russian-sponsored conference was clearly meant as a counteroffensive and would no doubt stress the decadence of the West; to this end the Soviets were hauling out of retirement their fabulous defecting poet and chief

America-baiter. They were reactivating the voice of "oppressed and rebellious American youth" and were asking Jeremy once more—sadly, predictably—to do his outmoded sixties thing.

Abbot gazed out at the wooded hills and valleys of Hesse, blue and mysterious behind veils of mist and rain. On a distant ridge he discerned the silhouette of yet another castle; this part of Germany was lousy with ruined castles. Whenever Abbot's colleagues at the institute worried that he wasn't getting enough attention, one of them would take him to some ruin and march him about, then bring him home for coffee and *Kuchen*. It always struck Abbot as ironic: The rubble of World War Two had been swept away by an avalanche of American-style progress and prosperity, while the wreckage of the barbarous past had been conscientiously preserved and was now proudly displayed as the legacy of a great tradition. And so it was. The Germans were a fine people. They had developed a marvelous culture. It was just the first half of the twentieth century, and more particularly the twenty-five years of Nazism, which they hoped to scrub away with their tireless sanitary zeal. Surely, it was argued, that interlude had been but an unfortunate aberration of the German psyche.

Abbot was inclined to agree. Individuals were always more or less guilty of the crimes they committed, cultures always more or less innocent. If the German culture—Mozart, after all, and Brahms, Goethe and Schiller, Einstein and Freud—was not to be blamed for Hitler's evil, why should America as a whole take the rap for the cynical miscalculations of *its* politicians and generals? At least some of us stood up to protest, Abbot thought proudly—until he remembered that he hadn't been one of them. If he had lived in Germany in 1941, would he have been one of those to pull down the window shade and turn up the radio as the trainload of doomed Jews went rolling by?

Jeremy, Jeremy, you crazy bastard—you pathetic, awesome, God-struck bloody genius—what do you want of me?

Later this coming week, for just a few days, Sam Abbot and Jeremy Sawyer would find themselves once more in the same city, perhaps within a few blocks of one another, yet separated by that infamous barrier between East and West, the Berlin Wall. Surely this coincidence was not unrelated to the death of Mikos Pajorfsky or to the snapshot from Abbot's past that he'd been carrying. It was altogether likely, Abbot thought, that he would be given the opportunity to meet and talk with Jeremy—either that or he'd get himself killed in the attempt.

Somehow this as yet only hypothetical risk did not greatly trouble Abbot. Last week he had walked through the local *Friedhof,* and in the midst of all those crumbling headstones and angel-adorned monuments it came to him that his chief problem, these last few years, had simply been an excessive and irrational fear of death. He was forty-five years old, forty-five and counting. He had begun to feel the passage of time like a congealing substance within his own body, the cold gravy of mortality waxing the chipped china of his soul. Another man might have taken a mistress or embarked on a new career. Abbot drank. Afraid to face death head on, he had begun to measure it out in shots of gin and bourbon, a sip here and a sip there, don't mind me, ladies—I'm just priming this old cadaver for the undertaker.

Abbot watched the rainwater stream across the window of the speeding train. Occasionally the buildup of air pressure along the glass broke the film of water into a scattering of droplets, some of which flew off the glass and some of which clung. Abbot but vaguely understood the principles of physics at work in the phenomenon, but he could feel them applied to his own life. When the forces at work on a man's soul reached a certain pressure or pitch of intensity, something happened: a man changed, his being was broken apart and reformed in accordance with certain laws of nature. But were such moral revolutions ever a matter of will, of conscious and rational choice?

Perhaps, in the next week or two, he would find out.

It took the express train less than an hour to travel from Breiburg to Frankfurt. Abbot saw clearing skies, the sharp outlines of the Taunus Mountains, as the *Schnellzug* glided through the Frankfurt suburbs. He had visited the city twice before and felt reasonably confident as they entered the switchyards, then slid beneath the huge glass-and-metal canopy of the *Hauptbahnhof.* He was not exactly an innocent abroad, for heaven's sake—he should be able to take care of himself.

Nevertheless, he felt particularly vulnerable as he stepped down from the train and let the crowd carry him along the narrow strip of concrete toward the large, pavilionlike area beyond the gate. There was no sign of the young fellow he'd seen in Breiburg, but he would be hard to spot in such a crush. Greta had said that his contact would "make himself known" in the station— she hadn't said how. Abbot supposed this person wouldn't approach until he was sure it was safe. If indeed he would be met by anyone at all.

He browsed among the fruit and flower stalls, the bookshops and newsstands, then spent some time studying a billboard-sized map of the city. When no one in the vast, bustling station seemed to take an interest in him, he strolled over to a lunch counter (*Schnellimbiss,* as the Germans called it) and ordered a bratwurst and a glass of beer. There were several small stand-up tables in front of the lunch counter, separated from the flow of pedestrian traffic by a low fence. Abbot took a stance at one of these tables and ate his brat. Students with backpacks, a party of nuns with old-fashioned black satchels, the usual assortment of tourists . . . none of them returned his questioning gaze. Eventually Abbot became aware of a stout man in a plaid sports coat, standing at the next table. The man was sipping a beer and reading an English paperback—nothing unusual about that, since all the newsstands in the station sold foreign publications—but he was holding this book slightly off the tabletop so that Abbot could see its title: *Bottled Rage.* Abbot knew the man couldn't have purchased that book here in the station, because Jeremy Sawyer's first and only book of poems had been out of print for years.

The fat man looked up. He had a round, florid face and pale, sleepy eyes. His ginger-brown moustache was waxed at the tips and gave his ruddy face an old-fashioned military appearance, as if he were a survivor of the Bengal Lancers. Having caught Abbot's attention, he quickly slipped Sawyer's book into an inside coat pocket and brought out instead a Bundesbahn timetable.

"I say, can you read one of these bloody schedules?" he asked, in what was almost a parody of a British accent.

"Sometimes," Abbot said with a smile.

The man transferred his glass to Abbot's table. "I'd be most grateful if you could tell me if you think this particular train—you see, just here?—connects with the train from Basel, or whether one has to go all the way to Cologne to catch the damned thing."

Then lowering his voice but still speaking conversationally he added, "Greta sent me around to meet you. Did you know there's a chap in a tan mackintosh tagging along behind you?"

"I saw him get on the train in Breiburg," Abbot said. "Any idea who he is?"

"No, but I'll bloody well find out. You wait here till I've drawn him off, then nip round the other way and down to the U-Bahn station—know where it is?"

"Yes, I think so."

"Take the number thirty-seven train—it should be arriving in three minutes—to the Römer stop. From there you can walk straight down to the river and you'll see a footbridge. Cross over, and Greta will meet you on the other side. Can you manage that?"

Abbot said he believed he could.

"Jolly good. I'll be off then." And raising his voice he added, "Thanks awfully—and pleasant journey!"

The portly Englishman crossed to a newsstand, where now Abbot saw the young man in the tan trench coat looking over a rack of foreign papers. Neither man seemed to notice the other, yet Abbot could tell they were both alert and wary. They danced a little pirouette around the revolving rack of newspapers, keeping it constantly between them. Then suddenly the Englishman broke away and nearly ran for the far exit. The man in the tan trench coat glanced once at Abbot, then set off in pursuit of the Briton.

Abbot left for the U-Bahn. He bought a ticket from the vending machine and came down on the escalator just as the number 37 train burst from its tunnel. Abbot stepped on board with a handful of Saturday passengers and the doors slid silently shut. The train began to glide along the platform, then lunged into darkness.

Two stops later Abbot saw the sign for the Römer and got off the train. He rode the escalator up to street level and found that the weather had continued to improve: There was a pale sun beaming down on the Römer's pink façade and a mild southerly breeze blowing across its cobbled square. The sidewalk cafés were open and the bells of the cathedral were just striking the hour of two as Abbot went down the lane to the broad boulevard along the river.

He waited for a light, then crossed the street to the footbridge. The broad brown Main oozed with syrupy smoothness between its concrete banks. Abbot saw a few pleasure crafts along the far shore and a long industrial barge coming downriver. He climbed the steps and started across the bridge, one of only a few pedestrians. It occurred to him that, if he paused at mid-river to admire the view, he could make sure he was no longer being followed. He chose his spot, paused, turned back to the city's skyline. Its ice-blue shafts and slate-gray obelisks burst from the jumble of black-tiled rooftops as if raised by the wave of some medieval wizard's wand. Yet as Abbot had learned, even the "ancient" structures of Frankfurt were postwar; the real wizardry had been the city's nearly faultless recovery of its past.

Satisfied that no one was following him, he continued across the bridge, descended the steps on the other side and found Greta waiting for him—still wearing her vinyl jacket and faded, thigh-hugging blue jeans. Her long blond hair was puffed and teased by the wind; her dark eyes greeted him with warmth, and there was a shy, sly smile hovering at her freshly painted lips.

"Guten Tag, Herr Abbot."

"Guten Tag, Greta."

"Do you speak German?"

"Not very well, I'm afraid."

She shrugged. "My English is also not so good, but perhaps we can make do, yes? Do you like to walk?"

She indicated the gravel path that stretched along the river, between two rows of severely pruned trees. Abbot agreed, and they began walking. "So," she said, "Mikos gave to you the photograph, yes?"

"He did. What I'd like to know is where he got it and why he wanted me to have it. He seemed to think it was pretty important—"

"Very important," Greta said. "Some of this I can explain and some will be told by others. But first I must warn you that there may be for you in this much danger. What happened to Mikos was no accident, Herr Abbot. He was murdered."

Abbot felt unhappily vindicated, as if some fearful diagnosis on which he'd sought a second opinion had been confirmed.

"I thought as much, since the body was gone by the time I came

41

back with the police." He paused. "Do you know why he was murdered, Greta?"

She put her chin and her pert nose into the wind, letting her sun-bright tresses stream out behind. "Mikos was very brave man. He risk his life many times for the cause we both serve. I am proud to be his comrade. I found his body, Herr Abbot. My friends and I took it away because we did not want the police to—how you say? —to investigate, yes? We took the body, but it was the KGB who killed him."

"The Russians?" Abbot looked involuntarily over his shoulder. "What did Mikos have to do with the KGB?"

She drew him into the shelter of a kiosk so that she could light her cigarette. Exhaling a long stream of smoke, she glared up at Abbot with her fiercely dark eyes. "You are also a brave man, yes? You are not afraid to fight for what you believe in?"

Abbot sensed an undercurrent of sexual challenge in her voice; only brave men, she seemed to be saying, would ever stand a chance with her. "I don't know whether I'm a brave man or not," he said, "and I don't really know if I have any beliefs worth fighting for."

She seemed to find this confession incredible—a man his age, who had never been tested? Who was still unsure of his beliefs? He might have admitted that he was still a virgin. Hoping to salvage some remnant of her regard, he added, "I do care about my friends—I guess I believe in loyalty to people, if not to causes. The man in that photograph was once a close friend of mine. I'd like to help him if I can. That's why I'm here."

Greta nodded her satisfaction, then indicated that they should continue walking. Abbot saw a young couple pushing a baby carriage, another sharing a park bench and a picnic lunch. Although the trees and flower beds were still bare, there was a subtle scent of spring in the mild breeze. Abbot wondered at his own submerged feelings: Was he going to let this little blonde play him for a sucker?

"I will tell you something about our organization," Greta said. "Mikos and I, we belong to a group the Americans call ELF—the European Liberation Front. *Auf Deutsch,* we say *die Osteuropäische Befreiungsfront*—it means the same thing, yes? We are many nationalities—Germans, Poles, Czechs, Hungarians, even Russians, but all anti-Communists. Many of us are refugees, or we have family members still living under the Soviet dictators. That is why we must be very secret, yes?—like underground resistance during the last war. As they fought the Nazis, we fight the Communists. We work to make all Europe free; we will not rest until our brothers and sisters in the East have the same freedoms we have here in the West—that is our cause."

She pronounced the words "bruzzers" and "seestairs"; Abbot found her accent charming—he was considerably less charmed by the note of fanaticism in her husky young voice. Years of disillusionment with American politics had taught him to regard such anti-Communist rhetoric with a good deal of skepticism.

"Are you by any chance financed," he asked her, "by the CIA?"

She shook her head vigorously. "The Americans do not tell us what to do. We are European organization, run by Europeans. We know what is best for Europe. Sometimes the Americans like what we do and sometimes they don't. But we do not need the CIA's money. We have our own money. There are many rich people here in Germany who support our work. We are—how do you say in English?—'private enterprise,' yes? This is making us strong, and strong makes free."

Abbot could see the girl had her rhetoric down pat, and he almost admired her simple sense of right and wrong—admired it as much as he disapproved of it. "So how do you fight the Communists?" he asked. "Do you throw bombs, steal secrets, what?"

She glared up at him. "Whatever we can do, we do. It is a war, yes? They are the enemy—we find ways to make trouble for them. We have agents in all the East European countries. Sometimes they learn things which we can sell to the Western governments. Then we use the money to help people escape the Russian tyrants—we bring them here to new lives in the West. In this way we keep the hope of freedom alive in those countries."

"And Mikos? What was his assignment in Breiburg? I assume it had nothing to do with archaeology?"

"That was, how you say, his 'cover,' yes? In fact he was very famous professor in Poland—that is why he was allowed to teach and study here in Germany. But his real purpose in Breiburg, Herr Abbot, was to meet you."

"And to give me that photograph. But why?"

43

"He had a message for you. I myself do not know what the message was, but I know it must have been very important, because it came from the Stork."

"The Stork—yes, Mikos mentioned that name. Who in hell is the Stork?"

"He is our most important agent in the East. We do not know much about him, not even his nationality. Some people say he is Russian and that he has sworn an oath to overthrow the Marxist dictators. Others say he is Hungarian or Czech, but over the years he has helped many people to escape from the Communists. He has many spies, yes? He is very powerful—the Russians cannot capture him. He brings us many refugees—artists, soldiers, diplomats, scientists—all who want a new life of freedom. That is why they call him the Stork—he is a bringer of new life."

"I see," Abbot said. "Then I think I can guess why Mikos was sent to give me that photograph. Jeremy Sawyer has had enough of Communism—he wants to come home."

Greta didn't seem to understand and Abbot guessed that she herself had not yet been told about Sawyer. Nevertheless, she caught the excitement in his voice and looked up at him with eager bright eyes. "Then—you will help us?"

"I still don't know what you want of me. But if Jeremy really does want to leave the Soviet Union, and if there's anything I can do to help him—well, yes, by God, I'm ready to give it a try."

"And you are not afraid of the Russians?"

"Afraid?" Abbot thought of the scar-faced man he had seen last night outside the guesthouse—his own personal grim reaper. "Of course I'm afraid, but what's that got to do with anything?"

Greta obviously approved of this attitude and slipped an arm through his as a sign of their new relationship: *comrades.* Abbot felt his pulse rate quicken as her body drew close. He caught the clean scent of shampoo in her windblown hair and wondered if he could offer to buy her a drink, now that they were united by a common cause.

They were nearing the end of the riverside path; ahead lay a busy intersection where one of the major thoroughfares of Frankfurt crossed the river. Beyond the intersection stood the entrance to the old streets of Sachsenhausen, a popular area of small restaurants and beer gardens Abbot had visited once before. He was just about to suggest that they choose one of these spots, when he noticed that Greta was signaling to a large dark car parked just up the street. At once the car began to creep forward. Abbot tried to pull back from the curb, but Greta clung forcefully to his arm.

"Do not be afraid," she said. "We go now—we will meet the others."

"The others?" Abbot asked, as the long black limousine slid to a halt in front of them.

The back doors opened and two men jumped out. They were both the size of wrestlers and had faces to match. Abbot would have had to knock Greta down in order to break the hold she had on his arm. Unwilling to use that much force on a woman, he let her hinder his flight just long enough for the two men to grab his arms.

"Hey, goddamn it—!"

Then he saw that Greta had taken what looked like a large hypodermic needle from her purse. At first he foolishly thought she meant to protect him with it, then realized she had other plans.

"This will not hurt, Herr Abbot," she said, as one of the men jerked his coat off his shoulders. "You will sleep for only a little while—"

And before he could find a convincing counterargument, she had jabbed the needle, with the brisk efficiency of a nurse, through his shirt and into his upper arm. The last thing he saw was the look of tender concern in her dark eyes as she withdrew the needle.

t seemed to Abbot as the anesthetic wore off that he was in the dentist's chair back in Wisconsin, having his four wisdom teeth extracted. "Will it hurt?" he asked the dentist anxiously. "Will there be much pain?"

"Nein, Liebling," replied a husky female voice, "no pain."

Abbot opened his eyes. At first his vision was obscured by the drug—he saw only blurred light and a periphery of shadows, but he could feel movement, hear the hum of a powerful engine. Then gradually he made out the interior of a large, luxurious automobile. Leather upholstery, tinted glass, the subdued spangles of filtered sunlight. He was sprawled across the commodious backseat, his head and shoulders resting against something soft and sweet smelling. . . . Was this a woman's breast cushioning his cheek?

Abbot tilted his head back and in the dusky, dappled light saw Greta looking solicitously down at him. "Are you feeling better now?" she asked.

He remembered the large dark car pulling up to the curb, the two big bruisers piling out, the needle jabbing into his arm. In a sudden panic he tried to sit up, but a piercing pain between his temples drove him back into Greta's arms. She gently massaged his neck and shoulders. "There, there, *Schatzi,* it's all right—the drug will wear off soon."

"Good timing," said a voice in the front seat that Abbot thought he recognized. "We're almost there."

"Where?" Abbot asked, pushing the syllable through a considerable dryness in his throat. "Where are you taking me?"

"To see a man who will explain everything to you," Greta said. "He will tell you how you can help your friend, yes? But the place where we will meet him is very secret. That is why we had to put you to sleep—it is better for all of us if you do not know how to find this place again."

Abbot wasn't sure he understood that, and he disliked occupying a spot on the globe he couldn't name or locate on a map. He lifted his wrist and, after a moment's concentration, was able to read the dial: just after five o'clock. That meant he'd been unconscious for nearly three hours. They could have traveled well over two hundred miles in three hours. They could be in East Germany by now.

He felt the car slowing, then felt its heavy chassis sway as they made a sharp turn to the right. He tried to sit up again, but the pain was still too severe, and Greta brought his head back to her breast. The road was rougher now; gravel rattled against the underside of the car. Sometimes bushes scraped and squeaked against its flank. The rhythmic flickering of sunlight at the tinted windows suggested a wooded area. The car went up a steep grade and around several hairpin turns. Gravity pushed Abbot hard against Greta's yielding bosom, but she didn't complain. After a long, laborious climb, the car leveled off. There was a steady brightness at the windows now. The car came to a stop but Abbot felt a gust of wind against its side.

"Better use a blindfold," the voice in the front seat ordered. "He might remember the view."

Abbot began to protest, but the voice said, "It's for your own protection, old man." Abbot was sure now it belonged to the portly Englishman who had met him at the Frankfurt station.

Greta placed the blindfold over his eyes. The back door opened and strong hands helped Abbot out and held him steady on his feet. Apparently the two musclemen had been riding in the front as well—Abbot could feel their bulky, stolid presence on either side of him. Car doors slammed.

"Now then," the Englishman spoke reassuringly, "as soon as you feel up to it, we'll just walk for a short distance. Ready?"

By the time Abbot thought to count steps, they had already gone a considerable distance along what seemed to be a brick-paved walk. Another ten paces and the Englishman said, "Easy now—we have to go up four steps. That's right—there we are. Just a moment now—"

Abbot heard a key scraping in a lock, a door opening. They crossed the threshold and he was guided along an echoing corridor, then through another door. He heard drapes being pulled, lights clicking on. At last the blindfold was removed.

The portly Englishman smiled at him. "Jolly good, I expect you'd like a drink."

"Some water," Abbot said. The room was large and comfortably furnished as a sort of den or sportsman's trophy room. The mounted heads of hundreds of horned animals—deer, antelope, oxen, sheep—gazed sorrowfully at Abbot from the paneled walls. Over the fireplace there hung the head of a magnificent boar, looking as though he had only just thrust his tusked snout through the stone chimney in search of a good fight. A case with glass doors held a large collection of rifles, muskets, pistols, while between the mounted heads were hung swords, lances, sabers, rapiers, axes and other ancient weapons of destruction. Abbot found it a thoroughly intimidating room and, sinking down onto a leather sofa, observed that there was even a suit of armor standing guard in one of the dark corners.

Greta sat beside him like a mother comforting her child in the doctor's office. The Englishman brought him a glass of mineral water. "Sure you wouldn't like something in that?"

"Maybe later. Is this your place, then?"

"Oh, Lord, no. The chap we want you to meet will be along shortly. My name's Hedge, Brian Hedge. Sorry about the needle and all that unpleasantness, but this way, you see, we keep your options open. If you don't like our offer, you can walk away with an easy mind."

Abbot thought the easy minds would likely be on the other side, but he said, "What sort of offer are you going to make?"

"Our friend will explain," Hedge said. "Oh, that youngish bloke in the *Hauptbahnhof* was a countryman of yours, by the way—a CIA man by the name of Morrison. Apparently the Yanks picked up on that accident report you filed with the Breiburg police, and they sent Morrison to check you out. I expect you'll be hearing from him again."

"So the CIA knows that Mikos was one of your agents?"

"No doubt they do—they know most of us, thought I hadn't run into this chap before; he must be new. We get along quite well with the Yanks—most of the time. Of course this particular business *is* rather delicate—I'm sure you understand. We'd rather not bring the CIA in on this one, just yet. We don't know how Jeremy Sawyer would react to that sort of welcoming committee."

"Then that's what this is all about? You want me to help you get Jeremy out of the Soviet Union?"

Hedge lifted a hand to his ear, as if to call for silence, and in a moment Abbot caught the sound of hoofbeats passing outside the building. A rider on horseback—appropriate to the setting, Abbot thought.

"That's him now—the chap who can best answer your questions. I'm just one of the hired hands, you understand. Spent twenty years in the British Secret Service, I did. When they said I was too old to work in the field and tried to chain me to a desk I took early retirement and caught on here with ELF. It's an admirable organization in many ways. For one thing, there are the advantages of our independent status. We have a somewhat freer hand when it comes to dealing with Communist thugs and terrorists—"

"In other words," Abbot said, "you don't have to observe the law?"

Hedge looked amused by Abbot's naïveté. "My dear fellow, there's never any law in the spy trade, you know. It's all perfectly immoral and illegal—which is why it appeals to some of us with temperaments to match, I suppose. Don't you imagine that the CIA sometimes bends the law a bit? Of course governments have all these purely *political* concerns to worry about—what the public will accept in the defense of the realm and what it won't. We're blissfully immune to that sort of pressure in ELF, since we answer to no misinformed and essentially sentimental body of public opinion."

Abbot was going to ask if public accountability wasn't an important part of the democratic system they were trying to defend, but at that moment bootheels echoed in the hall. The door opened and a man in a leather riding coat and high riding boots stepped confidently into the room. Abbot rose to greet his host, thus confirming his impression that the man was well under average height—perhaps an inch or two shy of five feet. His body, however, was in perfect proportion to his stature, so that he seemed a sturdy and athletic specimen of a slightly smaller species. His dark hair was long and curly and touched rather elegantly with gray. He had a strong jaw and a quick, ingratiating smile, which displayed two rows of small, white, even teeth as he crossed the room to shake hands. Though Abbot didn't think he had ever seen the handsome face before, he felt as though he were shaking hands with a celebrity.

"Professor Abbot, how good it is to meet you." The little man possessed a deep melodious voice, without a hint of accent. "Welcome to my house and excuse, please, these elaborate and somewhat melodramatic precautions. I trust we weren't *too* rough on you?"

"Not too," Abbot granted, unable to resist such a warm tone and friendly smile.

"Good, good—that's all right then." The little man clapped his hands together, and Abbot sensed that, behind his informal manner, his host nurtured an extraordinary view of his own importance and dignity. "Won't you be seated, please? I've taken the liberty of ordering a light supper for us, which will be served presently. In the meantime, what about a glass of sherry, or some scotch?"

Abbot decided that he was ready for a drink. "Scotch would be fine. With a little ice and water, please."

"Spoken like a true Yank," Hedge said, and went to the bar.

The little man sat down in a leather armchair and smiled at Abbot. "Though my advisers insist that my identity be kept secret for the time being, I think I can give you my first name, at least. I believe Americans like to establish an informal relationship as quickly as possible. I'm Franz—and may I call you Samuel?"

"Sam," Abbot said.

"And how are you liking Germany, Sam? Do you note many differences between our universities and yours in the States?"

Abbot saw they were going to make small talk for awhile, in accordance with his host's odd sense of propriety. He gave his standard answer: "Yes, I like Germany very much. This is my second visit. The people are kind and courteous, the customs generally to my taste. As for the university, I guess the main thing I notice is that your professors have a lot more status than ours—they're treated almost like aristocrats."

At this Franz sighed. "There are no more true aristocrats in Germany, Sam—just a few obscure titles and a handful of ancient families. Hitler did away with all the rest. But yes, the German people have always held the academic profession in great esteem."

"Perhaps," Abbot suggested as Hedge brought him his drink, "even too much esteem. I'm used to being asked to work a bit harder for my pay than I do over here."

Franz looked as if this were rather a puzzling complaint. "Ah well, if one is not required to work for one's money, one has the opportunity to find other ways of being of service to society— that is the true function of an aristocracy. The concept has nearly been lost in modern times, I fear."

"Noblesse oblige," Abbot said, smiling.

"Precisely." The little man raised the glass of sherry Hedge had given him, and they drank to it.

Abbot looked around the trophy-filled room. "I take it you're a sportsman. Are all these beasties yours?"

Franz made a face—he had one of those pliable European faces which could screw itself, on the instant, to a sea of wrinkles, so that he looked like a wizened old man. "Heavens, no. I abhor hunting, or any violent sport. These poor creatures were all slaughtered by my ancestors, who had rather more bloodthirsty tastes. I suppose I should have them decently disposed of, but I seldom use this lodge."

"Only for clandestine meetings."

"Quite so." Little Franz appeared momentarily confused, as if he feared that Abbot might be mocking him. The Germans, Abbot had noticed, often displayed a limited tolerance for irony.

"Now then," he continued, "I assume you have been informed concerning the nature of our organization and the work that we do. The Americans have given us the rather amusing acronym, ELF, though the initials in German are somewhat different. In any case, we *are* elves of a sort, working in stealth for the good of mankind. We are committed to the cause of freedom—and to the honor and dignity of all men. We would be both honored and pleased, Sam, if you would be willing to join us in this endeavor."

Abbot took a sip of his drink and chose his words carefully. "As I explained to Greta, I may not share your political fervor or your intense dislike for Communism. . . . I guess some of us in America have gotten a bit cynical about the causes of world tension; I haven't blamed all our problems on the Russians since I was a freshman in high school."

"We know about your politics, professor," Brian Hedge broke in, "and we have no problem with your liberal attitudes—even if we do think you have a great deal to learn about the realities of life here in Europe. The point is that at present we seem to have a common interest—"

"You're referring to Jeremy Sawyer. How do you know he wants to leave the Soviet Union?"

"We learned of Sawyer's disenchantment," Franz said, "from an agent of ours who makes it his business to know whenever there is an important person in one of the Soviet slave-states who is ripe for liberation. You smile at my rhetoric, Sam, but in the struggle we're engaged in, propaganda is one of the major weapons on both sides. The Russians bombard us ceaselessly with their propaganda. We, in turn, do whatever we can to keep the hope of freedom alive in Eastern Europe. You may recall the considerable embarrassment your country suffered when your friend Sawyer defected in 1968. American interests were hurt all over Europe, but the damage was particularly great here in Germany, among the young, and especially among the intellectuals. The German Left made a heroic martyr out of Jeremy Sawyer. They interpreted his defection as proof that America had become an oppressive police state—that it no longer tolerated reasoned dissent."

"Which was, of course, precisely the point Jeremy wished to make." Abbot felt the need to elaborate. "You see, he always did have this Byronic impulse to the grand gesture, this urge to sacrifice himself to some great cause. I've often wondered what he thinks of his cause, now that he's been living with it for all these years."

"Apparently it hasn't been easy for him," Franz said. "We've learned that Sawyer has written an account of his defection and of his life in Russia, in which he records his progressive disillusionment with the Communist system and his realization that he made a terrible mistake when he abandoned his homeland. Perhaps you can imagine what a victory it would be for our side, at long last, if Sawyer's true story could only be told in full—which of course is impossible as long as he remains in the Soviet Union. We've already made discreet enquiries with a British publisher, Sir Godfrey Clemmons, who has expressed much interest in the project."

Abbot was familiar with the name. Something of a maverick himself, Clemmons had built his Fleet Street empire out of several scandal-mongering tabloids before turning to political journalism and the mass marketing of certain controversial memoirs. Whatever the merits of Jeremy's book—and Abbot felt sure they would be substantial—his memoirs would certainly prove controversial.

"And what role do you see for me in all this? If Jeremy's ready to come, and you have the means to get him out—?"

"Unfortunately," Franz said, "he is *not* quite ready to come. It seems that your friend harbors certain lingering suspicions concerning the publishing establishment in England and America. He tells us that he's afraid of being swindled of what he deems his masterpiece. Moreover, Sir Godfrey has certain qualms about Sawyer—particularly his willingness to accept editorial supervision. It's entirely possible, since no one has yet seen it, that Sawyer's manuscript will need a good deal of work after it reaches the West. That's why the crucial point, at this juncture, has become the selection of an editor."

"The selection of an editor? But surely that can wait until Jeremy's out of Russia!"

"One would think so, but on this point your Mr. Sawyer has become very stubborn. He has said he won't budge until we can assure him of your cooperation."

Abbot's gaze traveled around the room until it alighted on a particularly frantic and harried-looking gazelle above the gun case. "Jeremy—chose *me* to edit his memoir?"

"Apparently a magazine you edit—*Excursions,* is that its name? —came to Sawyer's attention in Moscow. They do get American journals there on occasion, usually smuggled in by traveling scholars. This particular issue contained a section on Sawyer, with an essay by yourself. Sawyer was most impressed. He claims you're the only man for the job."

"And Sir Godfrey Clemmons?"

"He would, of course, prefer to use one of his own editors, but he has reviewed your work and found you satisfactory. He realizes that, as an old friend, you may have more success working with Jeremy than anyone else could hope to have. All that remains, then, is for you to agree to accept the job."

Abbot was amazed to think that all this had been arranged without his knowledge or consent—including, apparently, even his assignment to the Breiburg exchange. He remembered how, just last December, his personal life in turmoil and his professional life at an apparent dead end, he was called into the office of the dean and informed that there was an unexpected opening for the spring semester at Breiburg. It had seemed at the time a godsend; now Abbot saw that it had been arranged elsewhere.

"What did you have to do to get me over here—bump off some unsuspecting colleague of mine?"

Hedge chuckled. "That would have been a mite drastic. It was enough to persuade the Hessian Ministry of Education that they really needed another American scholar on their payroll this term. Given our connections, that wasn't difficult."

"And then you sent Mikos Pajorfsky to take a room next to mine at the guesthouse, so that he could initiate me into the scheme. But why did you have to wait so long? We were next-door neighbors for over a month."

"Mikos had other assignments, which, for a time, took priority," Hedge said. "Besides, we wanted to be perfectly sure it was safe to proceed—that neither of you had aroused suspicion amongst the opposition. Then it seemed a good idea to give Mikos some token or sign from Sawyer which would vouch for the authenticity of his message. A courier from Moscow delivered that snapshot to Pajorfsky in the Stadtwald yesterday afternoon, just before he was killed."

Abbot gave that a moment's thought. "Then doesn't Pajorfsky's murder mean that the Russians know about Jeremy's disaffection? Won't they pack him off to some Siberian outpost where you'll never be able to get at him?"

"We're hoping that's not the case," Hedge said. "It's quite possible Pajorfsky's murder was not related to his current mission. We know who killed him, you see—or at least we think we do. It may have been purely a personal matter."

"Personal?"

Franz rose quickly from his chair. "If you'll excuse me, I'll just see what's keeping our supper. Herr Hedge, don't tell Sam a lot of nonsense about this Hangman fellow."

Hedge waited until the little man had left the room. "Poor chap—he really does abhor violence, you know. Doesn't like to hear about all the nasty things that go on in our business. And Mikos was one of his favorites—they worked closely together for some months this winter.

"Let me get this straight," Abbot said. "You think Mikos was killed by someone called the Hangman?"

"We read the description you gave the Breiburg police. It fits the Hangman to a tee. That's his nickname, of course. He was given it years ago by American and British agents operating in Eastern Europe. His real name is Nikolai Charnov; he's a retired colonel in the KGB, no longer actively employed by the masterminds in Moscow. He seems to have drawn up a list of his old enemies, and now he's going around Europe settling these old scores one by one. We think he'd been stalking Pajorfsky for some time."

Abbot turned to Greta. "And that's why you were looking for Mikos yesterday afternoon? You were sent to warn him?"

She nodded, her eyes bright with remembered terror. "Early yesterday afternoon we learned that our Moscow courier had been stopped at the East German border, then allowed to proceed. We are thinking it is maybe a trap, and I am told to warn Mikos before he goes to meet the courier. But there is an accident on the Autobahn and I am getting there too late—"

She appeared about the burst into tears, and Hedge said, "Now, now, Greta, we know you did your best." He turned to Abbot. "Greta always forms these strong attachments to whomever she works with—I hope you won't find that disagreeable."

"Greta and I going to work together?"

"Quite likely, if you sign on with us for Operation Nightingale— that's the code name we've given this particular project. We were thinking of making Greta your personal assistant, just as she was

Pajorfsky's. What do you say, Greta? Are you willing to work with Professor Abbot?"

To Abbot's surprise, Greta suddenly blushed and looked at the carpet. "I am good soldier," she said fiercely. "I will do as I am told, Herr Hedge."

"Of course you will." Hedge looked at Abbot with a merry light in his rather bloodshot and somehow soiled eyes. "She's really a good little scout, you know, and a crack shot—"

A pair of double doors opened, revealing an adjoining room, larger and more brightly lit, where a long table had been spread with a lavish buffet. Franz stood in the doorway and invited them with a sweeping gesture to come forward. "Please, let us partake of some refreshment. We can conclude our business afterward."

As Abbot entered the dining room he saw a variety of cold sliced roasts and sausages, several kinds of cheese, numerous salads and relishes, breads and rolls and muffins, all attractively displayed on silver plate and white linen, flanked by bouquets of fresh flowers and glimmering candles. A white-coated servant stood ready to assist the guests and to uncork the champagne. A light supper, indeed! As the guests heaped their plates, gallant Franz stood solicitously by, urging them to try certain delicacies. He had, Abbot thought, the quaintly mysterious air of one who had conjured this feast from under a cloak. Was this, then, how the secret agents of ELF conducted their business? If so, Abbot saw how he might learn to enjoy to the life of a spy.

As their supper neared its end, the servant produced a decanter of port and box of cigars. Abbot noticed they were Havana cigars and he was still carefully unwrapping his when Franz said, "I don't mean to pressure you, Sam, but you haven't given us your answer yet. Will you undertake this assignment?"

"I've been thinking about it," Abbot replied. "When I came here, I was ready to do whatever I could to help you get Jeremy out of Russia. Now that I know what you really want—well, I'm a little dubious. It could be quite a lengthy commitment, depending on how much work the manuscript needs. I do have my own career to consider."

"Sawyer has assured us," Franz said, "that he will provide you with a handsome commission—say, fifteen percent of all proceeds from the book. I am prepared to guarantee you a certain sum, myself, in the unlikely event that the book is not the success we expect it to be."

Abbot felt hard pressed to explain his reluctance. "It's not just the money. You've got to remember that Jeremy Sawyer and I haven't seen each other since 1962; we haven't corresponded since his defection in '68. Our relationship was always complicated, and no doubt we've both changed enormously since our Cambridge days. I'm not sure we could work together on this or any other project."

"Sawyer seems to think so," Hedge observed. "He seems to feel you're the one man in the bloody western hemisphere who can fully appreciate what he's done."

"That's very flattering," Abbot said, "but Jeremy has always flattered his disciples—he's always hinted that we're uniquely blessed in being able to understand his genius so well. I fell for that line when I was young—I'm not at all sure I want to fall for it again. I'd like to preserve what precious little individuality I've managed to achieve in the past twenty-some years."

Franz passed a silver-plated lighter beneath his cigar and puffed thoughtfully. "Your attitude is most understandable, Sam. It is often regrettably true that men of genius, men like Jeremy Sawyer, can be incredibly demanding and difficult to work with—which was just what Sir Godfrey was thinking, I'm sure, when he insisted on an editor who would be acceptable to both Sawyer and himself. On the other hand, I beg you to consider the great service you could render, not only to literature, but to the even greater cause—if one may say so—of human freedom and dignity the world over. You have the opportunity, Sam, to give the world a book which could change the course of history."

Surely, Abbot thought, Franz was exaggerating—yet he had no wish to undermine Jeremy's chance to escape. "I've no doubt," he said carefully, "that anything Jeremy Sawyer writes will be of interest—to some of us, at least. But who knows if that precious talent has survived its eighteen years of exile? Who knows what kind of a man Jeremy Sawyer is now or what sort of book he's written? Are you even sure that it *will* serve the cause of freedom, when it's finally published?"

"Ah, there is a risk," Franz admitted, drawing thoughtfully on his cigar. "There is always a risk when one endeavors to find and promote the truth. But I begin to see what I hadn't quite anticipated—that there is also a considerable personal risk to you in this venture. That deserves some thought, as you say. Your relations with your friend were not, then, always happy?"

"Oh, they were happy, all right," Abbot said. "I was twenty-two and he was twenty-four; we were as close as brothers for all of ten months. But ever since, I've had this tendency to measure my own accomplishments by Jeremy's standards. I seem to have spent my entire adult life in his shadow, my own identity dwarfed by my image of the man I knew. Now you want me to commit a considerable portion of my life to his new book, and to tell you the truth, I'm not sure I can afford it. How much of Sam Abbot will be left, I wonder, when Jeremy Sawyer enters into his glory?"

There was a heavy silence at the table, and Abbot felt as though he had perversely dashed the hopes of those who had brought him here. He did not really expect them to understand his complicated feelings where Jeremy Sawyer was concerned, but Franz, having refilled his glass and passed the decanter to Hedge, favored him with one of his warm and reassuring smiles.

"My friend, let me tell you a little story. I cannot, of course, provide the story with proper names, but surely you've guessed by now that I belong to an old and noble family. The room in which we are seated is part of an extensive estate, and this estate is but one of several which came to me upon my majority. In fact, I can trace my ancestry back to the liege men of Charlemagne—over twelve hundred years! But please don't think I'm bragging. I take very little pleasure in this magnificent heritage. On the contrary, I've always been oppressed and defeated by it."

He paused to run his eye over the remains of the splendid feast he had served his guests, the gloomy paintings of hunting parties in marsh and forest which adorned the walls. "My ancestors, so we've been told, were giants among men—not only in their physical stature, but in the proportions of their spirit—in their passions, ambitions, conquests, achievements. Even in modern times, my family has distinguished itself in business, banking, politics, diplomacy . . . whereas I, the last of this noble line—well, I'm sure you've noticed my modest stature. My accomplishments in this world have been equally modest, I assure you. When I was young, I was determined to excel at sports. No matter that I was smaller than the other boys, or that I had a sickly constitution. I tried to compete in games of strength and skill where I had literally no chance. Then, at the university, I decided to pursue a career in science. Mathematical and mechanical talent is said to run in our family, but I proved woefully inept at figures. I then set myself to making money. It didn't matter that I already had more than enough to last me the rest of my life—I needed to prove that I could amass a fortune of my own, just as my ancestors had. And yet, do you know something, Sam? The more I tried to make myself large, the smaller I became. The harder I worked at becoming the equal of my ancestors, the less of me there was. For years I made myself and everyone around me miserable, until finally, through a happy marriage to an excellent woman, I learned to accept myself as I was. I learned that one is not accountable for one's size, or even for one's talents. We all live in the shadow of our giants, and how do we come out of that darkness? Only, I think, by proving ourselves free men. And how do we prove our freedom? Perhaps we can only prove it by keeping an honorable pact with the past—by doing that which our conscience tells us must be done, if manhood itself is to have meaning."

Abbot gave this impassioned speech a few moments of respectful silence. "In other words, the only way I'll ever come to terms with Jeremy Sawyer is by doing something for him—something he couldn't accomplish without my help."

Franz smiled. "We understand one another very well, my friend. I am sure that, should we have the opportunity to work together on Operation Nightingale, we will become excellent friends."

Abbot thought so, too. He had never met a man just like Franz before—had never met any pedigreed aristocrats, for that matter—but he sensed he had something in common with the little man, something deeper than the distinctions of class, nationality, and wealth. They were most alike, perhaps, in the demands they made upon themselves.

"Well, what is it to be then?" Brian Hedge asked. "Are you in with us, old man, or not?"

"I've got to see Jeremy first," Abbot said. "I've got to talk to him about all this before I can give you my decision."

"We thought as much," Hedge said, "which is why our Moscow

agents dreamed up the ruse of a literary conference in East Berlin the same week as yours. We can arrange a meeting between you and Sawyer quite easily, if you're game for a little expedition to the other side. On the hush-hush, of course."

"I have to go into East Berlin to see Jeremy? I don't suppose he'd come to me in West Berlin?"

Hedge shook his head. "He won't cross over, even temporarily, until everything's been settled in regard to his book. Actually, it's much easier going the other way. American tourists go into East Berlin all the time, you know. The DDR runs a regular tour of the city, and our men in Berlin have worked out a simple and effective way of using those tours for our own purposes. It's all quite routine."

"But I'll be in East Berlin illegally? What happens if I get caught?"

"You won't get caught, old man. In addition to our regular crew, you'll have the personal services of the Stork."

"Ah yes, the Stork. Greta was telling me about the Stork. Sort of a modern-day Scarlet Pimpernel, is he?"

"You could call him that," Franz said. "The Stork is the most important agent we have in Eastern Europe. Our chief function here in the West is to support his work. We finance his network by the sale of intelligence on the open market, and by taking on certain tasks the Western governments are unable to manage on their own. We receive the refugees from Communism which he brings us, and we prepare them for their new lives here in the free world. In this part of the enterprise, I myself have been privileged to play a small but vital role—"

"Hmm, yes—the less said about that the better," Brian Hedge intervened. "Once we get our old chum out, Professor, you'll see for yourself how our system works. We'll find a nice, quiet place where the two of you can get down to work on that manuscript of his—"

"Assuming I agree to become Jeremy's editor." The vision of Jeremy and himself, holed up in some safe house to edit his masterpiece—while Greta stood guard, no doubt—was both charming and disconcerting, and Abbot felt compelled to resist the speed with which events seemed to be carrying him, once again, into Jeremy's orbit. "Can I get a look at this manuscript when I meet him in Berlin?"

"We understand he has some sample chapters to show you," Franz said. "After you've read them, we'll pass them on to our British publisher. If both you and Sir Godfrey are satisfied, and if Sir Godfrey's terms are acceptable to Sawyer, Operation Nightingale shall proceed."

The little man rose from his chair, and Abbot saw they were going to drink to Operation Nightingale. "I hope you won't be disappointed in the results," he said.

Franz raised his glass and smiled at Abbot. "I do understand your scruples, and I appreciate your honesty, but I must say, in all sincerity, Sam, I don't think Jeremy Sawyer could have chosen a better man for the job."

"Hear, hear," Hedge said.

"Hip, hip, hooray," Greta tipsily added.

Abbot downed the rest of his port with the glum sense of having been had, and he began to wonder if he would have to be drugged again for the return journey.

As it turned out, Franz and Hedge agreed that a simple blindfold would suffice. Abbot's husky escorts were summoned; before submitting to their strong hands, Abbot turned to Franz and thanked him for his hospitality.

"My pleasure entirely," the little nobleman said. "I shall look forward to our next meeting—and may all go well in Berlin!"

As they proceeded to the car, Abbot discovered that by wrinkling his nose and raising his eyebrows he could displace the blindfold just enough to admit light. The red-orange glow suggested that the sun was near the horizon. The two strongmen eased him into the backseat, and Greta slipped in beside him, as before. Abbot waited until he heard the front doors slam shut and the big engine rumble into life. Then, under the pretense of an itch beneath his blindfold, he managed to push up the band of cloth for a quick, one-eyed squint at their surroundings. What he saw was not the house they'd just left, but a panorama of hazy, bluish hills and deeply shadowed valleys. The setting sun accentuated this rugged landscape, and on the bronzed slope of the ridge directly opposite Abbot saw something very strange—apparently a shadow cast by the ridge behind or above them, yet so lifelike it almost seemed to move. Abbot raised the blindfold higher and

61

beheld the figure of a giant, crouched over with an ax or a club on his shoulder as he searched the valley for his prey.

Greta poked him in the ribs and whispered hoarsely, "No peeking!"

"Sorry," Abbot said, "I had something in my eye."

The car lurched forward and began its long, winding descent. Abbot did not try for a second look, and soon the glare of the sunset faded. Yet he couldn't shake the uneasy feeling, as the car bounced and swayed over a rough road for the next several kilometers, that they were scurrying out from under the giant's shadow.

t was a long drive back to the city, and Abbot, cut off from the outside world by his blindfold, concentrated on the humid, perfumed presence close beside him in the backseat. As darkness fell and the drive grew tedious, Greta put her head on his shoulder. "Comrades," she said, giving his hand a squeeze before she began to breathe deeply and evenly—a pattern broken only later by several whimpering cries as she encountered a bad dream. Abbot wondered at the dreams such a girl might have, and it occurred to him that, if there was any way to find out more about ELF and its operations before he became too deeply embroiled in them, it might very well be through Greta. Which was fine, since it gave him an excuse to buy her a drink when they got back to Frankfurt.

Well, Liz, what did you expect? A whole month and no letters! What's a man to conclude from that, and how is a guy supposed to survive, anyway, without some small amount of casual, comradely affection?

Liz, somehow picking up these thoughts on the other side of the Atlantic and sending back a message of her own, told Abbot it was all right with her if he wanted to solace himself with a cheap floozy—a Teutonic Brigitte Bardot—but as for the rest of it, she sincerely hoped he knew what he was getting himself into.

Abbot replied that in his opinion Greta was *not* a cheap floozy (though the comparison to Bardot was apt, even to the flawed complexion); as for her second point—did one ever know what one was getting into? Sometimes, Abbot told his sceptical wife, a man has to take a few chances. And maybe that was exactly what had been wrong with his life until now. In any case, he thought he could make certain decisions for himself from here on in, since it was clear he wasn't going to receive any council from home.

Nearing Frankfurt, Hedge told Abbot that he could remove his blindfold. Taking note of the signs along the Autobahn, Abbot surmised that they were entering the city from the northeast. His notion of German geography was still sketchy, but he knew now they had not crossed any frontiers, and he resolved to consult a good road map at the first opportunity. Perhaps he could get some idea of where they'd been.

"You might check your bank account on Monday," Hedge told him as they left the Autobahn. "You'll find there's been a deposit of twenty thousand deutsche marks, which should cover your expenses for the time being."

"That's very generous," Abbot said.

"Just our way of making you feel part of the family, old man. Oh, and by the way, if that Morrison chap should come nosing around again, we'd much rather he doesn't catch wind of Operation Nightingale. Some of your countrymen may still hold a grudge against Sawyer, and besides, we're convinced there's a rather serious leak in the CIA's European network. Whatever the Yanks find out, the Russians seem to learn straightaway. So if you value your friend's safety, mum's the word."

"I'll do my best," Abbot said, "but I've never been interrogated before."

"I doubt they'll give you the third degree. The Yanks tend to go easy at first—especially when they're dealing with American citizens."

"That's some comfort."

"We won't contact you again until you're in Berlin," Hedge said, as Greta yawned and began stretching herself awake. "Just go about your business, and I'll be in touch when I've set up the crossing. Do you want a code name, by the way?"

"Oh, I get a code name, too?"

"Well, it's not strictly necessary, but it might come in handy if you're ever in a spot. We were thinking of Troubador—how does that strike you?"

"Flattering," Abbot said. "I'll bring my mandolin."

The limousine pulled up at almost the exact spot where Abbot and Greta had been standing at two thirty that afternoon. Greta got out with Abbot, and the limousine pulled away. It was a mild evening, and the lights of the city glimmered brightly across the river. For Abbot it felt like coming back to earth after a brief ride on board a flying saucer. He'd had his close encounter—now all he had to do was find someone who would believe him.

He checked his watch and saw he still had nearly two hours before the last train left for Breiburg. "Buy you a drink?" he asked Greta.

She took his arm. "I know a nice place not far from here."

"Then it's all right for us to be seen together?"

"Why not? I was Mikos's research assistant, and you were his friend. We are consoling one another at his loss, yes? This is what you must tell the CIA, so it is better if we are also seen in public."

Glad to have that settled, Abbot let Greta lead him across the busy intersection and into the narrow, cobbled lanes of Sachsenhausen. They strolled beneath the old half-timbered buildings, through the festive atmosphere of a balmy spring night. The bars and restaurants were crowded with revelers, and an odd medley of European folk music and American jazz issued from open doorways. Greta chose an establishment with a large, sheltered *Biergarten,* where they found seats in a quiet corner, away from the concertina and several tables of drunken singers. She ordered two glasses of the local specialty, *Apfelwein,* and another regional treat, *Handkäse mit Muzik,* which turned out to be a soft, aromatic cheese with a dressing of raw, vinegary onions. Abbot saw the natives consuming large quantities of this combination all around them, but contented himself with just a few bites.

"Comrades," Greta said again, raising her glass of wine.

"Comrades," Abbot said, and drank.

"So now we talk and become acquainted, yes? Is okay if I call you Sam?"

"Please do," Abbot said.

"You have a family back in America, Sam?"

"Yes, a wife and three children."

"So—why do they not come to Germany with you? You are not lonely without them?"

"Oh yes, I'm lonely. But it would have been hard to take the kids out of school for such a long time. And my wife didn't want to leave her job."

"She works? This is important to her?"

"Very. She's a staff artist at the Natural History Museum in Nakomis. She does the bird exhibits—it's an excellent position. She got it just last year, after completing her second degree in zoology, so it wouldn't have been a very good time for her to take a leave of absence."

"And for you, it is not so good that she has this job? Now she is no more just your wife and the mother of your children? She is also now what you call a career woman, yes?"

"Well, two-career families are all the thing in America these days," Abbot said. "I encouraged Liz to pursue her interest in ornithology when the kids got older—I don't think we would have had any trouble with that, if everything else in our life had been what it should have been."

"Everything else?" Greta asked.

Looking at it from a distance, Abbot had trouble remembering, not to say explaining, just what had bothered him so much about his life—except that it was passing much too quickly. "I got sort of depressed when this journal I was editing folded, and I couldn't seem to find anything in academic life to interest me any more. I tried administration, but that didn't work. I started drinking heavily . . . but you don't want to hear all my sordid problems, do you? Tell me, how did you become such an ardent disciple of free enterprise and such a foe of Communism?"

She lit another of her cigarettes, then tossed her hair back from her eyes. "You make fun of me, yes? You do not think women can understand these things? Perhaps this is why your wife prefers to work in her museum and sends you off to Germany by yourself?"

Abbot smiled. "That could be, I suppose. I'm sorry if I seemed to be making fun of you. I'm genuinely interested."

She combed her long, scarlet-tipped fingers through her hair and fixed him with her dark eyes. "My family, they come from Prussia—what is now part of Poland. Before I am born, they have very big farm, much land. Then, after the war, the Russians come to our village. They put the Communists in charge, and the Communists take away all our land. My father, he tries to make protest, yes?—so they send him away to Berlin to work in a factory. This is very sad for my family, but the Communists do not care. They say, 'Go here! Do this! Do that!' and the people they must obey, because otherwise the Russians will come back with their tanks and their guns, like Hungary, yes?—like Czechoslavakia. I am born in East Berlin, where we live in a little flat, six of us in three rooms. My father, he says we must escape to the West so we can have there a better life. He works very hard to earn the money for our escape. I am still very small but I remember it clearly. Men come to our house late at night and take us into the city. We go down into a basement and find there a tunnel. We must crawl through this tunnel on our hands and knees. My mother goes first, then the children, then last of all my father. We are all waiting for him on the other side when suddenly we hear shots in the tunnel, and my mother, she starts to scream. She tries to crawl back in the hole, but the men, they take hold of her and drag her away. They take us to a refugee camp in the West, and we wait there for my father, but he never comes. By now we know he is dead, but still my mother will not believe it. To this day she waits for him."

"I'm sorry," Abbot said with a catch in his voice.

Greta blew smoke in his face. "Sorry, bah! Sorry is not enough! I am now soldier—I fight for what I believe in."

"And how did you come to work for ELF?"

"This is some years later, when I am student at university in Munich, yes? I have there a boyfriend—he is also East German refugee. Like me, he hates the Russians, and one night he asks me, do I hate them enough to do something abut it? 'Do what?' I say. 'If there was one here now'—we were sitting in a café—'I would spit in his eye.' 'Would you do more than that?' he asks me. 'Would you drive this knife into his ribs?' And suddenly there is a knife on the table between us, and I am knowing why my friend goes away for long periods and comes back half crazy, with a strange look in his eyes, like a murderer. 'Heinz,' I say, 'you have killed somebody?' 'No,' he says 'but I am going to, and I want your help.'"

Greta signaled the waiter for two more glasses of wine, then continued her story. "He tells me there is a Russian general attached to the embassy in Vienna who likes young girls. He is something in the KGB, very bad, he has murdered many innocent people. Heinz and his group want to kill this general, and they want me to go to Vienna as, how you say?—the bait, yes? I am supposed to make eyes at the general, let him take me to dinner, then invite him up to my room, where Heinz and his friends will be waiting."

"And did you do it?" Abbot asked, half afraid to learn the answer.

Greta shook her head. "I was very angry. 'I am not a whore,' I tell Heinz. 'Find some other girl to do your dirty work.' Heinz goes away and I do not see him again, but later I learn he is dead—murdered by the KGB. I am feeling very bad, because I was much in love with him, Sam. And then his friends come to my house and tell me about ELF and how I can avenge Heinz's death by joining their cell. So I think to myself, first my father and now my lover—it is too much. If I must make like whore to fight the Communists, okay, so I will. Ever since then, Sam, I am soldier. A soldier is not being whore when she uses what weapons she has—"

"Of course not," Abbot said, aware that his desire for the girl had become a dull ache in the back of his throat, the dryness of a considerable thirst. "Were you and Mikos—very close?"

She shrugged. "We were comrades, good friends—like brother and sister. He was not interested in sex—he had wife and children in Poland."

"Oh." Abbot felt ashamed of himself, as if the little archaeologist had rebuked him from his grave.

"In Poland is more old-fashioned than in America, yes?" Greta asked, smiling around yet another cigarette.

"I guess maybe it is, though some of us still lead pretty old-fashioned lives, even in the States."

Greta arched an eyebrow. "This is also why you come to Germany, perhaps? You are hoping maybe to sow some oats, as the Yanks say?"

"It may have crossed my mind," Abbot confessed, "but I haven't sown any yet."

"Why not? Germany is full of whores. There are sex bars in Breiburg where you can get what you want—plenty more here in Frankfurt."

"I've seen them," Abbot said, "but that's not what I'm looking for, Greta. I guess I'm more the romantic type." He checked his watch. "Gee, I'll have to get across town pretty quick, if I want to catch the last train back to Breiburg."

She looked at him quietly for a moment, her smile deepening with something Abbot interpreted as female intuition. "You don't have to go back to Breiburg tonight, Sam. My flat is just a few blocks from here. Mikos often stayed over when he had business in Frankfurt. I can drive you back in the morning."

"Thanks, but I might not be quite as trustworthy a houseguest as Mikos was. You'd better think twice."

Her dark eyes told him that she already had. "I am not afraid of you, Sam. Comrades should trust one another, yes?"

Abbot smiled. "Yes, I guess that's right. If you can't trust a comrade, who the hell can you trust? So let's have another drink—it's a lovely night and this is a nice place. And I feel younger than I have in years."

Greta didn't comment, but her dark eyes told him she understood.

It was late when they left the *Biergarten*. Despite those several glasses of wine, Abbot felt alert, energetic, his lust honed to a fine edge. Greta took his arm and led him along the narrow lanes, then across a broad boulevard where streetcars passed like high-minded phantoms, showering sparks at the junction of their wires. Abbot could see lightning flickering behind a scalloped bank of clouds now rising to the south. How appropriate, he thought—the end of a long drought.

But what if he had misunderstood? What if Greta showed him to his bed and retreated to her own room, shutting the door firmly behind her? Or what if she simply sat there waiting for him to make the first move, that damned female intuition shining in her eyes?

I'll deal with it, Abbot thought. I'll deal with it.

They walked down a dimly lit residential street, then through a gate and across a courtyard. Greta led him into a house and up a flight of stairs. Abbot was too keyed up to take particular notice of his surroundings; he felt as if he had crossed over some moral boundary into a new country where he was as helpless as a child, as vulnerable as a blind man.

She unlocked the door of her third-floor apartment and entered without turning on a light. Abbot followed and felt her body close to his in the darkness, her breath on his cheek.

"I am not making you sleep alone, Sam. Just so you understand, I am not a whore."

"No, by God, you're a soldier," Abbot said, embracing her, "the best little soldier I ever met!"

She gave him her smoky kiss.

In the bedroom, she lit a single candle on a low table near the bed, then began to take off her clothes. Abbot guessed the candlelight was meant to soften her imperfections and make her more beautiful for him, but she needn't have worried—he saw her through the rose-colored lenses of his lust. Her slender young body glowed in the dusky room like the apparition of a goddess.

He had stripped only to the waist when she came to him and put her nakedness trustingly into his arms. Her tongue entered his mouth, her nipples grazed his chest. He stroked the smooth contours of her back, cupped her plump buns. As her pelvis fit itself snugly against his, his imprisoned manhood arose, demanding release. Greta answered the call, sliding down Abbot's tense body until she was kneeling before him, where she deftly freed the captive. Liberated at long last from his celibate's dungeon, Abbot surrendered to the pleasure of the girl's gentle touch, her generous mouth. Too late he thought to warn her of his probable lack of control.

Greta professed not to mind; she said she was glad to please him in that way, and now, if he liked, he could please her. Abbot was sure he would do his best.

By eleven the next morning Abbot was satisfied that Greta's pleasure had been adequately seen to—or if it hadn't, there was certainly no more *he* could do to discharge his debt. Desperate for a change of scene, his senses saturated with Greta's musky womanhood, he suggested they go out for a walk.

Greta hopped out of bed to dress. Abbot lay quietly and watched as she slipped into her bra and panties. Opening the wardrobe in search of a blouse, she seemed to think of something and called him over. Reaching above the clothes rod, she showed him a hidden compartment beneath the top of the cabinet.

"I will give you key to my apartment. In case you ever need it when I'm not here, you should know how to find *this*." She brought down a large, evil-looking handgun.

"Good God," Abbot said, shrinking back from the weapon, "do you really know how to shoot that thing?"

"I am very good shot," she said. "You must learn too, if you are soldier. Look—here is ammunition, yes? The clip goes in here . . . then you pull back this lever, yes? Now squeeze the trigger and the gun will fire."

"For heaven's sake, put it away," Abbot said. "I'm not a gun person."

Greta smiled teasingly at him over her shoulder as she returned the gun to its hiding place. "I thought all Americans owned guns—they go around shooting 'boom, boom!' like in cowboy movies, yes?"

"I think that's been exaggerated," Abbot said, as he continued to look at the old-fashioned wardrobe with morbid fascination. "Have you ever—?"

"Shot somebody? No, not a real person. But Mikos took me out into the forest and let me practice. I can put a bullet into a man's heart at one hundred paces."

"And Mikos—was he—did he ever?"

"Oh yes, he was spy for very long time—I think he must have killed many Russians in his life. Mikos hated the Russians."

Abbot remembered the mild, whimsical little Pole with the anxious, evasive eyes and found it hard to believe that he could have been a hardened killer. A killer, perhaps, but not a hardened one.

"Just what were you and Mikos doing? What was his assignment before me?"

"I do not think I am allowed to tell you that, Sam. They do not want you to know too much about us yet. It was not very dangerous, however. It had something to do with Mikos's field of study—"

"Archaeology? You mean, you two really did visit various prehistoric sites?"

She nodded. "In this I was not so interested. Broken pots and bones, who cares? I drove the car and helped Mikos with his German; also sometimes I stood guard when we were in the forest, but I never went into—" She stopped, and her eyes showed that she was afraid she had said too much.

"Into what?" Abbot asked.

She shrugged, as if it really didn't matter. "Into the ground, yes? Sometimes Mikos would explore caves, or—how do you say—old graves and tombs?"

"Catacombs?" Abbot suggested.

"Yes, those." She shuddered. "I could not go with him. Always I remembered the time in the tunnel, when we escaped from East Berlin, and I could not go under the ground. Mikos understood. He didn't insist."

"Where were these caves or catacombs?"

But Greta shook her head. "This is what I cannot tell you, Sam—at least not yet. Do not ask me any more questions, please. Are we going now for our walk?"

It was a pretty day, a fair sample of what the German spring might offer after the prolonged winter. They walked to the river and along its bank, and Abbot could hear church bells ringing all across the city. As usual after getting what he thought he wanted, he was beginning to feel something akin to remorse. "Thank you," he said, "for taking pity on an old man."

"What is this 'pity'?" Greta asked. "What 'old man'? I do not like that kind of talk, Sam. You are not old, and I am not making love out of pity. It was what we both wanted, yes?"

"Apparently—though why you should want *me* escapes comprehension."

She clung to his arm as they walked silently for a while. Then she said, "Your wife, she is making you feel old? She is telling you you are not so much man as you used to be?"

"Oh no, Liz and I always had a satisfactory sex life. Up until a year or so ago, anyway. Then . . . well, by bedtime I was usually too drunk for making love."

"Last night you were not too drunk," she reminded him.

"No, I wasn't, was I?" There goes that excuse, he thought.

"And why did you drink so much? Your life, it was so empty without alcohol?"

"It must have seemed that way. I don't really know what happened, Greta, because it was such a gradual thing, but maybe it all started when our children began to grow up—when my son Jeffrey left for college—"

She tightened her grip on his arm. "I would like to have children one day—when I am all done being soldier."

Abbot sensed that this was not quite a non sequitur and didn't comment. They paused to watch one of the bright red-and-white tour boats pull away from its dock. Despite the mild weather, there were only a few camera-toting tourists on its deck.

"I would like to go to America one day," Greta said dreamily. "It is the land of opportunity, yes?"

"So they say. Also, as it often turns out, the land of lost opportunities. Sometimes I wonder if I should have stayed on in England, like Jeremy. . . . It might've made a big difference."

"You would have gone over to the Communists in 1968, like him?"

"No, I'm pretty sure I wouldn't have done that," Abbot said. "There was a girl, in Cambridge. Both Jeremy and I were sweet on her. I took a little too long making up my mind, and he proposed to her first. She accepted. He left her with a two-year-old child when he ran off to Russia, the bastard."

"Ah," Greta said, leaning her elbows on the railing to watch the brown water flow past the embankment. "If you had stayed in England, you would have been there to comfort her, is that it?"

"Something like it, I suppose. I've always wondered what became of her."

"You did not write to find out?"

"No, it would have been awkward. I was married myself by then. I had other responsibilities."

"I would like to meet this man that we call now the Nightingale," Greta said. "Perhaps I would spit in his eye for being such a fool."

"You're not coming to Berlin with me? I thought you were going to be my bodyguard."

Greta shook her head. "Because I escaped from the DDR, my passport is not always good in East Germany. Sometimes they arrest people like me—I could be sent back to my family's village. I will guard your body here in West Germany, Sam, but I cannot cross the border with you."

"Well," Abbot said, slipping his arm around her, "you're doing a damn nice job of it so far, kid."

They crossed the river, strolled past the cathedral with its ornate spires of chocolate-colored stone, then along the gallery above the current excavation of Roman ruins. "Everywhere you look in Europe, there's something buried beneath something else," Abbot remarked. "That's what makes it so fascinating—you can *feel* the past, right through the soles of your shoes."

"Yes, and it gives you corns and bunions," Greta said. "I think I would like it better in America, where the ground is solid and there are no holes to fall into, no pits full of skeletons."

Abbot wondered at the violence of her imagery. "You and Mikos found pits full of skeletons?"

"I don't want to talk about it," Greta said.

The shops were closed on Sunday, but there were a few couples window-shopping along the modern pedestrian malls. Greta held Abbot's arm and oohed and ahhed at the new spring fashions. Abbot regarded their reflection on the sheets of glass and thought that he did not look quite so ancient and weary with a vivacious young lady on his arm. Or was that simply another illusion, the latest in the several spells Greta had sought to cast upon him?

They had lunch on the sunny terrace outside the *Hauptwache*, and Abbot decided, since he still had half his round-trip ticket, to take the train back to Breiburg. After nearly twenty-four hours of Greta's energetic company, he was beginning to miss his privacy, to think almost fondly of that musty bachelor sanctuary, the guesthouse. Perhaps he really wasn't fit for human society anymore, except in small doses; or maybe he just needed time to adjust to everything he'd learned since Friday afternoon.

Greta went with him to the station and saw him to his train, giving him one last ferocious kiss before he climbed on board. "Come down to see me once before you leave for Berlin," she said. "I know many nice places in the city where we can walk and talk. It is quite safe, yes?"

"I'll try," Abbot said, "but I really have a lot of work to do before I can go."

He saw her waving to him as the train began to move, looking with her wild blond hair and large charcoal eyes like any man's fantasy *Fräulein*. How his drinking buddies, the Breiburg GI's, would love poor little Greta, Abbot thought, sinking back into his seat. Eventually, one of them might even do the honorable thing and take her to that land of opportunity she longed to see. Perhaps he ought to arrange a few introductions.

n the days prior to his departure for Berlin, Abbot taught his classes, dined with his colleagues at the *Mensa,* worked on his paper, and did his laundry. The police returned his passport on Monday, but had no further questions. Frau Graushen, whom he had successfully avoided on his return Sunday afternoon, was all smiles when he saw her on Monday and subsequent mornings, and life at the guesthouse went on as usual—almost as if there had never been a Mikos Pajorfsky.

Abbot stopped at his bank on Tuesday and found that, sure enough, twenty thousand deutsche marks had been added to his account. It was one of the vagaries of the German banking system that there was no way of telling where this money had come from—perhaps it was left there by elves, Abbot imagined himself explaining to an IRS auditor back in the States. He blew a portion of this windfall on a new blazer, a good pair of walking shoes, and a collapsible umbrella to replace the one he had left somewhere in Frankfurt.

That evening he dined alone at Zum Eulenspiegel and was safely home by dusk, where he sat at the open window listening to the intricate music of the blackbirds. When the last bird had piped its final note, Abbot turned on his small portable radio. Over the past month he had developed a safecracker's touch on the dial and could now bring into his room a voluble babble of German, French, Italian, Spanish and Slavic tongues. Tonight each voice seemed to be urging its point of view with particular passion, and Abbot imagined the night sky over Europe as an ideological battlefield in which these disembodied voices contended like Milton's warring angels over the fate of some paradise already lost.

At eleven he drank a small *Weinbrand* and turned to the Armed Forces Network for the news. The current siege of terrorist bombings and kidnappings continued. Various groups claimed responsibility for these outrages, which were in turn deplored and condemned by government officials the world over. Though he listened to these reports with new interest, Abbot heard no mention of a group calling itself the East European Liberation Front; nor were there any references to Jeremy Sawyer, the Stork, the Hangman, or Operation Nightingale, which led Abbot to conclude that either he knew more than the news media about these matters or the events of the past weekend were part of some elaborate and preposterous hoax.

But who would play such a trick on him, and why? And why would these mysterious practical jokers spend twenty thousand deutsche marks just to make sure he took the bait? Abbot poured a nip more brandy and thought through the possibilities. Perhaps he *was* being manipulated, deceived, exploited, by forces not yet revealed for purposes not yet known . . . but there was only one way to find out the truth, and that was to proceed as he was proceeding: cautiously, deliberately, toward his reunion in Berlin with Jeremy Sawyer.

In the meantime, Abbot found that he rather enjoyed being a "secret agent." Hints of danger and intrigue, and the sense that he was involved in matters of considerable importance, known so far only to a few, warmed the hours of loneliness, eased the pangs of memory, made him feel for a change entirely comfortable within himself, so that he began to wonder if he hadn't found in espionage, at long last, his true vocation.

On Wednesday Abbot taught his seminar in nineteenth-century American literature. *Moby Dick* was the classic of the week, and Abbot felt like an Ishmael to his own Ahab as he tried to explain Melville's metaphysic to a dozen sceptical young Germans. Returning to the guesthouse around four, he found his first letter from Liz tucked neatly into his mailbox.

Heart pounding with anticipation, Abbot took the letter up to his room, poured himself a stiff drink, and sat down to devour what promised, by the thickness of the envelope, to be a very long, newsy, possibly important epistle.

The first several pages contained an account of the children: Jeffrey was doing well at Berkeley and had just about decided to major in Asian studies (he couldn't get far enough away from home, it seemed); Charlotte had a date for the prom (you had to know Charlotte to know what a trauma was thus averted); and Emily's braces were coming off next week (*that* Abbot wished he could be there to see!). The girls were busy with baby-sitting jobs and homework but promised to write soon. Then Liz went on to talk about her job at the museum, the new exhibit on the fresh-water marsh that was taking up most of her time. Abbot looked anxiously for hints concerning her state of mind, but Liz's prose, like her conversation, was notably free from innuendos. Finally, on the last page, the artist-ornithologist tossed her husband these crumbs:

> I'm sorry this letter was so long in coming, Sam. I kept putting it off in the hope that I would know just what to say about *us*—but I'm afraid the past month has been quite inconclusive. I do miss you, dear, but (to be brutally frank) it's also been rather a relief not having you around. So far I guess the pain pretty well cancels out the peace, and vice versa. I think of you often and wonder how you're doing, and I hope you are having a *good time* (your last letter sounded kind of glum). Perhaps you should travel more, if things are dull in Breiburg. After all, it's a once-in-a-lifetime opportunity . . .

Abbot left the letter open on his desk and sat staring at it, as if—exposed to the unreal atmosphere of his room—Liz's pragmatic prose might vanish in a puff of smoke. If only she knew what a "once-in-a-lifetime opportunity" he *had* been given! Yet chances were that she wouldn't be too impressed. Spy capers were not exactly high on his wife's list of worthwhile activities.

All in all, Abbot was disappointed in the tone of Liz's letter, neither as affectionate nor as forgiving as he had hoped it would be. She was holding fast, her position hadn't changed, and, for the first time, Abbot seriously considered the possibility that his marriage was at an end. It hurt him to admit it, but facts were facts. These days he was trying to cultivate a due respect for reality.

He chose for dinner that evening an Italian restaurant on the Friedhofstrasse, and his route from the guesthouse took him through the old cemetery. Daffodils were dancing on the sunny slope beneath the somber line of cedars, and later, waiting for his meal, Abbot sipped a glass of wine and fell to reminiscing: those legendary April afternoons of 1962 when he and Jeremy had strolled along the Cambridge "backs," beneath the spires of King's and the rosy arches of St. John's. He could picture the long, low punts gliding over the sluggish river, the swans, the reeds, the drooping willows, and on the other bank those Wordsworthian clouds of yellow daffodils . . . while at his side Jeremy's deep, droll voice gave vent to yet another whimsical or extravagant notion.

Jeremy's voice. It was amazing how well Abbot remembered it, how he could hear, even now, its tone, its timbre, those American accents incongruously coupled with a penchant for British slang, that flair for obscenity mischievously mixed with a heady display of literary allusions and tropes. For over twenty years now that voice had intervened in Abbot's thoughts at odd moments, lamenting this, execrating that, remarking with outrage or compassion some irony of the human condition:

"Really, old bean, it's a jolly good trick if you can pull it off. . . . No, no, Sam it's not *that* way at all. . . . Oh, what a bloody fucking mess this world is in, and here we all sit, drinkin' our pints like bleedin' ostriches. . . . Don't whimper, Sam; it ill-behooves a critic to kiss ass, unless of course it's a lovely fat fluid flatulent Molly Bloom type of ass, in which case I'd kiss it quicker than any man alive, you know I would, now don't you, old bean?"

How strange it was going to be to hear that voice again! And equally strange to think that for years now Jeremy's chief language—or language of common usage, at any rate—had been Russian. Of course some great writers had changed languages in mid-career, but Jeremy wasn't likely to have found in the Russian tongue those riches of allusion and connotation, of tone and nuance, which distinguished his use of English. There was no way that voice could ever put everything it knew (about the world, about art, about the human heart) into a foreign idiom. And no way that Jeremy's Russian readers, however diligent, could fully fathom his genius.

So why did he do it? Was Vietnam that important? Granted that writers should speak to the great issues of their time and jolt, on occasion, the public conscience, but a writer who loses his natural audience, Abbot reflected, has little to offer any cause. Surely Jeremy understood that. What could have induced him, then, to have given up everything he had going for him in England—his job, his art, his growing reputation, his wife and child. . .

Ah, there was the truly incomprehensible sacrifice, Abbot thought as his dinner was served. He could understand how, in the heat of a man's moral fervor or political commitment, he might rate human needs ahead of artistic ones. But how could that same man then voluntarily desert his own family—especially such a family as fate had given Jeremy? Abbot asked the waiter to refill his wine glass and then cautiously, reluctantly, allowed himself to think about Patricia Wilding Sawyer.

She was an English girl, a daughter of the landed gentry, but masquerading for the year as a poor student living in London. Someone brought her up to Cambridge for a party and she promptly became one of Jeremy's gang of revelers and a particular pal of Abbot himself. Enchanted by her radiant gray eyes, delicate complexion, and abundance of exotically dark hair, Abbot was also quick to recognize and admire her keen mind, ready wit, and sweet disposition. For a while he even toyed with the notion of making some sort of romantic overture, but no more as a suitor than as a poet did Abbot feel capable of competing with Jeremy Sawyer, and once Jeremy made his intentions known, Abbot withdrew as quickly and gracefully as he could.

Was it outside that whitewashed country pub—commemorated in Abbot's snapshot—that Jeremy first expressed his interest in Patricia, and there that Abbot (knowing how short-lived most of Jeremy's passions were) muttered vague expressions of approval? I should have had my tongue cut out, Abbot thought, if I ever blessed that match! Not that it would have mattered. Jeremy usually got what he went after, and his engagement party climaxed a May brimming with banquets and balls, teatime picnics, and all-night drunks. Abbot was two or three days at sea before he was fully recovered from his hangover.

He finished his dinner and sat musing over a cup of bitter espresso. In all the news stories that had accompanied Jeremy's defection, Abbot had never seen an interview with the forsaken wife or a biographic profile of more than a few lines. He was glad she had been spared the glare of publicity (no doubt her wealthy and influential family had something to do with that), yet the paucity of news tormented him. He kept wondering if there was anything he might do, if he ought to send some brief message of sympathy and support. Yet what could you say to a woman whose husband had just deserted her for a new life in another country, and would she really want to hear from any of Jeremy's old friends?

Looking back on it, Abbot was appalled at the way in which most of the truly important decisions in his life had fallen to one side or the other by default. He was not in the habit, it seemed, of controlling his own destiny, nor of responding to his deepest desires and convictions. Suddenly he saw his life as an empty room in which a telephone rang ceaselessly, plaintively, each shrill cry piercing an oppressive silence. Wouldn't somebody please answer the phone? But there was no one there to stop the ringing, to find out what the caller wanted. Spiritually, there was no one home.

Abbot paid the bill and walked out into the mild spring evening. The light lingered longer there in this northern latitude, and the golden glow of the sunset above Breiburg's jagged line of rooftops and spires reminded him of certain medieval paintings in which saintly martyrs lifted their eyes to heaven as they assented to their fate. Better a cross of one's own, Abbot thought, than a life without meaning or conviction. If the phone were ever answered, what would the caller say?

Back at the guesthouse by dusk, Abbot sat for a while on the patio listening to his birds, then climbed the stairs. Tomorrow he left for Berlin, and he wondered if he ought to leave behind some final message for his family, full of blessings and forgiveness, a general absolution for them all just in case something went wrong. *"To be delivered in the event of my death or incarceration—"*

Already composing his letter as he unlocked his door and fumbled for the light switch, Abbot was a little slow to take account of the offensive odor: *Now who the hell's been smoking in here?* Then it occurred to him that whoever it was might still be waiting for him in the other room. He backed quickly into the hall and would have run for the stairs, had his way not been blocked by a large young man in a tan trench coat.

"Professor Abbot—good evening, sir. Could we have a few words with you?"

It was the fellow Brian Hedge had identified as an agent for the CIA. He looked and sounded more like a young Bible salesman, however, as he stuck out his hand with the words, "My name's Jim Morrison. I'm with the U.S. government."

"The government?" Abbot felt something of the might of Uncle Sam in the young man's grip.

"And this is my boss, Roland Kohl."

A tall, dark-haired man had appeared in the doorway to Abbot's apartment. The stump of a cigar protruded from beneath a dense but close-clipped black moustache. His curly hair receded from a sharp widow's peak, and his forehead displayed two deep horizontal creases above a pair of thick eyebrows and shrewd dark eyes. The eyes had pouches. The cheeks had jowls. Though no older than Abbot, the man projected a kind of paternalistic authority which Abbot felt an instinctive need to resist.

"How did you get into my apartment?"

"The landlady let us in," Morrison said, "at the request of the Breiburg police. We're sort of working with them on the Pajorfsky murder."

"Oh, do the police believe my report now?"

Roland Kohl smiled around his cigar. "I don't know about the Krauts, Prof, but *we* believe you. Want to step inside so we can talk this over in private?"

Abbot didn't think he had much choice. He led the way to his inner room and opened the window wide to clear the air. He saw no evidence that the two men had been through his desk and cabinets, but he supposed they had. There was nothing in the room to tie him to ELF or to Jeremy Sawyer, except for the old Cambridge snapshot, which was still lying on the desk blotter where he'd left it.

"We wouldn't turn down a drink, Prof," Roland Kohl said affably, "if you're having one yourself. A beer would do me—how about you, Jimbo?"

"A beer would be fine, if it's no trouble," Morrison said to Abbot.

Abbot got two beers from the refrigerator and poured himself a generous brandy over ice. When he came back to the main room he found Morrison paging through one of the books he'd taken from Abbot's desk. It was *Huckleberry Finn.*

"I used to love this book when I was a kid," Morrison said. "Does it mean anything at all to the Germans?"

"It does when I'm done lecturing on it," Abbot said. "You know I'm here with the blessing of the State Department, don't you? The Breiburg-Nakomis exchange is supported by a federal grant."

"So we've heard," Kohl said, wiping foam from his moustache with his sleeve. "Which makes me wonder what the State Department would say if it knew that one of its exchange professors has gotten himself mixed up with an illegal organization—one which, according to some estimates, *could* be pursuing policies contrary to the national interest."

Abbot sat down and took a careful sip of his brandy. Despite Hedge's warning, he really hadn't decided what he would tell the CIA, when and if they showed up to question him. Now that he had met these gentlemen, he found that he didn't want to tell them much at all.

"What organization is that?" he asked Kohl.

"Let's not beat around the bush," Kohl said. "Jimbo here saw you in the Frankfurt station last Saturday with a known agent for an outfit called ELF. Later that evening you were seen in a Frankfurt nightspot with Pajorfsky's former assistant, also an ELF agent."

"So there really is such an organization," Abbot said, trying to sound mildly interested. "I wasn't sure whether to believe them or not, it all sounded so preposterous."

"Oh, they're for real, all right," Morrison said. "What did they tell you, Prof?"

"Not a hell of a lot. I gather they're fanatic anti-Communists, so I don't really see how their activities could be 'contrary to the national interest.'"

"Their idea of how to fight Communism may be slightly different from ours," Kohl said. "Anyway, they're still on the list of organizations which are definite no-no's for American citizens traveling abroad. Your federal grant would dry up like that"—

Kohl snapped his fingers—"if Washington knew you were on their payroll."

"I'm *not* on their payroll. The girl, Greta, called me Saturday morning and asked if I could tell her anything about Pajorfsky's death. I thought I'd tell her what little I knew, since the Breiburg police didn't seem interested in pursuing an investigation."

"They couldn't find a body," Kohl said. "The cops never investigate a murder if they can't find a body. So you went down to Frankfurt just to oblige this chick and give her Pajorfsky's last words, is that it?"

"Sure—I'd gotten to like Mikos. We'd been living next door for a month, but I had no idea he was—well, whatever he was. It still seems rather incredible. Are you sure these people aren't just harmless cranks?"

Kohl seemed to be losing his patience. "Come on, Prof, cut the crap, would you? The girl told you all about ELF. Then you and she disappeared for at least eight hours, probably to meet some higher-up in the organization. Then you're next seen cuddling up to each other in a beer garden in Sachsenhausen. Our sources say you spent the night at her place—that sounds like a recruitment scenario to me, wouldn't you say so, Jimbo?"

"It does, I'm afraid," Morrison solemnly agreed.

"Now see here," Abbot said, "I think I've had just about enough of this. How do I know you two even work for the CIA? Where's your identification? If I'm going to be charged with anything, I want to see somebody in authority at the U.S. Embassy in Bonn. I want legal counsel—"

"Take it easy, Prof," Morrison said. "Nobody's charging you with anything—at least not yet. Rollie was just pointing out the problems you'd run into if some of your actions were, let's say, misunderstood. On top of which, you realize you could be putting yourself into a pretty dangerous situation. They play hardball in this league, Prof—look what happened to your pal, Pajorfsky."

Abbot took note of the technique Kohl and Morrison were using: First one of them tried to intimidate and anger him, then the other offered friendship and conciliation. Supposedly, he would run from Kohl into the arms of Morrison. It was a strategy he felt capable of resisting, as long as nobody pushed *too* hard.

"I appreciate your concern," he said to Morrison. "If you think

84

I'm in any danger because of what I witnessed in the Stadtwald, I'd certainly like your protection. But I can assure you I haven't joined any subversive organization, and I rather resent the insinuation that I could be bought by that young lady's sexual favors—"

He noticed that Kohl was looking at a slip of pale blue paper he'd found on Abbot's desk. It was the bank statement he had picked up yesterday.

"Or by twenty thousand deutsche marks, Prof? That's pretty goddamn cheap, if you ask me."

"Now Rollie, I'm sure the Prof can explain that deposit," Morrison said. "Let's not jump to any conclusions—"

"I don't have to explain anything to either of you until I see some identification," Abbot insisted.

Kohl looked as if he might be about to produce it. Instead, he replaced the bank statement and picked up the snapshot of Abbot and Jeremy.

"Want to tell us where you got this picture, Prof?"

"It was taken with my own camera, approximately twenty-three years ago, when I was a student at Cambridge University."

"You always carry it around with you?"

"Not always. I was hoping to get over to England later this summer, and I thought I might try to locate that pub—for old times' sake."

Morrison stood up to look over Kohl's shoulder. "Hey, that's you, isn't it, Prof? On the left? Who's the other guy? He looks vaguely familiar."

"He should, Jimbo," Kohl said, snapping a fingernail against the black-and-white image. "He used to get his picture in the papers a lot, ten, fifteen years ago. His name's Jeremy Sawyer—am I right, Prof?"

"Jeremy Sawyer," Morrison said with a puzzled frown. "Now where have I heard that name before?"

"You were probably still in grade school," Kohl said, "but the Prof and I remember, don't we, Prof? Jeremy Sawyer was a draft-dodging, Commie-loving, artsy-fartsy fag poet who ran off to the Soviet Union back in 1968 or thereabouts. I guess he was afraid he was going to get his fag's ass sent to Vietnam, right, Prof?"

"You've got the name right," Abbot said, "but Jeremy Sawyer

wasn't a fag when I knew him, and I doubt that he was ever a full-fledged Communist. And we didn't call it 'draft dodging' in those days—we called it 'draft resistance.'"

"Some of us called it one thing," Kohl said serenely, "and some of us called it another. I don't suppose you heard that Sawyer is scheduled to attend a literary conference in East Berlin next week, when you *just happen* to be attending another in West Berlin. Amazing coincidence, isn't it?"

"I read about the East Berlin conference in the *Herald Tribune*," Abbot said. "It did strike me as a bit odd, but I figured the East Germans were simply trying to upstage the conference I'll be at—which is sponsored by the United States Information Service, by the way."

Kohl scowled at Abbot. "You don't have to keep pushing your credentials in my face, Prof—I know you're one of the State Department's fair-haired boys. I'll still bust your ass six ways to Sunday if you violate the restrictions that come with a U.S. passport. I don't suppose you and Sawyer were planning a little get-together in Berlin, were you?"

The more Abbot saw of Kohl and Morrison, the less inclined he was to tell them anything about Operation Nightingale. If that made him an enemy of the American national interest—well, at the moment he wasn't feeling particularly patriotic.

"It would be nice to see Jeremy again," he said to Kohl, "but I'm not planning on it: I doubt that it could be arranged."

"Oh, it could be arranged all right," Kohl said, coming to stand over Abbot with his coat hanging open, so that Abbot could see the large handgun in its shiny leather shoulder holster, hitched snugly just below a damp armpit. "Your pals in ELF are very good at arranging things like that—they do it all the time. What I'd like to know is, *why* do they want you to meet with Sawyer? And why have you agreed to do it?"

Abbot was determined not to let himself be intimidated. "You're writing the scenarios, why don't you tell me?"

Kohl grinned down at Abbot, rubbing the knuckles of one large hairy hand into the palm of the other. "Oh, I better not do that, Prof. Some of *my* ideas might make you sore. And then you might try to take a poke at me or something, and I might have to break both your fucking wrists, and we wouldn't want that, now would we?"

Morrison quickly put himself between Kohl and Abbot. "Hey, ease up, guys, would you? I think we're both on the same side here, really. Let me just explain something to the Professor, before you two start busting up the furniture."

"Be my guest," Kohl said, and walked away to the window, as if he really needed a moment or two to compose himself.

"Now Prof," Morrison said, sitting down across from Abbot and looking earnestly at him (as if, Abbot thought, he were about to start quoting chapter and verse from those Bibles he was selling), "I know ELF told you they were an anti-Communist group, and that's true, they are. Over the years they've given the Soviets plenty of trouble in Eastern Europe, and that's fine with us—we don't have any problem with that. Our problem is just that lately they haven't been keeping us very well informed concerning their plans and operations. And that makes us kind of nervous, you see, because a private outfit like ELF—well, you can never tell what sort of crazy thing they might do. I mean, they might be tempted to go a little too far, and *then* what might happen? We could have World War Three on our hands, right? So that's why we've got to keep tabs on them, even if they claim to be on our side. Am I making any sense at all to you, Prof?"

"Sure," Abbot said, though privately he observed that his meeting with Jeremy was unlikely to ignite World War Three. "In principle I'd say that any political group that operates in secret and without public accountability is a threat to world peace. That's why I have a little trouble with your organization as well, Mr. Morrison—"

"Now that's where you're wrong," Roland Kohl spoke from the window, in a somewhat friendlier tone. "We're the professionals, Prof. We know our business, and we know when to draw the line. Unfortunately, we're not always allowed to function to the full extent of our capability. Congress put the CIA in a straitjacket a few years ago, and that's when we had to start relying on free-lance outfits like ELF to do some of our work for us. It's a bad deal, if you ask me. The whole trade's been taken over by amateurs. These days you've got a lot of cranks, weirdos, and two-bit losers passing themselves off as intelligence operatives, and frankly, it scares the crap out of me."

"The same thing applies on the Soviet side," Morrison said. "The KGB has a lot more freedom than we do, obviously, but they've had to rely on some pretty far-out groups as well. Talk about these terrorist scares all over Europe and the Middle East—you think we'd be having all these bombings and hijackings if the professionals were in control of things?"

"I see, so it's *our* terrorists versus *their* terrorists, is that what you're telling me?" Abbot asked.

"Sort of—only our terrorists are nicer than theirs." Morrison grinned. "Heck, Prof, we're not asking you to queer any deal ELF may have set up in Berlin—we'd just like to know what it is, so we can be prepared for the consequences."

That sounded reasonable, but Abbot wasn't convinced. What about the leak Hedge had mentioned? He guessed that, leak or no leak, Kohl wouldn't hesitate to warn the KGB of Jeremy's defection if he deemed it a matter of professional courtesy.

"I'm sorry. I'd like to help you," he said, "but I wasn't told anything about ELF's plans. Once she heard the details of Mikos Pajorfsky's 'accident,' Greta simply warned me not to get involved. I went off to do some sight-seeing, then met her later for a drink. Whatever happened between us after that—well, it was purely personal."

Kohl and Morrison exchanged bleak looks.

"Okay, Prof, you can't say you weren't warned," Kohl said as he made for the door. "Oh, by the way, you did get a look at the guy that ran Pajorfsky down, am I right?"

"I gave his description to the police," Abbot said.

Kohl reached into a coat pocket. "Take a look at this, would you?"

It was a black-and-white photograph, enlarged and somewhat faded, as if the negative had been used many times. One face in a group of several had been circled; he was a man in a military uniform, apparently taking part in some sort of ceremonial occasion, and probably caught by a telephoto lens from a considerable distance. Though the man was much younger than the man in the Mercedes, Abbot recognized the bony brow, the deep-set eyes, the mouthful of large teeth.

"That's him, all right," he said, glad that he could at last give

Kohl and Morrison some useful information. "That's the guy who killed Mikos Pajorfsky. But he's a lot older now—this must be quite an old photograph."

"It's the most recent one we have," Kohl said. "This fellow died in 1969."

"What?"

Abbot could read his own astonishment by the smile on Kohl's face. "His name was Nikolai Charnov. He was a Colonel in the KGB, Special Branch. *His* speciality was the assassination of Western agents in Poland, East Germany, and Czechoslavakia. He was so good at it that they called him the Hangman, after his favorite method of execution. When I took over the East German network in 1968, he had all my operatives scared to death. For every agent he killed, another two defected to the Russians to save their necks. I knew I had to do something, so I set a trap for Comrade Charnov, baited it with something I knew he couldn't resist, then planted a suitcase full of explosives where I knew he'd open it. Mikos Pajorfsky was working for us back in those days—he helped to set it up. For years, it was the last we ever heard of the Hangman."

"Are you trying to tell me," Abbot asked, "that Mikos was killed by a ghost?"

"I was in a building across the street when the bomb went off," Kohl said. "It broke the window pane I was looking out of. If there was anything left of Charnov, the Soviet doctors accomplished a small miracle by sewing him back together again."

Abbot remembered the glaze of scar tissue on the Hangman's face, and the single deep scar which pinched back his upper lip. No wonder the poor creature had seemed the survivor of a holocaust.

Morrison gave Abbot a business card: ATLAS IMPORTS, AMERICAN MARKETS FOR QUALITY PRODUCTS. There was a Berlin street address and telephone number on the card. "If you should see Charnov again, or if you change your mind about talking to us, call that number. One of us will get in touch with you in a jiffy."

"Thanks," Abbot said.

The men crossed the kitchen, and Abbot had the sudden, scary feeling that he was being abandoned to his fate. "Do you think this man Charnov killed Pajorfsky for revenge?" he asked Kohl.

Kohl paused in the hall to unwrap a fresh cigar. "Well, Prof, I thought sure I killed that son of a bitch, and I don't believe in ghosts. But enough people have seen Charnov, or somebody who looks a lot like him, to make me wonder. If it *is* him, he's probably trying to even up some old scores, and that might make me next on his list. Which is one reason why I'd like to find him first, *verstehen Sie?*"

"If I see him again, I'll certainly let you know."

Kohl smiled. "Yeah, you do that, Prof. Thanks for the beer."

Abbot listened to their footsteps clattering down the stairs; then he shut, locked and bolted his door. He left the window open, however, hoping to get the stink of cigar smoke out of his room.

TRAVELS OF A TROUBADOR

PART TWO

erlin seemed to perch like a bird with clipped wings on the brink of spring. In the concrete planters along each major thoroughfare there were blooming stalks of forsythia, purple and yellow pansies, blue and white crocuses. Each morning a tepid sun made a belated appearance in the hazy sky; by noon the air had warmed sufficiently to encourage Berlin's hardier citizens and off-season tourists to congregate at sidewalk cafés along the Kurfürstendamm. By four or five, however, when those same tourists gathered for cocktails in the gleaming chrome-and-glass lounge atop the Europa Center, a rising tide of fog had once again extinguished the sun and all but obliterated the truncated steeple of the Kaiser Wilhelm Gedächtniskirche just across the square.

Abbot's conference kept him busy in the mornings. In the afternoons there were free hours, during which the participants formed small groups to visit the Dahlem museums or the Charlottenburg Palace. Abbot did his sight-seeing with half a mind, waiting for some word from ELF. By Sunday he was convinced that the mission had been canceled. The Russians were wise to the scheme; they had called Jeremy back to Moscow; Abbot would never seen his old friend again. He was surprised at his acute sense of loss. Why was it so important for him to see Jeremy Sawyer again? Not just to *see* him, he realized the moment he framed the question, but to *hear* him as well. It was Jeremy's voice which had called him to Berlin and which seemed even now to beckon to him from the other side of the famous wall. That voice he had never forgotten, which he heard sometimes in his dreams. As if, Abbot thought, I have been waiting all these years for Jeremy's call to rouse me from my slumber.

On Sunday he stopped as usual at the hotel desk to check for messages. The clerk handed him a plain envelope, in which he found a ticket for one of the standard tours of West Berlin. Though Abbot had already taken such a tour upon his arrival in the city, he met the bus outside his hotel that afternoon at the appointed hour. Its first stop was the Berlin Wall, where, along with a hundred or so impatient pilgrims of numerous nationalities, he mounted the rough wooden stairs and filed along a crude plank platform overlooking the graffiti-adorned barrier and the no-man's-land beyond. In the hazy April sunshine, the forbidden zone with its mud and puddles looked perfectly mundane—something like the swath of desolation an advancing freeway might cut through an American city. It was hard to believe that men had actually been killed for attempting to cross that barren stretch of ground and that all these people had been drawn to look soberly at the site. What was it, Abbot wondered, they had all come here expecting to see? Another escape attempt? Another refugee cut down by machine-gun bullets as he lunged desperately for the top of the wall? No, for most of them it was probably nothing so bloodthirsty as that. They were looking instead, Abbot thought, for some evidence that the great division between East and West really meant something—that it was tangible and real and worth the blood that had already been shed to sustain it.

Perhaps that was what Abbot was hoping to hear from Jeremy as well, though he suspected that the message he was most eagerly awaiting was a good deal more personal. Whatever Jeremy had to say to the rest of the world, he had some other message for Abbot himself, something which only Abbot could understand. Standing on the platform, Abbot tried to imagine Jeremy's voice calling faintly on the cold wind that blew from the east. He was so successful that, for a moment, a distinct chill rippled down his spine.

He returned to the bus past the several shabby souvenir stands and lunch wagons that lined the approach to the wall. Brian Hedge was waiting for him on board, having taken the previously vacant seat next to Abbot's. He had an expensive camera and a pair of binoculars crisscrossed on his chest and he gave Abbot the sleepy-eyed glance of a total stranger.

"Quite a sight, isn't it?"

"Yes indeed," Abbot said.

"Does this bus stop at the Plötzensee Memorial, do you know?"

Abbot checked his brochure. "Yes, I believe it's the next stop."

"Mmm, quite worth seeing," Hedge said. "It was once a prison for Hitler's political enemies—those who dared to speak out against the Nazis. I wouldn't miss the execution chamber, if I were you."

"I'll be sure to have a look at it," Abbot said.

When they reached Plötzensee, Hedge remained on the bus. Abbot followed the crowd through the museum, across a sunny courtyard brightened by spring flowers, then into a dim and ugly room, the walls of which still showed the bullet holes of Hitler's firing squads. A guide addressed the tourists, giving his speech first in German, then in English, then in French. During the English segment, a bearded man in a soiled raincoat stood next to Abbot and spoke without looking at him: "There will be another ticket for you at the hotel desk this evening. It is for a tour of the eastern zone. Use the passport in the packet and leave yours behind. When the tour stops at the riverside restaurant, look for a man in a red plaid scarf."

The bearded man walked away as the guide changed from English to French. Abbot completed the tour and returned to the bus, but Hedge, as he had expected, was gone. Though glad to have received his instructions at last, Abbot wondered a bit at ELF's choice of locale: Could there have been a more ominous spot in all of Berlin?

That evening he dined with a group from the conference. They were all American academics traveling or working abroad, and having compared notes on their itineraries and grievances, they fell to the usual shoptalk of the profession. Abbot was not particularly interested in who was making big money off his textbook or who was about to grab some lucrative grant or distinguished chair. It reminded him, this kind of gossip, of why his career had turned sour just when it should have been moving into high gear, leaving him with the aching desire to escape his old life and begin anew.

The woman next to him turned suddenly and addressed him in a broad southern accent: "Professah Abbot, Ah've been wantin' to tell you how much Ah enjoyed your paper—"

"Thank you," Abbot said. The woman was not bad looking; they had exchanged glances and smiles at several previous sessions.

"Of course, Ah must say Ah think you're totally mistaken on a couple of points—"

Having wearied of the topic, Abbot had no wish to defend his thesis. "No doubt I oversimplified the problem—"

"Well, how could you help it, with that outdated and discredited sexist ideology you were usin'? Ah thought we all knew by now that those ideas were the creation of a corrupt system of female exploitation and oppression—didn't we know that, Professah Abbot?"

Looking around the table for another conversation in which to seek refuge, Abbot heard a man to his right say, "Have you been following the conference the East Germans are holding?"

There were a few groans and snickers. "Of course it's the same old party line," someone observed. "Socialist Realism rides again."

"Yes, but they do have Jeremy Sawyer as one of their speakers," someone else put in. "That ought to stir up a bit of interest, at least."

Several members of the group were too young to know who Jeremy Sawyer was. Abbot listened as others explained. Though there were some factual errors, he did not intervene. After all, how did he know that one of these people wasn't a spy for one side or the other? He had never had such an excellent reason for keeping quiet on the subject of Jeremy's defection.

"We don't know if he's written anything in the past twenty years or not," the man next to Abbot said. "Maybe he's written a lot, but the cultural commissars didn't approve."

"Then why bring him to a conference?" someone else asked. "Perhaps he's written a monumental epic in praise of Marxism and the Russian people."

"No doubt they've ground all the talent out of the poor bastard by now," another man said, and that seemed to conclude the conversation.

As the group broke up Abbot declined an invitation to attend a play for which tickets were still available, another to explore Berlin discos. "You're not coming with us?" the woman who had been seated next to him asked as they all parted in the lobby. "Ah was hoping Ah'd have the chance to change your mind about a few things."

"Oh well, we couldn't talk very much over all the noise," Abbot said. "Perhaps another time."

"Ah'll be leaving Berlin tomorrow," the woman said, and her eyelashes actually seemed to flutter as she looked up at Abbot. "Perhaps you'd like to meet for a nightcap in the hotel bar, say along about midnight?"

Abbot was planning to be sound asleep by midnight, but he told the woman he'd try to meet her—"if something else kind of important doesn't come up."

She gave him a reproachful look and went off with her friends.

Abbot checked at the desk and was given a packet bearing only his name. He took it up to his room and found that it contained a ticket for a bus tour of East Berlin leaving at eight the next morning. There was also a passport—a virtual copy of his own, except for the serial number and the photograph, which had apparently been taken with a telephoto lens sometime during the conference. There were no instructions inside the envelope. Abbot supposed he would be told whatever he needed to know by the man in the red plaid scarf.

He was beginning to understand the principle: They told you as little as possible so that, if you were ever captured and interrogated, perhaps tortured, you would have less information to divulge. They kept you on a leash, but you didn't know for sure how long it was or who had hold of the other end. If you started off in the wrong direction they gave the leash a tug to change your course—otherwise you were allowed to follow your nose. Abbot wished he hadn't thought of this analogy.

He went back down to the hotel bar for a drink, feeling oddly calm about the next day's adventure. Perhaps *resigned* was a better word. Maybe it was time to write that last letter home: "Dear Family, don't blame yourselves just because I've gone and done something foolish . . ."

No, Abbot thought, tell them that and they'll feel guilty for the rest of their lives. Better by far (if one were about to disappear into a Siberian prison camp) to leave behind no explanations, no apologies, no general absolution. Let 'em wonder whatever happened to Sam Abbot—maybe that way his reputation would outlive him by a few years, at least.

He finished his drink and left the hotel to stroll through the glassy, glittering arcade of the adjacent Europa Center—a futuristic garden full of neon flowers and tinsel foliage. In a small bar calling itself an English pub, he drank a pint of ale and observed two young American soldiers who were trying to pick up the German barmaid: "What time you get off work, honey? Wanna take a ride in a real, honest-to-God American jeep?"

Abbot wondered about the woman with the southern accent. Was she really interested in him, or could it be some sort of trap? He remembered Greta's story about the Russian general and decided he'd better forgo the midnight rendezvous. With any luck, he could be drunk enough to fall asleep by eleven.

He left the Europa Center and came out onto the square surrounding the war-damaged hulk of the Gedächtniskirche and its boxy modern reincarnation, a chapel and bell-tower nicknamed the Powder Box and Lipstick Case by the irreverent Berliners. Despite another evening of foggy drizzle, the usual crowd of young people had gathered in the square. With their skateboards and portable tape decks, their ragamuffin "punk" costumes and outbursts of break dancing, they created a carnival atmosphere, a feeling of desperate frivolity which Abbot was able to recognize, after only a few days, as one of the authentic moods of the city. Caught between East and West, a hostage to the fortunes of diplomacy, the West Berliners lived each night as if it were their last—an attitude which Abbot on this evening found chillingly appropriate.

Traffic streamed along the Kurfürstendamm. Fog-bloated neons traced their snaky reflections across wet asphalt. Abbot walked down the boulevard, admiring the expensive wares displayed in the freestanding glass cases outside the fashionable shops, admiring also the fashionable women who rustled by on the arms of their escorts with a flash of jewelry and whiff of exotic perfumes. Behind the misty windows of a famous café, Abbot saw elegant blondes and sultry brunettes seated at candlelit tables with distinguished, gray-haired men, their poses and expressions reminiscent of a scene from *Cabaret*. He turned up his collar and walked on.

In the next block he entered an area of cheaper restaurants and sleazy theaters featuring porno spectaculars and kung-fu marathons. There were several hookers working this block and the next, and one slender brunette came forward from the shadowed entrance to a porcelain gallery. She flashed Abbot a smile and spoke invitingly in German. Though he knew well enough what she had in mind, he said, *"Es tut mir leid, ich spreche kaum Deutsch."*

The girl grinned. "Hey Joe, I speak English, too. You want to come wiss me and make love?"

The words nearly broke Abbot's heart. Behind the girl, in the window of the porcelain gallery, he saw tiny shepherdesses and geishas, aristocratic ladies of the French court, gypsies and Indian maidens, each bearing a spot of red on her delicate china cheek.

"I'm sorry, no—no, I can't, really."

The tart shrugged and turned away. Abbot trudged on, feeling at least ninety years old. There had been something inexpressibly appealing about her soft voice and funny accent, the way her eyes had slipped almost modestly away from his as she spoke the words *make love*. Dressed all in white except for a pink scarf at her throat, she had projected a kind of innocence he felt incapable of defiling.

You sentimental idiot, Abbot thought, she probably does it fifty time a night. Yet the girl's image accompanied him through two more drinks and a circuitous return to his hotel.

It was eleven-thirty when he entered the lobby, and Abbot had just about decided that he *would* have that drink with Miss Southern Accent. But when he looked into the bar he saw that she was already deep in conversation in a back booth with one of the conference's Ivy League glamour boys. Her quick glance showed no sign of welcome or recognition.

You *are* an idiot, Abbot told himself as he went up to bed.

It was another chilly morning of pallid sunshine, the wind blowing briskly from the east, when Abbot reported to the East Berlin tour bus. He waited on the curb, weighing discomforts—his hangover versus the cold wind—as the tourists were logged on board one at a time. When it came Abbot's turn a young woman examined his passport and entered his name and passport number on her clipboard. Then she gave him a number: 36. He gathered that his was the thirty-sixth name on the list. He found a seat and waited for the bus to fill up. He realized that his nose was stuffy, his throat raw—he was probably coming down with a cold. Great. Maybe he could use that as an excuse to stay home in his hotel room and sip soup.

At last the bus pulled out. It was a short drive to Checkpoint Charlie, where they were shunted off into an adjacent parking area. The tourists filed off the bus and were told to line up by number in the drafty compound. There were several busloads being similarly processed by guards in the dark green uniforms of the DDR. To Abbot, the whole procedure smacked of some specious bureaucratic rigmarole, but he began to worry when he saw how closely the guards were inspecting each passport. Damn, why couldn't he have used his real one? Was this cloak-and-dagger stuff really necessary?

The guard completed his inspection of Abbot's passport and waved him back on board. Abbot returned to his seat with sweat trickling down his ribs, his heart rattling inside his rib cage. If this was the way he reacted to the scrutiny of forged credentials, his career in espionage was likely to be a short one. He was *sure* that guard was suspicious of something!

When the tourists were all back on board, the bus pulled out of the compound, crossed an area of vacant, gutted buildings and barbed wire, and stopped before an isolated three-story house. A young woman in a blue uniform came out and crossed over to the bus; it appeared that she was their English-speaking guide. Her breathy accent greeted them over the PA system:

"Good morning, ladies and gentlemen, and welcome to the German Democratic Republic. We are very happy that you come to visit our capital city, which is an interesting and important example of life in a socialist society . . ."

They drove through the old center of the city, past the Brandenburg Gate and along Unter den Linden. The massive public buildings and palaces of the Prussian empire had been restored, as the tour guide explained to them, "by the hard work of the German people and the sound management of our economic resources" and dedicated to cultural uses: a library, an opera house, a university. Abbot was impressed by the serene dignity, not to say grandeur, of each new thoroughfare, and he overheard a woman behind him saying, "Well, it certainly makes West Berlin look trashy in comparison, doesn't it?"

"That's the idea, I should imagine," her companion replied. "Of course the western sector was rebuilt in a few years, whereas this lot took nearly forty."

The different time frame of the socialist mentality, Abbot thought. It was clear the citizens of East Berlin lived at a different pace, according to a different scale of values. It was strange to see a modern city in which there were no neon signs, no billboards, no advertising of any sort, except for a few banners proclaiming what Abbot took to be Communist party slogans—he translated one as "We support the people's candidates." It was also strange to see a European city so devoid of traffic and pedestrians in the middle of the day. There were streetcars, but few riders, parks and public gardens, but hardly anyone to enjoy the timid sunshine and spring flowers.

"Where *is* everybody?" a lady near the front asked the tour guide.

"No doubt they are all at work," the tour guide said promptly. "You might be interested to know that at present we are having no unemployment problem in the Democratic Republic, and our people are enjoying this very much—"

After a circuit of the Stadtmitte, the bus set out for Treptow Park, where they were to visit the Soviet War Memorial. The driver took them swiftly through several industrialized areas and shabby neighborhoods, about which the guide had nothing to say. The bus bounced and lunged along at a speed which discouraged shutterbugs, and eventually they arrived at Treptow Park, where they were expected to leave the bus and walk a cold, cheerless quarter mile through the wintery park to a windswept terrace, from which they could admire a gigantic statue of a Russian soldier. The soldier was holding a small child in one arm, while from his other hand there descended an immense sword. He was gazing off across Germany with an angry scowl, as if to say that he wanted no more damned nonsense—that if the specter of fascism should ever rise again he would come down from his pedestal to lay about him with his mighty sword.

It was possible to cross the intervening gardens and enter the base of the statue, which was actually a shrine to the Russian war dead, but Abbot decided to forgo that pilgrimage in order the take the giant's measure from a safer distance. He hadn't expected to find himself so indignant at this display of Soviet might on German soil, but the entire tour was beginning to offend him with its pompous and predictable touting of the party line. Perhaps his brief association with the partisans in ELF had altered his perceptions in such matters, or perhaps the East Germans really did lay it on a bit thick.

By the time they returned to the bus, the chilled and sobered tourists were glad to learn that their next stop was a riverside restaurant where they might purchase hot coffee and goulash soup. Abbot knew this was the place where he was to meet his contact— the man in the red plaid scarf—and he felt his stomach turn over as they pulled into the parking lot. The tour guide explained that they had precisely one hour during which to refresh themselves; she urged them not to wander off.

Abbot didn't see how he could meet Jeremy Sawyer and return to the bus in just half an hour, then suddenly understood why he had been given a false passport. Of course he wouldn't be taking this bus back to West Berlin. Someone else, with a duplicate of his passport, would take his place. But then how in the hell was he going to get out?

I should have my head examined, Abbot told himself as he followed the busload of tourists around the restaurant building to the riverside terrace, where the scent of coffee and reek of grease drifted from several kiosks. A small gathering of natives—most of them probably government agents—were seated at the frost-glazed iron tables. Some of the tourists went inside to eat, while others chose the sheltered areas of sunshine. The river at this point was broad and marshy; greening willows showed along its banks, and a distant church spire rose on the far shore. Abbot saw no one in a red scarf.

He lined up at one of the kiosks, rendered an unusually large number of West German marks, then carried two steaming paper cups to a table near the river. The soup was spicy and hot enough to burn his mouth, but the meat was tough and the potatoes mere mush. So much for East German cuisine, Abbot thought. The coffee wasn't much better, but at least it didn't require chewing. The fresh air cleared his sinuses, and he watched a family of ducks bobbing along near shore. Good Communist ducks, he supposed.

Someone had taken a seat next to Abbot and was slurping away at a cup of soup. Abbot turned and saw that beneath his drab overcoat the man was wearing a red plaid scarf. He waited until the man had wolfed down his soup and lit up a cigarette. "When they call you back to the bus," the man said in clipped, clear English, "make a stop at the toilets. Use the third stall—it has a window you can open. Climb out and you will find a path which leads down to the river. I'll meet you there."

"And how do I get back to West Berlin?"

"We'll see to that," the man said, and rose from the table. Abbot watched him walk away and wondered if he could be the legendary Stork or simply one of his assistants. Or perhaps an East German agent setting him up for a trap? Abbot had never realized how much faith was required of a secret agent in enemy territory—faith, or gullibility.

He sipped his cooling coffee and waited until he saw the tour guide motion them back to the bus. Knowing tourists, she had probably allowed a few minutes for toilet stops. Abbot veered off and entered the door marked *Herren*. The interior was cold and vile smelling. The third stall—bearing a sign Abbot took to mean "out of order"—was empty. He entered and found, sure enough, a frosted window above the toilet tank. It wasn't large, but he thought he could get through it. Locking the door to the stall, Abbot cranked open the window, then climbed onto the toilet seat and looked out. A heavy stand of trees and shrubs grew behind the building, screening the path from busybodies on the terrace. Abbot eased his head, arm, and shoulder out the window. He pushed, squirmed, worked out a leg. For a moment he seemed stuck, his body too bulky and stiff to make it through the narrow aperture. At last he freed the other leg, then dropped to the ground. He reached up to push the window shut behind him, then hurried down the path. The woods remained dense, the path secluded. In a hundred yards he reached the riverbank.

The man in the red scarf came out of the scrub willows at the water's edge. "This way," he said and led Abbot through the bushes to a small clearing, where a wooden rowboat had been beached in the reeds. Another man sat in the boat, ready to work the oars. Red Scarf reached into the boat and brought out a rubberized canvas poncho. "Put this over your coat. Raise the hood."

Abbot did so, then climbed into the bow. Red Scarf, now clad in a similar poncho, pushed off and clambered astern. Abbot felt a cold wind and realized they were downstream from the restaurant terrace. The current was swift near shore and the oarsman let it carry the boat along, applying the oars as needed. On the bottom of the boat lay several cane poles, tackle and baitboxes, a small dip net.

"Do you like to fish?" the oarsman asked Abbot in English.

Both he and Red Scarf laughed. Abbot smiled nervously. "Is it legal here?"

"It is not so illegal as certain other things," the oarsman said, and both men laughed heartily again.

When they were several hundred yards downriver, Abbot saw a railroad bridge stretching across the channel. The oarsman pulled hard to cut across the current as they neared the bridge. By now, Abbot supposed, the tour bus had left the restaurant. Someone else, bearing his name and a duplicate of his passport, was on his way back to West Berlin. It was sort of like dying. You saw your body carried off to the grave, but your soul broke free and went a different way; you crossed a river and entered the underworld, where you talked to the spirits of your youth.

The boat crunched into rocks and bushes along the far shore. Abbot climbed out over the bow and pulled the boat up onto a wedge of sand. Then the two men stepped ashore, and together they hauled the boat out of the water and into the bushes around the pilings of the bridge. They put their ponchos into the boat and the oarsman covered it with a green tarp. As nearly as Abbot could tell, they had been seen by no one since leaving the restaurant a little over fifteen minutes before.

They climbed up the bank through a thicket and came out on a small gravel road, where a car was waiting. The driver, who had been standing beside the car smoking a cigarette, got in and started the engine. Abbot took the backseat, where he found a case of beer on the floor. "Have one," Red Scarf said, tossing back a bottle opener. "If we should be stopped by the police, we are four men using our day off for a country outing. You can pretend to be drunk and sleeping."

Abbot appreciated the ruse. He opened a bottle and took a swig. East German beer was definitely superior in quality to East German coffee, and the wind on the river had aggravated his sore throat. By now, Abbot had the curious conviction that he would probably be invisible to any East German policeman—perhaps because he wasn't here at all. No, he was home in bed at the guesthouse, having a silly dream.

They bounced along the gravel road until they reached a larger thoroughfare, where they turned to the south, away from the center of the city. Abbot saw a series of high-rise apartment complexes, several mysterious factories, storage tanks and pylons, then marshland and newly plowed fields. The men in the front seat conversed in German; they struck Abbot as excessively relaxed and casual about their mission. Perhaps they smuggled people into and out of East Germany all the time, yet their air of confidence was not entirely reassuring. Abbot would have been happier if they had seemed just a bit more on edge—after all, it was *his* life they were risking.

They had been driving for twenty minutes when Abbot saw another river or small lake gleaming through the trees. The shore was lined with small, cottagelike buildings—the vacation villas, he guessed, of party officials of modest rank. The setting was pretty, but most of the cottages could have used paint or repairs. Many seemed not to have been opened yet for the season. On the roof of one of these houses a man was working; he gave the car a brief signal with his hammer, whereupon the driver slowed and turned onto a lane that led between the cottages.

They pulled up behind another car parked outside a gray house at the water's edge. Abbot saw that they were screened from the main road by a stand of tall trees. Two men were working on a boat, which had been overturned on the beach, while another painted a short pier. Down the shore, another man was replacing the window glass in a shed. None of these individuals took particular notice of their arrival.

Red Scarf turned to Abbot. "The man you have come to meet is waiting for you inside. You'll find food and wine on the table— help yourself. The rest of us will wait out here. If you hear us toot the horn, it means there is trouble. Use the trapdoor in the bedroom and follow the tunnel all the way to the end. We will meet you when we are able. Go now—you have just half an hour."

Abbot got out of the car, feeling suddenly light-headed and weak in the knees. With all the things he'd had to worry about, it hadn't occurred to him that he would dread his first meeting with Jeremy Sawyer after all these years. Now it struck him that he hardly knew the man—had forgotten what he did know—could not expect to understand a person who had done what Jeremy had done. The whole trip, it suddenly seemed, was a terrible mistake.

Yet like the good soldier he was trying to become, Abbot went up the plank stairs and opened the door, stepping directly into the main room of the cottage. There were windows overlooking the water; a tall slender man stood at the windows smoking a cigarette. He turned to greet Abbot, but the light was behind him, keeping his face in shadow. It was instead the voice, and its wry, mocking tone, that Abbot recognized first.

"Why hello, old bean—and how have you been keeping?"

8

As often as he had tried to imagine his first meeting with Jeremy Sawyer, Abbot could not have predicted the queer formality, the wariness, not to say the outright hostility, of their initial encounter. Shaking hands, the two men circled one another like wrestlers seeking an advantage; when Jeremy spoke again, it was as though he meant to put a hammer-lock on his opponent:

"So! Life seems to have been good to you, Sam. You're looking remarkably fit. Well fed, at any rate."

"I've always had a tendency in that direction," Abbot admitted. "As for you, Jeremy—"

But he didn't want to say what Jeremy looked like. Did time pass more swiftly in the Soviet universe or grind more harshly against the human frame? In Jeremy's gaunt figure and pale, lined face, in his cloudy, anxious, irritable eyes, Abbot thought he saw a longer history of suffering, of difficulties endured and temptations surrendered to, than a mere eighteen years could account for.

"Yes, I know," Jeremy said, "I look like hell, don't I? Like death warmed over. It's the angina—it sucks the life out of you."

"Angina? You have heart disease?"

Jeremy grimaced, as if the pain might be nibbling away inside his narrow chest even as they spoke. It seemed impossible for him to stand still or to meet Abbot's eyes for more than a second. He prowled the room as if looking for hidden cameras or microphones. "A hereditary ailment, I fear. My father died of a heart attack in his early fifties." He ran his thin fingers through a shock of mostly gray hair, which had a tendency now, as in the old days, to fall across his eyes. "I hear they've developed some extraordinary new treatments for arteriosclerosis in the West. Ever heard of a surgeon names Hans Maienfeld?"

"No, I guess not."

"He's Swiss, runs a clinic and research lab near Geneva. They say he can do amazing things with lasers. No cutting involved. That's the part that scares me the most, you know—to get at the heart they have to saw through your breastbone, open you up like a goddamn birdcage, then wire you back together again when they're done. Can you imagine somebody doing that to you?"

"Sounds unpleasant," Abbot acknowledged.

Jeremy took a quick look out the window, as if he'd heard some noise Abbot hadn't. "In Russia it's worse than unpleasant, old bean—it's fucking fatal. Those Soviet surgeons have all the finesse of meat-packers. I'd rather die slowly, a day at a time, than let those butchers have a go at me."

"So *that's* why you want to leave Russia." Abbot was a little disappointed. As much as Jeremy despised Western capitalism, he wanted the advanced medical treatment it could provide. He was only human, after all; he loved his skin as much as other people loved theirs.

"Do you blame me?" Jeremy asked, as if he guessed Abbot's reaction. "It's hell getting old, Sam—feeling your body crap out on you. I was always a physical sort, you may recall—tennis, squash, skiing; it's bloody hell to find that one has become, at forty-eight, a fucking invalid. Which is something *else* I've had to cut back on," he added, with a lewd wink.

That wink bothered Abbot. Though he hadn't expected, under the circumstances, a full display of Jeremy's old wit, he might have hoped for a little more subtlety, a finer sense of discrimination. Had his memory somehow exaggerated Jeremy's brilliance, or had the man adopted a broader style to please his Russian audience?

"And otherwise, you're quite happy with your life in the Soviet Union? You're not sorry you went?"

It was, perhaps, too soon to have asked this question. Jeremy appeared to pull himself up; he glared at Abbot with reawakened pride, his old assertion of superiority. "What is it you want, Sam?

An act of contrition? A general repudiation of everything I've done, everything I've stood for, in the past eighteen years? 'Forgive me, Uncle Sam, for I have sinned . . .?' "

"That isn't necessary," Abbot said. "I was told that you've written a book about your life in Russia and that you want to have it published in the West."

Jeremy's lined and ravaged face broke into a smile—hardly a fetching sight, since it was clear he had no more use for Soviet dentists than for Soviet surgeons. "That book is my ticket to Switzerland, Sam. It's going to buy me that laser surgery and a nice long recuperation at some Alpine spa. In fact, I'm reasonably confident that it will make us *both* rich and famous. I'm offering you a piece of the action, old bean—how does that strike you?"

Abbot couldn't meet the hopeful, if wavering, light in Jeremy's ash-gray eyes. Instead he fixed his gaze on the dusty square of sky he could see from the cottage window. "Yes, they told me that you wanted me as your editor. That's what I'm here to discuss."

"So what is there to discuss?" Jeremy extended his thin arms like some ungainly bird about to take flight. "It's a gift, Sam, from me to you. That manuscript won't require much editing, but the London publisher—what's his name, the reformed muckrake and rabble-rouser?—he insists that I need an editor. Probably thinks I'll be some sort of prima donna, or maybe he's afraid I've forgotten how to write English prose. Damn nonsense, of course, but since I must have an editor to get a contract out of the old pirate, I thought you'd be an excellent choice."

"Why? Because you think you can bully me?"

Jeremy took a step backward and regarded Abbot with ironic amusement. "My, we *have* developed a touchy spot or two over the years, haven't we? No, Sam, I have no intention of bullying you. It was my fond hope that you'd be as excited about this project as I am. I saw that issue of *Excursions* you devoted to my work— shouldn't you have gotten my permission to reprint those poems and that essay, by the way?"

"Your former publisher gave us permission. We didn't think you'd care, since there was no money involved."

Jeremy waved off any objections he might have had. "Actually, I was bloody pleased, Sam. It was nice to know that I haven't been entirely forgotten in the States. That critical introduction you wrote was first-rate, too. You always did seem to understand my work better than other people—*that's* why I suggested you for this job. I felt sure you'd want to help. If I was wrong—"

Abbot watched Jeremy take another cigarette from his pack and tap it on his wristwatch. "I'll do anything I can to help you get safely relocated in the West. As for editing your manuscript—well, I hope your deal with Sir Godfrey Clemmons doesn't depend entirely on my participation."

"Apparently it does, old bean. At least, that's what these ELF chappies tell me. There's no hope of getting a contract out of that skinflint without a suitable editor, and you're the only one we've come up with whom we both feel we can trust."

"But surely," Abbot said, "you could find another publisher. Why not have ELF get you out, and *then* worry about where you'll sell the book?"

"Because, old bean, without an iron-clad contract, my life won't be worth a plugged nickel in the West. My memoir could embarrass too many people, on both sides of what we used to call the Iron Curtain. They will want, if at all possible, to shut me up."

Abbot didn't quite understand. "But how is a contract going to protect you? All they'd have to do, these people, is get hold of the manuscript before it goes to press . . ."

"Ah, *that's* what we need to counter." Jeremy grinned at Abbot, as if he found this war of wits with potential assassins an agreeable enterprise in itself. "Once I'm safely across, we'll make several copies of the manuscript and deposit them with various reliable custodians. That way, killing me will be pointless, since my death would only prove the truth of all my allegations. However, I'm not about to scatter my precious pages all over Europe without a damned good contract, don't you see? I'd be a bloody fool to risk losing the rights to a work into which I've sunk eighteen years of my life. Eighteen years, Sam! My thirties and forties, a writer's most productive period, and that book is virtually all I've go to show for it—my only capital, if you will. I might as well stay on in Moscow, heart disease and all, if I lose control of that manuscript."

Abbot felt sure Jeremy's fears were exaggerated—at least as far as his authorial rights were concerned. Perhaps life in Russia had made him slightly paranoid concerning the treacheries of the free-enterprise system. Abbot foresaw that his own role would be primarily that of a literary guardian. He was there to make sure the new kid, the bumbling refugee, didn't get robbed and exploited by the evil capitalists. Abbot supposed he could fulfill this function—provided the book was anywhere near as good as Jeremy thought it was.

"All right," he said, "I'll do everything I can to help you close the deal with Sir Godfrey." And then surrendering to a generous impulse, he added, "We want to get you out, Jeremy. We want to see you resume your place as an important *American* author— maybe the finest poet of our generation."

It was amazing what this profession of faith did for Jeremy's agitated spirit. On the instant, he seemed younger and stronger, convinced of his own roguish charm. He flicked his cigarette into the open hearth and crossed the room to put both bony hands on Abbot's shoulders. His long lean face was close to Abbot's; his tobacco-tainted breath assaulted Abbot's nostrils.

"Sam, my old friend, my good old friend, I knew I could count on you! And don't you worry about a thing, old bean. I shall value your advice on this manuscript. I shall take everything you say very seriously. In fact—" he laughed as though surrendering himself to some power or authority which transcended human control—"I'll do whatever you tell me to do with the bloody thing! How's that for a deal?"

"I expect we'll have our disagreement," Abbot said soberly. "I hope we'll be able to thrash them out. We'll just have to see how it goes, Jeremy."

Jeremy continued to hold him for a moment at arm's length, then suddenly remembered the food waiting on the table. "I say, you'd better grab a bite to eat, old bean. They'll be coming to take you back pretty soon."

Abbot wasn't hungry, but he sat down at the table across from Jeremy and surveyed the offering: a hard sausage, several hunks of cheese, a basket of bread and rolls. And a bottle of red wine, which Jeremy, taking on the office of host, was now pouring into his glass.

"Well, cheers," Jeremy said, raising his own. "First drink we've had together in a bloody long time, hey? Let's hope it won't be the last!"

Abbot acknowledged the toast, though his mind was still laboring to assimilate and assess the changes in his friend. He hadn't expected to find Jeremy so aged and frail or so pathetically eager to enlist his help. In the old days Jeremy would have been quite capable of handling all these matters himself—in fact, he would have insisted on it. Had life in Russia really broken his spirit? Once a man of ungovernable energies, Jeremy now appeared drained, exhausted, a weary ghost who was simply too stubborn—or was it too mean?—to die. Instead of the enthusiasm of his youth, he displayed only a dry, burned-out ferocity—the anger of a great disillusionment. Were *these* the ingredients, Abbot wondered uneasily, of a literary masterpiece?

"I think you have some sample chapters for me to read. Something ELF can send on to Sir Godfrey Clemmons?"

Jeremy produced a thin cardboard carton, which Abbot recognized as the envelope for a computer disk. "I hope you realize what a precious object this is in Mother Russia. Few of us ever get access to a computer—even privately owned copy machines are illegal. Your friends in ELF have the program which will print it out—a friend of mine put it into a simple code. It's just the first chapter and another from later in the book, but it should give you an idea of what I've got. Of course you understand the need for secrecy. If word got back to Moscow that I was peddling a manuscript in the West—" Jeremy drew one long thin finger across his scrawny throat.

"Understood," Abbot said. "I'll be as careful as I can. But you should know that Operation Nightingale may have been compromised already."

Jeremy cocked an eyebrow. "Oh?"

"ELF's agent, Mikos Pajorfksy, was killed last week in Breiburg, just before he was to give me that picture you sent as a sign. ELF thinks the murder was unrelated to Operation Nightingale, but I'm not so sure. Just before I left for Berlin, two guys who claimed to be American agents came to question me. They'd already guessed that I would be meeting you in Berlin; they may also have guessed why."

Jeremy frowned as he sawed off several slices of sausage. "Can you describe these men for me?"

"One was young, husky, boyish looking. His name was

Morrison. The other guy was about our age—curly dark hair and hard dark eyes. Smokes a foul cigar and talks like some actor's notion of a tough cop—"

"Roland Kohl," Jeremy said. "I remember him very well. He was one of the federal agents who began harassing me back in '67 when I first got involved with the British antiwar movement. He's a bloody fascist but a lot smarter than he looks. I'm sure *he* won't be pleased to see my story published—he plays rather a significant role in it, you see."

Abbot was beginning to wonder if the political message of Jeremy's book would prove entirely to ELF's taste. "So you deal with the events leading up to your defection, as well as your life in Russia. I suppose you have some pretty harsh things to say about both sides?"

Jeremy showed his bad teeth in another grin. "A plague on both their houses, that's what I say! I've had the dubious privilege of living in two rival worlds, and you'd be surprised at how much they have in common. In Russia the commissars rule your life, in America it's the banks and corporations. It's a toss-up, which is the more abominable dictatorship."

"But isn't the standard of living higher in the West?"

"Yes, and the standard of morality considerable lower. I'll tell you, Sam, the modern superstate is not a fit habitat for the human species—you can take my word on that. In Russia they stifle the human spirit, and in America they merely corrupt and defile it. Maybe in a small, neutral country like Switzerland I'll find the kind of society I can live with; the Swiss, so I hear, are contemptuous of everyone but themselves."

Then it ought to suit you to a T, Abbot thought of saying, but didn't. He had to remember that, as brash and arrogant as Jeremy seemed at one moment, the next he was like a man on the brink of an abyss. In fact he seemed to be picking his way along a narrow ledge, the hard rock of his ego on one side, the empty space of his terror on the other. Watching Jeremy's cautious progress, Abbot himself felt a sensation akin to vertigo.

"I think we'd better move quickly," Jeremy was saying. "I may have aroused a few suspicions in Moscow by coming here, and Kohl's interest makes me nervous. Can you fly to London to deal with this Fleet Street impresario? Take my manuscript along and press him for a contract. I'll authorize you to negotiate on my behalf. As soon as you're satisfied, let me know. The Stork claims he can get me out of Russia within forty-eight hours of receiving your signal."

"I'm supposed to be teaching a couple of courses in Breiburg," Abbot said, "but I guess I can extend my absence by a few days. I'll try to get a flight to London tomorrow."

"Good. Then there's something else you can do for me while you're in England. I'd like you to nip up to Cambridge and deliver a message to my former wife. You remember Patricia, don't you, old bean?"

Abbot's vertigo intensified, as if he were suddenly on a ledge of his own. "Of course I do. I was going to ask you about her."

"Not much I can tell you, I'm afraid. Last letter I got from her must be ten years old. But I'm sure she still lives in Cambridge. Her name is Eckersley now. She married a chemistry don, fellow of Christ's, I think it was. What I'd like you to get from her—" He paused, arched an eyebrow in response to Abbot's anguished gaze. "Why are you looking at me like that? You're not going to give me one of your boring rebukes, now are you, Sam?"

Abbot stared out the window at the wintery blue lake. On the far shore the willows had turned a yellowish green. A flight of ducks skimmed the water. "You had a child, I believe," he said to Jeremy.

"Yes, a daughter, but this Eckersley chap adopted her some years back. There's a lot about my relationship with Pat you don't know, Sam, so don't leap to any hasty conclusions. She turned out, you see, to be a true child of her class, after all."

"You mean she disapproved of your antiwar activities?"

"If that was *all* she disapproved of, we'd probably still be married. I made the mistake of taking her for a free spirit, an enlightened sensibility, when in fact she was a disgustingly conventional woman all along—all veddy proper and British, *dewn't yew kneow?* The marriage was washed up long before I left for Moscow. I do regret leaving the child, though—"

"I should think so." Abbot pictured the snapshot of his own three little ones in that immortal moment before the Christmas tree.

"God, Sam, you're so bourgeois! I remember that about you

now—all those tiresome middle-class pieties you used to throw at me. *You* should have married Patricia! The two of you would have made a perfect match."

"I always thought so," Abbot said.

Jeremy put down his wine glass and peered wonderingly at Abbot. "So *that's* why you left Cambridge so abruptly that summer! You were in love with her yourself, weren't you?"

"Don't tell me you weren't aware of that."

"I confess I wasn't. Not that it would have made any difference, I suppose, since I was quite gone on Pat myself at the time. But you might have spoken up."

"And then what? We would've settled it with a game of squash or a drinking contest?"

"Darts, most likely," Jeremy said with a rueful grin. "But you needn't think so ill of me. I didn't leave my wife and child without a certain reluctance—"

"Reluctance?" Abbot asked, as if he heard in the word proof of Jeremy's callous disregard of his family.

"Damn it, man, there were important issues involved! At least, *I* thought they were important. I don't know where *you* were during that war—"

"Clutching my II-S deferment and keeping my mouth shut. But then, I've always lacked your firm convictions in political matters. I don't pretend to know all the answers—"

Jeremy looked hard at him. "There are a *few* answers, old bean, which any human being who begs the right to inhabit this planet damn well ought to make it his business to know. But wait till you've read my book. Don't judge me until you have the whole story."

Abbot was going to ask Jeremy if he really thought his defection had made any impact whatsoever on America's policy in Vietnam, but they were interrupted by a knock on the door. Red Scarf looked in.

"We must be starting back in a few minutes," he said.

"We're nearly done," Jeremy said. When the door closed, he reached across the table to grasp Abbot's arm in his thin but still forceful fingers. Abbot was reminded of the way Pajorfsky had clawed at his arm that afternoon in the forest, as he lay dying on his bed of moss-covered rocks.

"Now Sam, you must get something for me from Patricia—something she's been saving for me all these years. It's a box of personal items I left behind—letters, diaries, a few snapshots and mementos of my student days—she'll know the box I mean. There are certain documents I'm going to need when the book is published—just in case I get hauled into court for libel and slander, or any other trumped-up charges the Americans or British might try to use against me. I have no intention of leaving Moscow until I know you have that box."

"But what if Patricia no longer has it?"

"She has it. I think she knows how important it is, and I do believe, cad that I am, that she still cares for me enough to have kept it safe. In fact, I'm bloody well counting on it. Without the documents in that box, my story might be better left unpublished."

"All right," Abbot said, "I'll get it for you if I can. Will she give it to me, do you think?"

"Yes, old bean—Pat always liked you. If you tell her you've seen me, and that I've sent you for the box, she'll give it to you. You won't have to tell her anything else. In fact, I don't want you to tell *anyone* about this particular errand until I'm safe in Switzerland. Not ELF, nor Sir Godfrey, and certainly not Roland Kohl—do you understand?"

"And how will I let you know I've got it?"

"I've thought of that. Inside the box you'll find an old tie clasp of mine—gold and onyx with an inlaid pearl. Engraved on the back is a Latin motto—I won't tell you what it says. Once you have the box and everything else is arranged, use that phrase in the report you make through your contact in ELF. Make sure he passes it along to me, verbatim. It will be our signal that the box is in your possession. I won't budge until I get it."

"And will the Stork wait for your decision?"

"He'll have to, won't he? ELF knows the conditions I've set. The fact that you're here shows they mean to meet them. To tell you the truth, Sam, I wasn't sure they'd be able to get you. I was afraid you wouldn't want to risk your neck."

"I guess they caught me at a weak moment," Abbot said. "My neck hasn't seemed all that precious, of late."

Jeremy sat back from the table, lit another cigarette and gazed thoughtfully at Abbot through the smoke. "So those middle-class pieties have finally begun to let you down, have they? Well, that often happens at our age—that's when *all* one's pieties begin to crumble. A man hears the banshee calling his name . . ." Jeremy's voice faltered; his eyes narrowed in recognition of some unspecified dread. Then he shook it off: "But not to worry, my friend. Between us, we'll put those ghosts to rest. And we'll make a pile of money off this book, I guarantee it. We'll be the most celebrated team since the Brontë sisters. Abbot and Sawyer—not a bad billing for a pair of Cambridge cut-ups, hey what?"

Abbot saw their business was concluded and got to his feet. "You might lessen your angina if you laid off the cigarettes, Jeremy—no doubt you know that."

Jeremy looked comically, cross-eyed, at the brown-papered cylinder between his nicotine-stained fingers. "What, you mean these things are bad for you? Good God, the Soviet doctors prescribe them for nearly everything!" He crushed it out and rose to walk with Abbot to the door. "Seriously, I couldn't hold together a day without the damn things, I'm afraid. But once I'm safely in the West, I shall embark on a new life: clean living, healthful habits, regular hours at my writing table. . . . I do think I've got a few decent poems left in me, if I live long enough to write them."

"That's what we're going to make sure of," Abbot said. "The poems may be even more important, you know, than this book."

"Ah, but without the book, I'd never live to write them." Jeremy put his hands once more on Abbot's shoulders as they stood at the door, a gesture which emphasized both his relative height and his emaciated condition. "Now, you know what skinflints these publishers are! I want an advance of one hundred thousand pounds—don't settle for anything less or the bastards'll take us for granted. Get the standard royalties, the best subsidiary and reprint rights—you know how these contracts read. I'm counting on you, Sam. There's not another man in the world I'd trust to handle these things for me. And of course I'm cutting you in for fifteen percent of everything I make—they told you that, didn't they?"

"Jeremy," Abbot said, suddenly aware of the enormous responsibility he was taking upon himself, "are you sure you want me to arrange these things for you? What if something goes wrong? We could be endangering your life—"

For once, Jeremy seemed relatively calm and unafraid. "Nothing's going to go wrong, old bean—I have the utmost confidence in you. Besides, my life is in danger already. We all have to face our terrors in this world, but, to paraphrase my old chums in the antiwar movement, 'Better dead than unread,' hey what? Now cheery-bye, Sam. Give my love to Patricia and the child, and throw a kiss at the queen for me. See you in Switzerland!"

Abbot went out the door and down the steps. He got into the waiting car, which promptly backed around between the cottages. The last thing Abbot saw before they pulled away was Jeremy's pale, haggard face watching him from the cottage doorway.

"So," Red Scarf asked, "your mission has been accomplished? You had a satisfactory meeting?"

"I guess you could say that," Abbot replied. "How am I getting back into West Berlin?"

"The way you came. There is another tour due to stop at the restaurant in forty-five minutes. On board the bus is another man with duplicate of your passport. He has made sure that he is the thirty-sixth man on the list, as you were. When the tour reaches the restaurant, he will disappear, and you will take his place. There will be one more stop on the tour, at Museum Island, and then you will be returned to your hotel. No problem, you see?"

"Let's hope not," Abbot said. "Will I be searched when we cross back into West Berlin?"

"Not likely, unless you have somehow raised their suspicions. However, we have something for you—" He handed back a thin paper envelope. Inside were numerous postcard views of East Berlin. "They sell these at the restaurant," Red Scarf said. "The East German guards will be pleased to see that you have purchased a set. Notice that the computer disk you were given will fit nicely in amongst the postcards. The edges have been treated with a weak paste, so they will cling together during a casual inspection."

"And if the inspection *isn't* casual?"

"Then you had better find some way to destroy the disk. It would be bad for all of us if the East Germans realized what they had, and sent it back to Moscow."

Abbot put the disk in among the postcards and slipped the

packet into his coat pocket. He watched the countryside roll past the car and kept track of the time on his watch. In three hours he would be back in West Berlin, his little excursion into the world of spies and foreign intrigue safely behind him. "I'm not sorry I had the experience," Abbot heard himself telling a friend at some point in the distant future, "but I'd be damned if I'd ever do anything like it again."

It seemed to take longer than he remembered to reach the road above the river, and several times Abbot felt sure they had come by a different route. He drank another beer from the case on the floor and told himself not to get excited—he was in the care of professionals. At last they swung off the main road, and Abbot's faith was rewarded with a glimpse of the river shining through the trees. The car let them out where it had picked them up. Red Scarf and his assistant led the way down the heavily wooded slope to the base of the railroad trestle, where they found the rowboat waiting beneath its green tarp. Together they hauled it out of the bushes and placed it in the water.

Going upstream, they had to use a small motor. The boat bounced along against the current, waves splashing over the bow, and Abbot was thankful for the rubberized poncho. By now his desire to get safely back to the West had become a constant wailing in his mind, so loud he was afraid the men in the boat might hear and mistake his urgency for cowardice. It was not cowardice, Abbot assured himself. Whatever he had been feeling these past two hours, it was an emotion more complex than fear.

The boat crunched into the rocks along shore. Red Scarf pointed to his watch. "The two-thirty tour bus has just arrived. The terrace will be full of tourists. Go around the toilets and order yourself another bowl of soup. You have fifteen minutes before departure."

Abbot took off his slicker and tossed it into the boat. What did you say to men who had escorted you on a secret mission? Thanks for the ride? Long live ELF? Abbot simply smiled and nodded, and Red Scarf gave him a curt salute.

Hurrying up the path, Abbot wondered if he had been in the presence of the Stork or simply three of his subordinates. Perhaps the mastermind had been nearby but out of sight during the entire episode. In any case, Abbot was impressed by the smoothness of the entire operation. At no time, so far as he could tell, had they been in any danger of discovery.

Perhaps the Communist superstate was more porous than it appeared. There were men, Abbot realized, who made a living out of this perilous hide-and-seek. Certainly, he could never be one of them; he preferred to do his sight-seeing with a valid passport, thanks very much.

He joined the tourists on the terrace without difficulty, gulped down more hot coffee and fifteen minutes later found himself on board the bus. They left on schedule and twenty minutes later disembarked at Museum Island. The tour guide—a different young lady who spoke from the same script—led them through great gloomy galleries which contained an extensive collection of Greek and Asian antiquities. Ordinarily Abbot would have found several reconstructed temples intensely interesting, but all he could think of now was that ugly modern construction which stood between him and his freedom.

At length they returned to the bus and filed on board. There were no more stops en route to Checkpoint Charlie. Abbot had anticipated that they would have to get off the bus one more time in order to be processed by the grim-faced guards in the bleak compound. He thought he could endure this final trial, but he was exceedingly nervous as they lined up by number in the compound. Was this any way for human beings to be treated? Catalogued and bullied like prisoners of war?

The guard looked at Abbot's passport, made a check on his clipboard, and asked Abbot to please step out of line. He signaled another official, who quickly escorted Abbot across the compound to a small guardhouse, where he waited while the rest of the tourists were checked through and allowed to reboard the bus. No one came to question Abbot or to approve his release. He watched in horror as the last of his fellow passengers boarded the bus. Its door closed, its engine roared, and very slowly it began to leave the compound.

"Hey, that's my bus," Abbot cried. "I'm missing my bus!"

The guard looked at Abbot without expression. "A ride comes for you soon," he said in English.

Moments later a green police car pulled into the compound. It stopped before the guardhouse and a young policeman with the self-righteous look of a storm trooper got out. *"Kommen Sie, bitte,"* he said to Abbot and held open the back door. As Abbot slid into the seat, the cop deftly slipped one end of a pair of handcuffs onto his wrist and snapped the other to the grill between the front and back seats. Abbot felt the panic rush up from legs and feet suddenly filled with a desperate need to run. "Hey, come on," he said with a laugh which was altogether too much like a whimper, "what is this? For Christ's sake, what have I done?"

The young cop didn't answer. He got behind the wheel and took them out of the compound, back into East Berlin. Abbot saw more bleak streets lined with ponderous public buildings. The streets were heavy with shadows; the somber light of late afternoon shone in the tall, narrow windows. A cold, wintery sky—the sky of certain unforgettable nightmares—made its appearance as the police car entered an immense square. In the center of the square Abbot saw a larger-than-life figure on a pedestal, at first just a black silhouette against the sky; then, as they circled the statue, he recognized the bald head and pointed beard, the sharp satanic features of Lenin. The car passed through Lenin's shadow and came to a stop before a barred gate. Beyond the gate Abbot could see the opening to an underground parking area, the massive, unadorned, tiny-windowed walls of what looked like a prison. He took one last, longing look at the dream-colored sky. Then the car bounced through the gate and down the ramp into darkness.

9

The plaque on the desk said WACHTMEISTER KONRAD BENZ. A *Wachtmeister,* Abbot recalled from his dealings with the Breiburg police, was the German equivalent of a sergeant, and he was glad to see that his case had not as yet reached a higher level. Sergeant Benz was perhaps fifty years old. His military brush cut was mostly gray. His pasty complexion was broken by patches of tiny red veins on his cheeks and nose, as if he might be a heavy drinker off duty. A cigarette hung from his thick lower lip, sprinkling ashes on his gray tunic. He looked at Abbot with the moist, sorrowful eyes of a basset hound.

"Your name?" His pencil was poised above another of those multicarboned official forms.

"It's on my passport," Abbot said. He could see his passport, along with the other personal items he'd surrendered, in a small box on the sergeant's desk. Were the postcards still there?

"Your name?" Sergeant Benz repeated.

"Samuel Abbot. A, B, B, O, T."

"*Danke.* Nationality?"

"I'm a U.S. citizen."

The sergeant wrote it down. "Present address?"

"In Berlin, or in the BRD?"

The sergeant gave him a patient, though slightly contemptuous glance. "Present address?" he repeated.

"The University Guesthouse, Breiburg."

"*Danke.* Occupation?"

"I'm a teacher—an English professor."

The sergeant's eyebrows rose slightly as he wrote it down. "Purpose of your visit to the DDR?"

"I'm attending a conference in West Berlin. At the Amerikahaus. I had a free day and thought I would take a tour of the eastern sector. Have I done something wrong?"

Sergeant Benz completed his entry on the form with his usual deliberateness, then raised his sorrowful eyes to Abbot. "Your passport is illegal, Herr Abbot."

Abbot did his best to act surprised. "That can't be! I'm a U.S. citizen. I got that passport before I left the States—"

Benz consulted a similar form, the pink copy, which had been waiting in a basket at his elbow. "Several hours ago, a man carrying a duplicate of your passport, except for the photo, was arrested when he tried to enter East Berlin on the same tour bus. He is an East German citizen named Leo Markweiler—a known criminal and traitor to the Democratic People's Republic. We would like to know how he came to be carrying a duplicate of your passport, Herr Abbot."

"So would I," Abbot said vigorously. "I don't know anybody named Leo Markweiler. I don't know anybody in the DDR! I just came to see the sights."

Sergeant Benz dragged thoughtfully on his cigarette. "And yet you did not enter East Berlin with the tour, since Herr Markweiler had your place on the bus—the thirty-sixth place, as we have determined. Obviously, you must have joined the tour at some point along the route."

Sergeant Benz looked at Abbot as if it pained him to conduct such an investigation and say such disagreeable things to an American tourist. Wouldn't the American please tell the truth and shorten the interrogation?

Abbot offered what he hoped was a plausible explanation. "Actually, I came in on the morning tour. If you check your records, you'll see I was on that bus. I got separated from the others in the museum—they left without me. It was such a fascinating place that I decided I'd just wait there for the next tour, and that's what I did."

The sergeant looked disappointed. He had been hoping, it was clear, for Abbot's cooperation. Now the unpleasantness would have to continue.

"That is not possible, Herr Abbot. Our tour guides never leave anyone behind—it is not allowed. A man carrying your passport *did* leave the eastern sector with the morning tour. We have a record of it."

"But maybe that was this Markweiler guy," Abbot said. "Maybe he stole my passport in the museum and made a copy of it—"

Sergeant Benz shook his head sadly. "Such a copy could not have been made in the few minutes available to Markweiler at the museum. It is the work of a professional forger and would take days to prepare. Clearly, Herr Abbot, you and Markweiler were planning to exchange places for a period of time this morning. We want to know why."

Yes, why, Abbot thought—my God, why? The sergeant had steepled his stubby fingers beneath his blunt chin and was waiting for Abbot's answer, but at the moment Abbot couldn't remember why he had wanted to see Jeremy Sawyer again, or why he had let himself become embroiled in such foolish and illegal activities. Did this damn cold war between East and West mean anything to him?

And yet the hour or so he'd already spent as a prisoner of the East German state had made a huge impression on him. He had not been treated badly, but the experience was both humiliating and demoralizing. He had been—there was no other word for it—*processed*. His personal items had been tagged and recorded, and he'd been given a receipt. Then he had been fingerprinted, photographed, led from one place to another, turned this way and that, and with each new empty and indifferent face, with each briskly competent, impersonal pair of hands, Abbot felt his human dignity denied, discredited, washed away on the tides of bureaucracy. He was not a man, he was a cow in the stockyards. It would be of no use to bellow about his rights; the people who were processing him would not have heard, would not have believed that a dumb beast could speak.

Perhaps it would have been the same in a Western prison— Abbot had never been incarcerated before, so he couldn't say— yet it seemed to him that he had been given an insight into the totalitarian state and how it operated. Little by little, a piece here and a piece there, they took away your identity, your precious individuality. Little by little, they turned you into a piece of meat—

they ground you to ideological hamburger. Abbot had no intention of giving in to such tactics, nor would he assist in the process by which the humanity of others was systematically denied.

"You're right," he said at last, "my passport is a forgery. I shouldn't have used it, I know, but I lost my real passport shortly after I arrived in Berlin. I don't know how—maybe my pocket was picked. Anyway, I applied at the U.S. consulate for a replacement and was told that it might take several days. I was afraid I'd have to remain in Berlin longer than I wanted to, and I was complaining to the bartender back at my hotel. He told me about a guy who could fix me up with a temporary substitute—just until my real one was replaced."

Sergeant Benz seemed moderately interested. "And who was this 'guy,' Herr Abbot?"

"I never learned his name. I gave the bartender a hundred dollars, and he took care of it. I see now that was a big mistake, but I didn't mean to do any harm."

Abbot was rather pleased with this invention, though he could tell Sergeant Benz was not convinced. "And the photograph?" Benz asked.

Damn, he'd forgotten the photograph.

"Well, you see, I had some extra prints left over from the photo I had taken in the States—I gave one of those to the bartender, along with my Social Security number and other details. It's all correct. I'm sure, if you inquired at the American Embassy in West Berlin, they could confirm that information."

By now Abbot was beginning to feel that he was only digging a deeper grave for himself. The sorrowful, hangdog eyes of Sergeant Benz had begun to change; they were taking on the glint of an animal who smelled blood.

"I think I'd like to talk to someone at the embassy in any case," Abbot said. "I have a right to legal counsel, don't I?"

Benz smiled, "When you are formally charged, we will of course notify your government. However, you have not yet been formally charged."

The implication, Abbot thought, was clear: A lot could happen to a guy in this country before he was formally charged. A guy might be goddamn lucky to live that long. He suddenly noticed that Sergeant Benz's hands were large and powerful, with thick, blunt fingers and knobby, reddened knuckles.

The telephone on the desk rang. Benz looked annoyed. He picked up the receiver. *"Ja, Benz hier."*

He listened for a considerable period, and as he listened his eyes lost their anticipatory glimmer; a sullen anger began to take its place.

"Ja, sehr gut. Ich verstehe." He hung up the phone and glared at Abbot. "You are being transferred to another department, Herr Abbot. It seems that our friends in the KGB wish to talk to you."

Abbot sat stunned while the sergeant summoned a young policeman and gave him orders in German. The policeman picked up the box containing Abbot's belongings and escorted the prisoner to the door. Abbot took a last look over his shoulder at the dog-eyed *Wachtmeister,* who was lighting another cigarette.

"The KGB?".

Benz smiled and tossed his match at an overloaded ashtray. "I think you would rather have talked to me, yes? *Wiedersehen, Herr Abbot. Viel Glück."*

Much luck, indeed, Abbot thought as the young cop escorted him down a long corridor. If the KGB had taken over the case, his goose was surely cooked.

They passed through several offices, through various gates and locked doors which opened automatically, with small beeps, at the push of unseen buttons. Typewriters clattered and radios squawked; a secretary glanced up from the open drawer of a file cabinet to watch the condemned man pass by. Presently they were in an elevator, descending. Abbot asked himself how much punishment he was prepared to absorb in order to protect Jeremy Sawyer, of if there was any point in trying to protect him at all. If the KGB had not yet made the connection between him and Jeremy, he might be able to buy Jeremy some time by sticking to his story, as feeble as it was—until, of course, they got around to decoding the computer disk in his packet of postcards.

Abbot had a moment or two during which to marvel at the enormous folly of the whole business. ELF was a pack of raving lunatics, Operation Nightingale was a joke, and he was an utter and abysmal fool for getting mixed up in any of it. Then the elevator doors opened on the subterranean parking garage. A police car was waiting at the curb and a husky young officer who looked vaguely familiar to Abbot snapped to attention, then opened the back door for them. The cop who had brought Abbot down from Benz's office seemed momentarily perplexed.

"*Nein, ich muss den Gefangenen*—"

But he never got to say what he was supposed to do with the prisoner, because the husky cop planted his fist into the young man's midsection and doubled him over. With one hand he relieved the stricken guard of Abbot's belongings, with the other he shoved him into the backseat. He turned to Abbot.

"Get in, Prof—quick!"

Abbot scrambled into the backseat and James Morrison got in beside him. The driver pulled away and started up the ramp. Beside Abbot, the guard groaned. Morrison casually reached across Abbot to place a large automatic against the guard's neck, "*Still, verstehen Sie?*"

The car bounced into the yard, pulled up before the gate and was waved on through. Morrison kept his gun at the guard's neck, his elbow pressing against Abbot's breastbone. Abbot wasn't about to complain, however. He didn't think he had ever been so glad to see anyone in his life as young James Morrison.

As they drove away from the police station, Abbot and Morrison exchanged places and Abbot went through his box of personal items. The packet of postcards was still there, the computer disk wedged among them, though Abbot thought the edges were less sticky than they had been, perhaps from having been handled a good deal.

The driver pulled onto a darkened construction site where another car was waiting in the shadow of a gigantic crane. "Go ahead, Prof—I'll be right with you," Morrison said.

Abbot told himself he didn't want to know what Morrison was going to do, but heard the sickening crunch of metal on bone before he had quite reached the other car. Morrison took off his policeman's cap and tunic and tossed them into the police car, which then pulled away. The second vehicle was a Volvo sedan with Swedish plates. Morrison took the wheel and told Abbot to look in the glove compartment, where he found two Swedish passports and visas for the DDR. "How's your Swedish, Prof?" the agent asked as they neared Checkpoint Charlie.

"Jesus, I don't speak a word of it!" Abbot said.

"That's all right, these guys don't either."

The evening fog had arrived during Abbot's detention, but the sky to the west was filled with red light, as if the fires of World War Two still burned. They waited in line as the East Germans painstakingly checked each car. When it came their turn, Abbot sat tensely beside Morrison as he showed their papers. One of the guards indicated that Morrison should open the Volvo's trunk. Another poked into the backseat with a flashlight, then got down on his haunches to look under the car. Abbot kept his eyes on the murky red glow in the west. When at last they were allowed to continue, he had some difficulty unclenching his fists.

Roland Kohl was waiting for them on the American side, just beyond the sentry's station. He climbed into the backseat, bringing with him the aroma of his cheap cigars.

"Welcome home, Prof. Enjoy your tour of East Berlin?"

"Not very much," Abbot said.

"Next time try American Express. I hear their tour stops at a better restaurant, and they don't make everybody hike across Treptow Park for a look at that stupid monument."

"I don't imagine there'll be a next time," Abbot said. "I didn't exactly feel at home."

"Nobody does, Prof—not even the folks who live there. Once around the park, James." He handed a pocket flask up to Abbot. "I'll bet you could use a snort of this."

Abbot lifted the flask to his lips, recognized the sweet-sour taste of Kentucky mash, let it fill his mouth and trickle down his throat. Instantly, a sense of warmth and well-being flooded his nervous system. Yet there was an old sense of shame and surrender, as well. He wondered if Kohl had received a report on his weaknesses, perhaps gathered from gossipy colleagues back home.

"That was a timely rescue," Abbot said, handing back the flask. "Thanks a lot. You fellows do this sort of thing all the time, do you?"

"Not exactly," Kohl said, "Berlin is my old beat. I've got friends on both sides of the Wall. When one of my informants found that card in your wallet—the one Jimbo gave you back in Breiburg—he naturally assumed you were my agent. He let us know that the KGB was taking a particular interest in those

Siamese-twin passports ELF gave you, so we figured we'd better move quickly. Otherwise, we would have set up some kind of exchange—one of ours for one of theirs. Better vibes that way, no hurt feelings. Did you have to mess anyone up too badly, Jimbo?"

"Don't think so," Morrison said. "One fella's going to have a headache for a while. The Prof here was a brick."

"Glad to hear it," Kohl said. "Of course, if he's going to play secret agent, he's going to have to get used to a few close shaves now and then. So how's your old friend, Jeremy Sawyer?"

Abbot did not reply.

"C'mon, pal," Morrison said with a smile. "We went to a lot of trouble for you. The least you could do is level with us."

"That's all right," Kohl said. "I reckon he'll talk when we administer the truth serum."

"You wouldn't," Abbot said.

"I prefer the pliers and the cattle prod myself," Morrison said. "Or, if he's really stubborn, the rats and spiders."

"Very funny," Abbot said.

"You would have found out how funny it was if we'd let them haul you off to Moscow, you chump," Kohl said. "Their interrogation methods haven't evolved much since the time of Ivan the Terrible, so I've heard. When the hell are you going to wise up? Right now we're the best friends you've got on this side of the Atlantic, wouldn't you agree, Jimbo?"

"Without a doubt," Morrison said, gazing raptly over his steering wheel.

"If the Rooskies really want you, they can come after you on this side of the Wall," Kohl continued. "It wouldn't be the first time they've snatched somebody off a West Berlin street. If you want to get your fanny back to America in one piece, my friend, you'd better start talking to us."

Abbot was beginning to think Kohl was right. He wasn't cut out for this cloak-and-dagger business; he hadn't the nerves for it, and certainly he hadn't the training. Wouldn't it be better to confide in Kohl and Morrison, who obviously knew what they were doing, and to let them take the responsibility off his shoulders? Yet what would happen then to Jeremy Sawyer? He had promised Jeremy he would go to London, to Cambridge. . . . He didn't see how he could back out of that now. The memory of Jeremy's haggard face, his desperate eyes, his poor broken silenced voice, would haunt Abbot for the rest of his life.

It was suddenly all more than he could deal with. "I don't know," he said with a groan that was very near to a sob. "Jesus, I don't know what I should do!"

Kohl passed the flask back over Abbot's shoulder. "That's all right, Prof," he said, a note of unusual gentleness in his voice. "That's what we're going to help you decide. Head for home, Jimbo."

They entered a residential district somewhere near the Charlottenburg Palace, where large and pretentious dwellings sat smugly behind high walls. Abbot noticed that they seemed to be circling a particular block. As they turned for the second time onto a quiet side street, a car parked at mid-block flashed its head-lights at them.

"We're clean," Morrison said, and swung the Volvo into a nar-row alley between two garden walls. He pulled up at a back gate.

"Here's where we get out, Prof," Kohl said. "Jimbo will cruise around for a while and pick you up later."

"So long, Prof," Morrison said, and gave Abbot a reassuring wink. The Volvo drove off, leaving them in heavy darkness.

Kohl unlocked the gate and led Abbot through an overgrown garden to the rear door of the house. They were admitted by a man who must have been watching for them, since Kohl didn't have to knock. The man wore a shoulder holster over his black turtleneck, and he looked at Abbot without interest. Kohl took his guest upstairs to a small apartment, where the large windows were sealed off by steel shutters behind heavy drapes. The faded wallpaper displayed a pastoral scene: nymphs and shepherds, a satyr lurking in the shrubbery.

Kohl replaced the pocket flask with a bottle of Jim Beam, brought ice and water from an adjacent kitchen. "Hungry?" he asked. "I could send downstairs for a sandwich."

"No thanks—I'm hoping this won't take too long."

"You never can tell," Kohl said complacently, and settled down across from Abbot with his own drink. "Cheers."

"Cheers." Abbot looked around the room. "Is this what's called a safe house?"

"As safe as the gold in Fort Knox. You can talk here, Prof. Nothing you tell me has to go any farther than the two of us."

"But I was told," Abbot ventured, "that there's some kind of leak in your organization—that whatever you know will eventually find its way back to Moscow."

Kohl did not look particularly surprised. "Now who could have told you that? Let me guess—it couldn't have been a certain plump Englishman by the name of Brian Hedge?"

"You know Hedge?"

Kohl savored the spit-soaked nub of his cigar. "Hedgie and I go back a long ways. He's had it in for me ever since the late sixties, when a lot of the old guard in British intelligence had to be put out to pasture. They weren't used to working with Americans, and they weren't about to take orders from us, but that's what it came down to. I was sorry Hedge had to be canned—I think he was probably a decent agent, once upon a time. But he never misses a chance to throw a little dirt my way. There's no leak, Prof. The Rooskies hear what I want them to, nothing more and nothing less."

"I also heard," Abbot said, "that you were one of those agents who began harassing Jeremy Sawyer back in 1967—that you were partly responsible for his decision to defect."

Kohl smiled around his cigar. "So old Jeremy's still sore at me, is he? I suppose you could say I harassed him—we played the game a bit differently in those days. Besides, I had orders from Washington. Our government had enough trouble with the Brits over Vietnam as it was, and here was Sawyer getting the students all riled up. . . . I was told to lean on him a bit, which I did. That doesn't mean I *wanted* to chase him off to Moscow or that I wouldn't be glad to see him jump off the Commie bandwagon, even now. If that's what ELF is trying to arrange, I'd go along with it."

"You would?"

"Sure. Times change. A guy in my business has to be flexible. I've got no personal grudge against Sawyer, even if it does cork me a bit to think of somebody cashing in on eighteen years of treason. But what the hell—if the publication of Sawyer's memoir will serve the national interest and embarrass the Soviets, who am I to complain?"

Abbot could not conceal his surprise. "You know about Jeremy's book?"

"Prof, *everybody* knows about that book. Do you think an old blowhard like Sir Godfrey Clemmons can keep his mouth shut about something like that, when he's had a couple of drinks at his club and he's trying to impress his cronies with his latest coup? Hell, even the Kremlin must know about Sawyer's book by now!"

"Then why did they let him come to East Berlin? Why haven't they done something to him?"

"Ever hear of giving a man enough rope to hang himself with? They can't do anything to Sawyer until he actually makes his move—and even then they'd need to nail him with specific charges to keep him in the Soviet Union." Kohl paused to relight his cigar. "My guess is they really don't give a damn about Sawyer's book. I think they're willing to risk whatever harm it might do them in order to accomplish something else. I think they're using Sawyer as bait."

"Bait?"

"Have they told you in ELF about this fellow called the Stork? The Russians have been trying to put the Stork out of business for years—in fact, he's probably Public Enemy Number One on the KGB's most-wanted list. If they could give a loud-mouthed poet back to the West for the chance to terminate the Stork, I think they'd send your pal home gift wrapped."

"But ELF wouldn't trade the Stork for Jeremy Sawyer, would they?"

"Not intentionally. But in their eagerness to get Sawyer, they might be taking a few too many risks—such as using an amateur like you. No offense, but you're what we call in the trade an 'urgent virgin.' You haven't had the training a reliable agent needs. You can be turned."

"The way you're trying to turn me now?"

Kohl glared at him. "If I wanted to turn you, Prof, I'd stand you on your head and spin you around so many times you wouldn't know which way was which. I'd have you so dizzy you wouldn't be able to stand up without my support. I'd break you into so many little pieces you'd never be able to find yourself again without my help."

From the look in those fierce eyes. Abbot believed Kohl could, if he wished, do all that and more. He was getting tired of resisting Kohl's authority. It would be comforting, he thought, to hide in the man's shadow, to accept his powerful protection.

"So what's your angle in all this, Kohl? You don't approve of ELF and you don't like Sawyer, so why do you care what happens to any of them?"

"Well, Prof, it's clear you don't quite understand the complexities of this business. Despite our differences of opinion on certain matters, I'm not trying to get rid of ELF, and I certainly wouldn't want to see some KGB hit squad blasting the hell out of the Stork. Some of the people he's delivered to the West have been rich sources of intelligence—very rich. To tell you the truth, my job would be a helluva lot harder without somebody like the Stork driving the Ivans nuts, and that's why I'd really like to buy into this operation. If things get rough, I've got men in the field who can fight as dirty as any son of a bitch in the KGB. And I just happen to think ELF is going to need my help before this business is over."

"But they don't want your help—and neither, for obvious reasons, does Sawyer."

"Yeah," Kohl sighed, "that's been my problem all along. That's why I can't approach them directly. If I'm going to give them the assistance they need, I'll have to do it through you."

"Through *me?* What you mean is that you want me to keep you apprised of their plans."

Kohl spread his arms. "How else am I going to be there when they need me? I need to know when and where they're bringing Sawyer out. I need to know what I can do, behind the scenes if possible, up front if necessary, to keep this thing from turning into a bloodbath. If the Russians get the Stork, they'll eventually get the rest of his network. They won't embarrass themselves by putting a lot of Soviet citizens on trial for treason—they have other ways of dealing with 'counter-revolutionary elements.' They could wind up killing a lot of people, and your pal Sawyer could be one of them."

Abbot emptied his glass and set it down. "And you have no interest in preventing the publication of Sawyer's book, or in pressing any charges against him for his antiwar activities?"

Kohl shrugged. "That's all water over the dam. I'm willing to let bygones be bygones. Jeremy Sawyer can sing any song he likes, as far as I'm concerned, and if he can get rich off his eighteen years in the Soviet Union, I suppose he's got it coming. I've got more important things to worry about, don't you see?"

Yes, Abbot could see how Jeremy's book would seem a trivial matter to Kohl, in comparison to the survival of the Stork and his Eastern European network. It was all very confusing. If Kohl was on their side, why was ELF so afraid of him? Either he was an honest man or he wasn't. Eventually, you had to trust somebody. You couldn't carry the burden all on your own. You had to choose your allies and stick to them. And so far, who had done more for him than Roland Kohl?

"All right," Abbot said, "if you will personally guarantee Sawyer's safe conduct to Switzerland, I'll do what I can to help you."

Kohl smiled and picked up a telephone. "Prof, you've got a deal. Let me call downstairs for some sandwiches and a pot of coffee. We've got work ahead of us."

It was nearly midnight when Morrison dropped Abbot on a side street a block from his hotel. "You've got your story now, if ELF wants to know where you've been all evening?"

"Righteous indignation," Abbot said. "Put them on the defensive. After all, it was their scheme that broke down and landed me in jail."

"Right. They must know by now that we got you out, so when they ask what you told us—?"

"You grilled the hell out of me, but I wouldn't crack. No doubt you've figured out plenty, but you didn't get it from me."

"Except the disk."

"Oh, yeah, the disk. Chances are you made a copy of the disk. Why do I tell them that?"

"Because they'll suspect it anyway. And because the East Berlin cops probably found it and made a copy of it, too. From this point on, it's better if nobody drags their feet."

Abbot opened the car door. "Thanks again for getting me out of there."

"My pleasure, Prof. See you in London."

Abbot cut across the square between the Gedächtniskirche and the Europa Center. His sinuses were clogged; his body ached with weariness and fever. He knew he had drunk too much, and he had the bad feeling that he had talked too much as well. Had he made a mistake in trusting Kohl? Too late to do anything about it now. There was only one part of his interview with Jeremy which he had kept secret, and that was Jeremy's request that he obtain a certain box from his ex-wife in Cambridge. For some reason, Abbot clung to that commission as the crucial point on which he meant to keep faith with his old friend. Whatever was in that box, whatever it meant to Jeremy, Abbot wanted him to have it from Abbot's own hands when the first entered the West. "Here's your contract," he imagined saying to Jeremy, "and here's your damn box, and now I'm done."

Though of course he wouldn't be done, if the manuscript still needed extensive editing, but Abbot wasn't looking that far ahead. Somehow he couldn't quite believe that the time would ever come when he and Jeremy would sit down together to work on that manuscript. It was in the realm of the purely speculative, like life after death or the existence of God. Either you had faith or you didn't, and at the moment Abbot's outlook was utterly agnostic.

Despite the late hour and another light rain, the square held milling groups of teenagers, the usual scattering of nocturnal wanderers. What was it Kohl had said—if the KGB really wanted him, they could come after him on this side of the Wall. Abbot quickened his pace, steered clear of the clusters of young people in punk regalia. A skateboarder with a Mohawk, warpaint on his face and bare chest showing at the opening of his black leather jacket, whipped dangerously close to Abbot, swiveled and seemed about to come after him again. Abbot broke into a jog, ducked in among several concrete planters, reached the entrance to his hotel, and lunged panting through the glass doors.

Feeling foolish, he looked back to see that the skateboarder was nowhere in sight.

Since the conference had ended with today's sessions, both the lobby and the bar appeared strangely empty. Abbot hoped he wouldn't have to deal with ELF until morning, but he checked at the desk for messages. The young clerk came back empty-handed. Then his face brightened.

"But your wife is already here in the hotel, Herr Abbot. I myself gave her the key to your room, not two hours ago."

"My wife?"

"Frau Abbot, yes. You were expecting her, were you not?"

"Oh sure, of course. Thanks."

Were it not too ludicrous, Abbot would have asked the clerk to describe his wife for him. Instead he went to one of the lobby phones and dialed his room: After several rings a woman's voice answered. "Hallo."

"Greta?"

"Sam, is that you? Where have you been? We've been much afraid for you!"

"I'm just down in the lobby. Are you alone?"

"Yes, I am taking shower,"

"But what are you doing in Berlin? I thought you said you couldn't come here safely."

"By train is too dangerous, but by plane is no problem. This afternoon Herr Hedge wired me money for plane ticket so I could join you. He is thinking maybe you are needing my protection, yes?"

"Where is Hedge?" Abbot glanced back over his shoulder at the empty lobby. "Have you seen him here in Berlin?"

"Tomorrow we see him. I take you to him. But *Liebchen,* what is the matter? Aren't you coming up?"

"Sure, I'll be along in a jiffy."

Abbot was still not entirely sure it was safe to proceed. Should he call the number Kohl had given him and ask for help? He could spend the night in the lobby, if need be, or move to another hotel . . . but Greta's voice had sounded perfectly normal, and Abbot was too tired to go running needlessly around the city. Greta was his comrade and, as he'd said in Frankfurt, if you can't trust a comrade . . .

Nevertheless he approached his room cautiously and stood listening outside before slipping his key into the lock. He eased it gently clockwise until the bolt slid back. Then, his heavy-handled umbrella ready as a club, he pushed open the door and stood back.

A cloud of steam escaped from the room, instantly clearing his sinuses and allowing him to smell a musky perfume, which he recognized as Greta's scent. He also recognized the lacy black bra and panties tossed carelessly on the bed, the husky voice humming some popular melody over the rumble of the shower. The ashtray on the bedstand was half full of Greta's crimson-smeared butts; a bottle of wine and two glasses stood waiting beside it. The carpet before the telephone was damp.

The splashing of the shower abruptly stopped; the rings of the shower curtain jingled. Abbot went to the bathroom door, reached out with his fingertips and gave it a push. Swirling clouds of steam obscured, for a moment, his vision.

"Sam, is that you?"

Abbot saw his young comrade like a water nymph bathed in forest mist and dew. Her hair was wrapped in a towel, her slender body glowed pink from the shower's heat. Abbot sank down exhausted on the rim of the tub, embraced her wet hips, pressed his face to the smooth slope just above her beaded pelt.

"Oh, Greta, I've had such a miserable time . . ."

She instantly began to massage his neck and shoulders. "There, there, *mein Schatz*. There, there."

10

I t was raining hard on Wednesday morning when Abbot and Greta took a taxi to Tegel Airport. Greta's mood had turned almost as foul as the weather.

"It's not fair," she complained as the cab crept along flooded streets. "I come all this way to be with you, to take care of you, and how much time do we have together? One day!"

"And two nights," Abbot reminded her.

"Bah, and you are too busy blowing your nose and sneezing to make love to me . . . well, two or three times, maybe, but today you are better and already you are leaving me again. It is not fair. I want to go to London, too. I've never been to London. Why can't I come?"

Abbot repeated what Hedge had said when they talked to him yesterday. Greta wasn't needed in London, since Hedge himself would be there if Abbot ran into trouble. Besides, they wanted to get the deal with Sir Godfrey closed quickly. Abbot's visit wasn't likely to last longer than a couple of days.

"But I am not slowing you down, Sam," Greta protested. "I think you do not want me along. Is all right in German city, yes? But in English city I am not, how do you say, enough of a 'classy broad.' You are thinking that the English will laugh at me."

"Of course not," Abbot said, "that's not it at all." Though privately he observed that Greta would indeed be an encumbrance in London—chiefly to his intention to slip up to Cambridge unobserved. He reminded her of the understanding they had reached in Frankfurt: They were soldiers, comrades-in-arms.

When circumstances permitted, they grabbed a night of pleasure, but when duty called—

"Bah," Greta said, and clung to his arm in the back seat of the cab. "I know what we said in Frankfurt. But with you, Sam, I am maybe feeling something else. I think I will write a letter to your wife in America. I will tell her that if she doesn't want you any more, she should give you to me. Then I can have your babies, yes? We can live in little house on the prairie, like on American TV." She squeezed Abbot's thigh (an unpleasant habit she'd developed of late) to let him know she was only teasing, but her words chilled his blood, nonetheless.

"Greta, please don't do anything of the sort. And please don't start thinking seriously about me until after I've settled things with my family. They'll be visiting me this summer, when the girls get out of school, and Liz and I will have to have a long talk about our marriage. If we can save it, we will. If we can't—"

Greta laughed bitterly. "Then you will give me a call, yes? But I think you will always want me only for your whore, Sam, and never for your wife."

There was, sad to say, some truth in that. A few hours with Greta was enough to satisfy an old man's lust, after which Abbot was reminded of how little he could enjoy the raucous company of a young woman who was a good deal more experienced in the ways of the world. He was sure Greta would make someone a fine wife, but for Abbot she seemed best suited for occasional and illicit use.

They arrived at the airport in an awkward silence and found Brian Hedge waiting for them near the baggage check-in. At his nod, they entered a small baggage office, where Hedge gave Abbot the printout of Jeremy's manuscript. Neatly bound between vinyl covers, it ran to just over forty pages.

"That's all?" Abbot asked, flipping through it.

"That's all there was on the disk," Hedge said. "Won't it be enough?"

"That depends on Sir Godfrey," Abbot said. "Were you able to get me an appointment?"

"He'll see you briefly this afternoon at four, simply to take charge of the manuscript. He says he'll need a day or two to make his decision, but he understands we need a contract by the end of

the week. As soon as you have one, you're to call this number"—
he wrote it lightly on the folder containing Abbot's ticket— "and
say you have a message for Mr. Simms. Got that? Simms, Never
mind the response. I'll meet you in precisely one hour in
Leicester Square, beneath the statue of Shakespeare. Bring the
contract with you."

"And if I can't get the terms my client wants by Friday afternoon?"

"Then I'm afraid you'll have to settle for whatever Sir Godfrey
will give you. For various reasons, the Stork is best able to trans-
port his goods on a Sunday, and he needs at least a day to set things
in motion. If we miss this weekend, we might have to wait another
whole week, and who knows what will have become of your friend
by then? If the East Germans found that tape among your postcards, and if they made a copy for the KGB—"

"I understand," Abbot said. "Damnit, why doesn't he forget
about the damn contract and get out while he still can?"

"That would certainly be preferrable from our point of view,"
Hedge said, "but we have a few days' leeway, at least. We've
learned that your client, as you call him, has returned to Moscow
as planned. He'll appear at a university forum on Saturday and
it's not likely the Russians will take any action against him before
that." He checked his watch. "You'd better run along now.
Lufthansa flights always depart on time."

Abbot turned to say goodbye to Greta, but she was standing
near the door with her back to him and she pulled her shoulder
away from his touch. Abbot decided to let her pout—it might
make it easier for him to do what he had to the next time he saw
her. He put Jeremy's manuscript into his briefcase and set out for
his gate.

The small jetliner took off into a driving rain and Abbot endured several anxious minutes as they labored upward through
dense, swirling clouds. At last the mist brightened and blue portals opened around them. The plane ascended through one of
these portals into the sunny heights and tipped its wings toward
England. To Abbot it seemed an allegory of sorts: While the people of East Germany remained in the shadow of the storm, he and
Jeremy had broken free into the sunshine and were flying swiftly
westward above a dazzling cloudscape of snowy peaks and glacial

ridges. At least it *seemed* as if he and Jeremy were flying westward together as he opened his briefcase and extracted the vinyl folder. In rescuing these forty pages from the Soviet censor, Abbot felt as if he had already won a measure of freedom for his old friend, and he was eager to acquaint himself with the nature of his booty. Of course it would be good, but would it be good enough to bring Jeremy everything he was hoping for? Only a masterpiece, Abbot thought, would satisfy Jeremy's expectations—and his own.

He began to read sceptically, looking for weaknesses, determined to forgive the author nothing, but the very first page lay claim to his interest and the next several won his respect. He put the folder aside only briefly when lunch was served and resumed reading with growing confidence and admiration. Here, at last, was Jeremy's true voice, the clear, lucid expression of his genius. This was the Jeremy he had gone to Berlin hoping to hear—not that quavering, querulous, posturing fellow who had greeted him in that dismal cottage beside a wintery lake. There, in the darkness of a shadow that seemed to cover half the world, Abbot had heard a voice, all right, but it wasn't the voice of his old friend, the voice he had remembered with affection, pride, envy and awe. *That* voice had been waiting for him all along, it turned out, in the pages of his memoir.

Not that Jeremy's style hadn't changed since the freewheeling days of his youth. Perhaps exile in a non-English-speaking nation had taught him something about the nature of language or had altered his attitude toward his audience. Gone was the witty wordplay, the lush imagery, the extravagant rhetoric which had marked those flashier productions of his Cambridge days. This writer, one sensed, was under orders from a higher power; he had truths to enunciate, prophesies to proclaim. The result was a lean, hard, yet passionate prose—the kind of prose, Abbot thought, that Tolstoy had written after his famous "conversion"; a prose that embodied as much as it described the hard-won truths of experience.

And what an experience it was. No other writer of his time, Abbot thought, had lived such an extraordinary life. It was always Jeremy's nature to throw himself upon experience as if upon a samurai sword, whereas Abbot himself would have cautiously put forth a finger to test the sharpness of the tip. Perhaps, then, it was in the nature of artistic genius constantly to risk its own extinction through a series of perilous and even rather fatuous encounters with fate. A lesser man would have dodged such tests of his mettle; a wiser would have waited for an occasion worth the risk. Jeremy's way was to seek the challenge first and explain it to himself later, usually brilliantly. The book carried a motto from Seneca: "*Quid est boni viri? Praebere se fato,*" which Abbot translated as "What is the duty of a good man? To offer himself to fate."

The first chapter was devoted to an account of the author's youth. In a few brief but vivid paragraphs, Jeremy established the background from which he had come: wealthy, world-traveling, preoccupied father and sweet, alcoholic, self-indulgent mother; a series of boarding schools in America and England; a few good teachers but more bad ones; a long, wretched period without friends or affection of any sort in which the boy learned to fend for himself, both emotionally and physically. Several harrowing pages described Jeremy's early adventures with alcohol, drugs, prostitutes, a few thoughts of suicide, an impulse to anarchy, and then, just in time, as it were, the discovery of literature and the true birth of the author's soul. The bulk of the first chapter dealt with the pleasures and passions of a young Cambridge scholar and gentleman. Clearly, it was a world in which Jeremy had thrived, one which he remembered with undisguised longing in his Russian exile.

Late in this chapter Abbot made his own appearance—scarcely more than a walk-on—and he was quickly established as a decent, likable sort, the voice of reason and moderation, and therefore just one of the many voices Jeremy had had to ignore on the way to his doom. Abbot was not entirely pleased to see himself so portrayed. He wished he could have shown Jeremy something darker and more demonic in his own character—though on reflection he saw he was judging by the author's standards now and not his own. Ordinarily, Abbot would have been glad to claim the character Jeremy had given him.

The final pages of the chapter covered Jeremy's romance with Patricia Wilding. Here, and here alone, the author seemed a shade too reticent, perhaps unsure of himself, in any case unequal to the task at hand. Could it be—preposterous thought!—that

Jeremy hadn't known his own wife as well as Abbot had? But probably there was more on their relationship to come. The chapter ended soon after their marriage. It was 1964. Jeremy's first book of poems had just been published to excellent reviews; he'd been offered a position at Warwick University, and Patricia was expecting their first child. Everything looked good for the future, but there was one ominous note: by voting *in absentia* for Lyndon Baines Johnson in the American presidential election, Jeremy felt sure he was casting a vote for peace abroad and progress at home. It was, he told the reader, the last time he ever voted in an American election and the last time he believed an American politician.

The other chapter obviously came from much later in the book. Teaching at Moscow University, Jeremy had come into contact with a number of Soviet writers and intellectuals. With persuasive realism, he portrayed the difficult, often poignant, always anxious life of the Soviet artist. One episode involved a secret gathering at a friend's home where unpublished poems were read aloud and subversive Western authors were discussed. Another told the story of a friend and colleague who always defended the Soviet censors as necessary for the health of the state, and who was rewarded by a one-way ticket to a Siberian secondary school. It was a bleak, oppressive, sometimes harrowing chapter, and by its close Abbot could see well enough why the author wished to leave the Soviet Union. The wonder—given Jeremy's rebellious temperament and his impatience with fools—was that he had been able to stick it out for as long as he had.

These two chapters made Abbot intensely eager to read the rest of the book—all those intervening chapters that would describe, presumably, Jeremy's involvement in the British peace movement, his harassment by U.S. agents and his decision to defect, his first years in Russia and his travels in the Third World as a representative of the Soviet cause. This, Abbot thought, would comprise the most fascinating material, and he could see why Jeremy had wanted to hold it back. Curiosity would surely augment the author's bargaining power, while the pages he had submitted would convince an editor of the author's narrative skill. There was little doubt in Abbot's mind that the two chapters were good enough to procure a contract. They were good enough, also, to convince Abbot that Jeremy Sawyer's genius still lived and that the recovery of that genius from the abyss of history was indeed a task worth undertaking. It was simply the most important thing that Abbot had ever been given the chance to do, and to turn away from that opportunity now would be a final and unforgivable confession of his own mediocrity. What is the duty of the good man? To answer the prophet's call. *All right, Lord,* Abbot thought to himself as he put the manuscript back in his briefcase, *I am here.*

The plane was losing altitude, and Abbot looked down through a sky of scattered clouds to see the coast of England emerging from beneath the wing. Twenty-five years ago he had seen that same shoreline from quite a different angle, on the deck of the boat train from the Hook of Holland. It was the end of an all-night passage and the end of Abbot's long voyage across the Atlantic, the beginning of his first adventure in a foreign land. He could remember standing at the rail in the misty dawn as the ship eased into the Harwich harbor, and he remembered the green hills and red-tile rooftops glistening in the gentle rain. As he had made his way to the customs shed, a single clap of thunder heralded his arrival. It was, he felt at the time, a prophetic blast. Yet twenty-five years would elapse before the message would be made clear, before the call could be answered.

Abbot was through customs and passport control by two. He cashed a Eurocheque in the airport and picked up a map of the city, a tourist's brochure and a list of budget hotels. The Underground station was adjacent to the airport, and Abbot plotted a course that would take him to the Russell Square area, where he knew he could find an inexpensive bed-and-breakfast. The journey beneath London took slightly more than half an hour. Abbot sat quietly in his corner of the carriage and surveyed the exotic faces of London's international population—one forgot, from visit to visit, how heterogeneous the city had become. Would he be able to spot the agents Kohl, or Hedge, or possibly even the KGB had put on his tail? Well, what did it matter? He was in England, after all. It was hard to believe that anything too unpleasant could happen to him in decent, sensible, well-mannered England.

He came up from the Underground to a bright and breezy afternoon. He consulted his list of bed-and-breakfasts and, working his way along Bedford Place, settled on a modest, well-kept establishment offering rooms without bath, but with a "full English breakfast," for twelve pounds a night. Abbot booked a room through Friday and paid in advance with another Eurocheque.

It was not yet three, so he unpacked his suitcase, washed up at the sink in his room, then put a selection of items—toothbrush, razor, soap, a fresh pair of socks and a spare necktie—into a small plastic bag, which he slipped into his briefcase along with Jeremy's manuscript. Consulting his London map, he decided he could walk to Sir Godfrey's place of business. His cold was nearly gone, and he was filled with an extraordinary sense of homecoming. The streets of London, with their quaint and whimsical names—Houndsditch, Threadneedle Street, Piccadilly, Charing Cross—seemed to beckon to him with the promise of a lost past regained; or, if not regained, at least there to be seen, hovering ghostlike all around him in the cool, bright air.

He walked down Southhampton Row to High Holborn, and it was as if he shed years with every step, becoming as he went that exuberant, impressionable fellow he had been twenty-four years before. Reveling in the sights and sounds of a busy London street—the shops, the crowds, the red double-decker buses and shiny black cabs—it came to Abbot that, whatever happened to Jeremy Sawyer and his manuscript, Sam Abbot was having his own little adventure. He was having, in fact, the time of his life.

From the sunny breadth of Holborn, Abbot entered the cobblestone quiet and afternoon shadows of Chancery Lane. Sir Godfrey Clemmon's publishing house, aptly named the Clarion Press, stood at the end of the lane, just across from the Royal Courts of Justice. That great, gloomy edifice of British law seemed to hover over Sir Godfrey's establishment as if awaiting his first false step. Abbot rode an elevator to the second floor, gave his name to a receptionist, and was presently ushered into a large, comfortable office. A wedge of blue sky from a set of bay windows put a fine gloss on the darkly paneled walls and leather armchairs. Sir Godfrey, a genial mountain of a man, with a mane of white hair and a florid, fleshy face, came around his desk to shake hands.

"Professor Abbot—a pleasure to meet you, sir. I've become quite an admirer of your work."

"You have?"

The publisher smiled as he poured two glasses of sherry from a decanter on his mahogany buffet. "Of course I wasn't familiar with it when your name was first proposed to me, a few months ago, but I've since remedied that oversight. *Excursions* was an excellent journal of its type, a pity it's been discontinued. And I particularly liked the series on contemporary poets you did for Academy Press—a publisher can appreciate a fine piece of work like that."

"Thank you, that's very flattering." Abbot wished he had read some of Sir Godfrey's books so that he could return the compliment. Unfortunately, he had always tended to avoid the memoirs of spies, politicians and generals, which were the Clarion's stock-in-trade.

They compared notes on the several people in publishing and academic circles they both happened to know. Finally Sir Godfrey cleared his throat with a rumble and said, "Now then, sir: I understand you have a manuscript you'd like me to consider for the Press."

Abbot presented him with the vinyl folder. "I've just come from Berlin, where I saw the author and received the manuscript from his hands. Actually, it was a computer disk; the printout was given to me this morning by one of our mutual friends. I read it on the flight over."

"And your impression?" Sir Godfrey's obsidian eyes, nearly hidden behind puffy lids and creases, watched Abbot shrewdly.

"I was impressed. I think it's going to be a terrific book, maybe one of the best books of the decade—of my generation, even."

"Then you are no longer hesitant to become associated with the project? I was told there might be some problem—"

"No, no, I'll happily serve as the book's editor, provided you and Jeremy really think I'm needed. On the basis of what I've read, I'm bound to say I think you could save yourself the expense and trouble of a middleman. However, the author *has* asked me to negotiate a contract on his behalf. He wants it all settled before he leaves the Soviet Union."

"So I understand. And I don't mind telling you, Professor, that under the circumstances I deem your participation absolutely essential. I know a bit about this fellow Sawyer, and I know he was a difficult young man, very high strung. I can't imagine that his years in Russia have made him any easier to deal with. That's why I intend to insist that your role as editor be written into the contract."

Abbot simply nodded; it seemed he was not to be let off the hook. "And how soon do you think you'll be ready to discuss terms?"

Sir Godfrey lifted the vinyl folder, as if weighing the demand it might make on his time. "Oh, by tomorrow, if you like. I understand your need for haste; the KGB is breathing down the poor chap's neck, so I gather."

"We have till the weekend," Abbot said, "and there's another job I'd like to take care of tomorrow. What about Friday?"

"Very well, then, Friday it is—should we say for lunch, at my club?"

"Sounds good," Abbot said. He had never dined at an authentic British club before, with an authentic knight of the realm.

"Leave your address with my secretary and I'll send my car for you at noon." Sir Godfrey walked Abbot to the door, his large but gentle hand resting on Abbot's shoulder. "You know, if all this works out to our mutual satisfaction, there's another project or two I'd like to discuss with you. I have rather a penchant, it seems, for these renegade American types, so perhaps what I need is an American editor-at-large to deal with them. Let's talk about it sometime, shall we?"

"Gladly," Abbot said, "though maybe I should limit myself to one renegade at a time."

Sir Godfrey's laughter produced the illusion of a minor earthquake. "Indeed, sir," he said, "I quite understand." And, one massive hand still resting on Abbot's shoulder, he guided him out.

Abbot strode up Fleet Street in an exalted mood, drawn by the immense dome and classical portal of St. Paul's. It was that hour of the afternoon when the city seemed to be holding its breath, poised on the brink of rush hour, and inside the cathedral it was particularly still. Abbot sat in a rear pew to admire the majestic sweep of the nave, the frescos and baroque ornamentation, the cool elegance of polished marble. This was one church Jeremy had cherished; in fact, he'd insisted on stopping by whenever they were in London. "I'd almost think," Abbot told him once, after an hour of intense veneration, "that you were inclined toward Christianity."

"Well, I am, you know," Jeremy said. "Any religion that can produce art like this can't be all bad. The modern view of man is trivial in comparison; it lacks the grandeur of a coherent mythology."

"But you were just telling me—"

"Yes, yes, I know what nonsense I was spouting back in the pub. But then, there are pub truths and cathedral truths, don't you see, old bean? It's best not to get them mixed up. The fact is, I'd convert to Anglo-Catholicism in a minute if the English hadn't taken out all the hellfire and damnation. I don't think I could get seriously involved with a religion that didn't threaten to roast my backside over a bed of coals."

And was that, Abbot wondered now, why Jeremy ultimately turned to Communism—because its universe still offered the threat and promise of punishment? But it was always dangerous to take Jeremy seriously when they were merely talking. He was capable of saying *anything*, but only when he expressed himself in written form was he entirely serious. And Jeremy, to the best of Abbot's recollection, had never written on the subject of religion.

Nor had Abbot. In fact, it occurred to him that there were all sorts of subjects on which he had never expressed an opinion in writing. Perhaps, when Operation Nightingale was concluded and Jeremy's voice had been heard, Sam Abbot would have a thing or two to say for himself, as well. In the meantime, he had work to do. He needed to find out when he could catch a train up to Cambridge, but he didn't wish to broadcast his intention to whomever might be following him by going directly to the Liverpool Street station. Leaving the cathedral by a side door, he found a phone box in the little park to its rear and dialed the number for British Rail provided by his tourist brochure. A woman's pleasant voice gave him the London-Cambridge schedule, and Abbot jotted down several departure times in his pocket calendar. If he caught the eight-fifty, he could be in Cambridge by midmorning with a full twelve hours at his disposal before the last train returned to London that night.

First, of course, he would have to make sure he wasn't being followed when he left for the station, and that represented a challenge to which he'd already given considerable thought. No doubt they'd be watching his hotel, but it wouldn't cost much to take another room, and he had those twenty thousand deutsche marks to spend if he needed them. Better to make a move after nightfall, he reasoned, but he could start now by leading any surveillants on a tour of London. There were many places in the city he was eager to visit once again, and it occurred to him that, if he really put his mind to it, he could have his pursuers so footsore and weary by day's end that they'd be positively grateful when he gave them the slip.

Dusk found Abbot sitting in Parliament Square, resting his own feet and digesting a supper of fish and chips. The illuminated face of Big Ben looked down on his left, the towers of Westminster Abbey rose to his right. The square was an island of tranquility in a roaring sea of traffic, and, since pedestrian access was limited by iron fencing to several crosswalks, it was ideal for Abbot's purpose. He was watching a new arrival on the square—a nondescript little fellow in a gray nylon car coat, but Abbot was learning to take note of faces, and he was fairly certain he'd seen this guy twice before: once at the tube stop near St. Paul's, where Abbot had purchased a three-day pass, and once again in a pub along Haymarket. A few wisps of gray hair over a yellowish scalp, a weedy little moustache, and ears that were, once you thought about it, a size too large for his head. It was the same guy all right, and he took a park bench just down the row from Abbot, beneath the pugnacious scowl and hunched figure of the square's guardian spirit, Sir Winston Churchill.

Fine, sit there, Abbot thought. We'll both take a breather, and then I'll give you a run for your money. This spot, like many others he had visited in the past three hours, was rich with memories, for it was here, after a weekend of dissipation with two London working girls—who had let them invade their Bayswater flat and who had probably lost their lease as a result—that Jeremy had discoursed on one of his favorite themes: "the poet as man of action." Recalling the soldier-poets of the Renaissance—Sidney and Spenser and all the rest—Jeremy maintained that modern poetry needed to reclaim this "virile heritage." "We've had enough of these limp-wristed faggots," he said, warming to this theme, "enough sniveling, whimpering, self-pitying bastards. What we need now in the profession are some real men—"

"Like you and me," Abbot suggested.

"You're damn right, like you and me, old bean. Damn the whole business otherwise, don't you see? A poet can't be weaker than other men; he must be stronger. How can his words be taken seriously if they're not supported by actions? These days we need poets with courage, integrity, vigor, stamina, guts—"

"Balls," Abbot offered.

"Ah yes," Jeremy said, "most of all, balls. Primarily, balls. Absolutely, positively, without question, balls."

Well, Jeremy, Abbot thought gazing up at Churchill's stout silhouette in the deepening twilight, you certainly did your best to show the world a poet with balls. Now let's see what I can do for editors.

He got to this feet and walked briskly toward the nearest crosswalk. He was carrying his briefcase in one hand, his collapsible umbrella in the other, and he arrived just as the bobby working the intersection blew his whistle and halted traffic. Abbot picked up his pace as he entered the pedestrian flow, then broke into a run on the other side of the street.

There was an Underground station just up Bridge Street, and Abbot had already observed entrances on both sides of the busy thoroughfare. He went down one stairway and up the other, emerging on the Victoria Embankment. The sidewalks here were clear and Abbot ran beside the river, the London sky holding its faint violet tint above the flickering globes that lined the walkway, the water calm between tides, distant traffic a muffled humming in his ears. He didn't look back but ran at full tilt, hoping those hours spent jogging in the Stadtwald had given him the stamina to outlast his pursuers.

Finally, reaching the Hungerford Bridge with his breath nearly gone, Abbot ducked into the shadows and waited. After a moment he heard running footsteps. He held his umbrella by its soft end, his briefcase in his other hand—a club and a shield. The runner swept past his pillar, then abruptly put on the brakes. It was the balding man in the gray car coat, and Abbot stepped out of the shadows to confront him.

Abbot hadn't known exactly what he would do, but when the pursuer's face showed recognition and his hand went for something inside his coat, Abbot swung the wooden handle of the umbrella hard against the man's neck, then caught him from the other side with his briefcase. The little man went down, and something clattered across the pavement. Abbot kicked whatever it was away and ran on, beneath the bridge and down the steps of the Charing Cross station. Once beyond the ticket windows, the tunnel diverged to different lines. From the Bakerloo line's tunnel he heard the rumble of an approaching train. *All right,* he thought, *Bakerloo it is.* He rushed down the steps and arrived on the platform just as the train pulled in. He stepped on board, then watched at a window for the bald-headed man. A late rush of passengers, just before the doors closed, might have hidden him from Abbot's gaze, but the odds were against it. Abbot rode two stops to Piccadilly Circus, got off and took the long escalator up to the street. He waited at the exit, but the bald-headed man did not emerge from the Underground. Nor did Abbot see anyone else who looked remotely familiar, or anyone who lingered in his vicinity.

He strolled up Shaftesbury Avenue, through the crowds and bright lights of the theater district, then north on Charing Cross Road. Sometimes he stopped to gaze in shop windows or to examine the photographs in the lobbies of several theaters, but he could detect no one on his tail. Not yet satisfied, he returned to the Underground at Tottenham Court Road station.

It was getting late. Abbot's legs ached and waves of weariness washed over him, but he rode the Central line to Notting Hill Gate, transferred to the District line and rode two more stops to Paddington. He walked up Praed Street and stopped in a pub, then took his pint of bitter to the window where he could watch the street. After half an hour he left the pub and proceeded to Sussex Gardens, where there were several inexpensive hotels on his list. In fact, the street was lined with such establishments, and he had no difficulty finding one with a VACANCY sign still hanging in its front window. He rang the bell, was admitted by an anxious, smiling man with a Middle Eastern accent, and obtained a third floor room, scarcely larger than a broom closet, for ten pounds a night, including breakfast.

Secreted thus in the midst of London's enormous transient population, Abbot unpacked his toothbrush and razor—also that bottle of whiskey and the *Evening Telegram* he'd picked up earlier—and congratulating himself on his cleverness, settled in for a quiet night. However, the stress and excitement of the day's chase returned to disturb his dreams, and all night long Abbot fled from faceless pursuers through a labyrinth of London streets and tunnels. Finally, near dawn, he led his shadows into a vast, dense forest, where tall pines rose like black cones in the moonlight. At the bottom of a steep ravine littered with leaves and debris, he encountered the Polish archaeologist enjoying a picnic lunch. "It is time to redeem your raincheck, Herr Abbot," Pajorfsky told him, delicately placing a napkin to his bloody lips, and then his eyes glazed over with terror. Looking over his own shoulder, Abbot saw the spectral figure of the Hangman emerging from the forest, and he awoke on the edge of a scream.

11

A bbot arrived in Cambridge at eleven the next morning, to the best of his belief unfollowed. He purchased a city map at the station newsdealer's, then looked up the Eckersleys' number and address in the telephone directory. Now for the hard part—the task he'd been dreading most over the past two days. What did you say to a woman you once loved—though she couldn't have known that—a woman you hadn't seen for twenty-four years, a woman who could well ask—though he knew she wouldn't—where you had been when her need for friends was at its greatest . . . what did you say? Ah well, Abbot told himself, dial the number and find out.

The phone was answered on the second ring by a crisply civil female voice. "Eckersley residence."

"Is Mrs. Eckersley there?"

"May I ask who's calling, please?"

Abbot shut his eyes. "I don't know whether she'll remember me. My name's Sam Abbot—I'm an old friend, from America."

"Just a moment."

He waited, watching through the phone-box window as perfectly composed and rational strangers, creatures from another universe, strolled through the station. Then—

"Sam! Is it really *you?* Are you here in Cambridge?"

"At the station. I was in London on some business and thought I'd come up for a look around. Any chance of seeing you today?"

"Of course! You *must* come for lunch. I want you to meet my daughter Chris—you were just talking to her. Oh, and if I ring Stephen at the lab, he might be able to join us as well."

"Professor Eckersley? I'd like very much to meet him," Abbot said, though he imagined he would find it easier to talk to Patricia about Jeremy if it were just the two of them.

Perhaps she was thinking along those lines as well. "Maybe I *won't* call Stephen—he usually takes his noon meal at the college, and you'll be seeing him this evening. You *can* spend the evening with us, can't you, Sam? In fact, we'd love to have you stay over—"

"I'm afraid I haven't given you much notice," Abbot said, "and I don't want you to go to a lot of trouble. There's something particular I need to talk to you about, Pat."

"Ah well, there's a great deal I want to talk to *you* about, Mr. Abbot! But I daresay it will wait until you get here. Now, what time should we plan for lunch?"

"Whenever you say. I thought I'd take the bus downtown and stroll through some of the colleges. Say, twelve-thirty?"

"Splendid. And can you find us?"

"I've got a map. You're just off Grange Road, right?"

She laughed. "Good old Sam—always planning ahead. Don't you ever make mistakes?"

"Oh, I've made a few," Abbot chuckled. Yet he was secretly pleased by the thought that she still retained an impression of his character—flattering or not scarcely mattered; at least he was remembered!—and he wondered if he would meet some long lost image of himself as a young man when they finally sat down to talk.

He caught the bus outside the station and watched apprehensively as they neared the center of town. A parking ramp, a shopping center, a block of high-rise apartment houses—these were not hopeful signs. Yet the city's ancient core had escaped such ravages of progress, and Abbot stepped down from the bus in St. Andrew's Street, across from Christ's College, with a surge of sentimental reverence that nearly brought tears to his eyes. It was—thank God—all just the same.

He walked along the narrow, meandering lanes, past the medieval colleges with their high blank walls, their ornate gateways offering glimpses of green-turfed central courts. He gazed in shop windows, dodged bicycles, observed the young men with their blazers and their long college scarves tossed gallantly over one shoulder—the way *we* used to wear them, Abbot thought—

and it was all beautifully just what he remembered, just what he had hoped it would be. "A little paradise," as Jeremy called Cambridge in his memoir, "perhaps the only community on the face of the earth built not by merchants and monarchs, but by scholars and poets, thus the world's only true Utopia."

Not strictly accurate, Abbot knew; the merchants and monarchs had done their share, even here. Yet Jeremy's point was still valid: Cambridge was unique among the cities of the world in its dedication to learning, its long and intimate association with the arts and sciences, its devotion to what people used to call the "life of the mind." It was the only city in which Abbot himself had ever felt completely at home, and he wondered now what fantastic turn his life might have taken, what sort of person he would have become, if only he had never left. Not that he could have made a permanent place for himself in Cambridge. He lacked Jeremy's money and family connections, Jeremy's brilliant record and extraordinary talent. Now that he thought about it, Abbot wondered how he had ever managed to worm his way in for even a year. Surely, that wasn't him. *He* had never walked these sacred and exalted streets, except in some preposterous dream.

This disbelief in his own vivid memories grew stronger as Abbot strolled through the crowded market square with its colorful awnings and pyramids of fruit. He bought a bouquet of jonquils for Patricia, then proceeded along Benét Street to King's Parade, where he stood for a time, admiring the soaring gothic glory of King's College Chapel. Yes, he had seen those lacey white spires before, that clear April sky, but not in *this* life. Perhaps he had borrowed some other—a life that had been his for a year and had to be returned when the spell wore off. There had been, he was ready to say, precious little enchantment ever since.

He walked along Trumpington Street to the massive, fourteenth-century gate of St. George's College. With a tremor of anticipation, he passed beneath the heavy arch and along the murky passageway, then down several worn steps and through another arch, and there it was—the great good place of his youth, its rosy-golden walls and square plot of unadorned but very thick grass basking in the moderate English sun. There was the chapel and there the library; there the staircase to the dining hall and the Junior Common room. After a moment's inspection, Abbot was even able to determine which window along the dormered upper story marked Jeremy's old room and which one, almost directly across from it, had been his own—but he simply couldn't believe he had ever actually *lived* behind that window or sent signals from it to his friend whenever it was time to close the books and venture out for a pint of beer, a ramble along the backs, a hotly contested game of squash. Perhaps, Abbot thought, I was simply the college ghost—the one they always talked about, the one Jeremy and I were always hoping to see.

Standing on Silver Street Bridge, staring at the broken reflection of willows and gray stone walls in the wake of several placid swans, Abbot asked himself why he had become the missing person in his own life story. Was it Jeremy's fault that he seemed, in retrospect and in comparison to his friend, to possess no substance, no depth, no ultimate reality? Or was that simply Abbot's way? Other people lived life; he took pictures. Others pursued their passions, their dreams and illusions, while Abbot collected impressions and filled up mental photograph albums, documenting a world in which the photographer himself did not exist.

It was in this melancholy frame of mind that Abbot arrived, at precisely twelve-thirty, at a modest brick home on a quiet street on the west side of town. He unlatched the garden gate and went up a brick walk to the front door. He was ready, he thought, for almost any surprise or revelation, except the one he got, when his ring was answered by a striking young woman whose long, curly black hair and radiant, smoke-blue eyes recaptured almost perfectly the woman he remembered. Her smile was full of warmth and welcome, yet edged with that mischievous spirit of irony that Abbot remembered from years back. He was at first unable to speak.

"Hello, you must be Mother's old friend, Mr. Abbot," the girl said, extending her hand. "I'm Christina—won't you come in? You look as though you'd seen a ghost—is the resemblance that striking?"

"It's uncanny," Abbot said, stepping across the threshold. "But then, I already feel as if I've traveled back in time this morning."

"Ah yes, Cambridge never changes." Christina took Abbot's coat and set his briefcase on a corner chair. "Mummy's waiting for you in the library."

It was the sort of residence Abbot would have expected of a Cambridge professor—comfortable, but hardly splendid; cozy and cluttered, its furnishings a bit eccentric, as if the occupants had better things to do than to fuss over matters of interior decoration. The library, lined from floor to ceiling with bookshelves and warmed by a gas fire, also boasted a sunny alcove, lush with greenery. From this alcove emerged a woman his own age, her short dark hair handsomely touched with gray. At once Abbot decided that he liked the little double chin, the creases around her eyes and at her neck; they made Patricia Eckersley real for him, vulnerable and human, in ways her beautiful and perfect daughter was not.

"Sam, you brought me flowers? How *sweet!*"

She accepted the bouquet with one hand, took his paw with the other. On the continent or in America, Abbot reflected, they might have embraced, or even kissed. But not in England. Alas, not in England.

Yet the light of welcome in Patricia's gray eyes was as good as a kiss—or even better, since Abbot knew it was genuine.

"We nearly killed the poor chap with our trick, Mother," Christina said. "I do believe he suspected witchcraft."

"Oh, I *am* sorry." Patricia kept his hand in hers. "I guess I was just a little nervous about seeing you again, Sam. I wanted to remind you of the old me, before you saw the current version."

"Now that I've seen both," Abbot offered, "I don't know which is lovelier. But, having seen me, Pat, you can see you had nothing to worry about. I'm scarcely a well-preserved specimen."

She stepped back and surveyed him from head to toe, that gently mocking twinkle in her eyes. "Hmm, rather distinguished, I'd say. I think I like you better without so much hair."

"I used to have too much?"

"Well, for someone who never combed it or had it cut, and probably didn't wash it very often, yes. That receding hairline suits you better, I think—much more intellectual. Don't you think so, Christina?"

"Oh, definitely," the girl chimed in. "Mummy was showing me a picture just before you arrived, and I said, 'Egads, really Mum, he has way too much hair!' "

"I didn't know you had any pictures of me," Abbot said. He remembered quite well that he had only three snapshots in which Patricia appeared—none of them as clear and sharp as he would have liked.

"Ah well, you mustn't be smug about it," Patricia smiled, "but I do have a few. Perhaps we'll look at them later. Now, can I offer you a glass of sherry before lunch?"

"Yes, please."

They moved to the sunny alcove, where they sat down amid the ferns and philodendrons while Christina went off to the kitchen to complete the preparations for lunch.

"She's an extremely beautiful girl," Abbot said.

"Christina's the great vanity of my life," Patricia said. "Rather like a magic mirror, which can always flatter you with your youthful image. But of course Chris is smarter than I ever was—she inherited her father's brains."

"Better his brains than his looks," Abbot said with a laugh. "Yours suit her much better, I'm sure. Is she at the university?"

"Girton College, but she's living with us this year. She says it gives her more freedom, and an automobile to boot. Stephen spoils her terribly, I'm afraid."

"Then . . . everything's worked out well?"

"Oh, marvelously. Though it hasn't always been so pleasant. Chris and I went through some rocky times after Jeremy's departure, but I'm sure you don't want to hear about that. Suffice it to say that Stephen saved both our lives, and we're endlessly grateful to him."

Abbot guessed she had had it on her conscience to make such a statement early in their conversation, especially since Stephen wasn't there to speak for himself.

"Does Christina know about her father?"

"Yes, I explained it all to her when I thought she was old enough to understand. We've always treated Jeremy's political activities as openly and rationally as we could. Still, it is rather hard for a child, when most people consider her father a coward and a traitor."

"It that how you see him?"

She reached out to touch the withered leaf of an African violet. "I don't know how I see Jeremy any more—*must* we talk about him, Sam? Tell me about yourself. What have you been doing all these years? What brings you to England? The last we heard, you were working on your doctorate at some rather impressive institution on the West Coast."

Abbot briefly outlined his life and accomplishments, such as they were, and was just showing Pat the family photos he carried in his wallet when Christina called them to lunch.

They ate in a cheerful room overlooking the rear garden, where several fruit trees were already in blossom. Though both women disclaimed any culinary expertise—"You know what they say about English cooking," Christina joked—Abbot found the meal delicious. The conversation remained sprightly and relaxed, and Abbot was conscious of the fact that he had succeeded in making himself charming. He even observed during one of his stories about life in Germany that mother and daughter exchanged a glance which seemed to say, on Patricia's part, "You see, I told you you'd like him!" and on Christina's, "You're right—he is a dear, sweet old thing!"

The dear, sweet old thing, meanwhile, reveled in the attentions of two lovely women and, though it might have been disloyal, couldn't help reflecting that *his* daughters never would have greeted an old family friend so charmingly; nor would Liz and the girls have given anyone the impression of being such amiable and like-minded companions.

It was going on two o'clock when Christina finally rose from the table. "I'm terribly sorry to run off, but I can't miss my lecture. Awfully good meeting you, Professor Abbot. I hope we'll meet again."

"I hope so, too," Abbot said, rising to see her off. "If you're ever in America, be sure to let us know. My daughters would love to meet you"—and could learn a thing or two, he added privately.

"I may very well take you up on that," Christina called back as she left the room.

"I was hoping you'd let us take you out to dinner this evening," Patricia said. "You really should meet Stephen. I'm sure you two would hit it off."

Abbot gazed down into the dark well of his coffee cup. "Pat, there's something I haven't told you yet."

"I thought there might be," she said.

"I've seen Jeremy."

"Ah, so you've been to Russia. And how did you like it?"

"No, I saw him in East Berlin, a few days ago. It was arranged by a group that calls itself the European Liberation Front. They specialize in smuggling dissidents out of the Soviet bloc."

He raised his eyes to see how she was taking his news and found her staring out the window at the blossoming trees in her garden; her profile, highlighted by the window, was perfect and expressionless. The face of an angel. Her beauty could still make him ache.

"Go on," she said at last. "Is Jeremy planning another change of loyalties?"

"If all goes well. He has a book he wants to publish in the West. In fact, that's why I'm here in England—to negotiate a contract for him. I'm to serve as his editor once he's gotten safely out of Russia."

"I see." She got up from the table and came back with a cigarette case and a lighter. It was the first time he'd seen her smoke, and she did it awkwardly, as if it wasn't really her custom. He thought he could detect a certain fear, almost panic, in the light that now shone in her gray eyes.

"I've always believed that at some point Jeremy would want to leave Russia," she said. "That's why I waited for him—why I wouldn't marry again, why I forced my poor child to grow up without a father. There was money enough, and no end of kindly uncles, but then that's not quite the same thing as having a father in the house, is it? Finally, when Jeremy had been gone ten years and Christina was already twelve, I accepted Stephen's proposal. I thought ten years was long enough to wait. I still think it was!"

Abbot noted the force she gave her words. "I entirely agree. You had a right to think of yourself."

She smiled sadly. "I'm afraid I wasn't raised to think of myself, Sam—not at the expense of my family. English girls, at least the girls in my class, were always taught to be dutiful wives, to put their family first. I thought such selfless devotion was the one thing I was good at. It turned out to be the one thing about me Jeremy simply couldn't abide."

"Then he was a fool," Abbot said with a strength of feeling that surprised him. "He didn't deserve someone like you."

Her smile, he thought, turned a shade reproachful. "I'd say he simply had a different view of marriage. I tried to accept his view, and after he left I spent ten years blaming myself for driving him away—for not being tolerant and flexible enough to understand what he needed. But I think I finally did learn, in the end"—she drew on her cigarette in a rather self-conscious way—"to think of myself. I see now that such an approach makes perfect sense: If one isn't happy with one's life, one can hardly make others happy. I must be very stupid, because it took me a long time to learn that simple truth."

"I'm sorry," he said, "I know this must be very upsetting for you. I don't want to interfere with the new life you've made for yourself, and I don't think Jeremy does, either. He may not return to England at all. I think he intends to live in Switzerland, after his operation."

"His operation? He's ill?"

Her concern, Abbot thought sadly, gave her away. "He has cardiovascular problems, like his father. He needs a bypass, but he's afraid to have it done in Russia. He's heard of some Swiss surgeon who uses lasers—"

"Ah, poor Jeremy, he always was a great coward!"

Abbot thought that a peculiar pronouncement at first, then reflected that perhaps there *was* an element of cowardice in the way Jeremy did things—such as sending Abbot as his emissary to reclaim his precious box from his abandoned wife.

"Patricia, I was sent here by Jeremy. I wouldn't have come, I assure you, if I hadn't wanted to see you again, or if I had thought my visit would cause you pain . . . but you see, Jeremy thinks you may have kept something for him all these years—something he wants now that he's about the leave the Soviet Union."

"A box," she said at once, and Abbot wondered at her promptness. Had she been waiting for someone to claim Jeremy's box?

"He says it contains some old letters, diaries, mementos, and that he left it with you before his defection. Apparently there's something in that box, some document or other, which he thinks he'll need when his book is published—in case he's ever required to prove the truth of his story."

She rose from the table and stood by the window, and for a moment Abbot wondered if she was looking for intruders amid the shrubbery.

"I do have the box," she said, "but not here in Cambridge. Years ago, not long after Jeremy's departure, a man came to ask me about such a box. He claimed to be a friend, but I didn't trust him. I knew who he was. A rather unpleasant American—one of those government agents who had been hounding Jeremy about his antiwar activities. He frightened me, and I wouldn't give him the box. I knew without being told that Jeremy had left something important in my keeping and that someday he would return to claim it."

"This American," Abbot said, "was he a tall man, with dark curly hair and very dark eyes? Bushy eyebrows, maybe a moustache?"

"It's been so long, Sam—but yes, I think so. I remember he had rather a crude manner, like one of those tough private eyes in American films—"

"Roland Kohl, was that his name?"

"That rings a bell. Do you know him?"

"We've met. In fact, he and his associate got me out of East Berlin when the border guards arrested me. He's still working for the CIA, but he says he's no longer out to get Jeremy. In fact, he says he wants to help him get safely out of Russia."

"I wouldn't trust him," Patricia said.

"I don't. But then, I really don't trust anybody in this whole affair—not even Jeremy himself. I keep thinking there must be more to it than I'm being told—that Jeremy and I may be little more than pawns in somebody else's game. But I promised Jeremy I'd arrange a contract, if I could, and that I'd collect his box."

"And you'll be meeting him again, when he reaches the West?"

"Yes, I expect so. We'll have some work to do on his manuscript—how much I don't know. I've only read two chapters, Pat, but they were really excellent."

She sat down across from Abbot once again and reached out to put her hand over his. "You were always one of his most avid admirers. Are you sure—?"

"—that the book is good? Oh yes, no question of it."

"I mean, are you sure you want to work with him, Sam? Perhaps you should follow your own advice and think of yourself first, before you become any more involved in Jeremy's dirty business."

"Dirty?" It seemed a peculiar adjective.

"Well, it's all dirty, isn't it? Politics, propaganda, sabotage—Jeremy always had a fatal fascination for that sort of thing. You left in 'sixty-two—you didn't see what sort of person he turned into. He became quite a fanatic, you know. All those rallies, marches, riots—he thrived on the atmosphere of violence and intrigue. And even during those last few weeks before his defection, when the Americans were trying to have him sent home to face charges, I don't think I ever saw him happier. He was in his glory."

"That's a side of Jeremy's character I don't understand," Abbot said. "But the man I saw in East Berlin wasn't enjoying himself. He seemed to have had quite enough of politics. He was bitter, burned out—just a shell of his old self."

At once he saw he shouldn't have told her this—that the image of a ruined, embittered Jeremy could still cause her considerable pain. Yet it also helped her to make up her mind.

"All right, I'll give you the things he sent you for. They're his, and he's welcome to them. But we'll have to travel some distance. You came up by train?"

Abbot nodded.

"Fortunately, I can use Stephen's car. I'll leave a note for him—he has tutorials this afternoon."

"I'm sorry to put you to so much trouble," Abbot said. "Perhaps you could simply give me directions or a map I could follow?"

She shook her head. "It's at the family's country house, and you might have trouble getting past the caretaker. Besides, I'd like to take you there. It will give us a chance to spend some time together, and to talk about something besides Jeremy."

"How far are we going?" he asked.

"It's in the Cotswolds—about a three hours' drive. With luck we can be there and have your box by suppertime. I know a charming little inn where we can dine, and then I'll drop you in London on my way back to Cambridge."

"Sounds fine—but what will Stephen say?"

"Oh well"—and she gave Abbot that mischievous smile—"I

don't have to tell my husband *everything* now, do I? Just give me a few minutes to get ready and we'll be on our way."

By three they were driving across the flat fenland west of Cambridge in Stephen's Jaguar. The day was balmy and clear, and Abbot was reminded of the many outings they'd made from Cambridge in the spring of 1962—he and Jeremy and Patricia and numerous others, always off to see some church or castle, to eat and drink and explore the countryside. Abbot tentatively mentioned a few of these excursions and found that Patricia remembered them well. In fact, she remembered some adventures Abbot had totally forgotten.

"You and I were always the ones who wanted to stay until the museum or whatever it was had closed," she said, "while Jeremy was always anxious to get to the pub."

"Ah yes, he could put away the beer in those days, couldn't he? There was many a time he drank me under the table—"

"Don't talk as if you admired it!" Patricia said.

"Well, I did, in those days. We were young wastrels, out for a good time. . . . I've since learned, of course, that moderation is more to be admired. Not that I have any great merit in that line myself, unfortunately."

"I can't imagine you a problem drinker," she said. "You always struck me as having too much character for that. In fact, Stephen always reminded me a bit of you—I think that's possibly why I was first attracted to him."

"Really?" Abbot was both pleased and disappointed by this news. If she had found, in due course, another Abbot, she no longer needed the original. "And how is Stephen like me?"

"Oh, he's very gentle, and sensitive, and kindly toward others, and he's really much too modest and unassuming, but that's all part of his charm—"

"Stop," Abbot said.

"You dislike hearing yourself praised?"

"When I don't deserve it. I think you left out 'weak, vacillating, easily discouraged, morally lazy.' . . . I felt rotten about leaving you in the lurch after Jeremy's disgrace, Patricia. I blamed myself for years for not coming to your rescue."

"To my rescue? But what could you have done? You had a life

and family of your own by then, and I had a family here in England to look after me. I wasn't totally abandoned, like some Victorian heroine cast out into the storm."

Abbot said nothing. After a time, she added. "The opportunity you had to rescue me, Sam, came much earlier—before I married Jeremy. I sometimes wondered why you let me go so easily."

"Oh Lord, so did I," Abbot said. "I wondered that a lot! I guess I just assumed that, against someone as brilliant as Jeremy Sawyer, I didn't stand a chance."

"That was very foolish," she said, "You were always my favorite."

"I was? But . . . you accepted his proposal . . ."

"It was the only one I got. I decided that you had other things on your mind—perhaps a girl back home. Jeremy really seemed to need me; he was tragic and vulnerable in a way you certainly weren't. I suppose I thought I could help him—you know, 'save him from himself,' that sort of thing. You know what idiots young women are!"

Abbot was too amazed to speak. Finally, he said, "There *was* a girl back home, but I didn't start thinking seriously about her until I lost you. What you took as my preoccupation was a major act of will, Patricia. I was schooling myself not to think of you, because I felt I had no chance. I guess I was always too ready to concede the victory to Jeremy."

"Are you sure," she asked him, "that you didn't want Jeremy to live your life for you, so you wouldn't have the beastly bother of it yourself?"

That might have described his relationship with Jeremy in some areas, Abbot thought, but not where Patricia Wilding was concerned. "It would have been no bother loving you," he said. "The only difficulty was in trying not to, once I'd given you up."

She kept her eyes on the road, her voice playful. "I do wish you'd consulted *me*, Sam, before you made your magnanimous gesture. It might have saved us from a pair of mistakes. I hope yours proved less disastrous than mine, by the way."

Abbot didn't know how to respond, since ordinarily he didn't regard the first forty years of his life as any sort of disaster at all. Yet obviously *something* had gone wrong with both his marriage and his career. Had it all started—those middle-aged doldrums, the drinking, the desperation—with that one horrendous mistake he'd made back in 1962?

"Well, I suppose we've reached the age where it's natural for people to start second-guessing themselves," he offered. "Who knows if we'd have 'got on,' as you say over here."

She gave him a quick smile, as if she knew the answer to that one and thought he should, too.

"Even Jeremy was second-guessing himself, when I talked to him in Berlin," he added, feeling perhaps that he needed Jeremy's presence in the conversation at this point.

"Jeremy—doubting himself? That's hard to believe."

"I think he must have quite a few doubts—more than he's willing to admit. By the way, I've been wondering about something you mentioned back at the house—when we were discussing Jeremy's 'dirty business'—something about sabotage?"

"Those charges were never made public," she said; "but it was something else your government tried to use against Jeremy. You see, there was an unfortunate incident at a U.S. Air Force base not far from Cambridge. A group of protesters tried to break into one of the security areas. They were stopped by guards, and while their van was being searched a bomb went off, killing two of the protesters and an American soldier. The other protesters got away, and there was never any proof that Jeremy was one of them. But this man, Roland Kohl, threatened him with prosecution if he didn't give up his antiwar activities and return to the States."

"It's almost as if they *wanted* to drive Jeremy to the Soviets," Abbot said. "Kohl claims he was only following orders from Washington."

"No doubt he was. Your government has always behaved terribly, you know—it's why America has so few friends in the world."

In this comment Abbot heard the old Patricia—the Cambridge radical and peacenik, whose politics had not differed significantly from her husband's. Abbot asked, as they left the fens for the gently rolling country of central England, how she had come to lose her own interest in politics.

"I don't know that I did, actually. Stephen and I are active in the Liberal party, and we work for several good causes. But with Jeremy, it wasn't enough for him to espouse radical causes; he had to adopt a radical life-style, as well. I think it was that weekend we spent at a commune in Yorkshire which finally did me in, as far as the counterculture was concerned."

"A commune? In Yorkshire?"

"Oh yes, we had them too, just like yours in the States. Free food, free drugs, and free love. And every sort of madman imaginable, preaching every sort of weird doctrine under the sun. We were supposed to 'get into ourselves,' as it was called in those days, although Jeremy was interested primarily in getting into other women's sleeping bags. When I objected, he called me a disgusting prude and a brainwashed slave of the upper classes. It was quite a dreadful scene, and after that I tried to stay away from politics—of Jeremy's sort, at any rate."

"He must have been pretty far gone by then," Abbot said. "Was he doing a lot of drugs?"

"Some, though Jeremy's preferred vice was always alcohol. God, we had some bloody battles over his drinking, too! He claimed he had to 'explore the depths' before he could 'scale the heights' of his art. I said that was all just an excuse for his wretched self-indulgence. He said I had a totally inadequate understanding of the artistic temperament. Which was true, I suppose. But I didn't give up easily, Sam. I still thought I could save Jeremy from himself. All I accomplished, I see now, was the final destruction of our love. In the end, I was just something else that was driving him away."

Abbot heard the old hurt and sadness in her voice and was sorry to have been the prompter of so many unhappy memories. She in turn reminded him of what it was all too easy to forget—that Jeremy was indeed, at times, a great bastard. His evil temper, his vicious tongue, his enormous ego—Abbot had seen only a few hints of Jeremy's dark side during the year they spent as cronies, but he didn't doubt it was there.

"I don't think you drove him away, Pat. I think Jeremy felt he had an appointment with destiny. It was something he had to do—his martyrdom, so to speak. He wanted to be a hero."

"And is that what he is? Do you see him as a hero, Sam?"

Abbot gave it some thought. "I'm not sure just what Jeremy means to me right now. I guess that's what I'm trying to find out. Once a man like Jeremy takes a certain position and lays claim to a certain territory, you can't just turn away and ignore him. That's where I made my mistake in 1962, and again in 1968. It cost me a lot to keep my mouth shut when Jeremy was being pilloried in 'sixty-eight. I've been paying for it ever since. That's why I've got to help him now, if I can. It's the only way I have to cancel the debt."

Patricia was braking for a flock of sheep lethargically crossing the road up ahead. The Jaguar came to a full stop, and she turned to him, showing him the full beauty of her soft and luminous eyes.

"Sam, I don't know if Jeremy deserves a friend like you. He takes advantage of people, you know. He uses them, exploits them, makes them his vassals and disciples. . . . It would be quite terrible, really, if one didn't sometimes feel that possibly, after all, he's in the right."

Abbot heard the sheep bleating as they plodded across the road. He could smell their rank odor, and he saw the shepherd boy with his long staff prodding the stragglers into the roadway.

"Yes, that's the odd part of it," he said. "That's Jeremy's great strength—the suspicion we all have that he's right and we're wrong, that *his* vision of the world is the one we really ought to live by. Once you've admitted that possibility—"

But Abbot didn't quite know how to complete the proposition, and the last sheep having crossed the road, Patricia threw the car into gear and gunned the engine. The Jaguar leapt forward, and it was sometime before either of them spoke again.

12

Traffic was slow around Oxford, and it was early evening when they reached the road to Wilding Park. The family estate lay in a sheltered valley of the Cotswolds, not far from Stratford-upon-Avon, and the forest through which they drove had, to Abbot's romantic eye, a particularly historic and yet fanciful character, as if it might still harbor in its more secluded nooks the rollicking rustics and lovelorn princes of Shakespearean comedy. Patricia pulled up before the caretaker's house and told Abbot to wait in the car while she informed the old man of their arrival.

"He's deaf as a stone and won't understand a thing I say, but if I don't let him see me close up he might come after us with his shotgun."

"By all means, allay his concerns," Abbot said. He gazed down the long avenue that led to the main house. It was lined with tall trees, their massive trunks green with moss, their spreading tops alive with raucous flocks of birds. Patricia had already explained that the house was opened now only on holidays and special occasions, when Wildings gathered from far and wide to commemorate the traditions and revive the pleasures of English country gentry. Abbot supposed that meant shooting parties and fox hunts, sumptuous banquets and games of whist while somebody's niece tortured the piano. He could see how such weekends would have annoyed and bored Jeremy Sawyer, though Abbot himself would have liked them just fine.

Patricia returned and they drove into the park. They left the central avenue before they reached the main house, but Abbot saw its graystone gables and chimneys across an open meadow. They skirted a broad pond, whose still waters reflected the fading blue of the sky, then followed a winding road, which crossed and recrossed a swollen brook on its way into the wooded hills. The road became narrower and rougher, in places nearly impassable, and finally ended in the yard of an old stone cottage. When the car stopped, Abbot heard singing birds and the music of the hidden brook. He could smell the dense, damp forest and feel the chill of the spring evening. With its steep thatched roof and small shuttered windows, the cottage looked like something in a fairy tale—a refuge for two children lost in the woods.

"This is what we've always called the Honeymoon Cottage," Patricia said. "Jeremy and I spent some happy times here when we were first married—before I began to bore him so dreadfully. It's seldom used now, and I didn't think I'd ever want to come back, so this is where I hid the box."

She unlocked the front door and led the way inside. Apparently there was no electricity, but she had brought along a flashlight from the car, and they followed its beam through the dusky rooms. Even in its present state, with its furniture covered and the musty smell of disuse in all the rooms, Abbot found it a charming refuge. Its charm was diminished, however, by the thought that this, in all likelihood, was the place where Jeremy and Patricia had consummated their marriage—the place where his own loss had become irrevocable.

In the kitchen, Patricia asked him to hold the light while she stood on a chair and reached above the cupboard to a small space beneath the eaves. She stretched, groped, and then brought down something wrapped in black oilcloth. When she put in on the kitchen table and removed the covering, Abbot saw it was an ordinary steel file case—the kind he used at home for storing insurance policies and the like.

"Do you want to check the contents?" she asked him. "I have a key."

"Not now," Abbot said. "I don't really know what Jeremy wants out of this box or why it's so damn important to him—do you have any ideas?"

She looked away. "I'm afraid Jeremy didn't confide in me

much, the last few months before his departure. I was simply his banker."

"Well, I'll sort through it when I get back to London. It's obvious no one's been into this case for years—look at the dust on the oilcloth."

He took the key from her and they left the cottage. Patricia locked up, then stopped on the way to the car. Abbot understood that she wanted a moment or two alone with her memories and went on ahead. When she joined him, he could barely make out her face in the twilight, but her voice was a bit too bright and shrill. "What a dismal old place! Shall we find that inn I told you about?"

"Yes, let's," Abbot agreed, reflecting that it was well past the customary hour of his first drink.

The Black Swan, outside Cheltenham, was everything an American tourist could ask for in an English country inn, yet was blessedly free of tourists on this Thursday evening in April. Patricia requested a table in one of the inn's small private rooms, and they were seated by the plump, jovial landlord, who looked as though he had studied for his part by reading the novels of Fielding and Smollett. The fire was cheerful, the candles romantic, the heavy oak beams and rough plaster walls undeniably authentic, and the menu excellent. Abbot asked the innkeeper if he could manage an American dry martini "on the rocks" and was assured that he could. Patricia ordered a glass of sherry.

"This is a marvelous place," Abbot said, when they were alone. "I'm so glad you thought to hide Jeremy's box well away from Cambridge."

Patricia smiled. "So am I, but I'm afraid it's going to be rather late for driving back by the time we finish. Would you mind awfully staying over? They have some charming bedrooms, and the price is quite reasonable."

"I'll ask the landlord to reserve two of them for us. I don't have to be in London until noon tomorrow, but perhaps you'd like to call your family?"

"I don't think that's necessary. I told them in my note that it might be an overnight, and Chrissie can reassure Stephen that you can be trusted to look after me."

"I'm sorry I won't get to meet Stephen. I would have liked to have appraised this extraordinary resemblance you say there is between us."

"Oh, I wouldn't call it extraordinary. You're just similar types—you adhere, I should think, to the same moral code. Like you, Stephen would go to incredible lengths to help a friend, then deny that he deserved any credit for putting himself out, since he was only making up for past failures."

"Is that how I put it?" Abbot asked. "My, how pompous."

"You see?" she said, laughing at him with her lovely eyes, "even now you brush aside anything good anyone might say about you. Your humility is endearing, Sam, but you carry it to a fault."

Their drinks arrived. Abbot proposed a toast. "To old times."

"Ah, let's not drink to everything that's behind us," she protested. "To the present, and to us."

"To us." Abbot wondered at the look in her eyes as they lowered their glasses. He had had the feeling, since leaving the Wilding Park cottage, that she was making up her mind about something, and a kind of determined frivolity had come over her as soon as they reached the inn.

"Tell me more about me and Stephen," he ventured. "Do we look anything alike?"

"Not really. He's quite a bit older than you."

"Oh?" For some reason, Abbot had pictured Stephen as a man in his early forties—brisk, purposeful, athletic in a subdued, donnish way. "I didn't think *anyone* could be older than I am," he said, laughing.

She smiled and reached for the single long-stemmed red rose that adorned their table. "I doubt very much if you've reached Stephen's age in one particular. You see, it was understood when we married that sex wouldn't be part of our relationship."

"I see." Abbot was embarrassed and looked out the window. All he saw, however, was the reflection of a man and a woman seated at a table, and he had the peculiar sensation of spying on himself from outside in the darkness.

"I thought it would be easier that way," Patricia was saying. "Stephen needed a home and companionship after his first wife died, and my daughter needed a father. It didn't seem to me at the time that I needed anything in particular for myself—but of course I was wrong about that. A woman can deny her feelings for years—Englishwomen are particularly good at that, they say—but eventually it all catches up with her. Some confident young wretch comes along—one of her husband's students, perhaps—"

"You don't have to tell me this," Abbot said.

She lit a cigarette. "Why shouldn't I? Would you rather go on thinking of me as that innocent virgin you lost to Jeremy when you turned coward and ran back to America?"

Abbot took a sip of his martini. "I guess I deserve that, but it didn't seem like cowardice at the time, Patricia—just good sense."

"Cowardice always seems like good sense," she said, holding him with her eyes, "until you come to count your losses. You shouldn't have given me up, Sam. It wasn't fair to either of us."

"I see that now," Abbot said.

"I was yours for the taking, you know."

He nodded, miserably.

"And I still am."

He requested, as it turned out, only one room from the land-lord, and when they had finished eating, and after they sat talking for a time before the fire with coffee and brandy, they climbed the narrow, creaking stairway to what had become in Abbot's imagination a bridal chamber—a room which had been waiting for them, under some form of enchantment, for twenty-four years.

"I'm not as beautiful as I was then," Patricia whispered as, kissing her, he helped her out of her clothes. "I'm old and fat, Sam—I couldn't stay beautiful forever."

"Nonsense. You're lovelier now than ever. I like these extra pounds, these firm full curves—you were just a skinny kid back then."

"I was? Really? You beast, Sam—you're teasing me."

"You like my receding hairline, I love your double chin," he said, burying his face in her neck.

The bed was soft and deep; they sank down into the feather ticking as if into some magical sky of buoyant clouds. The air in the room was cold, and Abbot pulled the comforter over them, then continued undressing her beneath it.

"You remember *Lady Chatterley's Lover?* We had a very serious

conversation about that novel one afternoon, over tea. I was ravenous with lust for you, Patricia. I wanted to be your Mellors and
teach you dirty words."

"Oh, and I was ravenous for you, too, Sam. I kept hoping you'd
say the word *fuck,* so I could show you I wasn't shocked—that I
was ready—but you never did."

"I was a great fool. I never guessed."

"You *were* a great fool. I never guessed, either. We were so
bloody innocent then. The whole world was innocent then. Oh,
Sam—!" She gasped as his hand found what it was looking for.

"So this is Lady Jane?"

"Yes . . . and this is John Thomas?"

"The one and only."

"At long last they meet."

"Are you ready for me, love?"

"Yes, love. Say *fuck* to me, love, and . . . oh, yes, bring the bonny
lad home."

The clock had struck one, but occasional lorries still grumbled
and whined along the highway, trembling the timbers and floor-
boards of the ancient structure. Abbot was too happy to sleep. He
held her warm nakedness close against him and ran his fingertips
wonderingly, tenderly across her skin. She stirred.

"Sam? Will you be angry if I tell you something?"

"Of course not. You've told me lots already."

"More than you wanted to hear, I'm sure. But this isn't another
sordid tale of my extramarital transgressions. This confession is
important. You need to hear it."

"Fine"— nuzzling her neck and ear—"so tell me."

"You're better than Jeremy."

"Better? You mean, at making love?"

"In every way, Sam. Do you know, I never had an orgasm with
Jeremy. He said it was because I was frigid, because Englishwomen were too inhibited to enjoy a good fuck, but I learned
later that I was quite capable of orgasms with the right sort of
lover."

"So I noticed," Abbot said, letting his hand stray lower on
her hip.

"Jeremy's problem was that he really didn't care that much

about screwing. He was always in a hurry to get it over with, so he could get back to his poem or his critical essay or whatever it was he had on his mind."

"When people are young," Abbot said, "they don't know that much about making love. It takes years and years for a couple to develop a full appreciation of their sensuality. Liz and I—" He stopped.

"Yes, go on. You and Liz?"

"Well, we learned a lot together. It just kept getting better for us—and then it stopped."

"Yes. Why?"

"I don't know. I thought it was just old age creeping up on us. Maybe I was remembering you."

"That must have been it. Tell Liz I'm sorry, I didn't mean to ruin her marriage, but you and I had a long-standing obligation to one another, don't you think? We had to have this night together, Sam. Jeremy had to go to Russia and you had to go to Germany and everything had to happen just as it has, so that we could finally have our night. The universe was off-kilter and needed this tiny bit of adjustment that only we could give it."

"And now that the balance has been restored?"

She sighed. "Oh, I suppose now we'll go back to being the dutiful, self-sacrificing, abhorrently decent people that we are." But her hand, ambling across Abbot's abdomen, had found that part of his anatomy which was hardly inclined, under the circumstances, toward renunciation.

"You'll go back to Stephen, and all your young lovers, and I'll go back to Liz?"

"And to your German tart, don't forget her—unless of course Jeremy persuades you to stay in Switzerland as his indentured slave."

"Not bloody likely," Abbot chuckled, surrendering himself to the pleasure of her touch. Then, presently: "Isn't there any hope for us, Pat? No way we can work it out?"

"I don't know, love. But let's not think so just yet. It's sweeter if we believe that this is our one night together—the only night we'll ever have."

"And it's not over yet," Abbot said, pushing up on his elbow and reaching down to part her thighs.

"No, darling," she said, opening her legs to receive him, "thank God it's not over yet."

It was over, however, or certainly seemed to be, when, after a stop at London's Victoria Station the next morning, she dropped him at his Bloomsbury hotel—one sign of which he took to be the bright, ironic tone of her farewell. "Good-bye, Sam. Give my regards to the Great Ego when you see him. Tell him his good little wife has finally learned to enjoy herself, will you?"

Abbot wondered unhappily if their night of love had been for her simply a way of sending some such message to her former husband—if, even as a lover, he was fated to be only Jeremy Sawyer's emissary. Her smile softened and she put her fingertips gently against his cheek.

"I'm sorry, Sam—that was a rotten thing to say, after last night. I *wasn't* trying to prove anything, you know. To you or him or myself or anybody."

"You proved something to me," Abbot said. "You proved that I never should have given you up without a fight. Will I ever see you again?"

"I don't know, love. Let's take a few weeks to think things over, shall we? I never really expected to see you again, and I just sort of followed my impulse yesterday. Now I'd like some time to reflect on what it all means."

"I'll write to you when Jeremy's safe in Switzerland," Abbot said. "Will you want to see him again?"

She shook her head. "I don't think I could stand that. But do let me know what happens, Sam. I hope everything goes well—for both of you. Take care of yourself."

Abbot stretched across the gearbox for a last kiss. For several minutes, neither of them gave much thought to the busy London street. Then a rising volley of horns forced Patricia to pull away. "Good-bye, Sam. I love you, and I loved last night!"

"I love you, too," Abbot said, and got out of the car. With a throaty roar and puff of exhaust, the Jaguar pulled away from the curb and was quickly lost in traffic.

Abbot climbed the stairs to his room, full of strange, melancholy reflections. There was, of course, no way of knowing what his life would have been like if he had stayed on in England and married Patricia Wilding. It was even more impossible trying to weigh one life against the other—the one he'd lived and the one he hadn't. All those years with Liz and the kids, those good years when the kids were young and he and Liz were still very much in love—would he have given up any of that happiness, even for a lifetime of nights like the one he'd just spent?

The sad thing, Abbot thought, unlocking the door to his room, was you couldn't have them both. One life to a customer—you pays your money and takes your choice. Either way, you lost too much. Either way, it all went by too quickly.

In this respect, the Latin motto on Jeremy's tie clasp was indeed appropriate. Abbot had found it in the file case this morning before leaving for London and put it into his pocket. The rest of the case's contents—mostly letters from Jeremy's draft board, from a London legal firm, and from the office of the U.S. attorney general—he had left undisturbed. At Victoria Station, he put the case into a locker, where he could claim it before flying back to Germany. Such an arrangement had seemed superior to keeping the box in his hotel room, where it might easily be stolen.

He took out the tie clasp and read the inscription once again: *Respice finem*—"Reflect on your end." Tolstoy's Ivan Ilyich, Abbot recalled, had had that motto engraved on a medallion that hung from his watch chain. Jeremy had been a great admirer of Tolstoy, even before he went to Russia.

He had little more than half an hour to get ready for his luncheon with Sir Godfrey. He washed and shaved at the little sink in his room, put on the last clean shirt in his suitcase, worked on his sports coat and trousers with a tube of spot remover. Even so, he felt distinctly shabby as he went downstairs to wait for Sir Godrey's limousine—the archetypal mongrel American, in over his head, as usual.

The car arrived at noon, as promised, and took Abbot to the area known as Lancaster Gate, where the broad and quiet streets were lined with large, sedately whitewashed townhouses, one of which contained Sir Godfrey's club. The great man was waiting for him in the lounge. A waiter escorted them to their table in a formal dining room—white linen, bone china, sterling silver, plush carpet, old masters on the paneled walls. At the tables around them, Abbot saw several faces he thought he ought to recognize from newspaper photos or British television. He had a sense of having penetrated one of the inner sanctums of the Empire—a world in which they didn't even know yet that the Empire was gone.

Sir Godfrey did his best to put Abbot at ease. He had read Jeremy's chapters and he liked them very much. Of course two chapters weren't an entire book; it remained to be seen if the rest of the story would fulfill expectations. But, in view of the extraordinary circumstances, and the understandable need for some sort of commitment, Sir Godfrey was prepared to offer an advance of fifty thousand pounds.

That was, unfortunately, well below the amount Jeremy had demanded in Berlin. Abbot bided his time through soup, fish, roast beef, and the trifle. The wine changed from white to red at mid-meal. Sir Godfrey told stories of his adventures in sensationalistic journalism and dropped famous names as if they might have been old friends of Abbot's, as well. Abbot realized he was being plied, charmed, worked on. When they got to coffee and cigars he held firm: one hundred thousand pounds as a nonreturnable advance on royalties or no deal.

They settled at sixty-five.

Jeremy would be disappointed, of course, but the contract would reserve American rights, reprint rights, and most other subsidiary rights for the author. If the book was a success, Jeremy would be amply rewarded over an extended period of time.

Sir Godfrey's limousine took them back to the Fleet Street offices, where certain forms were filled out and certain papers modified according to Sir Godfrey's instructions. Abbot read through the completed contracts and signed each copy as Jeremy's agent. Then Sir Godfrey signed. They drank a glass of brandy to celebrate the closing of the deal.

"I hope our faith in Mr. Sawyer has not been misplaced," Sir Godfrey said. "If it hadn't been for you, Professor, there would have been no contract. You are, as far as I'm concerned, the vital link in the whole business."

"Someday," Abbot said, "I hope I'll hear you tell Jeremy Sawyer that, to his face."

He left the offices of the Clarion Press with two copies of the contract in his coat pocket, found a call box along the Strand and dialed the number Brian Hedge had given him in Berlin.

"London Towne Escort Service," said a sexy female voice.

Abbot wondered if he'd misdialed. "I've got a message for Mr. Simms—"

"Mr. Simms? Hold on, luv . . . ah, here we are. He said for you to look for him in the usual place at the usual time—is that clear?"

Abbot said it was.

He strolled down the Strand with an hour to kill and sat awhile in Trafalgar Square, near the central fountain, watching swarms of pigeons whirling around Lord Nelson's column. The British, he thought, were much given to self-sacrifice. The principles on which the Empire were founded had been drummed into the brains of schoolboys, passed on from generation to generation like the secret, sacred lore of the tribe. What was it Jeremy had said in his first chapter? "To live for any considerable period of time in England is to be awakened to a beautiful possibility that exists within each human heart: the possibility of martyrdom."

And was not martyrdom, Abbot wondered, the biggest ego trip of them all? Now that his mission was nearly complete, he found himself feeling oddly depressed and disgruntled about his role as Jeremy Sawyer's emissary. The more he tried to remember what he liked about the man—his generosity and warmth, his wit, his high ideals and noble aspirations—the more qualities Abbot uncovered that were less than admirable: Jeremy's arrogance and pride, his contentious and sardonic nature, his touchy artist's ego . . . and the more Abbot recalled these traits, the more he realized that, at some basic and intuitive level, where friendships are made and broken, the chief feelings he had preserved for Jeremy over the years were those of anger, fear and a deep, abiding envy.

Yet what did his personal feelings really matter? It was easy to say that Jeremy was a cad and a scoundrel and an all-American jerk; he possessed that peculiar capacity all great men possess, which in a sense defines greatness: the capacity to force others to judge by his standards. High up in the pale blue of the London afternoon, Lord Nelson stood forever enthroned as the epitome of British heroism. Each day he cast his shadow across a million lives as the sun passed from one sainted shoulder to the other. In Abbot's imagination, Jeremy Sawyer stood upon a similar pedestal. Even in his embittered and enfeebled condition, even after exile, shame and self-repudiation—or perhaps because of those things—Jeremy epitomized the Artist Triumphant.

In more ways than one, Abbot thought sadly. Even in Abbot's arms, Patricia hadn't been able to put Jeremy out of her mind, hadn't been able to stop herself from talking about him. No matter how many lovers she took, she would always remain faithful to Jeremy's memory, shackled to her image of herself as Jeremy's wife. Which was, Abbot supposed, as it should be. He was an old-fashioned man—a bourgeois, as Jeremy had said. He believed in fidelity. Too bad he never managed to practice it.

It suddenly occurred to Abbot what, at this point in the whole affair, he really needed: He needed to get drunk. Not just moderately inebriated, but soused, plotched, drunk as a skunk. Dead drunk.

It was, after all, his last night in England, and probably the end of his immediate involvement in Operation Nightingale. Once he gave Hedge a copy of the contract and sent the password to Jeremy, his work was done. All in all, he thought he had handled himself rather well. He deserved a night off, a night reserved for his private use. There was a certain ritual he meant to perform. His love for Patricia Wilding needed embalming and burial. Pickled, he would pronounce the last rites.

At the appointed hour Abbot entered Leicester Square from a side street and looked around. The massive neon billboards that lined the square were already blazing, though the soft light of early evening still illuminated the tops of the budding trees in the small, as it were imperiled park. Nighttime crowds had begun to gather, and there was a lengthy queue outside a cinema whose marquee advertised a new spy thriller—the latest in a popular series featuring an aging matinee idol whose double took all the hard knocks. Abbot saluted a life-size cardboard image of the old phony as he passed.

He entered the park through a gate in the wrought-iron fencing and followed a walk past beds of hyacinths and snapdragons. A statue of Shakespeare stood in a quiet corner, and the Bard was looking quizzically up from a sheaf of foolscap, as if wondering what had become of *his* theater. Nearby, Brian Hedge sat on a park bench reading an *Evening Standard.* Abbot sat down beside him.

"Been off on holiday, have you?" Hedge asked without looking up. His voice was soft, but Abbot heard his irritation.

"I had to give Sir Godfrey time to read the manuscript, so I went up to Cambridge yesterday for a look around."

"Cambridge, was it? You might have let us know that was where you were headed. Was it really necessary to brutalize one of our agents?"

"Was he one of yours? I didn't know—I thought maybe he was one of Kohl's men. It even crossed my mind that he could be somebody from the KGB."

Hedge harrumphed. "If he'd been one of theirs, you wouldn't be here to talk about it. That was bloody foolish, lad. Jacoby meant you no harm; a KGB man would've killed you on the spot. From now on, I trust you'll leave that sort of thing to the professionals."

"Gladly," Abbot said. "Tell Jacoby I'm sorry. Anyway, I've got the contract. Everything's set." He slid a copy of the contract across the bench and Hedge quickly covered it with his newspaper. "I'm saving one for Jeremy when I see him."

"Very well, Abbot—well done. And we can tell our friends in the East that everything is arranged?"

"You can. And tell Nightingale from me, '*Respice finem.*' It's a signal we arranged in Berlin—just so he'll know the message came from me."

"*Respice finem?* Anything else?"

"Just that I'd like to know when and where I'll being seeing my friend."

"Greta will explain all that," Hedge said, sliding an envelope toward Abbot's thigh. "Your ticket back to Frankfurt. You're on the one P.M. flight tomorrow—you can try to get an earlier one if you like, but that's the flight Greta's planning to meet. She'll drive you back to Breiburg, where you are to await further instructions."

"Then—I won't be part of Nightingale's welcoming committee?"

Hedge gave him a sharp look. "It's scarcely a committee. These operations can sometimes prove a bit dicey—especially if the opposition gets wind of them. You'll see your friend soon enough, I dare say."

And before Abbot could argue the matter, Hedge pushed laboriously to his feet, set his face toward Piccadilly and, plump and imposing, plodded off.

Abbot watched him go, then left the bench himself. Will Shakespeare was still studying the square in some consternation, and above his perplexed profile a red-green-blue neon rippled through its several phases. Beyond the neons and the darkening rooftops, the evening sky was a fading, wilted rose.

Some several hours later, Abbot pushed through the frosted glass doors of a Soho drinking establishment and entered a street flaring with neons and illuminated plastics—a winking, blinking, bewildering array of come-ons for a gaudy lineup of cabarets, clubs, erotic cinemas and bookshops. He knew he was somewhere north of Piccadilly and south of Oxford Street, but it was sometime since he'd bothered to look at a map and even longer since he'd given a damn where he was. He staggered on the uneven pavement, saw neons dancing and looping above the narrow street in a manner clearly beyond the current technology of sign making, and leaned against a lamppost to regain his equilibrium.

It was that hour of the night when Abbot's mood teetered precariously between goofy euphoria and black despair, when he knew he should get himself off the street yet wasn't sure he could face the silence and emptiness of his little room. If he pushed on—another pub, another pint of beer, another drunken conversation with some nocturnal wanderer as far gone as he was—he would come eventually to the abyss. But what did that matter? When you set off on a serious bender, it was demeaning to pull up short of your goal. Abbot felt he had been demeaned quite enough lately, and he was sick and tired of it. He was sick and tired of a lot of things, and if that mousey little ELF agent—what was his name, Jacoby?—were to show up now, Abbot would probably knock his goddamn block off.

"I would, by God," he muttered to a passerby, then pushed himself off the lamppost and managed several steps along the street before finding it necessary to seek yet another stabilizing support. I'm not this drunk, he told himself, clinging to an oddly wobbly postal box. My head will clear in a moment. Just take it easy . . .

The pubs were closing and the sidewalks crowded with men on the prowl. Most of them, Abbot noticed, were middle-aged foreigners like himself—some black and some brown and quite a few yellow. But all of them slinking along with that same hungry, furtive look in their lust-lorn eyes. God, he had seen this street a thousand times. There was a street like this in every city on the globe, and somehow he always managed to find it. There was a street like this running through his dreams.

A woman came out of an alley and locked herself on to his arm. "Hello then, luv—are you lookin' for a good time?"

She was a slight, waiflike creature, no longer young, her face heavily made up and her eyes unnaturally bright. Looking down at her from his woozy altitude, Abbot inhaled her powerful scent and beheld for a confusing moment the image of his lost love. "A good time?" he asked the painted face. "What the hell is that?"

"You know what that is, luv," the woman said, using her slight body for leverage against Abbot's unsteady legs, turning him from the bright, busy street into an unlighted lane that reeked of garbage. "My place is right along here. You and me could have a lovely party, luv."

"A party?" Abbot pictured hats and horns and noisemakers —no thanks. Yet there was something about the woman—the pressure of her hand, the weight of her slender body as she guided him along the lane, even her whore's potent perfume— that he found poignant and appealing. Perhaps the poor thing needed somebody to talk to, somebody kind and gentle who would sit down and listen to her problems.

"Here we are, ducks," she said, pulling him toward a shadowed doorway. "It's just in here and up a few stairs—you can make it."

Abbot wasn't sure he could. Moreover, he had taken an immediate dislike to the old, dingy, somehow sinister building, the door of which yawned before him like an open grave.

"Look, lady, I'm sorry—I've spent all my money. I can't pay you. Maybe another night, okay?"

"That's all right, luv," she said, wrestling him across the threshold. "It won't cost you a thing, I promise. This one's on the house."

On the house? Now that's a switch. Could she have been smitten by his roguish charm? Perhaps she had mistaken him for that other fellow, that Roger Connery or whatever his name was. He would have to explain to her that being a secret agent was not such an exciting job after all. You got sent places, you did things, it wasn't much . . .

"Right up these stairs, luv. You can make it, that's a good boy."

Abbot leaned heavily against the stair rail. The interior of the building was cold and damp; the stairwell was poorly lighted and smelled atrociously of piss and vomit. At the first landing a door opened and a thin-faced woman looked out at them with dead, drugged eyes. Her dressing gown sagged open to reveal slack, corpselike breasts. She laughed a harsh echoing laugh and slammed her door.

The little tart was alternately pulling and pushing Abbot up a second flight of stairs. He swayed against the rail and a wave of nausea came over him as he peered down into the black well. "Come on, darlin', *please*," the whore said, using all her strength to get him moving again. "We're almost there."

"Where?" Abbot thought to ask her. "Where are you taking me? What's going on, anyway?"

It occurred to him that she could have an accomplice—that he could be on the verge of getting rolled. There wasn't much cash left in his wallet, but he did have his Eurocheques and his American Express card, the key to his hotel and to the Britrail locker where he'd left Jeremy's box. . . .

Suddenly Abbot knew he was in serious trouble. He pulled his arm out of the woman's grasp and turned to head down the stairs, then saw that a man had come out onto the landing below.

He was a tall man, dressed all in black, and his face, in the dim light of the bare bulb that hung above the landing, was as white as a fish's underbelly. The alcohol seemed flushed from Abbot's blood by a rush of pure terror as he recognized the scarred and snarling visage of the Hangman.

The two men looked at each other, and Abbot remembered that moment on the bridge outside the guesthouse, when at his curt "*guten Abend*" he had been allowed to pass. There was no chance of getting by this time, he knew. The Hangman had already started up the stair, and Abbot had basically two options:

He could throw himself over the railing and down the well, or he could keep climbing the stairs. Perhaps at the top he could find a place to hide, another way down, a door to bolt and barricade. He grabbed the woman by her shoulders and, convinced of her treachery, pushed her roughly down the stairs at the advancing Hangman. Then he made his run for the top.

He turned, climbed, turned again . . . finally there were no more stairs. A long corridor led to an open door, and from the door a strong breeze was blowing, as if a window might be open in the room beyond. The fresh air helped to clear Abbot's head. He heard footsteps on the stairs and ran down the corridor and into the room, slamming the door behind him. There was, however, no key in the lock. He ran his fingers along the door and frame, searching for a latch, a bolt, a hook—then heard the creak of a rope, felt rather than saw the shadow pass over him as something swung suspended in the center of the room.

He turned, his back to the door, and saw the body hanging from the light fixture. The body circled slowly from its heavy rope, as if propelled by the breeze blowing in through a large double window. As the face rotated toward Abbot he recognized the features of the balding man in the gray nylon car coat—the agent Hedge had called Jacoby. As if to rebuke Abbot for the ill treatment he had suffered at his hands, Jacoby was putting out his tongue and glaring fiercely at him from a face turned quite purple.

The door panel shattered beside Abbot's ear and a gloved fist sought his neck. He lunged across the room, stumbling in his panic against the hanging body. Jacoby's corpse spun away, and as the Hangman entered the room Abbot careened toward the open window, hoping for a fire escape, a nearby roof, a ledge he could walk to safety, but there was nothing—nothing but night and wind and a drop of several stories to the street below.

Abbot swung around to face what he had to face and, determined not to go down without a fight, landed a punch or two before the Hangman drove him to his knees with a series of short, sharp, paralyzing blows. Stunned, Abbot felt himself hauled across the room and flung face down onto the musty mattress of a squeaking bed. A powerful hand held him there as the Hangman went methodically through his pockets. Resistance was futile; he

was like a small animal beneath the claw of a predator—
something to be devoured at leisure. When the Hangman found
what he was looking for—Abbot knew it had to be the key for the
locker at Victoria Station—he left his victim sprawled breathless
on the filthy bed and went to another part of the room. Abbot en-
tertained a brief, mad hope of being, in his utter insignificance,
spared. Then his head was yanked back and the coarse, heavy
rope brushed his ears. He felt its weight on his shoulders; the fi-
bers bit into his neck as the noose was drawn tight.

Abbot bolted for the door but the Hangman had him on a
leash now and yanked him back, then sent him stumbling toward
the open window. Abbot hit the wall and slid to the floor, where
he saw to his horror that the rope was tied to a water pipe beneath the sink. He began frantically wrapping the rope around
his hands. The Hangman grabbed a wrist; Abbot kicked him
away. There was a noise on the stairs, a woman's scream. Abbot
yelled for help but the Hangman wasted no more time. He lifted
Abbot by one arm and one leg and pitched him headfirst out the
window, launching him like a paper airplane into the cool London night.

THE STORK
AND
THE NIGHTINGALE

PART THREE

here was sunlight at the window; birds chirped and rustled in the vines which clustered close around it. Abbot had been dreaming of home and drifting in and out of sleep. In one of his dreams Liz told him that she wanted to quit her job at the museum and have another child. "At our age?" Abbot started to say and then decided that if his wife really wanted to get pregnant he was certainly willing to accommodate her.

A nurse came into the room and put a thermometer into his mouth. Then she took his pulse, peered into each eye and made certain notations on her chart. She put fresh water into the glass with the jointed straw beside his bed and measured out another ration of pain pills and sedatives. She removed the thermometer, read it, shook it down, made a note on her chart.

"Feeling better now, aren't we? There are two American gentlemen outside who would like to talk to you, but the doctor says not to use your voice too much, all right?"

Abbot nodded. He didn't want to use his voice at all, since it greatly aggravated the soreness in his throat. He'd had his tonsils removed at a later age than most and remembered the postoperative pain quite well; this pain ran it a close second. There were gauze bandages beneath his chin and across his throat, and both his hands were bandaged so that just his fingers and thumbs were exposed. He had only vague memories of the manner in which he had come by these injuries. Intermittent dreams of falling, and of drifting weightlessly above the planet, made him think that at some point in his misfortunes he had tried to fly.

Kohl and Morrison came into the room and drew up chairs to

the right of his bed. Abbot had no trouble remembering who they were, though for a moment he couldn't think why they had come to see him.

"How are you feeling, Prof?" Kohl asked.

"Terrible," Abbot croaked and indicated with one of his bandaged hands that he would like a sip of water.

Morrison held the glass for him. "You're darn lucky to be alive. The Hangman doesn't usually screw up like that."

Oh yes, Abbot thought—the Hangman. He knew there was a part of it he had managed to forget.

"If Charnov had taken the time to tie your hands behind your back, you'd have been a goner," Kohl said. "A drop like that would've torn your head clean off. Maybe he heard Jimbo here coming up the stairs and got a little rushed. The doc says there's no permanent damage to your throat. The worst you got were those rope burns and a mild concussion when you swung into the wall."

Abbot turned to Morrison. "You caught the Hangman?"

The young agent grinned sheepishly. "Well, I tried, and I've got a few bruises to show for it." He pointed to a yellowish patch on his cheekbone. "I had to let him go once I saw that rope hanging out the window. I untied it and lowered you down to the street—it probably wasn't more than another six or eight feet."

"I wonder why the Hangman didn't just throw you out the window without the rope," Kohl said. "I'm not sure the old bastard still has all his buttons."

"Wait a minute," Abbot said, as yet another ghastly image flashed through his mind. "There was someone else—Jacoby, I think his name was—"

"Yeah, he was the agent ELF had following you around London. Charnov got rid of him first. Any idea why he was trying to kill you, Prof?"

Abbot tried hard to think, but the events of the previous evening were jumbled and distorted. He'd been drinking heavily, he remembered that. There was a woman . . . a flight of stairs . . . he knew something was wrong when—

"The key!" Abbot cried, hurting his throat by raising his voice. "He's got the key!"

"What key is that, Prof?" Kohl asked, as Morrison offered more water.

Abbot sipped, swallowed hard. "To a locker at Victoria Station. It's where I put Jeremy's box. . . . What an idiot!"

"Jeremy's box?" Kohl said. "Is *that* why you gave us all the slip on Wednesday night—so you could go off somewhere and collect something for Sawyer?"

Abbot nodded miserably. He remembered that Kohl himself had been interested in such a box shortly after Jeremy's defection, but he saw no point in denying anything now.

"Do you remember the number of the locker?" Morrison asked.

"I wrote it down . . . my pocket calendar." Abbot pointed to his jacket, which was hanging with his other clothes in the wardrobe across the room. Morrison went to get it.

"Why didn't you tell *us* about the box?" Kohl asked. "I thought we agreed to work together on this thing."

"I'm sorry," Abbot said, "Jeremy warned me not to tell anyone—especially you, Kohl. He said there was something in that box he had to have in order to substantiate certain allegations . . ."

Morrison came back to the bed with Abbot's little datebook. "Here, is this it?" He showed the page to Abbot.

"Yes, G-217. It's in that bank of lockers near the Airways bus terminal."

"Jimbo, get somebody over to Victoria right away," Kohl said. "Have them get that locker open and report back to us here."

Morrison took the phone from Abbot's bedstand to a table across the room and dialed a number. Abbot knew it was hopeless. Surely, the Hangman had collected his prize by now.

"How long have I been in here?" he asked Kohl.

"They brought you in around midnight, so it's been nearly fifteen hours now. They gave you a sedative around two A.M., and we had to wait for it to wear off before we could try to question you. This private room you're in is compliments of the Agency, by the way. Nobody from ELF has shown any interest in you."

"But we've got to warn them," Abbot said. "Operation Nightingale has to be canceled. Jeremy said he wouldn't leave Russia until he knew I had that box in my possession."

Kohl lifted his bushy eyebrows. "So what's in there that's so important? Did you get a look at the contents?"

"I didn't go through everything. A lot of letters, mostly, and some legal papers concerning his draft status. . . . All I wanted was the tie clasp Jeremy told me about, so I could send the signal."

"Tie clasp?"

"There was a Latin motto on the back. *Respice finem.* Listen, Kohl, we've got to get in touch with somebody in ELF. Jeremy mustn't leave Moscow—"

"It's too late for that," Kohl said and withdrew a folded newspaper from his coat. "Take a look at this."

Abbot saw it was Saturday morning's edition of the *Times.* The brief second-page article Kohl had circled bore the headline POET KIDNAPPED IN MOSCOW, SOVIETS CLAIM. Abbot skimmed the column below:

> Tass, the official Soviet news agency, reported early today that Jeremy Sawyer, American-born poet and antiwar activist of the 1960s, was kidnapped off a Moscow street Friday evening by agents of the U.S. government. Sawyer, who renounced his U.S. citizenship and fled to the U.S.S.R. in 1968, was reportedly walking near his home when the kidnapping occurred. A spokesman in Washington has categorically denied the charge. . . .

Abbot put down the paper and turned to Kohl. "*Did* your men kidnap Jeremy?"

"Naw, of course not. The Kremlin sends whatever it likes over the wire. Chances are they've known about Operation Nightingale all along. They probably prepared this story as a way of covering their tails, so if Sawyer gets killed, they can blame it on the 'terrorist thugs' in the CIA. If he makes it to the West, they can say he was removed from the Soviet Union against his will. When he asks for political asylum, they can say he was brainwashed, and when his book comes out they can call it a forgery. Assuming that Sawyer *does* surface in the West, which doesn't look too likely at this point. The Russians are playing this one as if they wrote the script."

Morrison lowered the phone and said, "I've got an agent who's already at Victoria, chief—he's going to have security open that locker for us."

"What do you mean," Abbot asked, "'as if they wrote the script'? Are you suggesting that Jeremy's escape is some kind of a ruse?"

"That's a distinct possibility," Kohl said. "Maybe Sawyer has no intention of defecting again; maybe he's simply setting the Stork up for his pals in the KGB. But I read those two chapters you brought back from East Berlin, and I'd say the guy really has had a belly full of Communism. It's more likely that somebody inside ELF—somebody close to Operation Nightingale—is keeping the Russians informed. What happened to you last night just about proves it."

Abbot couldn't think how last night's events proved anything except that he was a damn fool. He sank back on his pillow with a groan and waited for Kohl to continue.

"Consider the timing," Kohl said. "Sawyer told you that he wouldn't leave Moscow until he received your signal. I assume you sent that signal through Brian Hedge when you met him at six P.M. yesterday in Leicester Square. It was already nine P.M. in Moscow, and that Tass story had to have been released by ten in order to have made this morning's *Times*. That means the KGB got your signal almost as soon as Sawyer did. They released their story and then, knowing it was too late for Sawyer to change his mind, they sent the Hangman to collect your box. Since they no longer had any need for you, and didn't want your version of events to contradict theirs, they told their assassin to dispose of you in his usual manner. If Jimbo here hadn't been on your tail as well, their order would've been carried out."

Abbot was much impressed by the thought that someone in the Kremlin—a man he had never met, and to whom he had done no wrong—had calmly ordered his execution, simply because he was no longer needed, or because his knowledge of events might someday prove an embarrassment. It made him want to cling fast to that knowledge—his own few scraps of truth, whatever they might be—and defend them against all comers.

"But how did they know I had a box of Jeremy's papers?" he asked Kohl. "Nobody in ELF knew about that box, and I made sure I wasn't followed when I went up to Cambridge—"

"An ingenious maneuver, Prof, but probably pointless. The Russians must have known that Sawyer left some important papers in England, and that he'd need to collect them if he ever tried to change sides again. They probably had somebody waiting at the station or watching the Eckersley house. I'm assuming that's where you got Sawyer's box. How is Mrs. Eckersley these days?"

"Let's leave her out of this, Kohl. She's suffered enough on Jeremy's account—I don't want her subjected to any more harassment."

Kohl raised his eyebrows at Abbot's adamance. "Sure, sure. I'm not going to bother the lady. And now that they have Sawyer's papers, the Russians probably won't bother her either. Come to think of it, I guess I can figure out what was in that box. . . . Did Patricia Eckersley tell you about a certain incident at our Waverly base, a few weeks before Sawyer flew the coop?"

"She mentioned that several people were killed during an antiwar protest when a bomb went off. She said you were trying to connect Jeremy to that incident, and that was another reason for his defection—"

"Your pal was in pretty hot water by then," Kohl said. "You see, that wasn't just another antiwar protest. Highly sensitive intelligence documents were being stored at that base, awaiting transfer to Washington. Some of those documents, concerning our network of operatives in Eastern Europe, were found missing after the explosion."

"And you think Jeremy stole them?"

"Well, let's just say they fell into his hands. An English civilian working at that base was later convicted of selling NATO secrets to the Russians. He could have passed those documents to Sawyer in the confusion that followed the blast. You see, I never did buy the notion that the boys in the Kremlin were such great poetry lovers—I think Jeremy had something more substantial to bargain with: a list of our key agents behind the Iron Curtain. Of course, in order to set up his deal, he had to have been in contact with Soviet agents here in England. If he kept a record of those negotiations, it's probably in the box you got for him, left behind as insurance that the Russians would live up to their end of the deal. Maybe Sawyer was even planning to buy his way out of Russia at some time in the future, by selling us information on Soviet agents in England."

For Abbot, who had always considered Jeremy's defection a rash and impulsive act of misguided idealism, Kohl's theory was hard to accept. It was one thing for Jeremy to have gone to Russia as an heroic martyr, faithful to a cause that transcended national loyalties; it was another for him to have gone as a spy and traitor, selling information at the cost of innumerable human lives. Could Jeremy have done such a thing? Abbot remembered the decrepit shell of a man he'd met in East Berlin—embittered, cynical, full of schemes and vain ambitions—and thought yes, *that* man could have done it. But what, then, of the man who had written the two chapters Abbot read, the man he was ready to call one of the great writers of his generation? Was it possible there were *two* Jeremy Sawyers?

Across the room, Morrison said something, hung up the phone and turned to Kohl. "The locker was empty, chief."

"Well, that's that," Kohl said. "Don't feel too bad, Prof—that box wouldn't have done your pal much good by this time, anyway. The Soviet agents he knew in England have probably all been put out to pasture by now—except for one who, I'd be willing to bet, is currently working for ELF."

"The mole?" Morrison asked.

Kohl nodded. "One of the reasons I was never able to nail Sawyer for that Waverly business was that he had the protection of somebody pretty high up in British intelligence. They were still running their own show in those days, and every time I tried to interrogate Sawyer I was told to lay off. Now who do you think was in charge of the Waverly investigation for the Brits?"

Abbot sat up. "Surely not . . . Brian Hedge?"

"The one and only. By the time I was able to get around Hedgie and put some real heat on Sawyer, he was off to Moscow, carrying a list of our best agents behind the Iron Curtain. A few months later Hedge was forced to resign his post in British intelligence. He took a long vacation, as I recall, then went to work for ELF. So who's got a better reason for wanting to make sure old Jeremy doesn't return to publish his memoirs?"

Abbot lay back with a sense of total despair; he had begun to like the portly Englishman. Was there no one in this wretched business he could trust?

Kohl had taken out a wrapped cigar and was rolling it nervously between his fingers. His asphalt eyes looked down at Abbot with an amused, perhaps kindly, curiosity.

"Well, Prof, I suppose you've had about enough of this kind of work by now. I bet you'd like to catch the next flight back to the States—and I wouldn't blame you, not one bit."

Abbot glared up at him. "What else do you want from me, Kohl? You see the condition I'm in."

"Yeah, terrible. I guess it all depends on how badly you want to help your friend. But like I say, I wouldn't blame you if you said to hell with the whole mess at this point. Would you blame him, Jimbo?"

"Not at all," Morrison said. "The Prof's a brick."

"Tell me, goddamn it! What can I possibly do for Jeremy now? Why *should* I do anything for him?"

"Ah, well, those are two very different questions," Kohl said. "Let's take them one at a time. The Russians knew about Operation Nightingale, and yet they let it proceed as planned. They put out a cover story to make it look as though Sawyer was snatched by the CIA. Chances are they've set up an ambush at some point along the Stork's route—probably where he crosses the border between East and West, or maybe just this side. Now, if we knew where and when Sawyer's coming in, we might be able to get there with enough muscle to even up the odds."

"You'd risk an international incident," Abbot asked, "to protect a man you consider a traitor?"

"Ah, that's the second question," Kohl said. "Jeremy Sawyer is not my major concern; the Stork and his network are. Suppose Sawyer makes it into West Germany. And suppose there's a KGB reception party waiting for him somewhere on this side of the line. Think of the propaganda value to the Russians if Sawyer's death occurs in a Western democracy and if it can be blamed on ELF, which the Russians have always said is run by the CIA. I'm trying to spare us that embarrassment. The Agency gets enough bad press these days without having Operation Nightingale hung around its neck."

"The Commies would love to get rid of ELF," Morrison added.

"There's not another organization in Europe that's giving them more grief right now. And by discrediting ELF, they can put pressure on the Bonn government to crack down on other pro-Western groups."

"They can do more than that," Kohl said. "If ELF comes out of this looking like a band of right-wing fanatics, the West German money that's been financing their activities will dry up awfully quick. These fat-cat industrialists may enjoy dabbling in espionage, with dreams of a reunified Germany leading them on, but let someone yell 'neo-Nazi' at them and they'll run for cover. After all, they've got lucrative worldwide business interests to protect. The last thing they want is to stir up old fears and hostilities."

"What it comes down to," Morrison observed, "is that nobody trusts the Germans—not even the Germans."

"So you need to know where ELF is bringing Jeremy in," Abbot said. "About all I know for sure is that the Stork's delivery is scheduled for sometime on Sunday."

Kohl twirled his cigar. "This little nobleman you told us about—the guy with the hunting lodge or whatever it was—did he seem to be in charge of Operation Nightingale?"

"I think so. He said something about assisting refugees to make new lives for themselves, and he seemed to be familiar with Jeremy's poetry. I'd recognize a photograph, if you have one—"

Kohl shook his head. "We know most of the field agents in ELF, but a few of the really important people have managed to keep their identities secret. It's not likely we'd have a photograph on file." As if unable to resist any longer, he slipped the cigar out of its cellophane wrapper and sniffed its shaft. "The precautions they took with you—the drug, the blindfold—suggest that not only the man but the place where you met him could be important. Any idea where that was?"

This was a question they had covered in Berlin, but Abbot made an effort to summon any relevant details. "It had to be at least three hours from Frankfurt, and in an easterly direction—"

"That would put it somewhere along the East German or Czech border," Morrison said. "The Hartz mountains maybe, or down around Coburg—"

"The land was hilly, but not mountainous," Abbot said. "The one glimpse I got suggested a range of low, wooded hills—

sparsely populated." He suddenly had a thought. "Caves and catacombs!"

"How's that, Prof?"

"Mikos Pajorfsky's field was European archaeology. Greta told me they spent a lot of time this past winter visiting certain prehistoric sites below ground—places where she was afraid to go. She wouldn't tell me where any of these places were, but I remember Hedge saying that Franz and Mikos had worked closely together."

Kohl got up and crossed to the window. "Caves and catacombs. Germany's got plenty of those. There are also some mineral deposits along the East German border, particularly in the central uplands. Several mines in the Hartz had to be closed when Germany was partitioned, because they had entrances on both sides of the line."

"Is it possible," Abbot asked, "that Pajorfsky located certain Bronze Age mines which wouldn't show up on modern geological surveys—mines the Soviets wouldn't know about?"

"The Stork's escape route," Morrison said, "that's got to be it!"

"That *could* be it," Kohl corrected him. "It's worth checking out, anyway. Prof, how are you doing? Feel up to a little travel?"

"You want me to go to Frankfurt and question Greta."

Kohl nodded. "It looks like our best chance. We need to get in touch with this guy Franz and persuade him to accept our help. At the very least, he's got to be told there's a Soviet spy in his organization. You'd be a lot more likely to get somewhere with these people than we would—"

"And wherever they take you, we can track you," Morrison said.

"I know it's a lot to ask—" Kohl paused.

Abbot sat up. The pain in his head was excruciating, but it quickly subsided to a tolerable level. He swung his legs over the side of the bed and Kohl and Morrison each took an arm as he tried to stand. At first he felt nauseated and dizzy, but after a moment his head cleared. There were numerous aches and pains in his neck, shoulders and arms, but they didn't inhibit his movement, and they didn't get worse as he proceeded cautiously around the room.

"Good boy, Prof," Kohl said. "You're a pretty tough little nut after all, aren't you?"

"Thanks," Abbot groaned, "but from now on I'd like to avoid the rough stuff, if it's all right with you."

Morrison said, "Prof, from now on I'll stick to you like a wad of bubble gum. Nobody's going to lay a hand on you, if I can help it."

Abbot was glad to hear it, though he had the curious feeling—perhaps it was only a euphoric reaction to his medication—that his enemies had seriously underestimated him; he was not to be so easily, so casually disposed of, and he almost looked forward to another opportunity to demonstrate his durability.

After a few turns around the room, he checked his watch. "I've missed the flight back to Frankfurt Hedge booked for me. Greta was supposed to meet me at the airport."

"We'll get you a seat on the next flight," Kohl said "You can send a wire to Greta and let her know your new arrival time. Jimbo, would you go by the Prof's hotel and pick up his bags? I'll see to his release from the hospital."

The doctor who came to give Abbot a final checking over shook his head in dismay. "You'd do much better to spend the night with us. A concussion like that can have serious aftereffects, and you really shouldn't be using your voice at all."

"Sorry, doc, we've got important business in Germany," Kohl said. "I'll make sure he gets medical attention over there."

The doctor grunted his disapproval, but relented at last and wrote Abbot a prescription for headaches and nausea. "Get this filled before you go to Germany," he said, "and try to stay off your feet as much as possible for the next few days."

An hour later they were at Heathrow. Morrison met them at the check-in counter with Abbot's bags and tickets for the seven P.M. flight to Frankfurt. "We sent a wire to your girlfriend, Prof, and put a little present in your suitcase. It's a traveler's alarm clock with a homing device. The signal has a range of thirty miles. If you get in real trouble, push the alarm button down, and it will send a distress call. But don't worry—I intend to keep you in sight the whole time."

"What about a gun?" Abbot asked. "If the Hangman comes after me again, I'd like to be able to defend myself."

"Too risky," Kohl said. "You'd never get a gun through airport security, and if ELF found it on you they'd immediately conclude you were acting as our agent. Besides, I don't think you know how to shoot a gun, Prof."

That was true, though Abbot thought he might learn pretty quickly with the Hangman in his sights.

"What puzzles me," Kohl said as they proceeded along the concourse, "is how Charnov got into England with that mug of his. You'd think every customs officer in the British Isles would double-check the passport of a guy with a phiz like that."

"He could have worn some sort of disguise," Morrison suggested. "They can do fantastic things with latex now. The Hangman probably has another face for use in broad daylight."

"That's a cheery thought," Abbot said. "He could be anybody! Well, almost anybody . . . he'd have to be as tall as you guys, for instance."

"Elevator shoes," Kohl said. "He's probably a shrimp with bionic arch supports."

"Doctor Strangetoes," Morrison chuckled, and Abbot reflected that it was nice to know secret agents really did have a sense of humor, after their fashion.

At the departure gate it became apparent that Kohl wasn't going with them. "I've got some loose ends to look after here in London," he explained. "I'll grab a flight early tomorrow morning and catch up with you guys when I can. Jimbo will keep me posted on your position."

Morrison had obtained seats together in first class—"on the Company." Once airborne, he proved a talkative and congenial traveling companion.

"Poor Rollie, he's really sweating this one out."

"He is?" Abbot hadn't noticed an unusual degree of anxiety in either agent.

"You've got to know him the way I do. The greatest triumph of his career—the single stroke that made his reputation in the trade—was getting rid of the Hangman. It really bothers him that the old boy is back in business. He's been edgy as hell these past few months."

The plane rose up through a hazy twilight and Abbot looked back at the lights of London strung out along the Thames. "I guess you know your boss pretty well. You two seem pretty close."

"He's taught me a heckuva lot. It's been really great, working for a legend like Roland Kohl. Of course, it isn't like it used to be when Rollie first got started. He made his mark in the old, free-wheeling days, before those Washington politicians got so uptight about our intelligence activities. They called Rollie in to testify before one of their Senate subcommittees once. I guess they gave him quite a grilling. He almost lost his Berlin post, had to pull a lot of strings over in the Pentagon to get it back."

"Oh, and what was he charged with?" Abbot asked.

Morrison shrugged and looked out the window. "Oh, you know, the usual stuff—running too free an operation, making too many deals with unsavory characters, breaking a few laws—but Jeez, Prof, everybody knows how the Rooskies play the game! Do they worry about a few laws when their national security is at stake?"

"No, I guess they don't," Abbot said.

"It's been hard as heck on Rollie, trying to keep his network viable, what with all the restrictions they put on our budget back in Washington."

"I suppose that's one reason why Kohl is so anxious to save the Stork," Abbot ventured.

"You know it. Rollie's always had a lot of admiration for the Stork. The guy's phenomenal—the best in the business. And he gets to run his own show, without all these politicians breathing down his neck."

Morrison sounded almost jealous, and Abbot supposed there were fraternal and filial rivalries in the espionage trade, as in any other profession. He could imagine young James Morrison recruited off some Ivy League campus after a few ROTC courses had commended him to the watchful eyes of his instructors. What kind of postgraduate training would such young men be given? Abbot imagined a secret school for spies, in rural Virginia perhaps, where bright, healthy, good-natured young fellows like Morrison were transformed into efficient, dedicated, lethal machines for the covert implementation of United States foreign policy. Finally, the young agents would be turned over to the old pros like Roland Kohl, who would teach them in the field all those dirty tricks of the trade they could no longer put into the congressionally monitored textbooks. The whole process no longer struck Abbot as quite so lamentable as it would have several weeks ago. A lot had happened to change his outlook in the past two weeks.

A stewardess came to take their drink order. Morrison requested a beer, while Abbot contented himself with a cup of tea for his sore throat.

"On the wagon, Prof?" Morrison asked.

"Just testing," Abbot said. "I may never use the stuff again, if I can make it through the next twenty-four hours."

14

For Abbot, who had never expected to become such an ardent admirer of German ways, it was a curiously gratifying homecoming. The Frankfurt *Flughafen* seemed clean and bright and well maintained after the decay and neglect one noticed in London; the people looked happy, healthy and eminently sane; even the sound of German voices over the airport's PA system struck Abbot as pleasant and reassuring. He turned to express some of these feelings to Morrison and discovered that the young agent was no longer at his side—in fact, Abbot couldn't spot him anywhere in the large hall where the passengers from Flight 029 were waiting for their luggage. Apparently Jimbo had decided it was time to render himself invisible. He had told Abbot he would be close by but out of sight once they reached Germany.

Abbot found his suitcase and duffel bag, put them both on a trolley and pushed them through the customs bay marked NOTH-ING TO DECLARE. He wasn't stopped; the automatic doors slid open to reveal the usual crowd gathered at the barrier, jockeying for position and watching anxiously for whomever they'd come to meet. A hundred pairs of eyes glanced at Abbot and rejected him; then he found a pair that didn't. Greta was waiting on the fringe of the cosmopolitan throng. Abbot was surprised by how good she looked to him after their brief separation; her young sexuality crackled in the large hall like a short circuit in one of the overhead lights. Her dark eyes were full of welcome—and then astonishment.

"Sam—your throat and hands—what has happened to you?"

"An accident," Abbot said. "I'll tell you about it. Is there some-place where we can sit down and have a cup of coffee?"

She led him through the airport's maze of corridors to the golden arches of a well-known American chain. Abbot was going to protest and then decided that a *Viertelpfunder,* as the Germans called it, wouldn't be half bad. He'd been fed only liquids in the hospital and his stomach was growling.

They sat in a corner booth, away from possible eavesdroppers, and Abbot gave Greta a short account of his adventures in London. "I've got to talk to Franz—the little guy you first took me to meet. He's the one in charge of Operation Nightingale, isn't he? He's got to be warned: The Russians know all about Nightingale; they're laying a trap for the Stork; they're trying to discredit your entire organization."

Greta shook her head in confusion. "But my instructions from Herr Hedge were to take you to Breiburg and to wait there for his call—"

"If we wait for Hedge's signal, it will be too late. The chances are that Hedge is a Russian agent."

"Sam! What are you saying? Are you sure of this?"

"Hedge knew Sawyer back in England—he probably helped to set up Jeremy's defection. It's possible that Jeremy took a list of U.S. agents into Russia with him and left a list of Soviet agents in England—" He saw that she couldn't absorb everything he was telling her. "Hell, it's all too complicated. You've got to get me a meeting with Franz—tonight, if possible."

Greta ran her scarlet-tipped fingers through her wild tangle of hair. "I am not used to making decisions, Sam. I don't know what to do."

Abbot reached across the Formica table to take her hand. "Trust me," he said. "I was nearly killed in London. I've had the Hangman's rope around my neck, I've looked into his eyes. . . . Trust me, Greta. I know what I'm talking about."

She gazed solemnly into his eyes, as if she expected to see there the horrors he had experienced. Then she made her decision:

"All right. Wait here while I phone."

"Who are you going to call? Not Hedge, I hope."

She shook her head. "There is another man here in Frankfurt we can talk to. He is a member of the *Herrschaft*—how do you say?

—the ruling committee, yes? If he believes your story, he will arrange a meeting with the man you call Franz."

"Okay, fine, let's start with him."

Abbot nibbled at his hamburger while she was gone. A few bites and he lost his appetite, but the warm coffee soothed his throat. He watched the people in the restaurant, thinking that he might be sitting in an exact replica of this establishment anywhere back in the States. They used to feed the kids at the golden arches when they were traveling. . . .

Greta returned with a look of accomplishment. "All right, we go now. He will meet us in one hour."

They took an elevator down to the vast underground parking garage. Greta's dusty, dented sports car was waiting in one of the numbered rows. Abbot put his luggage into the trunk and buckled himself into the peeling leather bucket seat. As he expected, Greta was an enthusiastic and aggressive driver. He hoped Morrison had arranged to have a car waiting for him at the airport, preferably with another German driver at the wheel.

They picked up the Autobahn and drove north, passing the several exits which would have taken them into the city. "Where are we headed?" Abbot asked.

"A spa in the Taunus mountains. It is on the way to Breiburg but some kilometers off the Autobahn—very secluded. The man we meet, he is also official of big Frankfurt bank. He has many connections in the government. Therefore he is very cautious."

"Fine, I'm all for caution," Abbot said. "Did you bring your gun, by any chance?"

She glanced at him. "In glove compartment. You want to see?"

Abbot opened the compartment and took out the gun. It was an old, heavy, World War Two–style Luger; Abbot supposed its firepower was no match for modern weapons, but it was better than nothing. "Is it loaded?"

"Check and see. You remember, I showed you how."

Abbot experimented and learned that he did remember how to remove the clip. The gun was loaded, all right. He replaced the clip with a pleasing sense of competence. Nonetheless, he knew Greta was a better shot. "You carry it," he said, and put in into her purse.

"You are much worried," Greta said.

Abbot watched the two rivers of light, one white and one red, that zigzagged into the mountains. Rain struck the windshield, blurring the lights between each sweep of the wipers. "Yeah, I'm worried. But I'm not scared, Greta. It's curious that I'm not scared."

"You are learning to be brave man," Greta assured him and for a while, watching the steady flow of traffic through the streaming windshield, Abbot almost believed her.

They left the Autobahn at Bad Neuheim and followed a country road through the wooded hills. Though Abbot saw headlights from time to time in the rearview mirror, he could not be sure they were being followed. Ah well, at least Morrison could track them with the aid of that homing device in his suitcase. Abbot imagined its signal as a rope he could cling to as he inched his way into a new abyss.

They came down a winding road and into the tiny village which surrounded the spa. Abbot had heard that the Germans were much enamored of their spas and convinced of their curative powers, but he had never visited one before. He was surprised by the size and opulence of the hotel, the classical elegance of the baths, the extensive formal gardens. They drove through a park where, despite the rain, a brass band was playing a spirited march in a sort of gazebo. Greta parked on a dark side street across the park from the baths. She checked her watch.

"We are early yet. I am told always to park my car some distance away from meeting place. It is better, yes, if we must make a run to escape?"

"You're the professional," Abbot said. "Tell me about this guy we're going to meet. Do I get to learn his name?"

"His name is Rinzelmann; he is official with bank——" She paused, and he could feel her looking at him in the dark. "Sam, you are still angry with me? I am acting very foolish in Berlin—— I'm sorry, it is not like me."

"That's okay. I guess I wasn't very considerate either—I had a lot on my mind." And still do, he thought.

"You are not yet giving me *real* kiss," she said shyly. "Now is good time, Sam—I am missing you very much."

Abbot put his arm around her. After a moment he found a way to kiss her without his bandages getting in the way, but he kept one eye on the street. Where the hell was Morrison?

"This is no good," Greta exclaimed, pulling away from his kiss. "You are not the man I took to my bed two weeks ago. It is different for you now, yes?"

I keep changing, Abbot thought. Pretty soon I won't know myself at all; I'll look in the mirror and see a total stranger. "I'm sorry," he said, "I guess it is different. I met someone in England, you see. Jeremy Sawyer's former wife."

"Ah, the one you should have married? And it was still the same? The sparks flew?"

"So to speak. But nothing will come of it. She's married again. In addition, I think she's still stuck on Jeremy, though she won't admit it."

"So it is between me and Liz, yes? Then I know how it will go. Liz will win. You are good man, Sam—I am not angry. We are still comrades, yes?"

"You bet," Abbot said and kissed her forehead.

Greta looked at her watch again and said they might as well start for the meeting. She locked up the car and gave Abbot a second set of keys. "All of a sudden I am having, how you say, bad vibes, yes? Maybe I am a little bit psychic—when trouble is coming I often get goose bumps. Do you think it could be a trap?"

"You know this guy Rinzelmann. Can we trust him?"

"Yes, I am sure. But what if his line is bugged, or what if we are followed from airport? If there is trouble, you must not worry about me. You must save yourself, Sam, so that you can deliver your message to Franz."

"I can't do that if I don't know where to find him. Why don't you just tell me how to find Franz? It's the place you took me, right? Is that where they'll be keeping Nightingale?"

She paused to consider. They were crossing the park and had come to a halt beneath the pink canopy of an ornamental fruit tree. The rain had stopped but water still dripped from its branches and the pathway was littered with fallen blossoms.

"No, we must meet Herr Rinzelmann—it would be very bad for me now if I didn't follow instructions. But kiss me, Sam. Hold me tight—make the goose bumps go away."

Abbot took the girl in his arms and kissed her as tenderly and earnestly as he could. Her slim body folded itself expertly into his and after a few minutes he no longer had to force himself to concentrate on their kiss. He heard the band playing from across the park, and his mind swung out in a wide circle, watching the two of them as if from a moving camera as they embraced in a pool of shadows and fallen blossoms. At last Greta broke the seal between their lips and put her head on his chest.

"Yes, that is better. I am not so frightened now. You must let me go ahead with the gun. If I tell you to run, you must run. Don't wait for me—I meet you later at the car."

Such an arrangement seemed hardly chivalrous, but she was, as he had said, the professional. And she did have the gun.

They walked across the park and Abbot saw the bright lights of the bathhouse approaching through the trees. To one side of the building, there was an awning-covered terrace where waiters in white tuxedos delivered glasses of water to the people at wrought-iron chairs and tables. The rainy evening had kept the crowd small, but a string trio serenaded the water enthusiasts from a corner of the terrace. Garlands of colored lights gave the terrace a look of holiday cheerfulness. The people were well dressed, elderly, but not, so far as Abbot could tell, particularly infirm. In fact, they appeared to take a robust satisfaction in their slightly cloudy beverage. Greta led Abbot along the hedge that lined the terrace until she spotted the man they were looking for.

Seated alone at a corner of the terrace, Herr Rinzelmann was a slight, fair-haired man whose pink, cherubic face made him look much younger than he was. Even a trim blond moustache, a touch of gray in his silky hair and a very fashionable white linen blazer could not make him look like the executive officer of a major world bank—or, Abbot thought, like the leader of a ring of spies. His blue eyes were merry, though guarded, and his manner urbane. His English, like that of many educated Germans, had an almost comical Oxbridge elegance.

"I'm pleased to meet you, Herr Abbot, though the circumstances are indeed a bit melodramatic. This spa has a carefully limited clientele—I think we are safe enough. Would you like to try a glass of our famous mineral water?"

Abbot thought it might hasten his recuperation and agreed to try a glass. Herr Rinzelmann snapped his fingers and a waiter hurried over. Their order placed, Rinzelmann lit a cigarette and peered shrewdly at Abbot through the smoke.

"Now then, I understand you have important information concerning Operation Nightingale. I am not immediately involved in this operation, but I can convey your message to those who are."

"I'd like to talk to Franz personally, if I could," Abbot said. "We have reason to believe you have a Soviet agent in your midst—one whose major aim, at present, is to sabotage Operation Nightingale."

"We?" Rinzelmann asked, inspecting the tip of his cigarette. "You are speaking of yourself and the *Fräulein* here?"

"No, I'm speaking of"—Abbot supposed his name would have to come up sooner or later—"an American agent named Roland Kohl. Perhaps you've heard of him—"

The German nearly jumped from his chair. "I am indeed familiar with the name of Roland Kohl! He is not to be trusted, Herr Abbot. We have specific instructions from the Stork not to permit this man to involve himself in Operation Nightingale. You must not believe anything Kohl tells you—he could be a Soviet agent himself."

"Oh, I don't think so," Abbot said, but he suddenly remembered that there had been several times when Kohl's concern for Jeremy Sawyer and the Stork had struck him as not quite genuine. It was also obvious, now that he thought about it, that Kohl also could have had an agent waiting for Abbot in Cambridge, and therefore could have known he had Jeremy's box, could have seen Abbot put it in the locker at Victoria Station, could have signaled the Russians. . . . In fact, every piece of evidence Kohl had used against Brian Hedge could have been used against Kohl himself.

The waiter was returning with Abbot's glass of water on a tray. A towel was draped over his other arm. Even before Abbot quite recognized the dark cylinder protruding from beneath the towel, before he could take the time to reason what it meant or ask himself what to do about it, he was on his feet. "Get down," he shouted, but the gun had already made a short, explosive *phoo!* Herr Rinzelmann was driven backward, a gigantic red carnation blossoming on his white shirt, a look of extreme displeasure in his blue eyes.

Abbot hit the waiter hard with his shoulder, driving him into the adjacent table. They crashed to the floor together and Abbot got both his bandaged hands on the waiter's wrist. The gun spoke again—*phoo! phoo!*—and Abbot felt its flame lick his cheek. Then Greta knelt down beside the waiter and placed her Luger against his temple. Abbot shut his eyes, but the roar of the gun was accompanied by the spattering of something warm and wet across his face. When he opened his eyes, he saw to his horror that the top of the waiter's head was gone.

"Run!" Greta yelled.

People were screaming and running for cover across the terrace. Greta had taken a crouching stance with her Luger held out at arm's length, sweeping the crowd as she tried to cover Abbot's escape. He scrambled to his feet and started toward the hedge. A car was approaching along the drive on the other side of the hedge—a large gray Mercedes, which Abbot immediately recognized. The side window was down and a white face leered at Abbot over the blunt muzzle of a submachine gun as the car drew even with his position.

"Look out—" he yelled to Greta and dove for cover behind one of the overturned tables. He heard Greta's Luger bark once, and then it was buried in a terrible crash of gunfire, shattering glass, bullets ricocheting off iron and stone. Abbot lay on the terrace floor and felt shards of glass and bits of plaster raining down on his back and legs. Then something else, something heavy and yet soft, fell jarringly beside him. He opened his eyes and saw Greta's face, her eye open and staring sightlessly into his. Blood was gushing from a wound in her neck and trickling from the corner of her mouth. The Luger was still clutched in her right hand.

Abbot pried the gun from her fingers. The rage of gunfire had ceased; the car was accelerating along the drive. Abbot jumped to his feet and aimed the Luger, but before his finger could overcome the stiff resistance of the trigger the Mercedes careened around the corner of the building and disappeared.

He turned, gun in hand, to survey the carnage on the terrace. Three bodies. The overturned chairs and tables were speckled and splashed with blood. Windows were broken, plaster fallen from the brick walls. The affluent, elegant, elderly people were just coming out of hiding, crawling toward the safety of the interior. Some were whimpering, crying for help; several were bleeding. Abbot knelt down beside Greta's lifeless body. He knew she had tried to return the fire from the Mercedes; she died fighting for *his* life. He put his hand against her cheek. Her lips were already blackened with blood, but the ferocity of her glare hadn't softened. *Run,* she told him with her dark eyes. *Get away—warn the others!*

He heard the first bleats of a siren coming from across the park. *Comrades,* he thought, stroking Greta's hair. "So long, kid," he said aloud and then got to his feet. Several people were watching him and Abbot knew they would give his description to the police. By morning it would be in the papers: CRAZED TERRORIST MURDERS THREE.

He vaulted the hedge and ran into the park.

It was after midnight when Abbot reached the outskirts of Breiburg and the first of the Autobahn's several exits. As tired as he was, he knew better than to leave Greta's car parked outside the guesthouse, so he cruised the nearby campus until he found a university parking lot which held several other vehicles. He wedged the sports car in between two vans and left his suitcase in the trunk. It was a short walk through the orchard to the guesthouse, and Abbot approached cautiously, checking the front from a distance, then jumping the small drainage ditch and groping his way through the dark and dripping back garden. He did not turn on the yard lights but came up the walk from the garage and fumbled his key into the lock of the front door. At the last moment he thought of his mailbox, checked and found two letters. He put them into his coat pocket, entered the chilly lobby and climbed the stairway to his room.

At this hour of the night the guesthouse was always as quiet as a tomb, and Abbot felt like a weary, wicked ghost making guiltily for his coffin. Driving the Autobahn he had been haunted by Greta's dead stare—the third time in two weeks that he had looked into the eyes of a corpse and tried to read the meaning of that fixed gaze. He told himself that Greta was, by her own definition, a soldier—that she was prepared to die for the cause she so fervently believed in. But he couldn't help remembering the young, frightened girl who had put herself trustingly into his arms and clung to his kiss in the shadows of the rain-wet park.

Her Luger hung heavily in his coat pocket, along with the several rounds of ammunition he'd found in the glove compartment, and it occurred to Abbot that, if only he could be stubborn and resourceful, wily and patient and much tougher than he'd ever been in his life, he might find an opportunity to avenge her murder. It was, at this moment, only the hard, cold lucidity of his anger that kept him from breaking out in sobs.

He paused outside his room, took the gun from his pocket and released the safety catch. Holding the weapon in his right hand, he unlocked and opened the door with his left. Only the stale, dead air of his closed-up rooms greeted him. He moved cautiously through the kitchenette, looked into the bathroom, then into the bed-sitting-room. He pulled the heavy green drapes, turned on the lamp beside his bed, shut and locked the hall door, slipped the triple-dead-bolt lock into place and put the gun down on the counter. In a curious way, the Luger consoled him and soothed his nerves; it had become the precious relic of a loved one. It seemed to put him in touch with Greta's ferocious, warlike spirit, from which he had drawn the courage for his escape.

He reached into the cupboard and got down his bottle of gin. "Well, Sam, that was a short ride on the wagon," he said aloud as he poured out a stiff drink—no vermouth, just a little ice to cut the bite of the gin. He went into the bathroom and began taking off his clothes. They were spattered with blood and there were dried rust-colored specks still clinging to his face. His eyes looked wild, his hands trembled and he felt sure that none of his colleagues here in Breiburg or back in America would have recognized him at this moment.

He found the two letters in his pocket and carried them into the other room along with his drink and dirty clothes. One letter was from his wife. The other bore the name and emblem of a hotel here in Breiburg. Abbot put them both on the desk unopened. There was no way he could fit Liz's news of home and family into a consciousness so filled with thoughts of death and vengeance. If her letter could wait till morning, so could the other. He sat at his desk, bone tired, sipping his gin and gazing morosely down at the photograph of Jeremy Sawyer and himself outside their English country pub. Their innocence and bravado seemed to belong to a different world altogether—a Golden Age, before the Fall. Abbot wanted to give each of the young men a hard shaking.

Now what? He needed help. That was obvious, but where he could turn for it wasn't. His first impulse, when he'd made it panting back to Greta's car, had been to dig that alarm clock out of his suitcase and push the button that would send a distress call to Morrison. But Morrison was probably out of range of the device—otherwise, why hadn't he come to their assistance? Unless, of course, Herr Rinzelmann was right about Roland Kohl—in which case, Abbot thought, he needed Morrison's help like he needed a pair of concrete overshoes. The young agent had saved Abbot's life twice, but Morrison was too much under the spell of Roland Kohl to function as an independent entity. There was no way Abbot was ever going to persuade him not to trust his boss.

These reflections had led Abbot to remove the alarm clock from his luggage and to toss it out the car window as he drove from the village. He needed time to think, to recover from the shock of this latest horror. The last thing he wanted, he decided on the way up to Breiburg, was to have Roland Kohl telling him what to do.

There seemed, then, only one place where he could go for help, and it was the place he had set out to find when he and Greta were attacked. He retained a vivid impression of the little nobleman he knew only as Franz, and he felt certain that Franz was one man he could trust. Franz was not a professional spy. He was a recent initiate, like Abbot himself, and he was moreover a man of principle and deep moral conviction. Abbot could not have been mistaken in his estimate of the little man's sincerity and goodwill.

But how was he going to find Franz without Greta's help? Tomorrow he would search her car for clues—a marked roadmap, a parking permit, something of that sort. He would search her apartment in Frankfurt if necessary. He would work on the problem and come up with something. But not tonight. He didn't think he should trust his own reasoning powers until he'd had a few hours' sleep.

He turned out the light and got into bed. The first thing he saw when he shut his eyes was the carnage on the bathhouse terrace. Abbot opened his eyes and stared at the blackness of his room. At last his lids lowered and he was immediately confronted by a vision of Greta's dead eyes and bloody mouth. Open, closed. There was Jacoby twisting purple-faced at the end of his rope. Open, closed. There was Mikos Pajorfsky glaring at Abbot from his muddy ravine. *Oh, go away,* Abbot thought, *for Christ's sake, go away!* At last he saw the river of headlights and taillights winding over the mountains and he concentrated on these, letting them lead him swiftly into sleep.

The telephone woke him at eight. His neck and shoulders had stiffened overnight; he got out of bed with difficulty and crossed the room in considerable pain. His brain still wasn't quite functioning as he lifted the receiver.

"Hello?"

"Prof, is that you?"

Morrison. "Yeah, it's me."

"You sound terrible. Hey, what happened last night? I lost you and the broad leaving the airport—she sure drives like a maniac."

"Drove," Abbot said. "She's dead."

"Dead? Gosh, what happened? You and she didn't get mixed up in that mess I heard about on the radio this morning, did you?"

"What mess is that?"

"Some kind of terrorist attack at a spa in the hills west of Bad Neuheim—three people were killed and several others injured. Come to think of it, the cops are looking for a guy who kind of fits your description."

Abbot was silent for a minute. "Jimbo, why didn't you track us using that device you put in my suitcase?"

"I tried to, Prof, but I lost the signal shortly after you left the airport. There must have been some sort of malfunction, or maybe somebody used a jammer, I don't know. I went into Frankfurt and staked out the gal's apartment, figuring you'd show up there sooner or later. Fell asleep about three and just woke up a little while ago. Heard the news while I was having breakfast. Are you okay?"

Abbot considered. "Yeah, I'm okay. Have you heard from Kohl?"

"He's arriving at the Frankfurt airport at nine this morning. I

214

thought I'd pick him up and then come on to your place, get there about ten-thirty. Don't go anywhere, okay?"

"Okay," Abbot said.

He turned on the radio, started heating water for coffee and ran a bath. Standing at the sink, he removed the bandages from his hands and throat. The wounds were ugly and Abbot saw there had been an unpleasant discharge overnight. He bathed the wounds gently with warm water and applied some of the salve they'd given him in the hospital. Then he returned to his bed-sitting-room and opened the drapes on a bright spring morning. The orchards across the way had erupted into clouds of pink and white blossoms. The surrounding hills, gray and wintery when he last saw them, had turned a vibrant green. Yet in the rich orchestration of the season Abbot could find only a cruel irony: Greta was still dead.

He was soaking in the tub, the portable radio at his side, when the local news came on. The young AFN announcer, probably stationed in Frankfurt, gave a good deal of attention to matters which directly concerned Abbot:

"Police are continuing the search for a suspect in the terrorist-style slayings that occurred late yesterday at a spa north of Frankfurt. Two of the victims have been identified. They are Otto Rinzelmann, forty-two, deputy assistant director of a major Frankfurt bank, and Greta Länger, twenty-six, an East German refugee believed to have been involved in an anti-Communist organization known as the European Liberation Front. A third victim remains unidentified. At least six people sustained minor injuries when a burst of gunfire raked the terrace of the spa's central bath shortly after ten Saturday night. The suspect is described as a male Caucasian in his mid- to late forties, approximately five feet ten inches tall, weighing one hundred and eighty pounds, with thinning brown hair and brown eyes. He is believed to be armed and dangerous. In other news this morning. . . ."

Abbot was draining the water from the tub and toweling himself dry when he heard:

"Officials in Washington continue to deny Soviet allegations that American-born writer Jeremy Sawyer has been kidnapped by agents of the U.S. government. Sawyer, a Soviet citizen since his defection in 1968, was reportedly abducted at gunpoint on a Moscow street Friday evening. Meanwhile, there are rumors in London this morning that a major British publisher has contracted for a new book by Sawyer—an autobiographical account of his eighteen years in the Soviet Union. Soviet spokesmen have termed the report 'ridiculous' and, we quote, 'an effort by the CIA to disguise its brutal and cynical violation of Sawyer's legal and human rights.' And now for a look at the weather. . . ."

Abbot went to pour his coffee. So it was starting already—the propaganda war Kohl had predicted. No doubt the charges and countercharges would escalate over the next several days, until Jeremy himself could appear before the world press and give an account of his actions. The sooner the better, Abbot thought. Neither he nor Jeremy would be safe until the whole story came out.

He took his coffee into the bathroom and began replacing his bandages with clean strips of gauze. Should he believe Morrison's story or shouldn't he? After all, Kohl had sent Abbot to Frankfurt to learn Jeremy's point of arrival. Why, then, would he set up an ambush? Yesterday, Kohl had been utterly persuasive, and yet now . . . I'm no good at this business, Abbot thought miserably. It was a trade, clearly, in which a man could trust no one but himself. Abbot's habit for years had been to give others the benefits of his doubts, while reserving the severest scrutiny for his own actions. That, he thought, was what was known as being a "man of good will." In the spy trade, it could also make you a dead man.

The radio announcer was talking about yet another terrorist kidnapping—sixteen Swiss and German businessmen taken hostage in Beirut. Abbot turned off the radio and went into his bed-sitting-room to dress. He saw his wife's letter on the desk and, in his distracted state, tore open the envelope and extracted the several sheets of paper. The first sentence, however, claimed his attention: "Dear Sam, this is a difficult letter to write—"

Abbot put the letter down and gazed out the window at the bright blue sky. He didn't think he could deal with this now, yet how could he concentrate on his immediate problems when his wife might be telling him that she wanted a divorce? He read on:

... but I have to tell you that I don't see how the children and I can join you this summer, as planned. I know you've been counting on it, but Charlotte really needs to get a job in order to start saving for college, and Emily may have to take a course in summer school—her math grades are starting to worry me! But the real reason, Sam, is that I just don't feel ready to pick up our marriage or to pretend that everything is the same as always between us, that we can go on as before. . . .

Abbot lay the letter aside. The customary qualms and scruples of married life seemed as remote to him now as the doings of some creatures of another age, whose domestic affairs might have been guessed at from items found beneath tons of volcanic ash. Perhaps he would do Liz and all of them a big favor and get himself killed sometime in the next twenty-four hours. The insurance proceeds would be sufficient to provide for the kids' college expenses, and Liz could sell the house to provide for her own needs. He hadn't done badly for his family, all told. . . .

Oddly, these reflections had a calming effect on Abbot's nerves. If he was prepared to think of himself as a dead man, he certainly didn't have to fear for his life. And if the books were cleared at home, he was free to deal with the task at hand. Whether he lived or died was a matter of little consequence. What really mattered was Jeremy's safety and the survival of his manuscript. It was—it had always been—the one cause Abbot could commit himself to, and he committed himself to it now with renewed fervor as he turned to the second letter.

Inside the emblazoned envelope there was a handwritten letter covering two sheets of hotel stationery and a third sheet of graph paper, which seemed to be some sort of hand-drawn map. The letter was dated April 27, just three days ago, and looking ahead to the end Abbot saw that it was signed by Marguerite Pajorfsky. He read:

Dear Professor Abbot,

I had hoped to see you when I came to Breiburg to collect my late husband's belongings, but they told me you had gone to Berlin for a conference. I am writing this letter and mailing it before I return to Poland so that I can say certain things I would not dare to put into a letter from my tragic homeland. I am sure you can understand why.

Before he died, Mikos mentioned your name to me as someone who might be recruited to the cause, and I learned from his colleagues that you were the one who found his body and reported his murder to the police. I thank you for any kindness you may have shown my poor Mikos during the last minutes of his life and for your effort to see that justice was done. Sadly, Mikos will never lie in a marked grave where his family can visit him, but we shall revere his memory all the same. He was a patriot, and a very good man. . . .

At this point there were several stains, perhaps from teardrops, on the letter, and the word *man* was slightly blurred, as if Mikos's species might have been in some doubt. The letter continued:

Those who killed my husband went through his room and removed all his personal papers and research notes. However, in his office at the university I found the enclosed, hidden in one of his books. Because Mikos told me something of his work for the Liberation, I know it must be important, but I do not know to whom I should give it and I cannot take it back to Poland with me. Therefore, I am sending it to you, in the hopes you will know what to do with it, or to whom it should go.

Again, many thanks for your kindness to my dear husband and wishing you well, I am yours, most sincerely, heartbroken but filled with hope for the liberation of my homeland.

Marguerite Pajorfsky

Abbot examined the sheet of graph paper and saw from the scale at the top of the page that 1 centimeter on the map equaled 0.5 kilometer; therefore the total area represented was not large, running 19 kilometers north to south, 16 kilometers east to west. On such a scale, there were no geographic features he could recognize, though he guessed that the jagged line penciled darkly across the graph might represent an important border—possibly that between East and West Germany. If so, the map showed a strip of borderland of some 300 square kilometers.

There were other lines, which probably stood for roads or foot trails, and some wiggly lines in blue ink, which were clearly rivers.

Shaded patches seemed to indicate areas of wooded land, and the rugged contour of the terrain was suggested by a variety of short, semicircular strokes. Only one village was shown on the map, and it was labeled only as *Dorf,* whereas nearby a series of rectangles seemed to mark the walls or fortifications of a square marked *Schloss.*

Great, Abbot thought. We've got a village and a castle somewhere within twelve kilometers of the East German or Czech border; there must be several hundred of those!

There was one other interesting feature on the map: a system of parallel dotted lines, punctuated by occasional circles. Each circle was numbered, one through eight, and the network extended from a wooded, hilly area just north of the *Schloss* to a final circle well to the east of the thick dark line. The dotted lines were interrupted in places by slash marks or large *x*'s, yet after a moment's study Abbot saw that—supposing the dotted lines to indicate a system of underground tunnels—one could get from one side of the frontier to the other without going above ground.

It was Mikos Pajorfsky's prehistoric mine—the escape route he and Greta had been exploring on their expeditions throughout the winter. Now, if only he knew where in hell along the frontier it might be!

Abbot got out his road map of Germany and spread it open on the desk. None of the features detailed on Pajorfsky's map were likely to show up at this larger scale, but Abbot ran his eye along the border looking for possible regions. Since there was only one village in an area of some three hundred square kilometers, the population was usually sparse for cozy, crowded Germany. It also had to be an area both hilly and forested, with at least one road passing within ten kilometers of the border. Abbot checked the Hartz mountains first; then, reflecting that the landscape he'd glimpsed was somewhat less rugged, he lowered his gaze to the Rhön uplands, east and south of the city of Fulda. He noticed that there was an Autobahn which should carry one to the region from Frankfurt in something under three hours. East of Fulda to the border the country seemed quite sparsely populated.

Abbot's map showed a quantity of tourist attractions, including certain castles and ruins. He began checking these throughout the Rhön and found several candidates for the *Schloss* on

Pajorfsky's map. He crouched over to read the fine print which spelled out their names: Bieberstein, Auersberg, Hirschwald, Dunkelheim, Riesenschatten . . . Abbot stopped. *Riesenschatten?* He reached for his German-English dictionary and quickly confirmed his suspicion that the word translated to "giant's shadow"—an unusual name for a castle. Often these old castles took their name from some historical event or some striking feature of the local landscape. And hadn't he seen—?

Growing excited, Abbot turned to his *Guide to Germany,* a comprehensive reference book Liz had given him as a going-away present last January. The book had an extensive section on castles, and under Riesenschatten Abbot found an entry which he scanned eagerly:

235. Northern Bavaria, eastern Rhön, 35 k. north from Schweinfurt. Hereditary home of the von Klarbach family, not currently open to the public except by special arrangement with the *Graf,* Franz von Klarbach. A portion of the castle, in ruins, dates from the 12th century. Another portion, in which the family maintains a summer residence, is a striking example of the 19th-century gothic revival. The chapel (15th-century) has a fine set of gold candlesticks and medieval icons from the eastern provinces. Beneath the old castle lies the family crypt, where the Klarbach princes, legendary in the region for their warlike spirit and their cruelty, are entombed. Martin Luther is said to have preached a sermon here in 1543, and both Schiller and Goethe were guests at the castle during the long tenure of "Albert the Enlightened." The castle takes its name from a peculiar rock formation on the summit of the hill on which it stands, which throws a distinctive shadow on the adjacent ridge. According to local legend, a 12th-century Klarbach, cursed by the bishop of Fulda for his bloodthirsty ways, has been forever imprisoned in the rock.

Abbot put down the guidebook with a sense of triumph. The little nobleman was Franz von Klarbach; the site of their first meeting, if not in the castle itself, was close enough to have provided Abbot with his glimpse of the famous shadow. And since Pajorfsky's map showed a tunnel, which terminated in East Germany, within ten kilometers of the castle, Abbot knew now where

Jeremy Sawyer would spend his first night in the West. Like Franz, he would sleep in the Giant's Shadow.

Abbot dressed quickly and put some clean clothes in a duffel bag. Should he wait for Kohl and Morrison or go ahead on his own? Some intuition told Abbot not to wait. He had a number he could call if, after having talked to the *Graf*, he decided to let Kohl know where to find him. It was only fair to Franz, whom he now saw as his protector, not to bring the CIA down on him without warning, and there was no telling what Roland Kohl's real purpose in all this might be.

He was still debating the matter, however, when his doorbell made its harsh ring. Abbot jumped as if someone had shot at him through the window. He put Greta's Luger into his bag, along with several rounds of ammunition. Pajorfsky's map went into one pocket, his road map into another. He left the apartment and went quickly down the stairs to the last landing above the lobby, where, crouching down, he could see James Morrison at the front door.

What the hell? It was only nine o'clock. Had Kohl's plane come in early, or was there some change in plans? Abbot watched as Morrison gave the bell another ring and then, having made up his mind about something, took out a set of keys. Much to Abbot's surprise, one of Morrison's keys opened the lobby door. Morrison entered and made for the stairs.

Abbot retreated hastily to the second floor, where he slipped into a small closet used for cleaning supplies. He heard Morrison's firm, unhurried step pass his closet and continue toward the third floor. Chances were that Morrison also had a key to Abbot's room; if he went in he'd see a cup of coffee, still warm, on the counter. He would see the letter from Pajorfsky's widow on the desk and know that Abbot had come upon a clue.

Abbot left the closet and went quickly down the stairs, glad he'd chosen a pair of rubber-soled shoes. Nearing the front door, it occurred to him that Morrison could have left Kohl or someone else to watch the house from the street. He crossed the lobby to the lounge, which had a set of sliding doors looking out on the back garden. Several residents of the guesthouse had appropriated the patio for a bit of Sunday morning sunbathing, but their eyes were covered with towels and they didn't see Abbot slip by them on his way to the shrubbery that screened the rear of the house from the street.

Abbot waited in the bushes until he was sure the coast was clear, then jumped the drainage ditch, ran across the street and into the orchard. He scurried beneath the fragrant trees until he reached the parking lot, where he'd left Greta's car. He made sure the car wasn't being watched, then slipped along the driver's side and unlocked the door. The interior still harbored Greta's distinctive scent—sharper than the blossoms in the orchard—and Abbot was inspired to bolster his nerve with a little fantasy. "Okay kid," he said, turning to the empty bucket seat beside him, "let's see how fast this old crate of yours will go!"

15

Despite an alarming tendency to shudder at its higher speeds, the old crate did pretty well, and Abbot was driving through the Rhön hills southeast of Fulda before noon. He came down into a long valley between two steep and heavily wooded ridges. The black soil along the river had recently been plowed, but aside from a few sheds Abbot saw no human habitation until he reached the village of Klarbach at the valley's eastern terminus. High above the village, the slate-gray fragments of an ancient set of fortifications protruded from the green slopes. Higher still, against the bright blue sky, Abbot saw the stark outline of the castle's tower.

He drove through the village, past a succession of tall, narrow, half-timbered houses. Near the river he found a lovely old *Gasthaus,* its darkly stained façade brightened by window boxes burgeoning with pink and red geraniums. Abbot parked the car and entered the restaurant. He chose a table on the sunny riverside terrace, where he could look up at the castle high on its hill. A young waitress in a peasant's blouse and girdle came to take his order.

"Ein Glass Bier, bitte—Wurst und Salat." And then, before the waitress could depart, he asked in German if it were possible to visit the castle on the hill.

She shook her head sadly. The castle was no longer open to the public—it was *"ganz privat."*

Abbot expressed regret; he told the girl he had come a considerable distance to see it.

The waitress looked at him shyly. "Yes, you are an American, I think."

"Ah, you speak English," Abbot said. "Tell me, I've heard such wonderful things about Schloss Riesenschatten and its collection of icons. Isn't there some way I could arrange a tour? Through the *Graf,* perhaps?"

"I do not think so, *mein Herr.* The castle is never open when the *Graf* and his family are here."

"Oh? Is the *Graf* here now, then?"

"Yes, but not his family. They are in Würzburg, I think. There are several children who go to school there."

"Your English is very good," Abbot said.

"Thank you." She gave a little curtsy and went to place his order.

Abbot sat looking up at the castle. If only there were some way to send a message to the *Graf* that wouldn't be intercepted by Brian Hedge. Maybe Kohl was wrong about Hedge, or maybe he had intentionally misled Abbot, but it was better, Abbot had decided, to take no chances. First he wanted to tell Franz everything he knew, everything that had happened to him since their last meeting. Perhaps the little nobleman could make some sense of it all that Abbot couldn't.

The waitress came back with his beer. *"Entschuldigung,"* Abbot said, "I wanted to ask—there are supposed to be some interesting Bronze Age digs in this region. Can you tell me anything about that?"

"Digs?"

"You know, places where they dig up old things from the past—bones, pottery, weapons, that sort of thing."

"Ach so, eine Grabstätte?" She looked a little horrified, as if Abbot had confessed to certain ghoulish pastimes. Then the light dawned: "Ach, you are *Archäologe,* yes? We have had many come here over the years, but not so much now. There is *eine Höhle*—what would you say in English, a cave? It was once *ein Grabmal*—a tomb, yes? But it is also on the *Graf*'s land and closed to the public."

Abbot could tell the girl was genuinely sorry to be of so little help. He imagined that the villagers would have been glad for a tourist attraction like the castle or the ancient mines to highlight Klarbach's picturesque charm. With his friends at the institute,

Abbot had visited many medieval ruins and restorations, but never had he come across a village so authentic and relatively unspoiled, yet so suggestive of the romantic, fairy-tale Germany most tourists wanted to see.

The waitress was about to depart when she turned abruptly back to Abbot and, leaning confidentially over his table, said, "The *Graf,* I am afraid he is a little—" and she made the circular motion with her index finger at her temple which universally signifies an addled intellect.

Abbot looked up at the castle with a new anxiety. Was it possible he had misjudged the little nobleman, or could it be that the man he had talked to was not, in fact, Franz von Klarbach? Perhaps the *Graf*'s local reputation served some well-thought-out purpose; for instance, if one were exploring an ancient copper mine, one might need certain pieces of equipment, local laborers or technicians. Such a project might go on for some time, and the only way it could proceed so close to the border without attracting unwanted attention on the other side, Abbot reasoned, would be if it seemed a harmless bit of amateur archaeology by some local quack. Nonetheless, Abbot was not greatly reassured by the young woman's impudent characterization of the *Graf.*

The waitress brought his bratwurst and potato salad, and Abbot ate quickly, forcing the food over the lingering soreness of his throat. He left the restaurant and returned to the car. There were no signs marking the way to the castle, but Abbot chose a narrow, winding road and took it out of the village, up the steep hillside and through a dense forest of pines and freshly foliaged hardwoods. Greta's little sports car had begun to sputter, its heat-gauge needle rising into the danger zone, when Abbot spotted a modern chain link fence zigzagging through the trees. Barbed wire was strung along the top of the fence. Another turn in the road and he found himself confronted by a reenforced gate, which wore the predictable sign "PRIVAT—EINTRITT VERBOTEN." Beyond the gate there was a small gatehouse; a stony-faced guard watched through the window as Abbot backed the car around before the gate.

Somehow, he didn't much care for his chances of talking his way past that guard. Nor did he want to entrust the guard with a message for the *Graf.* He would have to find some other means of entry.

Heading back down to the village, Abbot came to an intersection and stopped to check Pajorfsky's map. Yes, he remembered correctly: This road skirted the hill on which the castle stood and climbed an adjacent ridge. It might at least give him another vantage point from which to reconnoiter.

He followed the road and eventually reached the treeless summit of the ridge just south of the castle's hill. He pulled off the road and got out of the car, taking a pair of binoculars he'd found beneath the seat. All around the summit stretched a hazy blue-green panorama of hills and valleys beneath a brilliant midday sky. Several small white clouds sailed complacently westward. A breeze blew along the ridge, rattling the dead grass of winter, combing the new grass of spring. Abbot heard birds twittering in a nearby thicket and saw a hawk circling with vigilant ease above the valley.

He walked along the road until he came into full view of the castle on the opposite ridge. A few paces off the road he found a firm, dry hummock on which to sit. He trained his field glasses on the castle and studied it carefully. As the guidebook had said, Schloss Riesenschatten consisted of two distinct structures. The newer building, set lower on the hill, was made of light gray, nearly white stone. Its roofs were sheathed with copper, which had oxydized to a lovely green, and there were many towers, turrets, spires and other ornamental excrescences after the manner of nineteenth-century romanticism. It could have been a castle in a child's fairy tale, full of charming princes and sleeping beauties, with maybe an ogre or two kept chained in the cellar for use on special occasions. The older structure, set just above it near the summit of the hill, displayed a strikingly different character. Built of dark, uncut stones, it was much larger than its successor—or would have been, before it started crumbling. Now only its shell remained, but those thick walls and blunt towers evoked the primitive arts of a much earlier age, a barbaric and brutal period when robber barons had ruled these German provinces with a ruthless abuse of power. Looking at the two castles, Abbot could easily imagine the progress of the von Klarbach princes over eight or nine centuries: from tribal warlords to feudal administrators, to

Renaissance dandies, to Romantic dreamers, to . . . what? How would one characterize the present master of the castle? Was he the man of honor and principle Abbot remembered, or the slightly wacko recluse the girl at the *Gasthaus* knew by his local reputation?

Perhaps, Abbot thought, he was a bit of both; the heir to a legacy such as the one he saw displayed on the neighboring hillside could hardly be anything but complex. Above the ruin of the old castle stood a shape more primitive still—the craggy outcropping of somber rock which had given the castle its romantic name. Though there was no sign at this time of day of the famous shadow, Abbot experienced an optical illusion of another sort as he ran his gaze along the slope of the ridge: What he saw was not a castle falling into ruin, but rock and stone—the basic elements of the earth itself—gradually submitting to the needs, the ideals, the vainglorious ambitions of the tiny yet tireless creatures who lived on its surface.

On a different day, under different circumstances, Abbot could have spent hours gazing upon this provocative scene. He could have lost himself in those questions of history and culture, human shame and human glory, which the castle seemed to represent. But today he had other concerns, and his scrutiny of the castle turned of necessity to the question of access. How could he get himself inside those walls?

What seemed at first a simple matter—go down the valley and up the other side—became increasingly problematic as Abbot studied the situation. Through the binoculars he could discern the silhouettes of sentries at several points along the ancient walls, and across the lower slopes he noted fences, wires, towers and antennas—evidence of an elaborate system of electronic surveillance. After a while he became convinced that certain rectangular patches of concrete in the old stone walls marked modern gun implacements, and shortly after this discovery he glimpsed a party of armed men, perhaps a dozen, setting out along the ridge toward some outlying post.

Schloss Riesenschatten, it was apparent, had been reborn as a modern fortress—a staging area for ELF's systematic subversion of the nearby frontier. Abbot couldn't see the strip of denuded land, the fences and towers that would surely mark the border between East and West, but he knew it was only a few kilometers away, and, for the first time, he gave serious thought to the risk ELF was taking by establishing an armed camp so close to such an intensely guarded border. Did they realize, these dilettante spy masters, that by challenging the territorial integrity of a neighboring state they were performing an act of war? Were they really willing to commit their government, and perhaps the entire Atlantic alliance, to so perilous a venture?

Abbot lowered his binoculars and watched a pair of hawks making lazy circles over the valley. What was it Kohl had said about those millionaire industrialists and their dreams of a reunified Germany? What if there were people in ELF crazy enough to risk a world war—or perhaps even to invite one—in order to achieve their goals?

Abbot scrambled to his feet and started back to the car, convinced now that he should have trusted Roland Kohl after all. It was an all-out confrontation between the Russians and ELF that Kohl was trying to avoid. Why had he been so slow to recognize the dangers? Abbot felt as though he had just looked around several improbable corners and down a long avenue of hypothetical possibility, and what he saw was literally unthinkable.

He was nearly back to his car when he heard another vehicle coming up the hill behind him. He ran the rest of the way, jumped in, fumbled the key into the ignition, pumped the gas pedal, and promptly flooded the engine. He was still torturing the starter when the jeep pulled up alongside. There were two young men in military fatigues in the front seat, one holding a rifle at the ready position. In the backseat sat Brian Hedge. He had a large revolver trained on Abbot's neck.

"Nice day for a drive, but aren't you a little far from home, old man?"

"I've got to see the *Graf,*" Abbot said. "Greta's been killed— she was gunned down last night. I was almost killed myself. I've got important information about Operation Nightingale, and I demand to see the *Graf*—at once!"

The Englishman seemed mildly amused by this outburst. "We know about Greta's death, and Otto Rinzelmann's, and we have a good idea of who's to blame. If you've led Roland Kohl here, Abbot, shooting's too good for you!"

"I haven't, I swear—but I've got a message from Kohl that the *Graf* needs to hear."

"A pack of lies, like as not," Hedge muttered, but he instructed one of the soldiers to ride with Abbot. "Follow us," he said, and signaled his driver to turn the jeep around.

After several tries, Abbot got the sports car started, and, prodded by his captor's rifle barrel, swung around in the narrow roadway. They set out for the castle.

Franz von Klarbach was even shorter than Abbot had remembered—so short that it was slightly embarrassing to stand over him and take his small hand. Yet the *Graf* seemed almost unaware of this difference in height and addressed Abbot with the confidence and authority of a man of stature.

"Sam, my friend—welcome to my home, and allow me to apologize for the armed guard that brought you here. The sentries reported someone on the ridge opposite, surveying the castle through binoculars, so of course we had to investigate. This is a particularly anxious time for us. Operation Nightingale has reached its final stages."

"So I understand," Abbot said. "That's why I need to talk to you—preferably alone."

There were three other men in the room to which he had been escorted by the armed soldier—a large and rather formal room, with a marble floor and fireplace, uncomfortable-looking antique furniture, and a set of French doors giving on a broad terrace. One of the men was Brian Hedge. Abbot did not know the other two.

"I think my advisers should be present," Franz said. "Let me introduce them. Hedge of course you know. This gentleman"—he pointed to the large, handsome, black man with graying hair—"is Major Joshua Marsh, USMC, retired. He is the commander of our security force here at the castle, as well as the chief commanding officer of ELF's antiterrorist brigade. Major Marsh has had a great deal of experience in protecting the lives of endangered VIPs—or in getting them killed, as the case may be."

Marsh stepped forward with a chuckle and a handshake. "Welcome to Schloss Riesenschatten, Professor. And let me assure you, I much prefer keeping them alive."

"And this is my personal secretary and very good friend, Günther Haas. Günther keeps track of my business interests and helps me to stay abreast of world developments. We've been together since our college days."

Günther also came forward to shake Abbot's hand, though with the stiffer air of a very formal and self-conscious German. A good deal taller than his boss, but less robust, Günther had a look both scholarly and businesslike. Behind thick-lensed glasses, his blue eyes had the myopic glitter of eyes which spent a considerable portion of each day before a computer screen.

"Welcome, Herr Abbot." He spoke in a rapid and heavily accented English. "We are glad to have you with us, though for your sake we were planning to wait a few days before sending for you."

"I couldn't wait till you sent for me," Abbot said, "because there are things you need to know. The Russians may have laid a trap for Sawyer and the Stork; they're hoping to use their deaths to discredit and destroy ELF. Someone inside your organization has been providing them with information on Operation Nightingale, and I think I know," he added, glaring at Hedge, "who that person is."

"Ruddy nonsense," Hedge responded. "He's been talking to Roland Kohl—and *that's* where the Russians have been getting their information!"

Franz frowned and sat down behind his immense desk. If it hadn't been for his manly face and graying hair, he would have looked like a small boy playing at his father's desk. "These *are* serious charges. Perhaps I should hear them, first of all, in private. I would rather not disturb the trust and harmony of our group, if I can allay Professor Abbot's fears. Will you all excuse us, please? You will, of course, be given the opportunity to answer any charges which may be made against you."

Abbot could tell that the three men were unhappy with this arrangement, but were used to obeying the *Graf's* orders without question. When they were alone, Franz offered Abbot a glass of sherry and a cigar. Abbot declined them both and launched into his account.

Half an hour later he had told Franz everything, right up to the moment when Abbot himself had had his frightening vision of the possible outcome of Operation Nightingale. "If I could have gotten to a phone, and gotten through to Kohl, I would have told him how to find you. You see, I'm really worried, Franz—I'm afraid this is going to lead to something none of us would like—something pretty awful."

Franz walked over to the French doors and studied the surrounding hills as he gave Abbot's account several minutes of silent thought. When he turned back, his face had not lost its friendly aspect. He seemed, if anything, more kindly disposed toward Abbot than ever.

"First of all, my friend, let me reassure you that we have no intention of provoking the Soviets to the point of war. Our aim, our strategy, has always been to weaken the Soviet regime internally—and to expose the tyrants before the court of world opinion. We acknowledge the horrors of nuclear war; that is simply not one of our options."

"And the reunification of Germany?"

Franz gave him a rueful smile. "Of course every German longs for the restoration of what we used to call the Fatherland, but most of us have recognized by now the futility of such dreams. We are, I hope you realize, *civilized* men and women, and we understand that ends, however noble, do not justify ignoble means."

Hearing Franz say it, Abbot was half persuaded that his fears were exaggerated. Of course, civilized people *had* done horrible things in the past. That was the mystery Germany presented to the human imagination.

"You may not want a war," Abbot said, "but Kohl thinks you've become so troublesome to the Russians that they'll want to put you out of business, any way they can. And this castle is sitting terribly close to the border—just inviting some sort of assault."

Franz looked off across the hills like a commander ready to defend his homeland. "Schloss Riesenschatten is a nearly-impenetrable fortress, my friend. It has stood firm for centuries against every manner of attack, and it is better defended now than ever. We have an armed guard of fifty-six highly trained professionals, equipped with an arsenal of the most sophisticated modern weapons. The Russians cannot bring their tanks and rocket launchers across the border, and the air space over our heads is, I can assure you, closely watched by NATO forces. If the

Russians want Jeremy Sawyer, they will have to come after him with a small, guerilla-type force, under cover of darkness, the hit-and-run tactics of the terrorists. And with such an attack I think we can deal."

"You might deal with it better," Abbot suggested, "if you let Roland Kohl put several hundred American troops into these hills on training maneuvers. That ought to make the Russians think twice."

Franz shook his head. "And risk the very confrontation you said you were afraid of? Besides, the Americans never bring their troops this close to the border—there's too much danger the other side might misinterpret their action and bring up troops of their own. You see, Sam, our proximity to the frontier is, in a sense, our best protection. Both sides must be very careful about what they do in an area such as this; there are long-standing rules and traditions which must be observed. Your intuitions when you looked upon the castle this afternoon were quite correct—we *are* an affront to the Soviets, and one they must bitterly resent. But there's very little they can do about it."

"Can't they find the entrance to your tunnel on the other side and close it up?"

"They may find it, of course, in time. But the mines that Pajorfsky explored for us are quite extensive—the region east of here is literally honeycombed with mines and caves. If they close one entrance, we shall open another. We shall be like mice to a barn—no way they can keep us out, or in."

"Then won't they send a cat, or an exterminator—someone like the Hangman?"

Franz looked sympathetically at Abbot. "Your wounds are quite severe, my friend. I'm sure they must be very painful, and that you had a most horrible experience. Yet permit me to say that we cannot allow ourselves to be intimidated by professional killers like the Hangman. Nor can we allow the Russians to import their barbarous methods of oppression into free societies."

"Of course not," Abbot said. "But right now I'm thinking of my friend's safety and the ultimate goal of Operation Nightingale, which is the publication of Jeremy's book. If Kohl is right, and if there is a traitor in your organization who's been feeding information to the KGB—"

Franz put his chin on his interlocked fingers and gazed hard for a moment at the desktop. "I am not yet convinced by what you've told me that there *is* a traitor in our organization or that he is our old friend, Brian Hedge. I will talk to Hedge, of course, but, as you yourself have observed, Kohl's 'evidence' could be used against Kohl himself. I do not see how I can violate the very specific instructions of the Stork and allow this American anywhere near our enterprise. Besides, ELF has always taken special pains to maintain its independence; we want no help from the CIA or any other government agency."

"Then," Abbot said, "I've got one last suggestion. Move Jeremy Sawyer to Switzerland as swiftly as possible, and announce his defection to the press immediately. As soon as they see him alive and well in Switzerland and telling his story to the world, the Russians will have to admit defeat. There will be no point in killing him then, and no hope of using his death to embarrass ELF."

"Yes," Franz said, "we had planned all along to transfer Sawyer to Switzerland within a day or so, and to arrange a press conference for him in Geneva or Basel as soon as he felt ready. But there have been, I am afraid, complications."

"Complications?" Surely there had been enough of those already.

"Yesterday a group of Swiss and German businessmen were taken hostage by Arab terrorists in Beirut. Negotiations are under way through Syria and other Arab countries friendly to Moscow for their release. Theoretically, this incident has nothing to do with Operation Nightingale, but both the Swiss and the German governments have asked us not to announce Sawyer's defection publicly until the hostages have been freed. And the Swiss have told us that they cannot grant Sawyer political asylum until their hostages are released. Nobody wants to embarrass the Soviets while asking for their cooperation in Beirut."

Abbot sank back in his chair with a groan.

"I'm sorry, Sam," Franz went on, "but it looks as though we'll have to keep Sawyer here and under wraps until this other crisis has been resolved."

"I thought," Abbot said bitterly, "you guys operated independently of any government."

"There are sixteen innocent lives at stake, my friend. Bonn cannot tell us what to do in this situation, but they have asked for our restraint, and the Ruling Council of ELF has agreed. Jeremy Sawyer shall remain my guest until we have clearance from the Swiss and German governments to go ahead. Perhaps it is just as well that you found us when you did. I will count on your help when I explain this situation to Herr Sawyer. Your presence may mollify him, to an extent—perhaps the two of you can even get started on his book."

"You mean," Abbot asked, "that I'm a prisoner here, as well?"

Franz's voice become particularly gentle and reassuring. "Not a prisoner, my friend, but a guest. Of course we can't let you tell Roland Kohl where to find us, and from what you've said I gather the police are looking for you. How could you explain what happened on Saturday evening without telling them a good deal more than we want them to know? But I assure you, Sam, you'll find my hospitality no less warm for all of that. In fact, I'm quite looking forward to your company—yours and Jeremy Sawyer's. We shall have capital conversations, I'm sure."

Abbot looked around the formal, elegant room, with its marble floor and magnificent crystal chandelier. His gaze fell on the sherry decanter and glasses on the marble-topped table near the fireplace. "I think," he said, "I could use that drink, after all."

bbot was installed in a large, airy room on the third floor of the new castle, from which he could look out at the barrel-shaped tower and craggy battlements of the old. He was left alone for a time, to unpack, wash up and rest after his journey. At five-thirty a servant knocked on his door and told him the *Graf* would be pleased to see him in the courtyard, if he felt up to a tour of the grounds.

Thinking that it couldn't hurt to know his way around, Abbot said he would be right down.

Greta's Luger was still in his duffel bag, and he decided to leave it there for now. He put on a sweater and went down to the courtyard, where fountains splashed and sparkled in the sun, while tiers of spring flowers waved and nodded in the light breeze. Franz and a groom were waiting along the drive with two magnificent horses.

"I should have asked if you were a rider," Franz said. "I thought we might take our tour on horseback—the trails are rather muddy this time of year."

Abbot, who hadn't been on a horse since he was allowed to ride the sorry nags that came to town with the carnival each summer of his childhood, expressed some misgivings.

"This beast," Franz said, patting the neck of a chestnut mare, "is quite a gentle and well-trained creature. Hang onto the saddle horn and leave the rest to me."

"Fine," Abbot said and was helped to his seat by the groom. Fortunately, he had never had much trouble with heights, for he seemed extraordinarily far off the ground.

Franz mounted his horse, a white stallion, and was at once as tall as Abbot. With a few clicks of his tongue, he easily controlled both animals and took them across the courtyard at an easy gait.

To Abbot, it was rather like trying to keep one's balance on a surfboard—something else he'd never done—but he began to get a feel for the horse's motion. They left the courtyard and crossed the slope beneath the ruin.

"This hilltop has been in my family for over twelve hundred years," Franz said. "The first Klarbach received this land, and permission to fortify it, from Charlemagne. For centuries it marked an outpost of the Holy Roman Empire and guarded an important trade route into the eastern provinces. When the kings of Bavaria revolted against the Hapsburgs, the Klarbachs became virtual monarchs in this portion of the kingdom. They were a harsh and ruthless breed of men and they sucked the peasants dry. Which is why, even now, the country around about is so sparsely populated—no one wants to live in the giant's shadow."

"I understand one of your ancestors is supposed to be imprisoned in those rocks," Abbot said, pointing to the outcropping at the summit of the hill.

"Ah, that's Arnulf, the worst of the lot. Our family's version of Count Dracula. We'll get a chance to see his shadow a little later, when the sun sinks lower in the west."

Abbot looked off across the hazy blue-green hills. "It's beautiful country."

"Beautiful, yes—though it's had a tragic history. I've often wondered—what is it about the German character, what qualities did we bring from the forests of central Europe that made us such a violent and volatile people? Sometimes I think we are still a race of barbarians."

"The Germans I've met have all seemed pretty civilized to me," Abbot said. "Certainly more so than the Americans."

"Ah, but you don't really know us," Franz said. "You haven't seen us at our worst."

They rode into a plantation of tall pines and followed a bridle path through the sudden gloom. Abbot reflected that it was in a forest much like this one that his adventure first began, and he wondered aloud if they were still entirely safe.

"Yes, my friend," Franz said, "we are still within the perimeter of the castle's defenses. In fact, I have been preparing for a situation like this one ever since I inherited this piece of land. Even as a boy I speculated on how I might defend this ground, given the capabilities of modern warfare. It's been an interesting exercise—though of course I hope I won't have to use the devices I've installed. Over there, for instance, you see a hunting stand, left over from my father's time. You wouldn't guess that it contains TV cameras and listening devices which keep this forest under constant surveillance. Nor would you guess that just beneath this bridle path there are plastic explosives, which can be set off at the touch of a button from our command center back at the castle."

"Let's hope they don't mistake us for intruders," Abbot said.

"Don't worry, they won't. Look, over there"—they had come out of the pines and were cantering along the side of a ravine which dropped steeply down to the larger valley—"you see that cow shed on the opposite slope? It's true that the cattle grazing on that side of the ravine use the shed for water and shelter, but we also have machine guns mounted there, which can command this entire ravine. Tonight, we will have soldiers stationed there."

"For someone who abhors violence, you take a great deal of pleasure in these preparations," Abbot observed.

Franz was silent for a moment. He appeared to be seriously troubled by Abbot's comment, and finally he reined in both horses. The two men faced each other as their mounts moved skittishly on the brink of a sharp incline.

"Do you think I take *too* much pleasure in these matters, my friend?" Franz asked earnestly. "I must tell you, my wife takes a very dim view of these proceedings."

"Your wife knows about Operation Nightingale?"

"No details—she has never had security clearance from the Ruling Council, nor has she ever wanted to know more about ELF than it would be safe for her to know. Nevertheless, she has accused me of wanting to live out certain fantasies. . . ."

Abbot tried to keep his horse well back from the precipice. Franz's sudden change of mood reminded him of the young waitress's theory of the *Graf*'s behavior, and he tried to make his response as reassuring as he could. "Maybe that's what Operation Nightingale has become for all of us—a way to live out our private fantasies of one sort or another. Is there anything wrong with that?"

Franz's handsome face grew even graver. "Ah, but you see what a costly venture this has become. How many dead already? And now we have those hostages in Beirut to consider. . . . Is it really worth it, I wonder? Is your friend's book worth its cost in human lives?"

That was a good question, one Abbot certainly didn't know how to answer. How good did Jeremy's book have to be to justify the deaths of Greta, and Mikos Pajorfsky, and those others Abbot scarcely knew? Had any work of literature ever had such a bloody birth, and what was there about Jeremy's genius that seemed to cast darkness instead of light, that poisoned those it tried to heal?

"I think," he said to the *Graf,* "we've already made our commitment. All we can do now is push on to the end—and try to make sure our comrades haven't died in vain."

Franz held Abbot at the brink a moment longer. "You really cared for Greta, didn't you, my friend?"

"Yes, I did." Abbot was glad to say it.

"I want you to know, I was against using her as—well, as an inducement to insure your cooperation. I felt it was dishonorable to you both. But I see I needn't have worried on that score. You are not a superficial man."

Before Abbot could reply, the *Graf* led both horses back from the ravine, and they resumed their course along the hillside. Letting his mare follow the *Graf*'s stallion, Abbot reflected that he *had* been a superficial man for most of his life. But perhaps the events of the past two weeks had forced him to look a little deeper. He hoped so, because it would be something to cling to if everything else went wrong. As it probably would.

They completed their circuit of the hilltop and returned to the castle by another route. The sun, which had been in Abbot's eyes on the return trip, had just begun to touch the western ridge.

"Ah, it's nearly time for Arnulf to make his appearance," Franz said, giving the reins to his groom. "Come along, Sam, if you want the best view of the old ruffian. It's a bit of a climb, but I think we can make it."

They left the courtyard, crossed a narrow strip of garden, then ascended a short flight of steps to the base of the ruin. A narrow passageway through the thick outer wall took them into the courtyard of the old castle. A small wilderness had taken root among the piles of rubble and broken walls, and Abbot heard birds chirping in the tangled shrubs. The walls were hung with vines as if with festoons, and in several niches sizable trees had taken hold and were reaching skyward along the walls. The tall arched windows of the intact western wall showed the golden gaze of the sunset; otherwise the courtyard was already in twilight.

Franz led the way over uneven ground, past several craterlike depressions and open stairwells, to the base of the tower. A small door gave access to a spiral stairway, which was lighted only by an occasional slit in the three-foot-thick wall. Abbot had to grope his way, guided only by the sound of Franz's footsteps and the feel of damp, rough stones against his fingers. Then a light appeared above them, a circle of brightness that grew gradually brighter until it became a patch of blue sky. They emerged onto the parapet, and Abbot's breath—what was left of it after so long a climb—was snatched away by the tremendous, dizzying view. With the wind blowing hard from the east and the sun sinking low in the west, they seemed perched on the rooftop of the world.

"Off there," Franz said, pointing down a long misty valley, "is the East German border. And in those hills just to the north lies the entrance to our tunnel. Now, if you'll look over this way, at that curious formation of rocks on the summit of our own hill, you will observe my least admirable ancestor, Arnulf the Blasphemer."

Abbot looked, but the rocks themselves did not suggest a human shape.

"Arnulf was a huge man," Franz said, "with a ferocious temper and a voracious appetite for the sacking of monasteries. The bishop of Fulda threatened to excommunicate him for these transgressions, and Arnulf responded by throwing the bishop into his dungeon for a year or two. When the prelate was finally released, he fixed Arnulf with his angry gaze and said, 'Arnulf, since you have a heart of stone'"—it was clear that Franz was enjoying this impersonation—"'and since you have crowned yourself king of this mountain, I pray that God will strike you dead and imprison your spirit for all eternity in that rock!' Here the bishop pointed his mitre at the outcropping. A bolt of lightning came down from the clouds; it forked as it descended, one bolt shattering the rock into its present shape, the other killing Arnulf dead on the spot. It was said that his body was completely disintegrated by the blast, so that there was nothing left to bury—and do you know, it's a curious thing"—Franz's eyes twinkled—"but in the crypt just beneath us, where all the von Klarbachs are buried, there is no sarcophagus for Arnulf, nor have we been able to discover any of his bones."

"So presumably he's still locked up in his rock," Abbot said, smiling.

"Presumably. The local peasantry believed that as long as Arnulf remained in his rock, the von Klarbach family would prosper and the world would be a happy place—except where his shadow fell, of course. Beneath the giant's shadow there could be only gloom and misfortune."

"And if Arnulf should escape his prison?"

"Ah well. Then the castle itself will fall, and the house of Klarbach along with it, and the end of the world shall be at hand."

"The end of the world?"

"To the peasants, the world was an impossibility without the von Klarbachs to look after it. I daresay it will get along without us well enough, if the time should come. But now look over here—" and he turned Abbot in the opposite direction, so that he could see the shadow of the hill on which they stood as it fell across the wooded ridge directly to the east. "Do you see him? Crouching there with a club on his back? That's Arnulf—*that's* the giant's shadow."

"I see him," Abbot said, and for a moment the shadow was so convincing he felt compelled to look at the rocks once again.

"He can be seen," Franz said, "from a number of points along this ridge and down in the valley. When you first saw him, you were leaving the hunting lodge at the other end of the park. I thought we had very cleverly kept you from learning our whereabouts, but the giant's shadow gave us away."

Abbot thought that Arnulf looked more like a hulking Neanderthal than a medieval warlord. Or again, that silhouette could have been interpreted as the shadow of a modern soldier, his pack on his back and his rifle protruding over his shoulder. In any case, the giant certainly imparted a sense of menace to the lovely spring evening and tranquil landscape, and it intrigued Abbot to think that he had done so every sunset for centuries.

The sun was at the horizon. Abbot saw flocks of blackbirds whirling around the castle ramparts. One flock, the path of its flight like the sweep of a scimitar, passed across Arnulf's rock, and for a moment the giant was himself shadowed by the swarm of crying birds.

A light supper was served that evening in what the *Graf* called the lounge—a large, informal room on the first floor of the new castle, where off-duty members of Major Marsh's security force were allowed to shoot pool and watch television. Günther Haas introduced Abbot to a stout, bearded man with an imperious manner—Herr Doctor Spring, a cardiologist from Munich, whom Franz had brought in to examine Jeremy upon his arrival. Abbot noticed that Brian Hedge was not among the party, and he asked Günther if the *Graf* had spoken to the Englishman.

"Unfortunately, no. Herr Hedge went out to inspect the castle's defenses this afternoon and has not returned."

"Well, I guess that proves it," Abbot said. "He's flown the coop."

"Proves what, may I ask?" Günther's blue eyes peered skeptically at Abbot through his thick glasses.

"That what I told the *Graf* this afternoon was correct. Hedge is the informer."

Günther took off his glasses and cleaned them with a handkerchief. Without magnification, his eyes were mild and slightly moist. "Herr Abbot, I am not sure what sort of information you brought us this afternoon, but I can assure you that Brian Hedge is no spy for the KGB. He has been with us for many years and he has been in close personal contact with the Stork. In fact, he is one of the few people in our organization who has met the Stork, face to face, and who knows his true identity. Do you think it likely that the Stork could have continued his work so successfully, if Herr Hedge were a Soviet agent?"

"Then why has he disappeared, if he has nothing to be afraid of?"

The *Graf*'s secretary smiled. "Ah, I did not say he had nothing to be afraid of. We all have many things to fear, Herr Abbot, especially tonight. But Brian Hedge has a way of coming and going which is somewhat uncanny. I expect we will see him again, when he wants us to."

Abbot poured himself another glass of the *Graf*'s good bottled beer. "So you've been working for Franz since your college days, is that right?"

"It is," Günther said, and Abbot sensed that he disapproved of Abbot's free use of the *Graf*'s first name.

"You two must get along very well. The *Graf* must be a good man to work for."

"He is an excellent employer. Also a close personal friend."

"And how do you feel about his involvement in ELF? You're not worried that the *Graf* has, perhaps, gotten in a bit over his head?"

Günther's blue eyes nearly bit at Abbot through the thick glasses. "Have you come here to sow dissension among us, Herr Abbot? Now you wish me to criticize the politics of my employer?"

"Don't get me wrong," Abbot said. "I like Franz—I like him a lot. But I don't think he's cut out for this cloak-and-dagger business. He's too introspective, too much a man of principle. He seems to have a guilty conscience about something and this is his way of offering recompense. Also, he likes defending his castle—it makes him feel like one of his illustrious ancestors."

Günther gave Abbot a guarded smile. "You are a perceptive man, Herr Abbot. Of course all Germans have a guilty conscience these days—this goes without saying. We are perhaps too much preoccupied with our guilt, but the world shows no signs of allowing us to forget it. In the *Graf*'s case, he is thinking of centuries of oppression and exploitation, carried on by his family, with this castle as their stronghold. Perhaps it is important to him that Schloss Riesenschatten shall at last be used for a just cause. Both the *Gräfin* and I have urged him not to become personally involved in the activities of ELF, but to no avail. He is, as you can see, quite a headstrong man."

The *Graf* was at this moment conferring with Major Joshua Marsh at the other end of the table. After a period of intense private dialogue, the two men rose and shook hands. Marsh went off and Franz began to work his way along the table, talking to his men, patting their shoulders, showing his concern for each one of them. At length he reached Abbot's end of the table.

"We rendezvous with the Stork in just over one hour," he said.

"I've decided that you may come along with us, Sam, if that's your wish. At your own risk, of course. We leave from the main gallery in ten minutes."

"I'll be there," Abbot said.

He went up to his room for a jacket, decided to bring Greta's Luger and slipped it into his pocket. He was beginning to feel rather naked without its comforting weight, its hard surface there to greet his fingertips whenever he felt uneasy.

Franz and the doctor—who looked like a young Orson Welles in his black trench coat—were waiting for him in the gallery. "We won't be leaving the castle by the main gate," Franz explained. "My ancestors had an escape route for times of siege, which we've refashioned to our purposes. If you've never toured a chamber of horrors, gentlemen, you'll get a first-rate exhibition along the way."

They descended a flight of stairs to a large wine cellar, then followed a damp, echoing tunnel cut into the bedrock of the hill. They passed through an ancient dungeon and torture chamber, where the von Klarbachs of old had administered justice to the fortunate subjects of their realm. Pointing to the remnants of a horrid machine made of iron, wood, and rotting leather, the *Graf* remarked, "An interesting way of collecting taxes, so I've been told. I leave it here as an incentive to pay my own."

They paused before a heavy iron door. "We must pass now," Franz said, "through the family crypt, which is located just beneath the courtyard of the old castle. In the interests of historical authenticity, I haven't electrified this portion of the route—you'll need these lanterns."

He lit three small kerosene lanterns and gave one each to Abbot and the doctor. Then he opened the heavy door, and Abbot noticed a peculiar odor in the damp, cool air which escaped the crypt—the reek, perhaps, of decaying von Klarbachs. Holding their lanterns at arm's length, they surveyed a huge vault, its arched walls and thick columns carved from the basalt core of the hill. Off the central chamber there were numerous, low-ceilinged alcoves fenced off by iron grills.

"I hope you don't mind a few bones," Franz said, as their light began to reveal the grisly contents of these alcoves. "It's the custom here in Europe, you know, to lay our dead in these subterranean rooms. When all the caskets and sarcophagi are taken, the bones of an earlier age must be removed to make room for the newcomers. Of course the bones must be saved, in accordance with the Christian faith, for their resurrection on the Last Day. And so you have a spectacle such as this—"

Shining his lantern into one of the unfenced alcoves, Franz exposed shelf upon shelf of disembodied skulls, glaring out at them with black sockets, grinning their horrible grins. For an instant Abbot imagined himself confronted by a mirrored multiplicity of Hangmen, but these were real skulls, ancient and yellowed and about as dead as anything could be. On the lower shelves, Abbot saw stacked piles of bones—thighs and ribs and pelvises, toes and fingers, all neatly sorted and awaiting the call of Gabriel's horn, when they might suddenly find themselves restrung on a human frame and decently clothed in flesh.

"You'll notice," Franz said, "that each skull is numbered, and some are adorned with flowers, crosses, and other religious emblems. In the castle library there is an immense registry which supplies a name for each numbered skull. When the castle was still open to tourists, this was the most popular part of the tour, but I felt rather bad about it, you know—as if I were displaying my mother's corpse."

"And were all these people von Klarbachs?" the doctor asked, greatly intrigued by the spectacle.

"A few loyal retainers may have received the honor of burial in the family crypt," Franz said, "but they're mostly kin. We were a large family and we've been living and dying on this hilltop for twelve centuries."

Abbot had the uneasy feeling that the skulls were watching them with intelligent interest, perhaps even a touch of ancestorly skepticism: "Who are these people, and why are they all so puny?"

They continued through the crypt, which was surprisingly extensive, and came at last to another steel door. The tunnel beyond this door was well lit and made of concrete that seemed to have been recently poured. It led, after a lengthy downward course, to a large underground garage at the bottom of the hill. There were several military vehicles parked in this garage, and Major Marsh and a company of six armed men had already arrived.

"You and the doctor will ride with me," Franz said to Abbot. "Major Marsh and his men will lead the way."

A jeep and an ambulance—both apparently U.S. Army surplus—were lined up at the outer door. When everyone was aboard, the lights were extinguished and the door rolled silently up. The vehicles drove without headlights into the blackness of the forest night.

Perhaps the driver of the lead car had infrared glasses or some other means of keeping to the road. At the wheel of the jeep, Franz followed the dim red brake lights of the ambulance. They proceeded slowly along a dirt track, hemmed in by the dense growth of the forest. Looking up, Abbot saw the stars shining brightly in the narrow opening between the pines.

"I will tell you a little about the place where we are headed," Franz said. "The natural caves and man-made catacombs we'll be visiting were discovered in the early nineteenth century and partially excavated at that time. The artifacts that were uncovered suggested a Bronze Age settlement, probably Celtic, dating from the first or second century A.D. However, there were also traces of a Stone Age community on the same site, going back perhaps ten or fifteen thousand years. There has always been a legend in this region that a race of people, not quite human, once ruled these hills. In some versions they're described as fairies or elves; in others they are giants or strange mythological monsters, half man and half beast. Some people say the von Klarbachs were descended from such a race, which might explain their often-inhuman ways.

"As for the copper mine, which opens off the catacombs—its existence was never suspected until my father, the former *Graf,* converted the site to a hiding place for Jews during the Nazi regime. As an aristocrat, my father held a commission in the German army, but he never joined the Nazi party, and he was horrified by what he learned of the death camps. He became one of a small group of German officers who took it upon themselves to rescue as many Jews as possible and help them escape to Switzerland. It was in outfitting the catacombs as a temporary shelter that he stumbled on to the ancient copper mine. Still, we had no idea how large it was, or that it might actually extend into East

Germany, until Mikos Pajorfsky began his explorations. Mikos completed his map just a few days before his death."

"And is this the first time the mines have been used to smuggle refugees across the border?" Abbot asked.

"The very first. However, if Operation Nightingale is successful, there is no reason why we can't bring many more in by this means, or send our agents into East Germany."

Abbot did not reiterate his belief that the Russians probably already knew about the Stork's new escape route. He was beginning to wonder if Kohl's fears weren't imaginary—or calculated deceptions.

They drove for nearly half an hour without leaving the forest, and Abbot guessed they were very close to the border when the lead vehicle came to a halt. The soldiers gathered silently into formation at the side of the road, their rifles at the ready. Abbot saw they were in a canyon of sorts: a wooded slope on one side of the road, a steeper, rockier ridge on the other. He could hear water running over the rocks and it was this stream bed they followed up the side of the hill. Major Marsh and his troops led the way; Franz, the doctor, and Abbot followed. It was rough going in the dark and Abbot slipped and fell to his knees in the muck. When he got to his feet he seemed suddenly alone, surrounded by an intense and impenetrable darkness. He was close to panic when Franz spoke softly just to his left: "Sam—over here!"

Abbot followed the voice and found a crevice in a rocky wall, wet with trickling water. He wedged himself in and squeezed through the narrowest part, rough wet rock against his cheek and pinching his shoulders. Just when he thought he was going to get hopelessly stuck, he broke out into a larger chamber. Several of the soldiers had lanterns and Abbot could see a much larger cavern opening off this anteroom. The flickering lights made shadows dance around stalagtites and stalagmites. Abbot heard dripping water and smelled the clean, cold smell of the earth.

"The ancient mine follows an underground river," Franz said. "We've bypassed most of the old excavations and the catacombs my father knew about; this is the part Mikos opened up for us. We're very close to the border here—that's why we couldn't show a light."

Abbot looked down a long passageway. "Are we going across?"

"No, we wait here," Franz said. "Earlier this evening two of our men went ahead to meet the Stork and his client and to guide them through. They should be emerging from that tunnel straight ahead of us"—he checked his watch—"any time now."

Abbot sat down on a flat-topped rock to wait. The soldiers had taken up positions around the cavern. Everyone sat quietly, their eyes fixed on the black hole in the cavern wall. It was like waiting, Abbot thought, for a miracle. Like watching for the resurrection of Lazarus, or the recovery of Persephone from the Underworld. He wondered if there were any gods to which he might pray for Jeremy's safe delivery from *his* underworld of oppression and silence. *Were* there any gods who were known to be particularly fond of poets? Abbot wished he had saved some tiny scrap of his childhood faith which he could call upon now, but like most men of his generation he had to face situations such as these with only a superstitious notion of something called "luck" to keep his hopes alive.

Presently, when he saw a light in the tunnel, he couldn't be sure his strained eyes weren't playing tricks on him. He turned to Franz, who saw it also. "Here they come," he whispered.

No one moved forward to greet the new arrivals. Abbot watched as the light grew brighter, became in fact several lights carried by a party of several people, who moved slowly along the tunnel. As they grew closer still, Abbot saw that two of the men seemed to be carrying something between them, something like a stretcher. A little closer and he saw it *was* a stretcher, with a body on it. Two more figures, a man and a woman, followed along behind. The two men, in uniforms that identified them as the *Graf*'s soldiers, carried the stretcher into the large cavern and set it down. The doctor started forward with Abbot at his heels. The white, stricken face on the stretcher belonged to Jeremy Sawyer.

"Good God, is he dead?" Abbot cried.

Jeremy's eyes flickered open; their shadowy gaze fastened on Abbot. "Hello, old bean. Not dead, as you can see, but considerably incapacitated by a recent spell of angina. These lads were kind enough to . . . I say, have we reached the other side?"

"You have," Franz said, kneeling down on Jeremy's other side. "Welcome to the Bundesrepublik, Herr Sawyer. I am Franz von

247

Klarbach, and this is Doctor Spring from Munich who will tend to your needs—"

The doctor was already listening to Jeremy's heart with his stethoscope. He took it from his ears and spoke rapidly to Franz in German.

"What's he say?" Jeremy asked. "Will I live to see Switzerland?"

"He's going to give you an injection," Franz said. "We have oxygen in the ambulance and a room equipped for cardiac care in the castle. You shall be all right, Herr Sawyer, now that your long and arduous journey is over." He looked around. "And where is the Stork?"

"He and his men left us as soon as we found the tunnel entrance," Jeremy said. "I should introduce my friends, Herr von Klarbach."

Franz looked up at the young couple who stood waiting at the mouth of the tunnel, packs on their backs and anxious, uncertain smiles on their broad, attractive faces.

"Yes, please do. We were not aware that you were bringing others with you."

"Katya and Dmitri," Jeremy said. "They are brother and sister—two talented young writers who decided to escape with me. They're very shy and don't speak much English—much German, either—but they're serious artists. Russia is no place for them—they need to see something of the world."

Franz looked hard at Jeremy's protégés, who seemed ready to bolt back into the tunnel at the first unfriendly word. "They are welcome, of course," he said at last, "though it is our policy to screen all those we bring over the border very carefully, Herr Sawyer. They will have to be searched and interrogated."

"Sure, sure," Jeremy said. "I'll explain it to them." He called the girl to his side and spoke to her in Russian. Her dark, frightened eyes leapt from Jeremy to Franz to Abbot, then back to Jeremy. Then she leaned over and put a kiss on Jeremy's mouth.

Jeremy saw Abbot staring at him as his stretcher was lifted. "Don't look so shocked, old bean. Katya and I are getting married, once I've had my operation. Good to see you, Sam. We'll have time to chat later, I trust."

Abbot watched as the stretcher was carried off. My God, the same old Jeremy. He still needed his entourage of admirers, his eager little groupies, though the escape from Russia could only have been complicated by their presence. Abbot had trouble believing the girl was any kind of writer at all. As for her brother, he looked more like a soccer player or a gymnast than a poet. He wondered if Jeremy had fallen prey to that oldest of pedagogical follies—the bestowal of imaginary talents upon an intellectually inferior child-mistress.

Franz gave instructions to Major Marsh concerning these two, and then they exited, one by one, from the cave. As he came out into the riverbed, Abbot heard an owl hooting from the wooded ridge across the canyon. To his ears it seemed a particularly derisive and ironic hoot, as if the bird were amused by the nocturnal prowlings of an inferior species. It struck him, as he groped his way back to the jeep, that they had all gone to an awful lot of trouble to facilitate a May-December romance, and he wondered what Patricia would think of her ex-husband's latest escapade.

17

J eremy's first day in the West commenced quietly enough, with the gentle patter of rain on the castle roofs and windowpanes. Abbot pulled himself out of bed at nine and went to the window. The hills of the Rhön were blurred and softened by mist; the battlements of the old castle gleamed darkly in the rain. Down in the courtyard he observed a component of Franz's security guard—twelve men in battle-ready gear—as they received their orders from Major Marsh and left for their posts.

Abbot recognized the symptoms of a major hangover. He had sat up late drinking cognac with Franz and Günther as they awaited a complete medical report on Jeremy's condition. The report, when it came, was inconclusive; without an angiogram and other tests which could only be performed in a hospital, Doctor Spring could not determine the extent of damage already done to Jeremy's heart or the likelihood of his recovery. However, Jeremy's heartbeat was strong and regular; his condition had stabilized, and he was resting comfortably. It was after three when Abbot got to bed, but he thought the session had had one positive effect: The friendship between himself, his host, and his host's secretary, had been well cemented.

Abbot dressed and went downstairs in search of black coffee. A servant directed him to the morning room, where he found the *Graf* reading the newspapers over the remains of a light breakfast.

"Good morning, Sam. What may we bring you? Eggs? Ham? I

know the English like a big breakfast; what about the Americans?"

"I'll settle for some coffee just now," Abbot said. "Have you seen Jeremy this morning?"

"Indeed I have. He and his friends chose to breakfast in their rooms. I'm afraid Herr Sawyer is already upset with me. Could you have a word with him? He resents being kept prisoner in what he calls 'this damn pile of stones.' I'm afraid I rather lost my temper."

Abbot thought that Jeremy must have been unusually obnoxious to have overcome the *Graf*'s good manners. "I suppose," he offered, "he's anxious to get to Switzerland and to check into that clinic he told us about."

"Indeed. He seems to have developed quite a fantasy regarding the curative powers of this clinic. He also kept raving about some box you were supposed to have gotten for him in England. Do you have such a box?"

Great, Abbot thought. Now Jeremy will have something else to rave about—my incompetence. Well, he supposed he would have to own up to his failure sooner or later. He gulped down a cup of black coffee and set out for the suite of rooms in the west wing of the castle which Franz had assigned to his guests.

Katya opened the door to his knock. She was dressed in a flannel nightshirt, which, despite its simple and modest cut, gave Abbot a good idea of what Jeremy saw in his young mistress. Jeremy was sitting up in bed, smoking a cigarette and watching television. The program, Abbot saw, was an American situation comedy which had been popular in the seventies, something about the the trials and tribulations of a single woman pursuing a career at a midwestern television station. It was dubbed, of course.

"G'morning, Sam," Jeremy called. "Come join us—we're just catching up on the decadent preoccupations of my former countrymen. Bloody hard to follow in German, though—perhaps you can translate for us."

Abbot saw a breakfast tray on a table and he wondered, from the rumpled condition of the bedclothes, if the television program had really been a matter of major concern.

"Didn't the doctor tell you to quit smoking?" he asked.

Jeremy snorted. "*That* German horse doctor! What the hell does he know?"

"He's supposed to be a respected cardiologist, from a first-rate clinic in Munich."

"Big deal," Jeremy said. "I want the doctor we agreed upon. I want Hans Maienfeld."

"Franz explained the problem to you. The Swiss won't grant you political asylum as long as their hostages are being held in Beirut. And the Germans have asked us not to embarrass the Soviets—"

"Embarrass the Soviets!" Jeremy mocked. "I'll fucking well embarrass the fucking Soviets, and the fucking Americans, too. What do I care about those bloody hostages? I don't need these little creeps in ELF to set up my show—I can take care of it well enough myself. All I need is that box you picked up for me in England. Do you want to bring it around?"

Abbot sat down beside the bed. The irritable station manager was giving the sweet-tempered heroine a terrific bawling out.

"About that box," Abbot said.

Jeremy crushed out his cigarette and swung around to face Abbot head on. "You *do* have the box, don't you, Sam? You sent me the bloody signal!"

"I had the box, when I sent it," Abbot said, keeping his eyes on the TV screen. "A few hours later it was stolen."

"Stolen?" Jeremy almost shrieked. There was a long silence, during which the heroine gave the ill-tempered boss a well-deserved piece of her mind. Abbot idly wondered at the hysterical laughter these remarks evoked from the American audience, since they were delivered in German.

"Stolen by whom?" Jeremy asked in a quieter voice.

Abbot held up his bandaged hands and pointed to the strip of gauze across his throat. "I nearly lost my life for you, Jeremy. It was a Russian assassin they call the Hangman."

Jeremy seemed to recognize the name. "The Hangman? But he's . . . Who told you about this bloke, Sam? Was it Roland Kohl?"

"I heard about him from Kohl, and also from an ELF agent named Brian Hedge. I think you know Hedge as well, don't you, Jeremy?"

"I seem to remember the name. He was in the British Secret Service, wasn't he? Now he's in ELF?"

252

"He was, until some time yesterday afternoon," Abbot said. "When I showed up—they weren't going to tell me where they were keeping you—Hedge took off and hasn't been seen since. He's probably on his way to Moscow."

"To Moscow?" Jeremy seemed confused. "What's this got to do with my box? Goddamnit, Sam, I thought I could count on you—on you, of all people! Couldn't you have let me know the box was stolen?"

"I was unconscious in a hospital bed until two o'clock Saturday afternoon," Abbot said. "By then, I think, you were under way. The Russians released a story about your 'kidnapping' late Friday evening."

"Oh, bloody hell!" Jeremy said and stared for a time at the television screen.

Abbot looked around the room. Like all the rooms in the new castle, it was spacious, airy, elegantly decorated in eighteenth- and nineteenth-century antiques. On the ceiling there were angels alfresco, and on the further wall a large mural in the colorful, allegorical style of late romanticism. It portrayed the temptation of a knight in shining armor by several fleshy nymphs, who were partially submerged in a dark pool in a rather gloomy wood. The nymphs seemed to be urging the young knight to remove his armor and join them in the black water.

"Now everything's ruined," Jeremy said at last.

"Not everything," Abbot said. "I do have a contract for you, Jeremy. Sir Godfrey liked the two chapters. So did I. They were magnificent. I'm anxious to see the rest."

Jeremy looked at him resentfully, as if Abbot had forfeited his right to read any more of the precious manuscript. "How much did you get?" he asked finally.

Abbot sighed. Another disappointment. "The deal on subsidiary rights is very good. Excellent, in fact. You'll be making money off the book for years."

"And the advance?"

"Sixty-five thousand pounds."

Jeremy lay back and looked up at the ceiling, as if asking the cherubs in the plaster to carry him away. "I told you to *sell* the bloody book, not give it away," he said at last.

"I'm sorry, on the basis of only two chapters it was the best I could get. I guess you should have picked someone else as your errand boy, Jeremy—I seem to have failed you all around."

Jeremy crumpled his empty cigarette pack and tossed it across the room. "Yes, damn it, you have!"

"Well," Abbot said, getting up from the bedside, "there's only one thing I can say to you then, my friend, and that's *go to hell.*"

He stalked to the door and had his hand on the knob when Jeremy called, "Sam, for Chrissakes, forgive me. I've got a rotten temper—you know that, I always did."

"It's gotten worse," Abbot said, remaining at the door.

"Yes, well, when you know the whole story, old bean . . . I'm in a bit of a pickle, you see, without that box. Does Roland Kohl know I'm here?"

"We've done our best to keep him ignorant of your location. Apparently we've succeeded, or he'd be here by now."

"Then we've done one thing right, anyway," Jeremy said. "What about Pat? Was she—well, was she pleased at the news of my planned return?"

Abbot answered carefully. "She wasn't indifferent to it. She's rebuilt her life, Jeremy. She waited ten years for you, you know."

"She didn't suggest that she had taken anything from that box, did she? For safekeeping, perhaps?"

Abbot stared for moment. "Jeremy! What the hell's in that box that makes it so damn important?"

"I'll tell you about it," Jeremy said wearily, "but not just now, old bean. Give me a little time to think things over, would you? We had a beastly difficult journey. I kept myself going with these things"—he lifted a vial of nitroglycerine tablets, which were supposed to relieve angina pectoris—"and by telling myself that all my problems would be over once I got to West Germany. Now I see they've only just begun. But give me some time, and we'll talk. All right, my friend?"

It was hard to resist Jeremy when he called you his friend. "I'm not going anywhere," Abbot said. "None of us are."

"''Tis true; 'tis pity; and pity 'tis 'tis true,'" Jeremy said, waving weakly as Abbot backed out the door.

From the foot of the bed, Katya continued to stare at the television, transfixed, as if she had understood not one word of what had passed between her lover and his old friend. It was odd,

Abbot thought, that at least the tone of their conversation hadn't aroused her interest.

Out in the hall, Abbot saw that a pair of French doors were standing open. They gave on a small balcony, where Dmitri stood smoking and gazing moodily across the hills, as if trying to see his homeland.

"Dobri dyen," Abbot said, using one of the few expressions he remembered from an undergraduate course in Russian.

Dmitri looked at him in surprise, as if he had never expected to hear his native tongue again. Then he unleashed a stream of Russian, none of which Abbot could comprehend, but which seemed in its hushed urgency to impart some important message. When Abbot's incomprehension gradually made itself apparent to the young man, Dmitri scowled and backed away. *"Nyet,"* he said gruffly, shaking his head, *"Nyet."*

Nyets to you, too, Abbot thought, walking back to the central gallery. Perhaps he had been soaking up too much of the anti-Russian prejudices of ELF associates.

He found Franz pacing the gallery. "Well, my friend? Any luck with our honored guest?"

"Only that he's now as mad at me as he is at you," Abbot said. "Did you check out the two Russians, by the way?"

"Our search of their belongings and our initial debriefing produced nothing suspicious," Franz said. "We have sent a message to our contacts in Moscow, asking for additional information on each of them. However, we've not yet been able to contact the Stork."

"Is that unusual?"

"Not particularly. Since he just made his delivery last night, he probably hasn't had time to resume his ordinary regimen. I must say, though, I was disappointed not to meet him. That was one part of Operation Nightingale I was greatly looking forward to."

"Everything else is quiet?" Abbot asked.

"Major Marsh reports that there were no attempts to infiltrate our defenses last night. You see? It's quite likely that the Russians *don't* know where we're keeping Sawyer."

Abbot still wasn't convinced. "Has it occurred to you that these hostages in Beirut may have been taken simply to freeze Jeremy in place? To make us keep him here for an extended period of time?"

"Indeed it has," Franz said. "That's a good deal of what worries me. You may as well know that an emissary of the Bonn government is coming to confer with us this afternoon."

"Coming here? Bonn knows you're keeping Jeremy here?"

"This individual—a ranking officer in the Foreign Ministry— has provided our only contact with the government for some time. He is extremely discreet; he understands that his special relationship with us requires that he keep all such matters strictly confidential."

That may have been true, but Abbot was beginning to realize that ELF's relations with the West German government were somewhat cozier than he had been led to believe. He wasn't sure why that should bother him, but it did. Perhaps a time was coming when a final choice of loyalties would have to be made.

He spent the rest of the morning in the library, browsing through the *Graf*'s many rare and antiquated books. The reign of Albert the Enlightened, as it turned out, was well documented in the castle archives, and Abbot was interested to discover that several American writers and philosophers had visited Schloss Riesenschatten during the course of their grand tours.

After lunch, the dignitary from Bonn arrived in a black, chauffeur-driven limousine. Abbot was not invited to attend this conference, so he waited in the library, doing his best to translate a few passages from the *Graf*'s extensive collection of German fairy tales. Franz and Günther were shut up with the dignitary for over an hour, and when he left Franz came directly to the library.

"Well, Sam, it is as we feared. The Russians have made their offer."

"Their offer?" Abbot asked, finding it a little hard to shake off the fairy-tale world of dwarfs and giants he had been deciphering.

"The Soviets will use their influence with the Syrians, who will use their influence with the Palestinians, to free the sixteen Swiss and German hostages . . . *if* we turn Herr Sawyer and his friends over to the East German border police."

"Bullshit," Abbot said.

The *Graf* was somewhat disconcerted by his choice of expletive. "I am very sorry, Sam. I know you have gone to much trouble and exposed yourself to grave personal danger—"

"You're not going to do it, are you?" Abbot asked.

"Unfortunately, it is not up to me. The Ruling Council will take the proposal under advisement. They will decide if the potential benefits of Operation Nightingale are worth the lives of sixteen individuals. I must be gone from the castle for a time, so that I can argue the merits of our project at a council meeting. I will do my best, I assure you."

"What a shame," Abbot said, "that Jeremy didn't try a little harder to ingratiate himself."

He was still seated, so it was possible for Franz, standing beside his chair, to put his hand on Abbot's shoulder. "It does not matter what I think of Herr Sawyer personally, Sam. I have read his poetry, and even more important, perhaps, I have known you. I will do my best for the man."

"Thank you," Abbot said.

"In the meantime, Major Marsh will continue to defend the castle as if the future of Operation Nightingale were not in doubt."

Though the *Graf* didn't say it, Abbot understood him to mean that it would be as hard for anyone to leave the castle, at this point, as it would be for anyone to get in.

By four that afternoon the clouds had begun to break, and Abbot went out to walk in the courtyard. Sheltered on two sides by the old castle and the new, the courtyard was open at both its eastern and western flanks to stupendous views Abbot watched as wads of cottony clouds drifted across the gray-green slopes and rose, like fairy airships, out of the shadowed valleys. He was finding it particularly hard to come to terms with the anticlimactic nature of his adventure. After all he had been through, after the people who had died that Jeremy Sawyer might speak to the world once again, it was depressing in the extreme to think that his voice might now be forever silenced by a return to some Soviet prison camp. What, then, had the whole bloody business been for?

If, throughout the last several days, Abbot had had anything to cling to, it was his firm conviction that in Jeremy Sawyer's voice he had heard the authentic call of the prophet. Yet was *that* the prophet's voice he had heard this morning, that petulant whine? Was that the Jeremy Sawyer he had gone to such lengths to save? Suddenly he was filled with anger, with fury. He wanted to take that false prophet by the throat and strangle the son of a bitch until, in spite of his paltry personal complaints, he coughed up some genuine truth.

It was in this nearly murderous mood that Abbot chanced to see Jeremy and his two protégés out walking on the terrace that flanked their wing of the castle. Who the hell are you, Abbot thought, and what have you ever done, that you should be the cause of so much grief and hardship? Sixteen people held hostage in Beirut. Another four murdered in cold blood. And there you are, strolling the *Graf*'s terrace as if you owned it.

It seemed high time that somebody speak frankly to Jeremy and that somebody demand a few explanations. *Had* he been involved in that bombing at Waverly? *Had* he sold intelligence secrets to the Soviets? *Did* he know anything about Soviet agents in England or elsewhere, and did he have *anything* to tell the world besides his own miserable woes and petty complaints? Was he, in short, a hero or a bum, a prophet worth listening to, or just another puffed up phoney?

There was nobody, it seemed, with a better right to ask these questions of Sawyer than Abbot himself, and feeling confident that he could now do so, Abbot strode across the courtyard and up the steps to the terrace. As he bore down on Jeremy, both Dmitri and Katya drew closer to their master, as if to ward off some hostile attack. It wasn't their protective stance which made Abbot pull up short of his goal, however; it was rather his sudden realization that the object of his wrath was a weak and defenseless, possibly even a dying man. And in Jeremy's lusterless, watery, pain-washed eyes, he seemed to see the answer to his demand for enlightenment. It was not the prophet's words, but his poor ravaged face which told the significant tale.

For Jeremy was ancient. As old as Jerusalem, as the patriarchs themselves, as the Hebraic prophet after whom he'd been named. He was the devastated human spirit, adrift in the twentieth century, savaged by two world wars and menaced by annihilation, exposed to every spore of evil that rode on the winds of history and infected all the unfortunate creatures of this wretched planet. He was, Abbot saw now, not history's master but history's victim.

There were suddenly no questions he wanted to ask.

"Filthy weather these Germans have, isn't it?" Jeremy asked, looking off across the cloud-dappled hills.

"It's clearing up," Abbot said.

They stood for a time at the balustrade. Jeremy seemed amused by Abbot's awkward silence. "Was there something you wanted, old bean?"

"Well, I was wondering . . . since it looks like we're going to be stuck here for a while—I was wondering if I could have a look at the rest of your manuscript."

Jeremy was silent for a moment. "You could, Sam, certainly, but it's all on microcomputer disks, like the one I gave you in Berlin. I don't know if they have the program here for decoding it."

"I'll ask Günther," Abbot said. "He's the *Graf*'s computer man."

"Anyway, the disks are stowed away in my bag somewhere," Jeremy said. "It would be a nuisance to get at them now. Keep working on the little Kraut, will you, Sam? See if you can't get him to let us go. I don't much fancy spending another night so close to the fucking border, I can tell you that."

"You're well protected here," Abbot said, "but I'll see what I can do when Franz returns from a meeting."

He had started away when Jeremy called after him: "We'll have that talk soon, old bean. I'm working up my strength for it."

"Sure, fine," Abbot said and went to find Günther.

Günther did not have the program for decoding Jeremy's disks. That part of Operation Nightingale had been entrusted to Brian Hedge alone, and Hedge had yet to make his reappearance.

"That's odd," Abbot said. "If Hedge had the code, why didn't he stick around to see what was on Jeremy's disks? If he didn't like it, he could have taken a powder then."

"Perhaps," Günther suggested with dry humor, "Herr Hedge remembers your friend's manners from their previous encounter and thought to spare himself."

The *Graf* did not return by suppertime, and Jeremy's party dined once again in their private suite. Abbot and Günther passed the evening drinking wine and talking (somewhat incongruously, Abbot thought, under the circumstances) about life in their respective countries. Günther had studied for a year in America and had many fresh and accurate observations. He had even more interesting things to say about life in Germany.

"You would have made an excellent German," he told Abbot. "You love the truth and despise falsehood—but only if they fit your a priori sense of how things are. This has historically been the great failing of the German people. As much as they love the truth, they have often failed to see the big lie when history has presented it to them. I think it is because they are afraid to look into the abyss."

"Well, I seem to have looked into a lot of abysses lately," Abbot said, "and I've run across quite a few lies."

"But the big lie," Günther said, "is the one you can't see—the one that's too deeply imbedded in the way you view the world. It's the big lie, I think, which catches up with all of us in the end."

"No doubt it does," Abbot said, but he was getting too tired and had drunk too much wine to think thoroughly through these matters, and he told Günther he was going to bed. "Tell the *Graf* I'll see him first thing in the morning. I hope he doesn't take any action before I've had a chance to talk to him."

"He will want to consult with you, I'm sure," Günther said.

Abbot was in his room, already in his pajamas and about to put out the light, when there was a soft knock at his door. He opened it to find Jeremy standing alone in the hall. Not only had he managed, apparently, to climb two flights of stairs on his own, but he had brought along a bottle of whiskey and two glasses. A cigarette dangled rakishly from the corner of his mouth and he grinned at Abbot with at least a ghost of his old charm.

"Care for a nightcap, old bean? I think I'm ready to have that talk, if you're in the mood."

Abbot was to think of it later as perhaps the strangest part of the whole affair—the most extraordinary of his many adventures. And yet all he did was listen. Listen in the darkness, for Jeremy had requested they put out the light, as Jeremy's voice spoke to him of things beyond his wildest imaginings. Listen as he had done back in their Cambridge days, when Jeremy might have arrived at his room at a similar hour, similarly craving a chance to unburden himself, a friendly ear, a silent audience of one. But what Jeremy had to say was, of course, drastically different from anything he could have told Abbot in those far-off days. For Jeremy had spoken then largely only of possibilities—things glimpsed in theory and speculated upon by his restless, questioning mind. Now he spoke of *experience*—of risks taken and dangers braved, of commitments made and vows broken, of temptations resisted and others succumbed to, of sufferings endured and pleasures greedily hoarded, of loneliness, exile, shame, remorse, terror, despair . . . but most of all, it seemed, of a great gamble confidently and foolishly undertaken—a gamble which in turn required another gamble, and another, until Jeremy's whole life became a series of desperately calculated risks.

Abbot listened in the darkness, saying nothing, seeing only the glowing red nub of Jeremy's cigarette as it burned brighter for a moment, then dimmer, twinkling in the darkness like a candle in a red glass jar, a vigil light left flickering in the cold and musty gloom of an empty church. And the whiskey bottle was passed back and forth, filling the glasses, though Abbot in fact drank little and no longer felt drunk, or tired, or in any way compelled to drink, sipping now and then only as if he were joining Jeremy in some ritual, some sacramental sharing that seemed appropriate to the occasion.

Jeremy's voice droned on, growing weary as the night passed and sometimes so husky Abbot was afraid he might have to cease, and sometimes he did cease for five or ten minutes at a time, resting, sipping his whiskey, reflecting on what he had just said or was about to say. Then the voice would resume again, in that same quiet, reflective, almost impersonal tone, as if Jeremy were not talking about himself at all but about some character he had invented for the purposes of his art, some third party whose actions he knew and understood but could not control. And along the way he told Abbot many things about life in the Soviet Union and in those Third World countries he had visited on behalf of his hosts, and all these places, eternally mysterious to Abbot in his ignorance, came briefly alive as Jeremy spoke of them, so that Abbot thought it would always be for him as if he had been there, too—as if he had lived those eighteen years with Jeremy behind the Iron Curtain—for it *was* an iron curtain, cold-war rhetoric aside—an iron curtain of mutual ignorance and misunderstanding. No man could move from one world to the other, the way

Jeremy had, without experiencing a sort of death and rebirth, which had left him, as it were, *different.* Crazed. Touched. As though some terrible twelve-headed god of Egypt or Babylon had put its poisonous spittle to his eyelids and made him his own.

There were surprises enough in Jeremy's account, and explanations enough, to keep Abbot awake and listening until nearly dawn. Then, during one of Jeremy's lengthy pauses, the whole story, or most it, having been told, Abbot fell asleep. And when he woke an hour or two later, Jeremy was gone.

At eight that morning, Abbot found Franz, still red-eyed from his all-night journey, drinking coffee in the morning room.

"I have something to tell you," Abbot said.

"And I have things to tell you, my friend," Franz said in a sorrowful voice. "I did my best for Herr Sawyer, but I failed. The council's decision is to send him and his friends back to the Russians."

"That's impossible," Abbot said, "you mustn't."

"I have no choice," Franz said.

"Yes, you do," Abbot said. "You can send for Roland Kohl. Let the Americans take charge of Jeremy. Then the Soviets and their puppets in Beirut will have to deal with them."

"And our hostages?"

"If you no longer hold Sawyer, the hostages will serve no particular purpose. Chances are they'll be released—those people already have plenty of American hostages. They can propose another swap, if they want to."

Franz thought it over. "But can we trust Kohl?"

"Yes, I know now that we can."

"Now?"

"I talked to Jeremy last night. Or rather, he talked to me. He told me the whole story."

"The whole story," Franz said, as if wondering at the enormousness of such a tale.

"It's funny we never guessed," Abbot said, "but it was right there in front of us all along. As Günther was telling me last night, we all have trouble recognizing the big lie. I'm afraid we've all been taken in, and now we're going to have to deal with a vastly altered situation."

Franz seemed to catch a glimmer of what Abbot was getting ready to tell him. "Jeremy Sawyer is not . . . who, or what, he seems to be?"

Abbot nodded. "If anybody should send Jeremy back to the Russians, or fight to save him, it's Roland Kohl. You see, Jeremy is Kohl's agent."

"His agent? But then—his defection eighteen years ago—it was all a ruse?"

"There's more," Abbot said. "You won't like this, I'm afraid, but we named our operation for the wrong bird. We weren't rescuing a nightingale at all, you see—"

Franz sat back and stared until Abbot finally said the words: "Jeremy Sawyer is the Stork."

18

Roland Kohl arrived in the village at midafternoon and telephoned the castle for permission to proceed. Franz, who was still suspicious of the CIA man, decided to send a party down to meet him. He suggested to Abbot that he might like to go along.

"Kohl has brought someone with him, you see."

"His aid, Morrison, I assume."

"Someone else," the Graf said. "Did not Herr Sawyer have a wife in England named Patricia?"

"Good Christ, has Kohl brought her here? Why?"

Franz shook his head. "He says she has something for Herr Sawyer, and that she insists on giving it to him herself."

"I guess I'd *better* go along," Abbot said, thinking he would have to prepare Patricia somehow for Jeremy's Russian mistress.

As was his custom now, he went upstairs for his gun, which he slipped into the deep pocket of his raincoat.

Günther and Abbot rode in the black limousine with the two hulking musclemen Abbot remembered from his first visit to the castle. A fine, misty rain was falling, and they found Kohl and his party waiting beneath the awning of a sidewalk café.

"Sam, your poor throat!" Patricia put her hand up to touch the wound, which he had left unbandaged this morning, hoping the air would hasten healing.

He put his arm around her and a light kiss on her temple.

"I'm okay, but what are you doing here, Pat? I didn't think you wanted to see Jeremy again."

"I didn't think so either," she said, "but I have something that belongs to him and I want to make sure he gets it. That way, he won't be able to blame *you* if things don't work out to his satisfaction."

"Something," Abbot asked, "that was supposed to be in that box you gave me?"

She nodded. "I had taken it out a long time ago, before I hid the box at Wilding Park. I know I should have given it to you in Cambridge, but I wasn't sure—forgive me, Sam—I wasn't sure you could be trusted to take care of it."

Abbot smiled. "You made the right decision."

Kohl stepped forward. "Shall we get started?" He was carrying a raincoat and a small attaché case.

Günther stopped him. "I'm sorry, Herr Kohl. My instructions are that you and Frau Eckersley must come alone and unarmed. You may leave your case and any weapons you are carrying with your assistant."

Kohl and Morrison exchanged a look which suggested that Günther's terms were not entirely unexpected. Then Kohl took out his large automatic and passed it to Morrison. "I guess you'll have to cool your heels here for a while, Jimbo. I'll be in touch."

"Right, boss. Let me know if you need any help."

"Will do," Kohl said and submitted to a frisking by one of their bulky escorts before getting into the car.

Günther rode in front with the big men; Kohl, Abbot, and Patricia in the back.

"So what happened, Prof?" Kohl asked as they started up the hill. "You change your mind about us again, or what?"

"Jeremy and I had a long session last night," Abbot said. "He told me everything."

"Everything?" Kohl asked, somewhat dubious.

"I can't think of much he could've left out. Why didn't you tell me he was your agent, damn it?"

"Why didn't he tell you that himself in Berlin? I reckon we both thought you wouldn't risk your neck for a spy. It was a crummy, second-rate poet you wanted to save."

"Please," Abbot said.

"Oh, well," Kohl said, "I don't claim to be a literary critic. But I know good spy material when I see it. One look at Jeremy Sawyer, addressing one of those Cambridge antiwar rallies, and I knew he'd be a natural genius."

"So you compromised him," Abbot said bitterly.

"Hell, he compromised himself. He dug his own damn grave with that Waverly business. I just showed him a way to get out of it."

"You gave him the documents to carry into Russia," Abbot said. "They were never stolen at all. You betrayed your own network."

"Only a few ineffectual agents who were probably working the other side of the street already. It had to be done, Prof. I had to send the Russians a message they'd believe."

"A message," Abbot said, "for the Hangman."

"That's right. He was their specialist in sanctioning foreign agents. Jeremy was carrying one document, relating to our network in Poland, which I knew would come to Charnov's attention. It led him to a certain flat in Krakow, where we'd planted a suitcase full of explosives—"

"So getting rid of the Hangman was Jeremy's first assignment. I should have noticed the proximity of the dates. And Mikos Pajorfsky helped you set it up?"

Kohl looked out the limo's window. "Mikos helped me set up a lot of things. He was a damn good man. I'll miss him." They were passing a large black van, parked at one of the turnouts on the winding road, and Kohl leaned forward to poke Günther's shoulder. "I suppose you checked those guys out?"

"Yes, they are with the public works—looking for a gas leak."

Kohl sank back in his seat. "And I suppose you believe *that*," he said with contempt.

"You know better?" Abbot asked.

"I know the Rooskies have got you spotted," Kohl said. "By now they've probably got strike teams in position all over these hills. We'll have a sweet time getting old Jeremy out of here alive, let me tell you."

Günther turned around and gave Kohl a perfectly vicious smile. "From now on, Herr Kohl, that will be your problem, not ours."

"I hope you fellows don't hold a grudge," Kohl said.

The gates were opened at their approach. They went up the long drive and pulled into the courtyard between the new castle and the old. Franz came out to greet them. Despite recent revelations, he gave Kohl and Patricia a formal and courteous welcome to Schloss Riesenschatten.

"Nice place you've got here, Graf," Kohl said, looking around the courtyard as if he might be interested in some choice German real estate. "Would have made a snug little fortress in the Middle Ages. But you're vulnerable to mortar fire from that ridge over there—or to a few sweeps from a low-flying plane armed with rockets."

"We do not expect an attack of that nature," Franz said. "This area is very closely patrolled by the Bundesrepublik."

"I'm sure it is, but your whole organization is a bit of an embarrassment to Bonn just now. I'm not sure how they'd feel about an armed fortress so close to the border—or about that tunnel you've opened into East Germany. And just when the two Germanies are in the process of 'normalizing' their relations—that could be a bit sticky, don't you think?"

Franz looked resentfully up at the tall American. "I don't think you need to explain the niceties of German politics to us, Herr Kohl. If I have understood Professor Abbot correctly, ELF is very much your own creation. We have been all along, it seems, mere puppets for the CIA."

"Not true, Graf," Kohl said in his most genial and conciliatory manner. "I let you guys run your show, for the most part. All I needed was the information Jeremy could send out of Russia with his refugees. As for the rest, I chose not to meddle. I didn't even know about this place, for instance—I would've been here before now, if I had."

"And what is it you want from us, Herr Kohl?" Franz asked coldly.

"I want my man. Sawyer deserves a Company pension and a nice, safe, quiet retirement, and I intend to see that he gets it. All I need from him are a few assurances."

"Assurances?" Abbot asked.

"Kohl, you said I could talk to Jeremy first," Patricia reminded him.

"Oh yeah." He looked at her with something akin to pity. "I'm not much into these tearful reunion scenes, lady. Why don't you and the Prof go ahead. Give Jeremy what you brought him. I've got a few more matters to discuss with the *Graf.*"

"You'll find Herr Sawyer—and the others—in their suite," Franz said.

Abbot took Patricia inside. As they were crossing the gallery he stopped and put his hands on her shoulders. She was still heartbreakingly beautiful, and now that he knew the whole story, or most of it, he found her more magnificent than ever.

"Pat, there's something I need to explain. I guess you still love the guy, huh?"

She gazed up at him. "Would you believe me, Sam, if I told you that it was for *your* sake I came here, and not for Jeremy's?"

"No, I guess I wouldn't."

"Then there's no point in telling you, is there? But if you're trying to prepare me for some drastic change in Jeremy, I don't think there's much I haven't already imagined."

"Including a young Russian mistress?"

She took just the quickest, tiniest breath. "I'm sure Jeremy couldn't exist for very long without some sweet young thing to minister to his vanity. So he brought a woman out with him, is that all?"

"A woman and her brother," Abbot said. "Jeremy claims they're talented young writers—the sort of people the Stork specialized in smuggling out of Russia. But he's planning to marry the woman after his operation."

"Fine. I'll wish him every happiness. Shall we get this over with now?"

"I guess we'd better," Abbot said.

He took Patricia down the long hall to Jeremy's suite and knocked on the door. As usual, Katya answered the door. She was dressed in a form-fitting black turtleneck and jeans, her long dark hair done up in a bun. She was a striking creature and she seemed to recognize Patricia at once as a woman with a prior claim to her lover. After a long, hostile look, she stood aside and let them enter the room.

Dmitri was at the window, smoking. Jeremy was sitting up in bed once again, watching more television. Abbot didn't know if he had been informed of Patricia's and Kohl's arrival, but he did a good job of feigning surprise.

"Pat, is it you? How bloody fine!"

He swung his long, bony legs out from under the covers and

started to get to his feet, then sagged back on his pillow as if stricken by a new series of chest pains.

"I'm not quite . . . as you see . . . at my best."

Patricia stood looking down at him, her eyes bright with unshed tears. "What have they done to you, Jeremy? You look terrible."

At this he took umbrage. "Well, Christ, woman, what did you expect? I'm practically a walking corpse. If these fools don't get me to Switzerland soon, they can bury me in that bloody crypt I saw the other night. What have you got there, love?"

He had noticed the paper she had just removed from her purse and she thrust it out to him. "Here—take it, it's yours."

Jeremy quickly took the paper and examined it. As he read, his expression underwent an amazing change. It was as if that single sheet of paper was enough to restore his health, youth, and vitality. For an instant, he was almost the old Jeremy.

"Pat baby, you're a doll! You've just saved my worthless rotten life, you know that, don't you?"

"I promised I would keep it for you," she said coldly, "and I have. Now at last our divorce is final. You have what you need and you can deal with Roland Kohl on your own. I do hope I never see you again, Jeremy."

She started for the door, but Jeremy, no longer disabled, jumped out of bed and went after her. In his funny, old-fashioned nightshirt, he did look to Abbot something like an ungainly, stilt-legged stork.

"Wait, Pat—wait, honey! There's so much we ought to talk about—"

"Oh, really?" Abbot was surprised to see those lovely gray eyes turn themselves into lethal weapons. "I can't imagine what you'd want to know about me, after all these years—or about your daughter!"

"Pat, that's not fair," Jeremy said. "I did it, you know, at least in part for you, and for our daughter. Kohl could have had us both sent to prison for that Waverly incident, and then who would have raised our child—those bloody, stuffy relatives of yours?"

Abbot picked up the paper which Jeremy had left on the bed. As he had suspected, it was a presidential pardon, signed by Lyndon Baines Johnson. Reading further into the document, he saw that it covered Patricia Wilding Sawyer as well as her husband. Jeremy had told him last night that she was the driver of the van in which the bomb was found.

Though it seemed uncomfortably as though he were eavesdropping, Abbot turned his attention back to Jeremy and Patricia, who were standing near the door. Jeremy was holding both her hands and gazing anxiously into her eyes, as if, having seen his wife again after eighteen years, he was determined to win her back.

"Christ, you don't know how I missed you, those first few years. I never intended to be gone so long, babe. I thought sure the job would be done and that I'd be back in England by the time Christina was old enough to ask about her old man. It was like going off to war, don't you see? A lot of my countrymen were doing that, just then. How was I any different?"

He had turned to Abbot, as if hoping for his corroboration. Abbot, instead, was reminded of a question Jeremy had not answered the night before. "But I always thought you were opposed to America's foreign policy—how could you have gone to work for the CIA?"

"It's easy enough, old bean, when they have you by the balls. Though in point of fact, my objections to U.S. foreign policy had to do with the war in Southeast Asia; Eastern Europe was something else. Pat and I had taken a tour of the Soviet Union in 1966, and we didn't like what we saw there—nor in Hungary, Poland, East Germany. Those weren't free socialist societies of the sort we used to talk about, Sam—they were bloody police states. Roland Kohl simply gave me the opportunity to fight the war I could believe in and avoid the war I was opposed to. Most of what I said when I got to Moscow about America's misguided meddling in Vietnam was perfectly sincere, and I hope it did some good."

"Not as much good," Roland Kohl said, entering the room, "as the stuff you told the KGB in private, Jer. That was your *real* contribution to world peace—getting rid of Nikolai Charnov, that murderous son of a bitch."

Jeremy drew himself up to face his old nemesis and taskmaster. "So, Kohl—you've found me, have you. Well, it doesn't matter now. I've got the pardon, you see. Patricia brought it to me."

"Sure, Jer. I brought her here so she could give it to you in person. Which ought to prove to you that I'm on the level. Roland Kohl never welshes on a deal."

Abbot noticed that Franz and Günther had come into the room after Kohl. With all these people standing around him, Jeremy seemed to become conscious of his nightshirt; he retreated to his bed and got once more beneath the covers. Katya, meanwhile, had joined her brother in one of the window alcoves at the far end of the room, where they watched the proceedings with wide, staring eyes. Abbot took Patricia's hand.

"Herr Sawyer," Franz said, "I understand that we have known you for many years under a different name. Allow me to congratulate you on a distinguished career—and for having deceived us so thoroughly."

"The *Graf*'s a bit pissed, Jer," Kohl said. "He thinks we took advantage of ELF for our little arrangement. I tried to tell him that you guys ran your own show."

"That's true," Jeremy said. "It was Mikos Pajorfsky who put me in touch with ELF. Mikos had friends at Moscow University and he told me about this new group being privately financed in West Germany. He suggested that we use their services to smuggle certain friends out of the Soviet Union. I'd become acquainted with a circle of dissidents, so I knew I'd have no trouble finding candidates for ELF's underground railroad. All I needed was a new identity."

"And so you became the Stork," Abbot said. "I should have recognized you in the romantic code name, Jeremy, and in the literary parallel. You were playing the role of the Scarlet Pimpernel, weren't you?"

"To the hilt, old bean, to the hilt. Which is not to say I had an easy time of it, juggling my dealings with ELF on the one hand, my dealings with Kohl on the other, and my role as a KGB informer on the third. That's three hands, isn't it? No wonder I got tired! In Moscow, every other comrade is a government spy. It was like walking on fucking eggs."

"Don't kid me, Jer—you enjoyed every minute of it," Kohl said. "Once we took out the Hangman, you could have come home and claimed your pardon any time you liked. But you were having too much fun, weren't you? It's a certain something in a man's character you learn to spot, a certain love of role playing and a talent for deception, that makes a great spy."

"Call it self-deception," Jeremy said, "and you've got it about right. I'll admit it, one year in Moscow and I was hooked. I wanted to get back to you and the kid, Patricia, really I did, but this bastard kept telling me how important my work was, and how I was performing this bloody great service—"

"And so you were." Kohl looked down at Jeremy with an almost-paternal expression. "Once I had you in place and got a sample of your effectiveness, I decided not to link you with the agency's regular network. You needed a separate sphere all your own."

"And so"—Abbot made a connection he hadn't seen before—"you arranged with Brian Hedge to become Jeremy's contact inside ELF."

"Good guess, Prof. Old Hedgie had agreed to take the rap for Jeremy's escape from England—somebody had to, in order to persuade the KGB they were getting the genuine article. Hedge's tarnished reputation and his well-known dislike of the Yanks made him a natural for ELF, which was determined to remain independent of the CIA."

"So Jeremy smuggled defectors out of Russia and Eastern Europe," Abbot said, "and ELF debriefed them here in West Germany. Then Brian Hedge passed the information on to you. But why did you keep trying to make me suspicious of Hedge?"

"I needed your help. Over the years, both Pajorfsky and Hedge drew closer to ELF and away from me. That was all part of the plan, to give them 'deep cover' and a free reign, but it became difficult keeping tabs on them. I began to think they were determined to freeze me right out of Operation Nightingale. Why didn't you just tell me you wanted to come in, Jer? We could have made a deal."

Jeremy glared up at Kohl from his pillow. "Yeah? What kind of deal?"

"The same deal we're going to make now," Kohl said. "What is it you want, retirement in Switzerland? An operation? A nice pension? I've got no problem with any of that. You deserve a peaceful old age, my friend—a nice, quiet life under a new name—"

"A new name?" Jeremy asked.

"Well, you can't very well let the KGB know where to find you. And the agency couldn't keep a bodyguard on the scene indefinitely—"

"But once my book is published," Jeremy said, "the Russians won't dare to come after me. The whole world will know my story. I'll be famous, Kohl. Not just among literary people, you understand. Everyone's going to read this book—*everyone!*"

He looked around the room, as if inviting his friends to share in his vision of glory. Patricia winced, and Abbot himself had a piercing insight into the appalling magnitude of Jeremy Sawyer's vanity. He had given up eighteen years of his life as a hostage to his art, and now he wanted his reward: the fame, the fortune, the critical adulation that went with being a hero and a celebrity—as if those past eighteen years had been at bottom nothing more than an outrageous publicity stunt.

Roland Kohl took out one of his big cigars, unwrapped it, sniffed it, licked the tip, bit off the nub and spit it delicately into his palm. "Well, that's the trouble with using a writer for intelligence work," he said to the rest of the group. "They're crazy enough to take the risks and play the roles, but they always want to brag about their exploits afterwards. I couldn't let you blow the whole network you set up over the years, Jeremy, you know that. The Stork was a great invention, but he had a large supporting cast. You'll put half the agents in Europe in jeopardy if you tell your story now."

"Including yourself," Abbot said. "The fact is that you don't want some of your methods and alliances known back in Washington, isn't that right, Kohl? It's your own reputation you're worried about."

Kohl blew smoke in Abbot's direction. "Prof, when I want your theories, I'll ask for them, okay? The fact is that four U.S. presidents have known about the Stork and the work he's done for us; it's those men, and the credibility of their administrations, that I'm trying to protect. Jeremy can have anything he wants from the agency as thanks for a job well done—anything except the right to ruin it all by shooting off his big mouth."

"I knew you'd take that position," Jeremy said. "That's why I decided to smuggle myself out of Russia without your help—and

273

I would have made it, too, if these damn fools had taken me to Switzerland, as they promised."

Kohl turned to Franz. "I guess he doesn't know about the sixteen hostages, huh?"

"He knows," Franz said. "Their lives don't weigh very heavily with him, I'm afraid."

"My heart bleeds for the poor buggers," Jeremy said, "but I happen to think I have something more important to offer the world. And *you*, Kohl, if you're willing to pay for it."

Kohl raised his bushy eyebrows. "You're ready to make a deal, Jer? Just for curiosity's sake, how much did the Prof get out of old Sir Godfrey Moneybags for the rights to your magnum opus?"

"One hundred thousand pounds," Jeremy said quickly, without looking at Abbot.

"Whew, that's a lot!" Kohl said, watching the smoke curl away from his lips. "I don't know if the agency could match that, Jer. Of course, a good health insurance program and a monthly pension might be worth more in the long run . . . and I suppose we could throw in a retirement bonus of fifty thousand or so. Dollars, not pounds."

"That's not enough, Kohl," Jeremy said, and Abbot was now amazed at the way in which he seemed suddenly willing to bargain his book away.

Abbot came forward: "Goddamn it, *nothing's* enough for the loss of that book! Don't give it to him, Jeremy. Make the bastard live with the truth, for a change. You've got nothing to hide!"

Both Kohl and Jeremy seemed to resent this intrusion. But Jeremy's eyes carried the sharper warning, and Abbot backed away from the bed. Quite angry, he went to the window where Patricia was gazing out at the soggy grounds. The rain was still slanting down. There was a noise coming from somewhere across the hills, and after a second he recognized it as the clatter of an approaching helicopter. In another moment he saw the ungainly craft rise above the crest of the hill. It hovered there, like a giant hummingbird, then disappeared behind the broken walls of the old castle. Günther had joined Abbot at the window.

"Were you expecting somebody?" Abbot asked him.

"I'd better look into this," Günther said and left the room.

Kohl, who seemed not to have heard the copter, was sitting at

Jeremy's bedside, complacently puffing his cigar. "Maybe you don't fully understand the situation, Jer. The hostage gambit was just Moscow's way of freezing you here at the castle, within striking distance of the East German border. Somebody's been keeping the KGB apprised of Operation Nightingale right from the start. They could have nabbed you back in Moscow, if they'd wanted to, but they let you get this far. They're setting something up, and I confess I don't know what it is. But I think you're still in a lot of trouble, my boy. ELF won't do a thing for you. Your only hope of getting to Switzerland, you see, is me."

Jeremy looked to Franz. "He is right, Herr Sawyer. As my guest, you would certainly receive my protection—but I have instructions to return you to the Russians by this evening."

"And if he decides not to do it," Kohl said, "the Russians will come and get you anyway. They've got enough men in these hills by now to blow this place away."

Jeremy pushed himself up on his elbows and called to his young mistress at the other end of the room. Obediently, she got to her feet and came to him, bringing with her one of the backpacks they'd carried in with them Sunday night. Jeremy gave her a pat, and she knelt at his bedside as he began to rummage through the pack. At last he extracted a plastic box; Abbot recognized it as a storage case for a dozen or more computer disks.

"Here it is, Kohl," he said, holding it up but out of Kohl's reach. "Here's what you want, you bastard—my life's blood, my genius, my sorrow and my shame. It's all on these tapes, and it will cost you two hundred thousand dollars to make sure it never gets into print."

Kohl laughed. "Two hundred G's? Jeremy boy, you've got delusions of grandeur! The agency would never cough up that much dough for a damn book!"

"Then maybe," Jeremy said, extracting another case, "they'd be interested in this. The six disks in this case are from the KGB's new computer in the Kremlin. They contain enough information on Soviet-sponsored terrorism around the world to keep you guys busy for years. There's everything you need—secret membership rolls and training areas, bank accounts, front organizations, supply lines, the lot."

275

Kohl's face had broken into a huge grin. "Jeremy, I always knew you were a genius. How the hell did you get hold of those disks?"

"There are men, even in the Kremlin, who disapprove of the use of terrorist violence against innocent people. They thought I could put such information to good use when I got to the West."

"They were *so* right," Kohl said and reached out for the case. At that moment, however, Katya did something extraordinary and unexpected. Grabbing a handful of Jeremy's lank gray hair and jerking his head back, she brought a large automatic out from beneath the rumpled bedclothes and rammed the barrel into Jeremy's exposed throat. Next to Abbot, Patricia gave a choked cry.

"Back away, all of you," Katya said in quite serviceable English. "One move toward me and this man dies."

"Well, I'll be goddamned," Kohl said, looking at the young woman as if he could appreciate a bold and clever move when he saw one.

Meanwhile, at the other end of the room, Dmitri had taken the pieces of a submachine gun out of one of his packs. He quickly assembled the weapon and then herded Kohl, Franz, Abbot, and Patricia away from the bed to a corner of the room, where they were quickly searched for weapons. Dmitri found a knife strapped to Kohl's leg, but the others were unarmed. Abbot suddenly remembered that Greta's Luger was in the pocket of his raincoat, which was draped across a chair near the door.

"You will consider yourselves our hostages," Katya was saying, her large gun still wedged none too gently under Jeremy's ear. "Klarbach, we have planted explosives throughout this castle. They can be set off either by me or by a radio transmitter on board the helicopter you heard moments ago. Now you will call the commander of your security force, and you will tell him that he and his men are to put down their weapons and present themselves in the courtyard for arrest in precisely ten minutes. Then you will call down to your gatehouse and tell the guard to admit the two black vans that are just now approaching. Any deviation from these orders and you will all die."

Franz looked to Kohl, who said, "You can test her on it if you want to, Graf, but I wouldn't advise it. Why the hell didn't somebody check these people out when they first got here?"

"We did check them," Franz said. "Their packs contained no weapons nor explosives—"

"The things we needed were deposited here weeks ago," Katya said. "Now make those calls, Klarbach, or we will kill the woman first, then this American"—her black eyes stabbed at Abbot as she searched her vocabulary for a descriptive term—"*pipsqueak.* Then the rest of you."

Franz went to a telephone near the bed. While he was talking, Katya released her grip on Jeremy's hair, put the plastic cases back into the pack, and carried it across the room to Dmitri's side. Jeremy, who had been unable to speak with his head pulled back and the gun in his throat, began to sputter inanely:

"Katya—Katya, darling, what are you doing? This can't be possible. . . . Why are you doing this to me?"

Katya swung the gun back in his direction. "Silence, you fool! I've borne the dishonor of being your whore long enough. It will give me great pleasure to kill you, you filthy capitalist spy!"

"That's telling him, girlie," Kohl said with a grin. "Do they still teach you kids to talk like that in the KGB? I'll bet you had old Marokofsky as one of your teachers, didn't you? He was always big on the 'capitalist swine' rhetoric."

"You be silent also, Kohl," Katya said, though not quite so contemptuously as she had spoken to Jeremy. "I am Major Katerina Oblonova of the Soviet secret police, and I have been unraveling your schemes for quite some time."

Kohl laughed and turned to Jeremy. "So you eloped with a major in the KGB! I always knew that pecker of yours would get you into trouble."

Jeremy, however, had turned quite gray. He fumbled on the bedstand for his vial of nitroglycerine tablets and he seemed to be having trouble breathing. When the vial slipped from his fingers and rolled across the floor, Patricia retrieved it and went to his side.

Katya followed her with the gun but did not interfere. "Pah, Englishwoman! You will let your men walk all over you, will you not? This is why England is decadent nation."

Patricia slipped a nitro tablet beneath Jeremy's tongue and cradled his head in her arms.

Franz put down the telephone. "Your instructions are being

carried out," he said to Katya. "If you find it necessary to destroy this castle and murder me, I beg you to spare the lives of my men and these innocent people."

Katya simply smiled.

Kohl said, "I don't imagine that's their scenario, Graf. I figure that, once they've disarmed your men and secured the castle, they'll kill the lot of us, then plant documents in your office to make it look like the whole thing was a CIA plot that went haywire. Is that the way you've got it planned, Major?"

"Not quite," Katya said. "These others will die. You will come with us, Kohl. There are people in Moscow who are very eager to make your acquaintance."

For once, Roland Kohl was stunned. He sagged back in his chair and stared at Katya for several moments before he could speak. "Jesus, what a chump I've been! It wasn't the Stork you were after, was it? It wasn't even ELF. All along, you were after me."

Katya offered another of her superior smiles. "We could have arrested the Stork at any time in the past year. It's the man who created him that we want. With ELF exposed as a neofascist cell and laid to your door, you will have no choice but to defect, Kohl. We will make very good use of your expertise in the KGB."

Kohl grimaced, then turned to Jeremy. "Well, chum, I guess I'll get a taste of what you had to live with for eighteen years. I hope that strikes you as fit punishment."

But Jeremy was in no shape to respond to Kohl's comment. He had begun to writhe and groan on the bed, and his face had turned a deathly white.

"He's in terrible pain," Patricia said to Katya. "Won't you let us send for the doctor?"

Katya looked at her former lover without interest. "He will be dead soon enough. You all will."

"Now there's one tough broad," Kohl said approvingly. "I gotta hand it to you, Major, you and your team set this one up pretty well. You had to hold old Jeremy here until I showed my ugly mug, so you snatched those sixteen hostages in Beirut, made it look like the work of Arab terrorists, and offered to help get them back if the Germans would cough up Sawyer. You knew that would smoke me out sooner or later. In the meantime, you were setting up this little coup ... but you overlooked one thing, Major. You forgot what a cautious man I am."

Katya swung her gun on Kohl. "So?"

"Well, you don't really think I would have come up here alone and unarmed, if I didn't have something pretty good backing me up, do you? Right now"—he checked his watch—"there are two hundred American soldiers taking up their positions on that ridge to the south, a similar number coming up the valley from the east. We've got the roads blocked, and there's another detachment guarding the entrance to the tunnel into East Germany. You'll never get out of here, Major—not with me or anyone else."

"You're bluffing, Kohl," Katya said, but her voice had lost its calm, cool arrogance.

Kohl shrugged. "Maybe I am, and maybe I'm not. You could be bluffing, too, about all the explosives you say you've got stashed around this castle. So we call each other's bluff and maybe we all get blown to smithereens ... sounds like a familiar stand-off, doesn't it?"

"I am not afraid to die for my country," Katya said. "However, we have another way of getting back to the DDR."

"That chopper? You'll never get to it, lady. We've got sharp-shooters stationed on that ridge over there. They'll pick you off the minute you come out in the open. We've also got a rocket launcher that'll knock your whirlybird out of the sky. It's hopeless, Major. You're outmaneuvered. ... Of course, what you *could* do, if you want to salvage something from this bungled operation of yours, you could make a deal for your safe conduct back to the border, with Sawyer's disks as your prize. That way, you get something to carry back to Moscow with you—so you don't look like a total failure—and we get old Jeremy here, for all the good he'll do us, and nobody gets hurt. Now doesn't that sound reasonable?" Kohl gave her his most engaging grin.

Katya seemed tempted; she turned to Dmitri, who nodded toward the window. Abbot looked out and saw that the *Graf*'s soldiers had lined up without their weapons in the courtyard. Major Marsh had them standing at parade rest, facing the two black vans which were just now coming up the drive from the main gate. At the same time, the helicopter could be heard approaching the hilltop from another direction, and in a moment its shadow swept swiftly over the courtyard.

"Come on, Major," Kohl said genially, "you've given it a good try, but there's no point in killing a lot of people for nothing. Let's call it a draw, shall we?"

The young woman seemed to make several desperate calculations. Her dark eyes raked the room, from Jeremy writhing on the bed, to Patricia, to Franz, to Kohl, to Abbot. She shouldered one of the backpacks and spoke rapidly to Dmitri in Russian. Then she turned to Kohl: "You will be our hostage, Kohl—you and two others. The woman, and"—she nodded toward Abbot—"that one. Klarbach, you had better find some way to warn the Americans that if they open fire on us we'll kill these three on the spot. My men will hold the castle until we're safely under way. Then, if you want to make a deal for your lives, you may do so. But remember, any tricks and I have the means to destroy this castle."

"Herr Kohl," Franz said desperately, "tell me how I can call off your troops."

"Well, you might try the Tactical HQ at Schweinfurt," Kohl said, as if it mattered little to him whether the troops held their fire or not. "Ask for Colonel Buzz Riley, Fifth Armored Division, on maneuvers, and use the code name 'Gatecrasher.' Chances are you won't reach him in time."

Dmitri motioned them toward the door with the muzzle of his submachine gun. Katya grabbed Patricia's arm and pulled her roughly away from Jeremy's bed. Unable to speak, his face white and his eyes bright with pain, Jeremy watched as the group gathered at the door. Abbot reached down and picked up his raincoat, casually draping it over his arm. No one seemed to notice. Sometimes it was an advantage, he reflected, to be considered a "pipsqueak."

Patricia sought Abbot's hand as they started down the long corridor. Katya and Kohl went first, her gun in his ribs; Dmitri brought up the rear. They crossed the central gallery and left the castle by the main entrance. A fine, cold mist struck Abbot's face. He put on his raincoat and felt the weight of the Luger in his deep pocket.

On the castle steps they were still out of sight of the southern ridge, where Kohl claimed to have sharpshooters. The black vans had already pulled into the courtyard, and they watched as a dozen armed men, in the black jumpsuits and ski masks of terrorists, took possession of the courtyard. The *Graf*'s men were led away, presumably to imprisonment somewhere in the castle. Abbot wondered if any of those ski masks hid the hideous white face of the Hangman. *If I'm going to die,* he thought, *I'd like to get one shot at that bastard—just one.*

Katya conferred with a tall man who seemed to be in command. He saw her point to the ridge, then to the grassy slope beyond the terrace, where the copter would be likely to set down. The tall man shook his head. Katya went to the van and was given a walkie-talkie, into which she spoke, her eyes circling the cloudy skies.

Kohl also looked up. "Nice day for a chopper ride," he remarked.

Abbot edged closer to him and hoped that Dmitri wouldn't overhear. "Kohl—I've got a gun in my pocket."

Kohl raised an eyebrow and gave Abbot half a smile. "Watch for my move," he said.

They could hear the helicopter making yet another pass over the hilltop. This time, however, it rose above the broken walls of the old castle and hovered there. Katya gave Kohl's shoulder a push. "Get moving, Kohl—up there!"

"You can't land that thing up there," Kohl protested.

"Our pilots can land anywhere," Katya said and shoved her pistol into Kohl's back.

Abbot saw the purpose of this maneuver: Within the walls of the old castle they would be protected from any sniper fire originating on the ridge opposite. By staying close to the northern wall, they could cross the courtyard and reach the ruin without coming into view of the southern ridge. Two of the terrorists, armed with submachine guns like Dmitri's, joined the party. The hostages were pushed and prodded up the short flight of stairs and through the passageway that led to the interior of the ruin.

The helicopter, meanwhile, had begun its descent, and its great blades had the effect of a hurricane within the enclosure. Flocks of birds fled their roosts along the pitted walls. The trees and shrubs that grew among the piles of rubble were stirred to a frenzy; dust and bits of grit filled the air. Abbot got something in his eye and, when he paused to rub it, felt the barrel of a submachine gun digging into his back.

Pummeled by the copter's wind and deafening clatter, Abbot lowered his head. Less than twenty feet to his right, there was a dark cavity—an open stairway to one of the castle's subterranean chambers. With his left hand he took Patricia's hand and squeezed; his right he slipped into his pocket, where it closed around the butt of the Luger.

And then Abbot saw Brian Hedge. The portly Englishman was crouched amid the rubble of the old west wall, some twenty feet above them and fifty feet to their left. His rifle was braced on a section of wall. The wind from the copter blades blew his sparse hair out from his round pink skull, and he looked like some doughty old campaigner of the Empire, defending His Majesty's outpost in one of the dark corners of the globe.

The helicopter hovered now over a spot of open ground in the center of the ruin. Abbot saw someone at the open hatch, motioning them forward. Katya pushed Kohl toward the copter. They had gone perhaps six paces when Hedge opened fire.

His first shot hit one of the terrorists and drew the fire of the other. Kohl spun, hitting Katya full in the face, then leapt on Dmitri. They sprawled on the ground, grappling for Dmitri's gun. Abbot pushed his Luger into the side of the other terrorist and, without quite meaning to, pulled the trigger. The man flew away from him with a bright red stain on his black suit.

Katya had scrambled to her feet with Jeremy's backpack and ran for the copter. Kohl was still struggling with Dmitri. "Stop her, Prof! She's got the disks!"

Abbot trained the Luger on Katya, but couldn't bring himself to fire.

Kohl did something violent and decisive just out of Abbot's line of sight, rose with Dmitri's machine gun and trained it on the fleeing woman. He released a blast that cut Katya's legs out from her; she tumbled into a pile of rubble several yards shy of the copter. At that moment Abbot saw the long, snakelike barrel of a machine gun protruding from the copter's hatch. He still had Patricia's hand clutched in his and he pulled her with him as he ran for the dark cavity he'd seen off to his right. They were still several strides away when the machine gun swung in their direction, and the air crackled around them. Abbot grabbed Patricia by the waist and jumped feet first into the open stairwell. They hit and rolled and then Abbot got his feet in front of him and brought them to a stop. He held Patricia tight and let her sob convulsively against his chest.

After a moment the noise of the helicopter began to grow louder and Abbot realized that it was climbing out of the ruin. He saw its whirling blades and knew it would soon rise above their line of cover. He was about to lead Patricia down the stairs and into the deeper shadows when the copter, pivoting slowly in order to sweep the ruin with its machine gun, struck its tail against the tall central tower. The craft managed to gain altitude, clearing the castle walls, but then seemed to veer out of control. Through a break in the ancient wall, Abbot was able to see the explosion as the copter struck the rocky summit of the hill. An orange ball of flame engulfed the hilltop, and out of the flame spiraled black smoke and debris. As the smoke began to clear, Abbot could see the wreckage scattered across the rocks. Burning patches of oil made the summit look like a smoldering volcano, and from Abbot's position it looked as though Arnulf's rock had been shattered into a new configuration.

Within the ruin it was peculiarly quiet. Abbot knew the rest of Katya's terrorist force would arrive soon. He began working his way cautiously up the stairs for a look around when he heard a scuffling near the rim of the well. Gun in hand, he slid up along the stone wall and looked over the side. Roland Kohl was dragging himself, and Katya's backpack, through the dust. His side was soaked with blood, and he seemed unable to use his legs.

"They got Hedgie," he said. "Does that stairway lead anywhere?"

Abbot was going to say he didn't know and then realized that he probably did. "To the crypt, I think—and to an exit at the bottom of the hill."

"Here—" Kohl swung Katya's pack over the side of the stairwell. "Take this and the girl and see if you can get out of here. I'll hold them off as long as I can."

"You'd better come with us, Kohl. You're badly wounded."

"Naw, Prof—it's just a scratch. Go on now—they'll be up here any second."

Abbot shouldered the pack, took Patricia's hand, and led her the rest of the way down the stairs. At the bottom they found an ominous-looking door of rusty iron. Abbot removed the massive wooden bar, tried the latch, and discovered that it worked. The door swung open and the damp, rotten-ripe air of the crypt wafted out to greet them.

Groping in the darkness to the left of the doorway, Abbot found a shelf, candles, matches. He pulled Patricia in with him and shut the door, then lit a candle.

"It's not pretty," he said, holding up the light, "but it's probably our only way out of here."

Patricia gasped at the alcoves full of skulls. "Oh, Sam, I don't know if I can—"

"You're doing just fine," Abbot said, leading her into the crypt. "Now all we have to do is find the tunnel that opens off this chamber, and—"

He stopped, because he thought he had heard a footstep somewhere in the crypt. He held up his candle. The low vaulted ceiling and short pillars created a complexity of shadows. When the candle flickered in the draft, all the shadows seemed to be moving. Abbot couldn't stand the suspense.

"Hello, is anyone there?"

"Prof, is that you?" a voice asked at his elbow.

Abbot spun around and saw James Morrison emerging from behind one of the pillars.

"What the hell are you doing here?"

Morrison grinned. "After you guys left me in the village, I started working my way up this hill—those were Rollie's instructions. A while back I found this tunnel and I was groping along when I thought I heard an explosion—"

"You did. And right now your boss could sure use your help. Through that door and up those stairs—"

"Rollie's up there? What's going on?"

"He's been shot—so has Hedge. The castle's been taken over by a KGB strike force. Kohl told us to go ahead with this—" Abbot lifted the pack an inch or two off his shoulder.

"Yeah, what's that?"

"One of Sawyer's backpacks. It's got the disks he brought out with him. Go on now, Kohl needs your help."

For an instant the young agent seemed confused, as if conscious of conflicting duties. Then his face cleared. "You wait here, Prof, while I check things out, okay?"

"We won't go far," Abbot promised.

Morrison made for the stairs in the light of Abbot's candle. He went out and shut the door behind him. Maybe it was that last glimpse of Morrison's young, anxious face in the daylight, but Abbot suddenly had a thought: *Brian Hedge had fired on the Russians.* Therefore, Hedge was clearly not the traitor. Did there have to be one? Katya had kept the KGB informed of Jeremy's plans as he made them in Moscow, but who told them what was going on inside ELF? And who told them about Abbot's movements—about the box he'd checked at Victoria Station and the meeting he'd set up with Rinzelmann at the spa?

Abbot slipped the pack off his shoulder and gave it to Patricia. "Can you manage this? See if you can find the tunnel—it should be right back in there somewhere. If you find it, keep going. If you hear shooting, don't stop. Run for your life."

"But Sam, what—?"

"No questions, go. Here, take the candle. Now get away from me."

He had to give her a violent push to get her started, but she went. Abbot groped his way back toward the stairs, until he could see the narrow slit of light beneath the heavy door. He sat down on the damp floor with his back to one of the pillars and his knees up in front of him. Then, holding the butt of the Luger in both hands, his right index finger curled around the trigger, he rested his wrists in the little notch between his kneecaps, barrel aimed directly at the solid rectangle above the slit of light, and waited.

Within moments, he heard a noise beyond the door. He heard the latch lifted, the hinges resisting with a prolonged creak. An inch-wide strip of brightness appeared. The inch grew to a foot and stopped. Abbot saw the hand in silhouette, the gloved fingers delicately extended as the door was pushed further open still, the hand quickly withdrawn.

He knows I'm waiting for him, Abbot thought. I'll get just one shot as he comes through the door. He tried to concentrate his entire being, all his senses and all his conscious will, on the sights of the Luger. The shaft of daylight from the open door reached almost to his hiding place. He held his breath, squinting along the barrel, counting one, two, three, four—

Slipping sideways, the tall, angular figure came through the open doorway with the submachine gun up and ready. There was just an instant when, the face caught by a scrap of daylight, Abbot recognized the white, ravaged visage of the Hangman. At once he squeezed the trigger and the gun nearly flew from his hands. A tremendous roar echoed in the crypt. The Hangman lunged into the darkness, his gun blazing. Abbot rolled across the floor. He heard the Hangman's bullets spraying the crypt, ricocheting off the stone walls and ringing against the iron grills. With a dreadful, ghoulish clatter, the skulls and bones of twelve centuries were torn from their resting places and scattered about the chamber. They flew through the darkness, careening off walls and rolling across the stone floors like a mad scramble of spooks desperately seeking their component parts at the blast of Gabriel's horn. Meanwhile, Abbot had come to a stop behind another pillar. Lying on his stomach with the Luger out in front of him, he aimed at the blaze of light from the Hangman's gun and squeezed the trigger. Once, twice, three times . . .

A last blast from the submachine gun tore at the pillar above Abbot's head, showering him with dust and bits of rock. Then the gun clattered to the floor and a black shape slumped into the shaft of light from the entrance. Abbot remained on his belly for several minutes. Then he got stiffly to his feet and went forward. As he bent over the body, he could see a bloody patch on the Hangman's chest and another at the side of his head. There was still enough left of the Hangman's face, however, so that Abbot could grasp the rubber mask and peel it up and off the lifeless head.

As he suspected, Roland Kohl had gotten his man the first time. Colonel Nikolai Charnov had not come back from the dead, nor had he been miraculously resurrected by Soviet science. The face behind the mask belonged to young James Morrison.

19

Bruised and swollen clouds obscured the mountaintops; sheets of rain descended the steep, gray-green slopes and hid the distant valleys in blue haze. Abbot squinted through the water-filmed glass of his rented car and struggled to make out the minimal road markings of this primitive *Landstrasse*. Whenever the clouds thinned and parted, he caught glimpses of yawning chasms and vast gulfs which gave him the sense of flying through these mountains in a small plane, as free of gravity as the occasional hawk or eagle he had seen soaring on thermal updrafts before the heavy weather rolled in from the south.

He reached Glarner, a tiny collection of sheds and chalets clinging improbably to the mountainside well above the timberline, shortly before noon, and he stopped at the local *Volq* to inquire the way to Chalet Meisterhof. The blond, toothy Swiss miss told him to follow the road on up the mountain.

"What, you mean it goes up from here?" Abbot asked. There was no continuation of the road shown on his map, and it scarcely seemed possible that a road could wind higher.

"*Ja,* it goes oop *und* oop," the girl said, pointing through the streaming shop window at a craggy peak which loomed darkly over the village.

Abbot trudged back to his car through the heavy rain. Perhaps he should wait out the storm or give up the idea of a visit altogether; he could always send Jeremy a postcard from Italy telling him that his hideaway was just too well hidden, even for friendly visitors.

Jeremy wasn't the only person he had come to see, however, and he had already gone too far out of his way and spent too much of the day on the venture to call it off now. That was becoming a sort of motto of his, he reflected, as he urged the gasping Volkswagen up the next horrendous slope and across an Alpine meadow. No matter how hard the way ahead looked, and no matter what pleasures, passions, and memories one left behind, it was always better to go forward. You saved the past— what little of it could be saved—only by carrying it into the future with you, step by step.

And so here he was, inching his way along a mountain slope where there really shouldn't have been a road, driving through a rain that seemed to be trying to turn itself into snow, even though it was still just early August, because his conscience told him there were still words to be said and issues to be resolved before he could get on with his life. For weeks now he had both looked forward to and dreaded this day, had marked it off on his calendar, and fenced it off in his life. This was for Abbot a true day of reckoning: the day on which he presented himself to Jeremy Sawyer for judgment.

They had not seen each other since that afternoon in April, when Operation Nightingale reached its violent conclusion. By the time Abbot and Patricia had escaped via the tunnel and walked to the village, West German forces had converged on the scene. The village was teeming with military vehicles and troops in full battle gear. It took Abbot a long time to get to someone in authority and present his information. To his relief, he found the crisis was already past. The *Graf* had come to terms with the remaining terrorists—their safe conduct to the border for the lives of all those in the castle—and a U.S. military helicopter had carried Jeremy Sawyer and Roland Kohl off to the American hospital at Mainz. Franz left for Würzburg soon after, to be with his family, and Patricia went to Mainz to watch over Jeremy's bedside. Abbot entrusted Jeremy's disks to the CIA man who had been dispatched from Bonn to wrap up the affair and received this individual's assurances that his own role would be buried deep in agency files. Günther Haas drove Abbot back to Breiburg and they discussed the probable future of ELF.

"Even though a major scandal has been averted," Günther said, "many wealthy men will get wind of what happened and withdraw their support. ELF may survive as an organization, but the *Graf* and I shall not be part of it."

"You sound relieved," Abbot said.

"I am, I can confess it now. I never liked this espionage business, Herr Abbot, and I don't see what purpose it serves. Last year several thousand people were allowed to leave the Soviet Bloc countries with a minimum of fuss; several hundred of these will eventually return to their homeland because they did not find life in the West to their liking. It's not exactly an Iron Curtain any more, and some of these Cold War strategies seem to me outdated and counterproductive. The European nations are learning to work together, and neither America nor Russia can prevent the development of a united Europe, which will include both East and West."

"And do you think Franz believes this?"

"He will," Günther said with a smile, "when the *Gräfin* and I are done with him."

It was another week before Abbot received a letter from Patricia, informing him that Jeremy had been transferred to Hans Maienfeld's clinic in Switzerland. She wrote that she had decided to remain close by, through the operation at least, because, as she put it, "the poor blighter really doesn't have anybody else."

A month or so later Abbot returned from his classes in town to find Roland Kohl waiting for him in the guesthouse lobby. It was a warm, sunny Friday in June; Abbot brought down a couple of beers and they sat on the patio near a trellis laden with red roses.

"Well, Prof, I thought you might appreciate a wrap-up on this whole business. I guess I owe you that much, anyway."

"You owe me more than that, Kohl. But there's no way you can repay what's been lost. You've done the world a great disservice."

"You're referring, I suppose, to Sawyer's book. How do you know it would have been so goddamn wonderful?"

"Because he told me the better part of it, that night before you arrived at the castle. If he had written his story even half as well as he told it to me that night, it would have been a masterpiece."

"Well, he can rewrite the damn thing if he wants to," Kohl said. "I only bought the disks he brought out of Russia with him, not his creative soul. Personally, I think I did you a favor by queering that deal, but you might want to talk to Sawyer about a cut of his two hundred G's."

"I'm not interested in the money," Abbot said. "I received a very generous check from the *Graf,* which more than covers my time and trouble. But it would have been a great book, Kohl—that's the tragedy."

Kohl aimed a jet of smoke at a low-flying wasp. "I think maybe you'd better go have a talk with Jeremy before you leave Europe. He still owes you a few explanations."

Abbot saw there was no point in trying to make Kohl feel guilty about the loss of Jeremy's manuscript. There were other matters he wanted to ask Kohl about.

"I've been wondering what took place between you and Morrison before he returned to the crypt?"

"Nothing. I'd passed out at the top of the stairs, waiting for the rest of Katya's gang to come after us. Apparently they never did. As soon as the chopper crashed, Franz was able to reason with them. Jimbo just took my Uzi and came back to the crypt to get those disks. Damn good thing you were ready for him, or I'd probably be cooling my heels in a Kremlin decompression chamber right about now, trying to think up new ways to keep myself from spilling my guts to the KGB."

"Then, you didn't have two hundred American troops on the ridge, or another party guarding the tunnel back to East Germany, or any of the rest of it?"

Kohl grinned around his cigar. "If you're going to bluff, Prof, you have to make it a *big* bluff. How the hell could I have mobilized a force like that in the time I had? Besides, no American commander would take his troops that close to the border on his own authority."

"Jesus," Abbot said. "Then they nearly won."

"They came awful close. Two things saved us—Hedgie's ambush and your Luger."

"Do you think Hedge knew there was going to be trouble?"

"He must have guessed it when you showed up with your tale of woe. It's too bad he didn't get in touch with me at that point—we could've straightened things out between us. But then, Hedgie always liked to play a lone hand. He was that sort of dude."

"And Morrison? He'd been impersonating the Hangman all along? Those bruises on his face were from *my* fists? God, Kohl, he could have killed me any number of times!"

"Not quite," Kohl said. "He wasn't instructed to kill you until after you'd collected Jeremy's box and sent the signal that would set Operation Nightingale in motion. Then he took his best shot. Twice. You wiggled off the hook both times."

"But the first time, in London, he lowered me to the ground. I was out cold and would have strangled in a few minutes—"

"He had to let you down, because there was someone else following you that night—another one of my agents who heard the ruckus and came rushing up the stairs. Jimbo just had time to whip off his mask and make like he was rescuing you when the other guy burst into the room. That was one reason I stayed on in London—to check out Morrison's story."

"Then you were already suspicious?"

"Hell, I'd been suspicious of Jimbo for a long time. That's why I never told him the Stork was my agent, or that Hedge and Pajorfsky were my men inside ELF. I never guessed, though, that he could be impersonating the Hangman. Like the rest of you, I bought the theory—against my better judgment, mind—that the great Russian assassin had somehow been resurrected from the dead."

It seemed odd, in the warm June sunshine, with the smell of roses in the air and bees buzzing among the trellises, with birds chirping and children playing in the nearby sandbox, to be discussing these horrors. "Why did he do it?" Abbot asked. "I mean, why the gruesome disguise? If he hadn't put on his mask before coming into the crypt, I might not have had the nerve to shoot at him."

"Ah well, poor Jimbo was a hopeless fruitcake, I'm afraid. Like most double agents, he had to cultivate two distinct personalities —one for each side. Since he played the clean-cut all-American boy for us, he had to have a completely different image for his alter ego. Actually, Jimbo wasn't nearly as young as he looked. One of the things I learned when I checked into his background was that he'd been a prisoner of the Vietcong for nearly a year. Probably they shipped him to Moscow for a crash course in psychosis. Jimbo was finally released in 'seventy-five. I reckon that's when Colonel Charnov really rose from the dead."

"But what was the point? What were the Russians trying to accomplish?"

Kohl puffed on his cigar. "It's the same old card game, Prof—the war of nerves that's been going on between us and the Russians since the end of the war. Charnov was a figure who struck fear into the heart of every NATO agent in Europe. When I got rid of him, it was like I trumped the Kremlin's ace. When they brought him back from the dead, they beat my trump with a higher one of their own. A ghostly Charnov was even scarier than the live one had been. Morrison's mission was to destroy ELF and to set me up for defection. The mask helped by making those of us who had arranged Charnov's death very, very nervous."

"And Jeremy's decision to retire from his role as the Stork and return to the West—?"

"Dovetailed nicely with their master plan. No doubt they refashioned it from time to time, as Katya fed them information about Operation Nightingale from her side and Morrison gave it to them from his. But you see, if Sawyer had played it straight with me right from the start, most of our problems could have been avoided."

Abbot considered that over a swig of beer. It was, in fact, the first alcohol he'd had in six weeks and he was pleased to note that it set off no irreversible chain reaction. From now on, he promised himself, he would confine his drinking to social occasions, like a normal human being.

"You know," Abbot said to Kohl, "I can understand your dislike of the Soviets and their methods, but hasn't it ever occurred to you that what you did to Jeremy Sawyer was almost as bad as what they did to James Morrison?"

Kohl gave him a hard look. "There was one important difference, Prof. Sawyer knew what he was getting into. He wanted the adventure, the excitement—hell, he wanted material for his damn book."

"Which you took away from him."

"Ah, so now we're back to the lost masterpiece, are we? Listen, you go see Sawyer in his new digs. We've got him well hidden, but I'll show you how to get there. Got a map of Switzerland handy?"

Abbot went up to his room to get one; Kohl marked the tiny village and the circuitous route through the Alps. When it was time for Kohl to leave, Abbot walked him to his car. They shook hands and Kohl slid behind the wheel. "You know, Prof, you've demonstrated a certain talent for this business. If you're ever interested in going on with it—"

"What, as your agent? Here in Europe?"

"Why not? These days a professor can go anywhere, do his research and talk to colleagues in just about any country on the globe—it's a damn nice cover. For instance, there's an international conference in Bucharest next year you might find interesting—"

"No thanks," Abbot said. "I don't like the games you people play with other people's lives. Life is *not* cheap."

"Not on this side of the Wall, old buddy," Kohl said, starting his engine. "You ought to try it on the other side some time. See you around, Prof."

And the big American vehicle drove away.

Abbot's Volkswagen topped a last rise, rounded a last curve, and there it was, perched on a narrow spine of rock just a few hundred yards from what appeared to be the absolute summit of the mountain: Chalet Meisterhof. The Master's Court, Abbot thought, a well-chosen name. And what a spot for a poet! Jeremy's operation must have been a success, if he was now able to breathe this rarified air and walk these steep trails. If a man had the physical capacity to live at such heights, what couldn't it do for one's spirit and imagination?

He parked before the chalet and was greeted, as he climbed out of the car, by a ray of sunlight from the clouds. To the south the sky was clearing; he could hear cowbells jangling on the slope below the chalet, and a last long peal of thunder rolled through the sky and echoed in the valley. As Abbot neared the front door, Patricia came out to embrace him.

"I'm so glad you made it! I was afraid this dreadful weather would hold you up."

He saw she wasn't going to offer her lips, so he kissed her forehead instead. Perhaps they had been lovers in another life. He had been given as many, it seemed, as a cat.

"You're looking as beautiful as ever, Pat. What a wonderful spot this is! Don't you love it here?"

"Oh, Sam, I don't even know what I'm doing here! I thought I could help Jeremy, but he's not recovering the way he should."

"Not recovering from surgery?"

"Physically, his recuperation has been quite marvelous. It's his spirit I'm concerned about—his mind. We've been here for nearly a month now and he hasn't even begun to work. He just sits on the veranda, or at the window on rainy days, and stares out at the mountains."

"Perhaps he's composing, or waiting for inspiration to strike."

"I think he's lost heart, Sam. I don't think he cares any more. But maybe talking to you will do him good. He's been looking forward to your visit for days."

That may have been true, but Jeremy didn't seem particularly glad to see Abbot. A certain reserve had come over their relationship, almost as if they were both embarrassed by the memory of that long night during which Jeremy unburdened his soul and Abbot had listened in silence. Did Jeremy feel he had said too much, opened himself too wide, allowed too many secrets to come pouring out? Abbot tried to think of some way to reassure Jeremy that it had been, quite simply, the most extraordinary night of his life—the high point of his own adventure.

Throughout lunch Jeremy seemed nervous and preoccupied. He talked mostly about his operation and the state of his health. He told Abbot the doctors had predicted a complete recovery, another fifteen or twenty years of active life—especially if Jeremy followed the regimen of diet and exercise they had prescribed for him.

"And I'm not smoking, either," he said proudly. "We live as gods up here, Sam, on nectar and ambrosia. Maybe I'll write a physical fitness book—I hear they're all the rage in the States now. How about something like . . . *The Spy's Guide to Surviving Stressful Occupations?* There's got to be some way I can make use of my experiences in that dirty business!"

"I've heard from Sir Godfrey Clemmons," Abbot said. "He'd be interested in a fictionalized account of your adventures, if you want to try one. You could publish it under a nom de plume."

Jeremy seemed uninterested in the possibility; he gazed out the window at the clearing sky and the mountain peaks across the valley, now sharply defined by the afternoon light. Like mountains in a painting or on a stage set, Abbot thought, they were almost too perfect, too ethereally beautiful, to be real.

"And whatever became of that little German nobleman," Jeremy asked finally, "who gave ELF the use of his castle? What was his name, von Klarbach?"

"I just spent a very pleasant week with the *Graf* and his family at their estate near Berchtesgaden," Abbot said. "Schloss Riesenschatten has been closed indefinitely, but the family has other properties. Franz has given up the spy business and is thinking of running for political office instead. When I left, the *Gräfin* was urging him to take the family to America. His children are mad to see Disneyland."

Jeremy smiled. "I may get around to visiting the States myself one of these days. Kohl tells me my presidential pardon has been declared valid by the State Department and I can get a U.S. passport any time I ask for one—under a new name, of course. It wouldn't be a hero's return, but it would give me a chance to see what they've made of the place since my last visit in the mid-sixties."

"You wouldn't approve," Abbot said. "The old counterculture has run its course; it's been enshrined as another piece of nostalgia. We're all quite mainstream now. The country's gotten very conservative, but maybe a little wiser than the last time the pendulum swung in that direction."

Jeremy shook his head. "I don't think nations ever achieve wisdom. Only individuals may sometimes become a bit wiser—and then at a terrible price. By the time a man reaches our age, Sam, he finds that he's traded his precious youth, his energy, his dreams, the best part of his life, and for what? A few paltry truths."

Abbot looked at Patricia, whose eyes told him that this was the sort of thing Jeremy had been saying a lot lately. "Then you no longer believe," he asked, "that poets should become involved in politics and world affairs—that they should give themselves over to some great cause?"

Jeremy scowled and looked away. "I don't know what the bloody hell I believe, Sam, and that may be the true beginning of wisdom. Or the end of my feeble attempts to attain the same, who knows? But you talk of causes. . . ."

Abbot waited, but apparently Jeremy had no more to say on that subject.

After lunch they went out on the veranda for coffee and dessert. The last of the clouds had blown away and the sun warmed the thin air. Abbot looked down the long valley, a river browsing through its deepest folds, and counted no less than ten tiny villages on the steep slopes. He saw the road he had taken winding indefatigably toward this summit, and it seemed to him a pilgrim's tortuous path to enlightenment, as it might have been portrayed in one of those fanciful German paintings of the Middle Ages.

"Well, Jeremy"—the time had come to speak his piece—"it seems that once again you've done much more for me than I've been able to do for you."

Jeremy seemed to scoff. "And what have I ever done for you, old bean, aside from giving you a bloody lot of trouble and nearly getting you killed?"

"But that's just it," Abbot said. "You gave me an adventure—the one great adventure of my life, as it turns out. When I came to Germany, I was scraping rock bottom. I'd lost my confidence, my self-respect—I thought my life was dull and meaningless, my accomplishments insignificant—"

"And now?" Jeremy asked, as if, in some courts, Abbot might still be convicted of these shortcomings.

"Now I see things in a different perspective," Abbot said. "I see the point of what you were always trying to tell me back in Cambridge, when we had those lengthy arguments about life and art—"

Jeremy looked genuinely interested now, as if he only wished he could remember what it was he used to tell Abbot. "Yes—go on."

"Well, I see that the intellectual life has to be translated into action before it can be tested and validated. Isn't that what you used to say? One makes one's beliefs and values true by living them, not just by writing about them?"

"Is *that* what I used to say?" Jeremy seemed both amused and embarrassed by the memory, like a man confronted with a youthful picture of himself—the proverbial baby on the bearskin rug. "And is that what you think I did by spending eighteen years of my life in the Soviet Union? Sam, Sam—you *do* want a guru to show you the way through life, don't you? You're still the same eager, greedy, gullible little bastard you always were! And you're still trying to buy your wisdom at the corner shop. But the truth of the matter is, you'll get nothing from me—not a drop of wisdom, old bean, not a fucking crumb. I got involved in a nasty, vicious and degrading business, and I let it destroy me—it's as simple as that."

"No, it's not," Abbot said firmly. "The book I read—those two chapters you gave me—they were great, Jeremy. It was a work of true genius. It could have been one of the great works of our time. If only you could write it again, from memory—"

But Jeremy waved the thought away. "That book was a colossal hoax, Sam. The first two chapters, which you read, were written years ago, when I first arrived in Moscow. I was lonely and homesick and had a lot of time on my hands. Moreover, I was full of doubt and guilt and it helped me to write those chapters. But that's all I ever did write. The rest of it—the part you never saw—was mostly just rubbish: alcoholic musings and ravings, the pilfered work of my students and colleagues, newspaper clippings—a grab bag of garbage. You see, after I'd been in Moscow a few years I was much too caught up in the intrigues and double dealings of a secret agent. I couldn't have written a coherent paragraph, much less an entire book! But I knew Roland Kohl was afraid I had such a book and I figured I could use those fears to milk the Agency for all it was worth. Do you think Kohl would have coughed up that bonus if I hadn't had a manuscript to hold over his head?"

Abbot was, for a time, too astonished to speak. He looked at the mountains as if they were cardboard cutouts, the tritely conventional scenery of a cheap amateur stage production. "You mean the whole business—all of Operation Nightingale, my negotiations with Sir Godfrey, and all the rest of it—was just a way of extorting a lousy two hundred thousand? Jeremy, people got *killed* trying to get you out of Russia!"

Jeremy's pale, anxious eyes fled away from Abbot's glare, and it suddenly occurred to Abbot that what he had been seeing in Jeremy's eyes all along, the thing he hadn't understood or recognized, was Jeremy's moral death. There had been a man living behind that face, once upon a time, but that man hadn't survived his Russian exile.

"And the night we talked? Everything you told me? That was—?"

Jeremy smiled. "Ah, that was the truth. The whole truth and nothing but the truth. The first time I ever told my story, and the last, old bean. You are the sole repository."

Abbot supposed that he should have felt honored. Instead, he felt almost guilty, as if he'd stolen something which belonged to the entire world. Jeremy's story was not a burden he wanted to carry all by himself. There was too much in it—too much that was dark and disturbing; Abbot foresaw that he might spend the rest of his life trying to penetrate that darkness.

Jeremy himself summed it up as he saw Abbot to the door. "Don't hate me quite so much, old bean. After all, if I played a nasty joke on you and Kohl and anyone else who still thought Jeremy Sawyer had a decent piece of literature in him, the joke turns out ultimately to be on me, doesn't it? I'll always be remembered, if I'm remembered at all, for the books I *didn't* write. Like Keats and Shelley and all those sad young poets of long ago, I sent my talent to an early grave. And what good is money, when I could have had . . . could have had. . . ."

For a moment, Jeremy's eyes shone anew at the thought of the literary immortality that could have been his. But the glow faded quickly, and Abbot said good-by without offering to shake Jeremy's hand.

Patricia walked with Abbot to the car.

"Do you have to stay with him?" he asked her.

"Where else would I go?" She gazed up at Abbot with those clear, delicately colored, always beautiful eyes. "Are you proposing to take me away, Sam? Because you know I can't go back to Stephen—I've burned that bridge behind me, and rightly so. Christina's making a life of her own, and the rest of my relatives—well, Jeremy was right about them. They *are* prigs. You see, I've always had just two choices—you or Jeremy. You're the only two men I ever loved."

Abbot held both her hands. "I'm meeting Liz tomorrow in Florence. She and the girls have just flown over from the States. My son, Jeffrey, visited me in Breiburg in July, and he sort of set it up—a possible reconciliation. We're booked into Venice for the week, and then we drive on to Vienna."

"So," Patricia said, forcing a bright smile, "you can't very well carry *me* off, now can you?"

"I can't make any commitments until I've given my marriage another chance, that's what it comes down to."

"Oh, I'm sure that means it's all over for us, then," she continued in the same bright vein. "If you give your marriage another chance, you'll make a success of it. You always get the things you go after, Sam—you're that sort of chap."

It struck Abbot as oddly, surprisingly, right. He *was* that sort of chap; funny it had taken him so long to learn it.

"Whatever Liz and I decide," he said, "I hate to see you giving up the rest of your life to that"—he looked at the chalet, where Jeremy's pale face could be seen at the window—"that charlatan in there."

"Don't worry, darling," she said, lifting up on her toes to kiss his cheek. "If I can't have you, he's a pretty decent second best."

Driving down the mountain, Abbot suddenly realized what Jeremy's confession meant to him. He pulled over and got out of the car. The air was clear and sharp after the rain and he could see Jeremy's chalet high on the mountainside. The valley below was beginning to fill up with the blue shadows of evening, but where Abbot stood there was still full sun. And then Abbot understood that, after all these years, he had finally come out from under the giant's shadow which had darkened his own life.

That night Abbot took a hotel room in Saint Moritz. He bought himself a good dinner at a restaurant overlooking the lake and then went out to stroll the hilly, tourist-jammed streets. At a *Tabak* he picked up a large, Roland Kohl–style cigar and a *Herald Tribune.* As he was waiting at the counter to pay, the headline caught his eye: DISARMAMENT TALKS SUSPENDED. Dateline, Vienna. He skimmed the first paragraph: . . . "abrupt change in the Soviet position . . . two sides still far apart . . . American public opinion not fully in support of . . . continued unrest in the Middle East . . . terrorist bombings in Athens and Cairo. . . ."

Abbot put the paper back and paid only for his cigar. He walked out into the chilly mountain evening and saw parties of tourists moving up and down the brightly lit streets. He saw elderly couples strolling arm in arm, families with small children in tow, groups of prowling young people, sweethearts, honeymooners. . . .

Tomorrow, he told himself, he would rejoin the flow; he would resume his normal place in the human community. But for to-night he was still, thank God, an alien. He lit his cigar, put his hands in his pockets, and started walking.